Peace, Love, and Crime

Crime Fiction Inspired by the Songs of the '60s

Edited by Sandra Murphy

Peace, Love, and Crime: Crime Fiction Inspired by the Songs of the '60s
Edited by Sandra Murphy

Cover Design by Ginny Glass
Cover credit: Holger.Ellgaard / Rock-Ola djukebox CapriII från 1965
Image Source: https://commons.wikimedia.org/wiki/File:Rock-Ola_Capri_II.jpg,
Adapted Work: http://store.untreedreads.com

ISBN-13: 978-1-95360-199-5

Also available in ebook format.

Published by Untreed Reads, LLC
506 Kansas Street, San Francisco, CA 94107
www.untreedreads.com

Printed in the United States of America.

Publisher's Note

This is a work of fiction. Names, characters, places, and incidents either are the product of the authors' imagination or are used fictitiously, and any resemblance to actual persons, living or dead, business establishments, events, or locales is entirely coincidental.

The publisher does not have any control over and does not assume any responsibility for author or third-party websites or their content.

Anthologies Also by Untreed Reads Publishing

Discount Noir
Flash and Bang
Grimm Tales
Moon Shot: Murder and Mayhem on the Edge of Space
The Killer Wore Cranberry
The Killer Wore Cranberry: A Second Helping
The Killer Wore Cranberry: Room for Thirds
The Killer Wore Cranberry: A Fourth Meal of Mayhem
The Killer Wore Cranberry: A Fifth Course of Chaos
The Killer Wore Cranberry: A Sixth Scandalous Serving
The Untreed Detectives
Year's End

www.untreedreads.com

For Earl Staggs, who loved to write a good story, and for Mary Harvey, who loved to read a good story, especially if there was a poodle in it. You'll be missed.

Contents

Introduction

Late one night, I watched (for the sixth time) the 1989 mystery/thriller, *Sea of Love,* starring Al Pacino, Ellen Barkin and John Goodman. At each of the murder scenes there is a record player with a 45 on the turntable (remember vinyl?). "Sea of Love" is playing on endless repeat.

Late-night ideas come easily and some of them are good, non-life-threatening, and legal to boot. The idea of an anthology using '60s music to inspire a crime popped into my mind and wouldn't leave. After all, the '60s meant rebellion, revolution and rock and roll. Love was free, peace was the goal of a generation, and if you weren't protesting, you were turning on, tuning in, and dropping out, on the advice of Timothy Leary. Drugs were colorful and in abundant supply. Fighting the Establishment, what could go wrong?

When I put the call out for stories for this anthology, I expected to get a lot of British Invasion music and folk songs protesting the war and encouraging us to celebrate life, even though I'd told writers to avoid the obvious. They dug deep, listened to YouTube performances, and recalled old favorites.

The result is an eclectic mix—Elvis, the Lovin' Spoonful, Nancy Sinatra, Crosby, Stills & Nash, Bob Dylan, Richard Harris, Billy J. Kramer and the Dakotas, Norman Greenbaum, B.J. Thomas and the Triumphs, Jan and Dean, Roy Orbison, The Drifters, The Beatles, Blind Faith, Moody Blues, Neil Sedaka, Frank Sinatra, The Zombies, Rolling Stones, Frankie Valli and the Four Seasons. The crimes they chose are just as varied.

Delve into the dark corners of the closet for your tie-dyed t-shirt and bell-bottomed jeans, fire up the lava lamp, and crank up the sound of '60s music to 11 as you read 22 tales of crimes committed during the Age of Aquarius.

Spinning their chosen tunes and the tale of its matching crime are Earl Staggs, Jack Bates, Linda Kay Hardie, Jeanne DuBois, Terrie

Farley Moran, Heidi Hunter, Merrilee Robson, Claire A. Murray, Michael Bracken, Maddi Davidson, Joseph S. Walker, Dawn Dixon, Karen Keeley, Paul D. Marks, Wendy Harrison, Mary Keliikoa, Maxim Jakubowski, James A. Hearn, C. A, Fehmel, Catina Williams, Josh Pachter and John M. Floyd, talented writers all.

The year 2020 has been a challenge in many ways. Thanks to Untreed Reads for taking on this project. Jay Hartman, Editor in Chief, and K.D. Sullivan, She Who Keeps Us All Under Control (as much as is possible with writers, creative types that we are) did an extraordinary job. K.D. only fainted twice when hearing there are twenty-two stories in an anthology that would usually host only a dozen. The stories were too good to pass up.

Thanks to Ginny Glass for the cover design that is exactly what I had in mind and more.

Readers, we couldn't do this without you. Writers and publishers need your support to keep the stories coming. Buy books from the publisher, locally owned bookstores, or ask your public library to carry your favorites. It matters.

Peace and love,
Sandra Murphy, St. Louis, 2020

Aunt Laverne and Elvis
by Earl Staggs
(based on "Please Don't Stop Loving Me," Elvis Presley, 1966)

Aunt Laverne is the star of my family. She's a tall and beautiful redhead, even though the red now comes from a bottle, and she has enough bubbling personality and charm for five people. She's so bright and vivacious, when she enters a room, she owns it and everyone in it. She's also rich, thanks to three wealthy husbands, one she divorced and two she buried. Yesterday was her eightieth birthday, and it almost turned into the biggest disaster to ever hit Texas. It started to go bad when Aunt Laverne shouted at the top of her powerful lungs, "Where the hell is my Elvis?"

For her birthday every year, she rents a ballroom in a hotel in Dallas, and unless they're in a jail cell or a hospital bed, the entire family gathers there for a party. Everyone brings food. Not that she needs food, of course. Aunt Laverne always hires a caterer to prepare several entrees, but her reasoning is that if each person brings a side dish of their own making, they'll have something to talk about and can have fun exchanging recipes. According to Aunt Laverne, that's a tradition in Switzerland. What Switzerland has to do with it, I'll never understand, but that's Aunt Laverne for you.

The most popular person in the kitchen crowd is always my husband. When he retired from Bell Helicopter five years ago, he bought some books on cooking, took an online course, and became very good at it. He became Lilburn Goodall the Great Chef in the family. and for the last three years, his recipes won the Watango County Thanksgiving Cooking Contest. I retired from the Fort Worth Police Force at the same time, but after six months of enjoying his fabulous meals and gaining twenty pounds, I decided to get out of the house before I turned into Mollie Goodall the Blimp. I found a job and became Mollie Goodall, the Sheriff of Watango County.

Each of my aunts and cousins brought a dish. Aunt Louise had her three-bean salad, just like last year. And the year before that, and the year before that, and so on. Okay with me. I love her salad. Cousin Thelma Lee brought an apple pie she claimed she made from scratch, although it looked exactly like a Mrs. Smith's pie I bought at Kroger recently. Her sister, Thelma Lou, arrived with a broccoli and carrot dip. It didn't look at all appetizing. Henry showed up with a big bowl of chili and a flashy woman half his age. Marilyn had covered her huge coconut cake. As she walked past, she gave me that little smirk I hated. We never got along. When she passed my Lilburn, she flashed him a big smile that I hated even more. Aunts, uncles and cousins each brought something, and placed their dishes on a long table at the front of the room. Cake covers, containers and boxes were stashed under the table. After dropping off their food, everyone made a stop at the coat room. There must have been seventy or eighty people in the room, half relatives and the rest, spouses or plus-ones.

Every year at Aunt Laverne's birthday celebration and any other family gathering, the same thing happens. All the women hover around Lilburn. They pretend it's about his cooking, but I suspect it's more than that, likely his good looks. Sometimes I feel I need to remind the horde of enthralled women that I carry a gun.

Yesterday's celebration began in the usual way. Aunt Laverne made her way to every table in the ballroom, stopping to hug everyone at least once. She talked about her adventures the previous year, asked to meet new members of the family through marriage or whatever, and then we'd enjoy the great feast.

After we were done eating, Aunt Laverne told the same story she told every year, the one about how she met Elvis Presley in 1966 when she was eighteen. He was touring, and she didn't have money for a ticket, so she came up with an ingenuous plan. She worked as a housekeeper at a local motel, so she put her uniform over her regular clothes, carried a bucket of cleaning supplies and walked right into the theater where Elvis would be. When a security guard stopped her, she convinced him she worked there. Once she made it past him, she found a closet near the stage, stashed the uniform and bucket, and waited. In the closet. For three hours, she waited.

She heard the band warm up and knew it was almost time. Hearing voices and footsteps in the corridor outside the closet, she pulled out another trick with a small compact mirror. She opened the closet door just a crack and held the mirror so she could see the corridor, an uncomfortable position. After ten minutes or so, she saw a group of eight people heading toward the stage, Elvis leading the pack. He was wearing a white suit coat, tight black pants, and a red shirt. He looked magnificent in anything, so it didn't really matter. When the men were almost at the closet, she stepped out right in front of them.

Elvis stopped short and said, "Whoa."

Three men, his protectors, known as the Memphis Mafia, stepped in front of him. One, she recognized as Red West, who'd gone to high school with Elvis. He said, "Step aside, girl. You don't want to get hurt."

"Don't hurt me, I love him. I just want to ask a question."

Red said, "Sorry, girl, but you're not allowed in here. You'll have to leave, or we'll remove you the hard way."

Elvis stepped in front of Red and grinned that gorgeous lop-sided grin of his. "Take it easy, Red," he said. "Let her ask her question. What's your name, girl?"

"It's La...La...Laverne," she said, completely awestruck that she was really speaking to Elvis.

"Well, Miss Laverne, what did you want to ask me?"

"Could you, I mean, uh, would you give me your autograph?"

Elvis gave her a full hundred watt smile then. She thought she would faint.

"What would you want me to autograph?"

She reached in her right pocket, then in her left and found nothing. How could she have forgotten to bring something he could sign?

"Wait a minute," she said. She opened the closet door and reached in for her bucket of cleaning supplies. She dug inside it, then said, "Here it is."

She held out a 45 rpm record she'd bought that morning. "It's you singing 'Please Don't Stop Loving Me.' It's from your movie *Frankie and Johnny*."

He laughed. Some of the guys behind him laughed too.

"I know," he said with that grin again. "Do you have something I can write with?"

She dug in her pockets again, found nothing, and felt totally stupid. How could she have forgotten something for him to write with?

Red West held out a ball point pen.

Elvis took the pen, slid the record out of its sleeve, and scribbled on the label. He handed it back to her along with the pen. "Here you go, Laverne." He nodded toward the stage. "I have to go to work now. It was a pleasure to meet you. Enjoy the show." He leaned forward and planted a quick kiss on her cheek.

Elvis walked toward the stage, the other guys behind him. Red West was the last in line. She handed his pen back to him.

"Keep it, Laverne," he said. "You got guts, girl." He gave her a wink and hurried to catch the others.

She thought she would die right there in that corridor. Or at least pass out. She stuck the pen in her pocket, held the record against her heart with her right hand, and held her left palm against her cheek where he'd kissed her.

Finally, she looked at what Elvis had written on her record.

"Laverne," he'd written. "Don't stop loving me." It was signed with a rapid scrawl of his name. "Elvis Presley."

At this point in the story, Aunt Laverne stopped talking and stood perfectly still. Tears made their way down her cheeks. I looked around the room and saw tear stains in many of the faces. Most of them had heard the story before—several times—but that didn't matter. The way Aunt Laverne told the story, even though it was a happy ending, put a little pressure on the tear ducts.

"Well, people," Aunt Laverne said as she patted her face with a tissue, "that's the story of how I acquired something very dear to my heart, and I cherish it as much today as I did then." She looked around the room. "Any questions?"

My cousin Thelma Lou raised a hand, then shouted, "Was that hair his own, or was it fake?"

Aunt Laverne giggled. "Believe me, honey. Everything about that man was real. Nothing was fake."

Lucy asked, "Did he do all his stunts in his movies himself?"

"No, dearie. He wanted to, but they wouldn't let him. You can't let the star get hurt."

Cecily, Cousin Howard's wife, asked, "Can I have the leftovers of that dish Lilburn brought?"

Aunt Laverne gave her a sad look. "Cecily, I hate to tell you this, but as usual, Lilburn's dish was all eaten. There are no leftovers."

There weren't any more questions either, so Aunt Laverne raised her hands in the air and said, "Would y'all like to hear the song Elvis signed for me?"

After a chorus of "Yes, yes, yes," she said, "Stay put. I'll go get it." Laverne hurried to the coat room.

Five seconds later, we heard her scream, "Where the hell is my Elvis?"

Everyone stopped doing what they were doing and froze. Mouths open, they all stared at the coat room door.

After two or three seconds, Aunt Laverne burst into the main room. "It's gone! It's gone! Someone took Elvis!" Her eyes were huge, and her face flushed red. She looked from one person to the next and finally settled on me. "Mollie, you're a cop! Do something."

By the time I got through the crowd, someone had brought a chair for Laverne and made her sit before she could fall. Hands over her eyes, tears oozed between her fingers.

"Don't you worry, Aunt Laverne," I said. "We'll get your Elvis back. Where was it?"

"It was…it was…" she stopped long enough to pull a handkerchief from somewhere out of her dress and blow her nose. "it was…in the pocket of my coat." She jerked her thumb over her shoulder. "Someone snuck in there and stole It."

"Are you sure you brought it? Are you sure you didn't leave it home?"

Her head bobbed up and down. "I'm positive. I even checked it when I put my coat in there."

"Could it have dropped on the floor and wound up under something?"

"I looked. Mollie. You know how long I've had it and how much it means to me."

"Don't you worry. We'll find it. It has a lot of sentimental value for all of us."

"Not just sentimental, Mollie. It's worth a lot of money. Collectors want it. Just last week another one called and offered forty thousand dollars for it. I'd never sell it, of course, not for a million dollars."

"That much, huh? Forty thousand dollars makes stealing it a third-degree felony in Texas. Did anyone in the family know about that offer?"

"Well, Marilyn was there to ask for another loan when I got the call. She might have overheard me mention the amount on the phone. I hated to tell her no, but I had to. She has to figure out how to take care of her finances."

"She has a lot to learn. You were right to say no."

"Do you think you can find my Elvis, Mollie?"

"I'll do my very best, Aunt Laverne. You just rest and relax."

During the party, someone had stolen the record from Aunt Laverne's coat pocket. Whoever did it was still here because no one ever left before the song. Whoever took it had to have somewhere to hide it.

I looked for my husband and found him on the other side of the room. One of my flirty cousins was standing very close to him, running her fingers up and down his arm. He caught my look and came over. "What can I do to help?" he asked.

"I hate to tear you away from your adoring fans, but if you wouldn't mind, would you check the coat room and make sure it's not there somewhere? Look under everything and check the pockets of the coats."

"Sure thing," he said as he hurried off. Good old Lilburn. Always there when I need him. Even when he's sometimes surrounded by predatory females.

While I waited for him to come back, I roamed around, looking for possible hiding places. There was nothing in the room except a bunch of tables and chairs that had been set up for us, the food table in the front, and the baskets, boxes, trays and Marilyn's big cake cover stashed under the table.

Lilburn came back and reported, "I checked the room end to end and top to bottom, and Elvis is not in there."

"Did you check coat pockets?"

"Only a few coats had pockets large enough. I found some interesting things and some yucky things, but not what I was looking for. What next?"

"Maybe we can find another copy of that record. I know it won't replace the original, but she can still play the song for everyone, and that's important to her. You're familiar with the stores around here. Do you know of any that might have old recordings?"

He thought for a few seconds. "A couple years ago, the guys at the coffee shop were trying to remember the words to an old song of Bobby Darin's, and I found it at this place on Denton Road. Their ads say they have every song ever recorded."

"Well, I doubt if anyone could have every song ever recorded, but it's worth a try. What was the name of the place?"

He thought a few more seconds. "It was Daddy-O's Records."

"Daddy-O's?"

He had his cellphone out and searched for the number. "Yup. There it is. I'll call for you."

He handed me the phone, and after two rings, someone answered.

"Daddy'O's Records. If we don't have it, we can get it."

"Well, I hope you have what I'm looking for," I said. "Elvis Presley singing 'Please Don't Stop Loving Me' from 1966."

"Give me a minute. I'll check."

I waited almost the whole minute before he returned. "You're in luck. We have that song."

I breathed a big sigh of relief. "That's great. Give me your address, and I'll come and pick it up."

When he told me, I realized I really was in luck. It was only ten minutes away.

I said thanks and hung up. I gave Lilburn his phone and said, "I'll be back in half an hour. Don't let anyone leave, especially my cousin Marilyn." I added, "And tell those women if they don't keep their hands off you, I'll shoot them."

He grinned and said, "Yes, ma'am, Sheriff."

I ran to my car and took off.

I arrived at Daddy-O's eleven minutes later. I'd have made it in ten but a minor traffic jam at an intersection had held me up. When I went in, there were two men wearing white t-shirts with "Daddy-O's" in big red letters on the front. The "O" was a picture of a record. Cute. It was definitely an Elvis store. Posters of him hung on every wall.

The younger man stood behind a cash register near the entrance. "Yes, ma'am," he said, "Can I help you?"

"I called a few minutes ago and was told you had a copy of an old Elvis record I wanted."

"You talked to my dad." He looked over his shoulder at an older man, somewhere near fifty, at a counter at the back of the store. "Hey, dad, customer for you."

"Hi, there," he said with a big smile. He was handsome, about six feet tall, with gray hair and a thin athletic build. "You called about an Elvis record?"

We shook hands and exchanged names. His was Tommy Cooper. "Nice to meet you," he said. "I pulled it for you, right here." He stepped behind the counter and held it up for me to see.

My heart sank. He had an album, not a 45-rpm record. The cover read, "Elvis – Movie Songs."

"I was looking for a forty-five." I sounded disappointed because I was.

He was disappointed too. "I'm so sorry, but this all we have for that song. I happen to like the song myself so I include it in my live shows."

"What kind of live shows?"

"I'm an Elvis Tribute Performer. Maybe you noticed my posters on the wall."

I looked around the walls again and moved over close to one poster. "This is you, not Elvis himself?" It sure looked like the real Elvis from a distance. The same hair and outfits. but up close, I could see a difference.

"I haven't done any shows for a couple years, but for quite a long time, I kept busy full time. I keep my outfits and my play list handy though, just in case I get the urge to do a show."

A nugget of an idea bounced around in my head until it became a plan. "Can we talk?"

A half hour later, Tommy Cooper and I were in my car and on our way. He had his black Elvis hairpiece and outfit in a small suitcase and his audio equipment in the trunk. I called Lilburn and told him the plan. I also told him I had a good idea how to find Aunt Laverne's missing record.

When we arrived back at the party, Lilburn was waiting at the side door that led into the kitchen so he could help Tommy carry in his stuff. Tommy explained the plan and told Lilburn what his role would be. I walked around to the front of the house, stopped by my car for a pair of handcuffs, stuck them in my pocket, and went inside.

Laverne sat on a plush chair someone had found in a back room and was much calmer than when I left. She was surrounded by concerned relatives. I waited for Lilburn to do his part. It didn't take long. He carried a speaker box into the room and plugged it in to a wall socket. He laid the microphone on top of the speaker.

The show was about to start.

I picked up the microphone, and announced, "We all came here to hear Elvis sing. Well, we're not only going to hear him, but this year we'll see him. Everyone, please take a seat. Elvis is in the building." I placed the microphone back on top of the speaker and reached over to the wall and dimmed the lights in the room.

About ten seconds later, Tommy entered from the kitchen. He looked great in the toupee of Elvis hair and in a white jumpsuit decorated with sequins. Tommy explained to me in the car that Elvis didn't begin wearing jumpsuits until a couple years after *Frankie and Johnny* was filmed, but that was the image people remembered, so that's what he gave his audiences.

I had described Aunt Laverne to him. He walked over to her and knelt on one knee in front of her. She was all smiles. "Laverne," he began, "I understand this is your birthday and this song of a favorite of yours." He reached for her hand and kissed it. The music started to play. Lilburn did his part by pushing the right buttons on Tommy's music system from the kitchen. Tommy stood up and sang "Please Don't Stop Loving Me" and he sounded just like the real Elvis.

When the song ended there was a loud eruption of applause in the room. Tommy said, in his best Elvis voice, "Thank you. Thank you very much."

Laverne was so happy, she couldn't stop smiling. She held her hands over her mouth, then reached out for Tommy. He leaned over and she planted a big kiss on his cheek.

Tommy then turned to the rest of the audience. "Anyone else have a favorite song?"

The requests came, one after another: "Jailhouse Rock," "Love Me Tender," "Don't Be Cruel," "Hound Dog."

Tommy said. "Let's do 'Jailhouse Rock.'"

The music began. He had taught Lilburn how to select a song from his recorded playlist. Lilburn is a genius with electronics and mechanical stuff, so it was no problem for him.

Tommy did the same bunch of dance moves Elvis performed in the movie as he sang "Jailhouse Rock."

Tommy entertained us for nearly an hour, and every song was a big hit with the audience. When it was over, Aunt Laverne held him in a tight hug and said something only he could hear. He blushed. Who knows what the old gal said to him? I was pretty sure I didn't want to find out.

It was my turn again. I picked up the mic. "Well people, wasn't that wonderful?"

Everyone applauded and Tommy did a long, low bow to them.

"Now," I said, "we have one more piece of business here today. It's about Aunt Laverne's missing record. I know who took it and I know where it is." I paused and kept my eyes on Marilyn. She had been my number one suspect from the beginning. When we were kids, she stayed overnight at our house. After she left the next day, I discovered my favorite necklace was missing. She had a couple scrapes with the law as she grew up, mostly from shoplifting.

As soon as I said I knew where the record was, her head swung to her left and she stared at that cake cover. I walked over and lifted the lid, and there was the record, still in its sleeve and sealed in a baggie. Red West's ball point pen was in the bag too. I took it over to Aunt Laverne.

"Oh my God, Mollie," she cried, "you found it just like you said you would. Thank you, thank you, thank you. I also want to thank you for bringing Tommy here today. It was an absolutely wonderful birthday treat."

"You're very welcome, Aunt Laverne. It was my pleasure."

Lilburn appeared at my side. He asked, "How did you know who took it and where it was hidden?"

"As for who it was, I wasn't completely sure, but Marilyn had some prior experience with stealing. For the where, she told me where it was when she looked at her cake cover."

"Well, it was good work. And you prevented the day from being a disaster. How much do we owe Tommy?"

"Absolutely nothing. After I told him Aunt Laverne's story, he said he was happy to do it for nothing."

"Well, you certainly made your Aunt Laverne very happy."

"Thank you, sweetie. And thank you for helping. I hated to take you away from your fans."

He laughed. "Oh that. You have nothing to worry about. After all, I know you carry a gun."

I saw Marilyn sneak out of the coat room and head for the door. I followed, my cuffs in hand. I was sure the judge would give her probation and not jail time since she never left the crime scene, but maybe this time, it would teach her a lesson.

The Preacher's Daughter
by Jack Bates

(based on "Voodoo in My Basement," the Lovin' Spoonful, 1966)

I had no intention of dying on the dirt floor cellar of a hippie commune.

Didn't matter how I saw things, though, did it? Regardless of the plans we make, the gods have their own ideas about our fates. Sometimes I think we're nothing more than tokens on a game board to them.

Earlier that day, I was in my office going through a stack of mail, all of which bore the big, red letter stamps of PAST DUE, when my receptionist Kelly knocked on my door. Normally she would just open it and walk right in like she owned the place. Kelly had a code though, and a knock meant she was bringing in a client and I should clean up my desk, stash the bottle of bourbon I kept on my blotter, and fix my tie. I did all of that just before she stuck her head into the room.

"Yes, Miss English?"

"I have a Pastor Meredith out here who'd like to talk to you. He doesn't have an appointment—" It was part of the Kelly Code for "pay attention and this could solve a lot of our financial woes." She also flashed me her "trust me on this" smile. Who was I to argue?

Kelly stepped back and motioned to the mysterious Pastor Meredith, a tall man, gaunt in the face. A half halo of hair, cut military short, stretched from ear to ear around the back of his head. There was no grip in his handshake. It was like clutching a days-old dead fish.

"Have a seat, Reverend." I gestured to the black leather sofa in front of my desk.

"Thank you for seeing me, Mr. Devlin. And please, you may call me Pastor Andy."

Something about the name he gave lodged in my head.

A ghost of a grin slipped over his face. "Yes. I'm that Pastor Andy. You've listened to my morning radio show, I take it."

"I've caught it once or twice." I wasn't a religious guy, but I still felt a tad guilty lying to a man with a gold cross pin on his lapel. "How can I help you, Pastor?"

"Do you have children, Mr. Devlin?"

"Came close. The war kind of interfered with my plans in London."

"You were stationed in England?"

"I worked for the O.S.S. Were you in Europe?"

"South Pacific. All over." He absently rubbed his left wrist.

"How did you go from gun pit to pulpit?"

"I made some foxhole promises. Told the Almighty if he got me through the war unscathed, I'd carry His message to whatever shore He sent me. Wound up in Warren, Michigan."

Warren was a growing automotive industry hot spot north of a struggling Detroit. The small but developing city in southeast Macomb County even had a tank plant that produced the M60 Patton for the wars after our war. Lot of guys came home and kept the factories and the war machine running for the next twenty years. I wasn't one of them. I opened Devlin Investigations ten miles north of where Meredith opened his church.

"Are you feeling all right, Mr. Meredith? You keep rubbing your wrist."

"Do I? I misplaced a rather expensive watch one of my sponsors gave me." He interlocked his fingers and cupped his palms over his raised knee. "Irrelevant to my visit."

"Of course. Forgive me for distracting you. You were saying?"

"Ever wonder why we were where we were, Mr. Devlin?"

"I'm not following you."

"Ever think to yourself, 'This is the world I fought for? This is the world my buddies died to save?' Gruesome murders in California. Decadent behavior in upstate New York. Race riots less than five miles from my congregational door. A Cold War gripping the planet. I look around and I see the devil hard at work."

I leaned back in my swivel chair wishing I had left the booze out in the open. "If you're asking me to hunt down old Mr. Scratch, Pastor Andy, I'm afraid you've come to the wrong guy."

He sighed, waved a hand like he was shooing away a fly. "I want you to find my daughter, Mr. Devlin."

I got the feeling he came to me reluctantly. Coming to me either meant the police had turned him down or failed him or both. There was also the possibility he didn't want to involve the authorities due to his celebrity stature in the community.

"I need to know some particulars. Do you have a photograph of her?"

"Not a recent one."

"How old is your daughter, Mr. Meredith?"

He leaned forward a bit and covered his left wrist with his right hand. "I know what you're going to say when I tell you, and before you say it, let me show you this."

He reached into his jacket and brought out a folded sheet of red paper. I could see where the small poster had been ripped from a telephone pole or a bulletin board. Someone had gone to a lot of work to design and print the flyer for a music festival in Port Pinnebog, a shipping community known for stockpiles of taconite ore, copper, and sugar from sugar beet farms. One of those Huron County farms had given up its fields for an event called the Soul Revival Music Festival. Three days of music, dance, freedom, spirituality and more. The names of fifteen bands, none of which I recognized, appeared on the belly of a demon that looked a lot like the one in *Fantasia*. To be honest, the festival probably would have gone unnoticed by most of the world had it not been for the body of a young, unidentified woman found in a tent by a member of a cleanup crew. After that, it was all over the news. Rumors persisted she was murdered by members of a cult.

And his daughter was missing.

"I found the flyer in my daughter's room along with all of her LP records. Albums I was unaware she possessed."

"Not the Pat Boone or Elvis Presley type of rock and roll?"

"More like psychedelic, acid rock. Devil music. Songs like 'White Rabbit' or 'Purple Haze' or 'Voodoo in My Basement.'"

"That's one of the bands on the flyer." I tapped the name on the sheet of red paper.

He turned his head away. "Yes. I saw. Have you ever listened to the song, Mr. Devlin?"

"I'm more into the Rat Pack."

"It's a song about a man who worships Satan. Plain and simple. It talks about how the man's son eats small children. Preferably girls. And I think of that young woman they found when it was over..." He slapped his hand down on the flyer the way he might swat a mosquito on his arm or a demon on a sheet of paper. "This is the crap my daughter was listening to before she ran off."

"And you think she went to this Soul Revival Music Festival?"

"I know she went. I watched her get into a van with a group of other misguided young people. They're going to change the world by smoking marijuana, growing long hair, being flower children." He worried like overly concerned parents who watch their only child learn to ride a bike. Calamity could happen at any moment.

"You watched her go. Meaning you couldn't stop her."

"She's twenty-two, Mr. Devlin. Living at home and working at Korvette's Department Store down at Ten Mile and Mound roads. They sell those records at that store! It's how she was introduced to that so-called music, of that I am certain." He drew in his upper lip and bit on it. He rubbed his wrist again.

"The festival was two weeks ago—"

"Please stop calling it a festival. It was never a festival. It was a hedonistic, orgiastic, bacchanal!"

He spoke and acted with no self-control. White, foamy spittle flew from his mouth. His outrage overtook him and he began to shake. He hooked a finger under his collar and pulled it away from his neck.

"Can't...breathe." His face contorted.

"Kelly! Get in here!"

I brought out the bottle of bourbon and poured some into a glass. I held the glass out to him. Pastor Meredith's eyes bulged. I knocked back the bourbon myself and set the glass on my desk.

Kelly ran into the office. She took one look at the minister and blamed me.

"Oh my God, Jack! What did you do?"

"Me?"

"Call an ambulance!" She undid the man's collar and loosened his tie. "Uncle Andy, it's Kelly. Relax. Take deep breaths. We've called for help."

Just before he passed out, Meredith glared at me and mumbled, "Find her."

Kelly stood up, her hands on her hips. "Great. You killed him."

"He's not dead. And by the way, you could have told me he was your uncle."

"I know how you feel about helping family."

"My family."

"How was I supposed to know? You wouldn't even help your mother find her dog last week."

"That's because that beast isn't a dog. It's a hound from hell. It chewed up my best Florsheim loafers. You know what a pair of Florsheim goes for?"

"I think my uncle could cover at least two pairs if you take the case."

"I kind of have to, considering I almost killed him."

Kelly wrapped her arms around my neck. She pressed against me. "Oh, Jack, thank you. I knew you would. And I'll help pay. You can take it out of my check."

"We'll work out the arrangements later."

She pulled back a bit. A familiar smile slipped over her face and her moony eyes peeked out from under slightly lowered lids. "Why, Jack Devlin, haven't we already been down that road?"

It was a road I wouldn't have minded traveling a second time. Kelly had been working with me for over five years. We'd shared a lot of laughs and a lot of tears. Yeah, I was older, but neither of us cared. We didn't see the gap in our ages as an obstacle. It wasn't as wide as the one between Fred Astaire and Audrey Hepburn in *Funny Face*. We were more like William Powell and Myrna Loy in *The Thin Man*. I leaned in for a kiss. Pastor Andy groaned and ruined the moment. Kelly said, "Just as well. He'd probably wake up long enough to ask your intentions and then lecture me about chastity, before conking out again."

I didn't get a chance to respond or kiss her anyway, because at that moment the ambulance arrived.

They loaded Pastor Andy onto a gurney and wheeled him down the hall to the elevator. Kelly sat on the corner of my desk talking to her aunt on my phone.

"He'll be fine, Aunt Claire. They said you can pick him up at South Macomb Hospital in a couple of hours." Kelly smiled at me with those moony eyes casting her spell over me. "Yes. He agreed to do it. I'm helping to cut costs. Don't be silly. Jack's practically family. Uh-huh. You, too." She hung up.

"Practically family?" I asked.

"If I didn't say that, she'd worry about paying you."

"Someone should. We're strapped." I pulled on my jacket and put on my hat. "Okay, partner, let's roll."

"Where we going?"

"Shopping."

"I thought you said we were strapped, Mr. Devlin?"

"Window shopping. I hate going into department stores by myself. I need to ask around Korvette's about your cousin."

"Ooo! While you're doing that, I can check out ladies' delicates. I need some new bras."

"What happened to your other ones?"

"I burned them."

She always made it interesting.

I expected the longhaired, freaky dude behind the counter on the Entertainment Media floor to ignore me, given my charcoal gray suit and black fedora. I figured he wouldn't trust me because I was over thirty.

"You're on a mission." He spread his hands on the counter. "I'm Bob. How can I help you?"

"It's my niece's birthday. She heard this band at a music festival up in the Thumb a few weeks ago and it's all she talks about. I want to get her their album."

"The band have a name?"

I unfolded the flyer. "Yeah. Here it is. 'Voodoo in My Basement'. Ever hear of it?"

"Heard of the song by the Lovin' Spoonful, my man."

"Lovin' Spoonful as in 'Summer in the City' Lovin' Spoonful?"

He snapped his fingers and gave me a thumb's up. "Right on! That's the band."

"Well, they seem—groovy."

"Spoonful? Great band."

"What about this band?" I pointed to name on the flyer.

"Probably a tribute band, Spoonful fans, covering their songs."

Bob opened a drawer and pulled out an opened copy of *Hums of the Lovin' Spoonful*. He held the disc by the edges between his palms and gingerly put it on a hi-fi turntable.

"Let me play the track for you. It's kind of a bluesy, folksy number I think is meant to echo the sounds of New Orleans. They—they, being the band—were trying all kinds of styles so maybe they were just looking for a new sound. But hey, what do I know? I only work here part-time. I'm a Philosophy major."

Of course he was.

The record dropped. He lifted the arm and set the needle down on the space between the tracks. The song started with bluesy guitar. Someone woo-hooing. There was some rhythmic, woodblock drumming that went "clop-clop-clop-CLOP…clop-clop-clop-CLOP…clop-clop-clop-CLOP." It reminded me of the drums heard in Jacques Tourneur's horror movie, *I Walked with a Zombie*. Nothing too explicit in the lyrics. To me it was just a fun little song with a quick, hypnotic beat.

I could see where it would get under Pastor Meredith's skin.

"What do you think?" Bob asked.

"I'm going to have to think about it."

"Yeah, that's cool. I can hold a copy for you."

"I'm really looking for something from this other band."

Bob shrugged. "That was probably the only time Voodoo in My Basement ever took the stage."

"Why is that?"

"Promoters need to fill spots. Word goes out for talent. People cover a dozen songs in a thirty- to forty-five-minute set. Those dudes probably just really dug the Lovin' Spoonful or psychedelic songs."

"Did you go?"

Bob shook his head. "Soul Revival? No. Missed that one."

"Know anyone who did?"

Bob turned to a salesgirl working the small electronics counter. "Hey, hey Paula. This guy has a question about the Soul Revival Festival."

Paula looked up from a catalogue. "You a cop?"

"No. I have a question about a band."

Paula shook her head. "To be honest, I don't remember a lot of the festival."

I laughed. "Must have been a real trip."

Paula nodded. "Oh, it was that and more. What was the band you were asking about?"

"Voodoo in My Basement."

Paula's eyes widened. She drew her mouth into an *O*.

"Having a flashback, Paula?" Bob asked.

If she could have, I think Paula would have flipped Bob the bird.

"On the way up to the festival there was a girl from Swimwear who had that song on a cassette. She kept playing it over, singing along with it and laughing."

"Laughing?"

"Yeah, well, she was high. At least I thought she was tripping. Kept saying how cool it would be if voodoo was real."

"It is real," Bob said. "By that, I mean a real religion people practice. I have a Religion minor."

Of course he did.

"You say this other gal works up in Swimwear?" I asked.

Paula shook her head as if she were clearing away the memory. "I don't think she works here anymore. I haven't seen her since that weekend. We got to the festival and she said, 'I'm free!' and off she went. That was the last any of us saw of her."

"You mean you left her there?" Bob kinda said what I was thinking.

"Well, it's not like she was a kid. I'm sure she got home."

"I know, but I mean, that girl who was murdered—"

"Got my bras!" Kelly announced to all as she entered the sales floor. "Did you get anything?"

"No…" I said. I must have been blushing because I could feel a little heat in my cheeks. "I was just asking about some music for my niece's birthday, dear."

"We should ask my cousin. She works here." Kelly looked at the two salesclerks. "Anna Meredith?"

Bob shook his head. Paula did the same.

Kelly smiled. "Well, it is a big store. We ready?"

I nodded to Kelly, then turned to Bob and Paula. "Thanks for all your help."

We walked out of the Entertainment Media Department. I caught Kelly by the arm.

"That was good back there, dropping your cousin's name like that. Funny thing, though, the salesgirl at the counter didn't recognize it and I'm pretty sure she was in the same van going up there. Did Anna work in Swimwear?"

"We could ask. It's right up the escalator."

"Isn't that where women's delicates are?"

"Oh, relax. It's not like you haven't seen them before…" She gave me that smile of hers, the one that always hypnotized me. Made me wonder why we broke it off in the first place. Then I remembered, it wasn't "we" that broke it off. It was me.

I let Kelly take the lead. She spoke to one of the saleswomen positioned at glass display cases around the floor. The saleswoman gave her a curt, impatient smile that looked more like a grimace.

"Returns are on the first floor in the Customer Service Department."

"I don't have a return. I'm looking for my cousin. I believe she works in this department."

"I see. What is the young woman's name?"

"Anna Meredith."

The woman thought about it before shaking her head. "I'm afraid we don't have anyone here by that name."

"Are you certain? I know she worked at this location."

"I'm the floor manager, Miss. I know my employees."

Kelly leaned on the counter. "Then you would know my cousin. Two weeks ago, she took the weekend off to go to a music festival up in the Thumb. No one in the family has seen or heard from her since. We're all just a little concerned about her."

"Two weeks ago, you say?"

"Yes, ma'am."

"There was a young woman who didn't show up for her Friday night shift. We tried calling the number she gave us but the man who answered said he's the custodian at a church. He said he never heard of her."

"What name did you give?"

"Hers."

"But that wasn't Anna Meredith?"

"Certainly not. It was Apollonia Mancuso."

"Oh. That's definitely not her. Sorry for the inconvenience."

"Not a problem. I'm sorry I couldn't help."

"Oh, you've been extremely helpful." I said.

The saleswoman gave me the once over. "What are you? Her muscle?"

Kelly stifled a laugh.

She took my arm as we stepped onto the down escalator.

"So why would Anna use a fake name?" Kelly asked.

"Why does anyone?"

"She didn't want the people she worked with to know who she was."

"Safe bet. Could be she didn't want people knowing her father was a radio evangelist. Might cramp her bohemian lifestyle. When we find her, we can ask her."

"Will we find her?"

I put my arm around Kelly's shoulder and hugged her close. "I promise. I'm heading up to Port Pinnebog in the morning."

"I'll make you breakfast before you go."

"What about dinner tonight?"

"You're taking me out. But first I want to stop by South Macomb General and check on my uncle."

The news was not good when we got to the hospital. Kelly's Aunt Claire spoke to us in the waiting room for the Intensive Care Unit.

"He's in a coma," she said in a low, guarded voice. "They have no explanation why."

Telling us broke her. She clutched Kelly's hands.

"Oh! Lord, please don't take him before he can be reunited with our daughter! He didn't mean the things he said! He regrets the actions he took!"

Kelly hugged her. "What happened, Aunt Claire? They were always so close."

"Oh! It was awful. Just awful! Andy told Anna she was opening the door to Satan with the choices she was making. She accused him of being a charlatan. He slapped her across the face. And then she left with those people from her job and she hasn't been back. I begged her to come home."

Kelly sounded surprised. "Begged her?"

"Have you heard from her, Mrs. Meredith?"

Kelly's aunt hesitated. "She called me a week ago. She knew Andy would be at the church recording his sermon for broadcasting."

"And you didn't tell Uncle Andy?"

"No. Anna begged me not to. She said she was fine but she could use a little money. She asked me to take the cash she had in her jewelry box and send it to her."

"Did you?"

"Yes. I wrapped six twenty-dollar bills in butcher paper and put it in a long envelope and mailed it."

"Was that the only time you heard from her, Mrs. Meredith?"

Again, she hesitated. "Anna called again yesterday and asked me to send them more."

"Them?" Kelly asked.

"The people she's living with. I told her I sent her all the money I found in her jewelry box the first time. A man got on the phone and told me to find a way to make it happen, and if I didn't, he'd tell everyone Andy was a phony who beat his wife and daughter. I couldn't let that happen. Andy just got syndicated."

"So you sent more dough?"

Aunt Claire was on the verge of tears. "I had to."

"Where did you get the money, Aunt Claire?"

Her hands flapped up and down. "I'm so ashamed!"

"Did you take some from—"

I stopped Kelly from asking her aunt what she didn't want to admit. "Do you remember the address she gave you?" I asked.

"Twenty-nine Hellebuyk Road." Aunt Claire turned away from us. "I know. I know. It's less than twenty miles from here. But I couldn't tell Andy. I was afraid he'd go after her and scare her away for good. Now it looks like I'll lose Andy."

"You're not losing anyone, Mrs. Meredith." I turned to Kelly. "Dinner is going to have to wait."

"I know." Kelly gave me that wrinkly nose smile. "Just make sure you don't miss breakfast."

A twenty-mile trip was a hell of a lot better than a two and a half hour ride up M-53 to the tip of Michigan's thumb peninsula. I'd be in northern Macomb County instead of the edge of the world in Huron County. Farm country. A place where guys in red plaid jackets and matching hats hunted pheasant with double barrel shotguns and long-haired dogs while women sold produce at roadside stands and children swung on rope swings tied to the rafters in the barn.

*

Number 29 Hellebuyk Road didn't look any different than the dozen or so other farms I passed.

Until I got there.

There must have been two dozen people plucking peaches off the orchard trees. I could see more in the fields, twisting ears of sweet corn off the stalks. Another group sat in the shade, snapping pole beans and dropping them into paper lunch bags that, when filled, got put in a wooden crate to be taken to the busy produce stand. On the sign over the bins of food, a cartoon bald man in a long garment took an extra-long step as he carried a bushel of fruits and vegetables. The words Hellebuyk Road Cooperative hovered above him.

It all looked very idyllic, but there was a current of danger humming under the *R.* Crumb world I saw before me. The haunting "clop-clop-clop-CLOP…clop-clop-clop-CLOP…clop-clop-clop-CLOP" echoed in my thoughts.

Three guys with arms the size of tree trunks stood outside the closed barn door clearly standing guard over whatever was being grown or stored in there.

I pulled in and parked at the end of a long row of cars. I took off my jacket, rolled up my sleeves, and tipped my hat back on my head. I kept my .38 in my pants pocket. Not ideal, I know, but I couldn't go poking around without looking suspicious if I had on my shoulder holster.

A young woman sat on the back porch. She played with a string of pearls draped around her neck with her cigarette hand. The bottom step moaned when I leaned my weight on it.

I gave her my best ten-dollar smile. "Beautiful Michigan day."

"Yeah, we get them every now and then. Produce stand is around front." She made a slight shift of her head and jetted smoke out of her mouth in the direction she wanted me to go.

"I'm not here for the peaches, Peaches. I'm looking for Apollonia Mancuso."

She eyed me. "Who sent you?"

"I have something to tell her. Is she inside?"

"You need to talk to Brother Horace."

"Who's Brother Horace?"

A scruffy looking guy with thick, curly hair and a thick, black beard appeared in the screen door. "I'm Brother Horace. Sister Apollonia is in the kitchen canning peaches. You want to talk to her, come inside." He held open the screen door stretching its rusted spring.

"I'd rather talk to her out here."

Brother Horace's nod was so slight I barely recognized it as a signal. By the time I turned around, the three guys from the barn were already behind me. The biggest of the three punched my lights out.

A bucket of cold well water woke me sometime later. Someone had tied a blindfold around my eyes and my hands behind my back. I sat on a wooden folding chair. I knew from the smell of dirt, I was in a farmhouse root cellar.

"Who are you and why are you here?"

"That you, Brother Horace?"

A fist flew into my jaw. I could taste iron, and it wasn't from the well water.

"I'll ask you again. Who are you and why are you here?"

"I was sent to find Apollonia Mancuso."

An uneasy stillness took over the room.

"Apollonia says she doesn't know who you are."

"Is she here?" I waited to be punched. "Apollonia—Anna—if you're here, I know it's because you want to be. Unless you're being held against your will..."

I thought for certain I would get punched then. When it didn't happen, I continued.

"I can't force you to go with me. If I did, then I'd be a kidnapper. I'm only here to tell you your father is in a coma and it doesn't look good. Your mother thinks if you go to him, it might bring him out of it."

"My daddy's in a coma?"

I heard someone other than me take a blow, a heavy slap.

"Did I say you could talk—"

There was a bit of a commotion. Something that sounded like a shallow gong rang.

Someone asked, "Holy—how did you do that?"

"Stick around and I'll do it again," the young woman said.

Then someone ran up steps. The ropes tying back my hands slipped away. I pulled off the blindfold. I stared at the young woman from the porch as she dug through one of the many apple boxes stored on metal shelves around the cellar.

Then I saw Brother Horace sprawled in the dirt, the rusty steel bucket used to throw water on me lying next to his head.

"You're Anna Meredith?"

"I want you to take me to my father." She removed a ragdoll from an apple box with the name Apollonia Mancuso on it. The doll, made of black fabric, had red button eyes and white thread *X*s for a mouth. Around the waist was a silver and gold wristwatch. She removed the watch and put it on her own wrist. I watched her pluck several hairs from the back of Brother Horace's scalp. Horace did not move.

"You crowned him good," I said.

"The S.O.B. had it coming." Her choice of words surprised me for the daughter of a preacher man. Then, in a more civilized tone, she added, "We should go. It's about to get crazy here."

I followed her into the backyard through the cellar doors. Farther up the road, the flashing lights of the local municipality flickered against the night sky. Members of the cooperative fled as sirens wailed.

In the car, she told me the cooperative may have started as a utopia, but it wasn't long before she realized it was just another Orwellian nightmare.

"Did he have anything to do with the murder of the young woman at Soul Revival?"

"Someone was murdered at the festival?"

I filled her in as we left the farm. Took us about an hour to get to South Macomb General, what with sheriff cars swarming in from all directions. Halfway there, she asked me to turn on the radio.

"Which station?" I asked.

"Any. It's going to be on all of them."

"What is?"

"Listen."

She stopped turning the dial in time to hear the repeated news flash: "Once again, police in Huron County have arrested Glenn Leland for the murder of nineteen-year-old Stephanie Schultz last month at the Soul Revival Music Fest in Port Pinnebog. Early reports indicate—"

Anna cut in. "Lovers' spat—the two had a quarrel earlier in the day…"

I turned off the radio. "How did you know that was going to be on the news?"

"I don't know. It's weird. I get premonitions sometimes. Drives my dad crazy."

"I'll bet."

"Make a left."

"That'll take us north."

"Suit yourself but they'll be checking cars. What will you tell them when they start asking questions?"

I turned left. In my rearview, I saw a long line of taillights.

We got to the hospital around ten. Kelly met us in the hospital lobby.

"How's dad?" Anna asked.

"It's a miracle. About an hour ago your father just woke up out of the blue. The doctors can't figure it out."

Anna looked at the watch on her wrist. "Yep. That's about right."

About the same time she took the watch off the black fabric doll, she meant. I'm not saying there was a connection between Anna putting the watch on her wrist and her father coming out of his coma, but it did make me wonder. Perhaps it was a question best saved for Brother Bob the Part-Time Record Salesman and Religious Philosopher. Or maybe it was a question best ignored.

Anna grinned at me. "Thanks for the ride, Sir Lancelot." We watched her go off to the elevators.

Kelly leaned into me. "What did she mean by all of that? If you're anyone's Lancelot you're mine."

"Mellow out, Guinevere. Remember, that love story doesn't have the best ending."

"Are we going for happily ever after this time, Jack Devlin?"

"Why? You have a bottle of Love Potion Number Nine in your purse?"

"Who needs a potion when I can just do this." She wriggled her nose like Samantha on *Bewitched*. I had no defense against it.

And then she kissed me.

Cooking with Butter
by Linda Kay Hardie

(based on "These Boots Are Made for Walking," Nancy Sinatra, 1966)

Nancy Sinatra gave me the idea to kill my ex-husband.

We'd just added her to our playlist, and when "These Boots Are Made for Walkin'" came on for the first time, I was on the air, jockeying those disks. Ha. Actually, today the music is all on a hard drive, played by computer software. We record our voice tracks before the fact, taking about forty-five minutes to record a four- to six-hour shift. My voice was on the air but I was in the studio, answering the phones and updating our website.

I knew the song was coming up, but when you voice-track, you only get to hear the first few seconds of the song as you introduce it. I wanted to hear the whole thing. It didn't disappoint. I was inspired to walk all over someone, and I had the perfect subject in mind.

While we were married, Pete had me completely under his control. He decided what I could do for fun. He decided who I could do it with—and who I couldn't. He gaslighted me often, telling me that I looked upset when I'd thought I was having a good day, and other illusions to mess with my mind. I thought the problems in our marriage were all my fault because that's what Pete wanted me to believe. I thought I'd married for love, but after the divorce I realized I'd married out of fear, fear of being alone.

Pete and I met when we both worked as disk jockeys at an adult alternative radio station in Fresno. We dated, got married, bought a home, populated it with Abyssinian cats. We were both 27. Fifteen years later, when he hit The Big 42, Pete asked for a divorce. Typical male midlife crisis. By that time, I'd moved on to a job at my favorite format: 1960s golden oldies. Pete worked for the same radio company, but at the modern rock station.

After Pete filed the divorce papers, my program director, Harry, was the first person I told. I discovered Pete was not a beloved figure around the station. Harry called our music director into the office.

"Hey, Jeff, Amanda's got some good news!" Harry said. "She and Putrid Pete are getting a divorce."

Jeff stuck out a hand. "Congratulations," he said.

In a daze, I shook his hand. That's when it first occurred to me that the divorce might be a blessing. I didn't have any idea the other jocks had such a nickname for him. It was pretty funny, now that I thought about it. I also realized some of Pete's quirks I'd overlooked were bigger faults than I ever thought. Pete's habit of skipping showers and not brushing his teeth affected more people than just me.

So when I came up with the idea of murdering Pete, I had a strong feeling the people at work wouldn't narc on me. If I didn't make it too obvious.

Initially I'd resisted, but soon realized divorce was the best gift my ex ever gave me. Working at the same company wasn't, well, working out. One of us had to go, and it wasn't going to be me. Nancy taught me that. Question one was how to murder him? Question two was, could I get away with it? I wanted that answer to be yes.

Pete kept coming into the oldies studio when I was on the air, despite Harry telling him to leave me alone. Pete's excuse was that he had to talk to me about the divorce. Pete was fighting me, because he thought he could dump me after 15 years without splitting our assets. He dragged his heels about providing financial details to my attorney until he was threatened with contempt of court. Every step of the way, he would come in and harass me in person, until I asked my attorney if I could get a restraining order. Instead she talked to his attorney, who told him to cut it out.

Meanwhile, the radio stations had a lunch thief, like so many offices do these days. The day after Nancy's song debuted on my station, I solved that mystery when I walked into the break room in time to see Pete grab Harry's lunch bag out of the fridge. Without making a sound, hardly breathing, I backed out of the room before Pete spotted me. Despite our friendship, I didn't say anything to Harry.

One of the things Pete harassed me about at work was my cooking. He'd seldom complimented me, but he always cleaned his plate. Now he came into the studio with the excuse of asking for my recipes. I didn't want to see him, much less give them to him. My homemade spaghetti with meat sauce was his favorite. I decided I would poison my own lunch and put it in the break room fridge, then wait for Pete to steal and eat it.

That night, I made my poisoned spaghetti sauce, my favorite oldies blaring. Pete was pissed because we'd had to sell our house to split the proceeds, since neither of us could afford to buy the other out. I took my settlement, my share of the equity in our house, and I bought myself a mobile home in a nice park. The homes were close together, but well-insulated, so I could listen to my music almost as loud as I wanted.

I've always liked to cook to up tempo songs, and today I added Nancy Sinatra to a repertoire that included the Turtles, the Kinks and the Zombies. The hardest part about cooking poisoned pasta sauce was remembering not to taste as I cooked.

I didn't have to research what poison to use. That had been given to me on a silver platter when I first moved to California after college 20-some years ago. I don't even remember who told me oleanders are poisonous. Oleander, the ubiquitous bush found all over California, especially along old highway 99 that bisects Fresno. It occurred to me that oleander leaves look enough like a common cooking leaf that perhaps someone arrogant could mistake them for bay leaves. Someone like Pete.

I did read oleander has a bitter taste. So does bay, which is why you only use one or two bay leaves, depending on size, when you cook a stew or spaghetti sauce. I decided to use an old, deep skillet to make the sauce in, one I could throw away once I'd finished. I didn't know how corrosive oleander leaves were, but I didn't want to poison myself cooking tomorrow night's dinner. I used a wooden spoon that I picked up at a thrift store. It would go in a trash bin too. Not both in the same bin, not near the house or studio either.

I made a small batch. I only needed enough to fill Pete's favorite margarine container. The health claims of margarine always seemed suspect to me. I never used the stuff because I prefer real butter. It was always a fight when we were married. I bought a tub of margarine at a store where they don't know me, scooped out the yellow glop and threw it away, keeping the container for the decoy lunch.

I always came in at 9 for my 10 A.M. to 3 P.M. air shift. I made sure Pete saw me come in with the container and put it in the fridge. The trap was baited, the decoy was set in the water. Now I had to wait in the bushes for the sitting duck. To mix a few metaphors.

"Amanda!" Jeff called out to me as I walked past the office he shared with the music directors of the other stations. "Did you bring us butter cookies made with real butter today?"

"Nope. I made spaghetti with homemade meat sauce last night. Maybe this weekend."

I recorded my voice tracks for the day and settled in to update the website with more community events. Pete burst in when I was deep into adding concerts to the calendar.

"Why won't you give me your recipe for spaghetti sauce, you selfish bitch?" he yelled without preamble.

"Go away," I said. Outwardly I hoped I sounded calm, but inside I was quaking. His verbal abuse always cut the legs out from under me.

Harry walked by just in time. "Pete, my studio is off-limits to you," he said. "Out! Next time I find you in here, you'll be suspended. Since the divorce is now final, you have no need to talk to Amanda at all."

With a glare, Pete stomped out. Harry patted me on the shoulder and left. I blinked back the tears I'd been holding in. I hoped that Pete would eat my spaghetti today and relieve me of my misery. I would have to wait a few hours for lunchtime.

Since I only brought the poisoned lunch, I didn't have anything to eat. Fortunately, I wasn't hungry today, which was unusual, but perhaps not, given the circumstances and the queasiness in my stomach. The enormity of my plan was beginning to sink in. But what could I do? I couldn't quit. I had good ratings, a good contract, and I liked my job. Pete refused to quit. He had decent ratings on the afternoon shift on the modern rock station, but more than that, he wouldn't give me the satisfaction. Even though he'd been the one to ask for the divorce, he still fought me every step of the way.

And that's when the Guess Who's "Undun" came on. I hadn't seen it when I was voice-tracking, because I was preoccupied and didn't announce it, so I didn't notice it in the middle of a long set of music. I felt like the girl Randy Bachman wrote about, the one he saw at a party, fall into a coma after taking acid. I was happy when the song ended and Aretha Franklin came on. Whew. This strengthened my resolve. Yes. I deserved respect, and I didn't see any other way to get it besides removing my major source of disrespect.

I usually ate lunch around 1 o'clock, so at that time I went into the break room to check out the fridge. The margarine container was gone. That's when I noticed the aroma of spaghetti sauce hanging in the room. He'd nuked it and gone somewhere else to eat.

My stomach dropped. It was happening. In a few minutes, I would be a murderer.

I was back in my studio answering phones when the commotion started. People were running up and down the hallway outside the studio's window. Harry stepped into the studio. He looked grim.

"I know you're divorced and he's an asshole," Harry said and stopped. He took a breath. "I wanted you to hear it from me. I think Pete is dead."

"What happened?" My voice shook, and I had to clear my throat.

"He was voice-tracking his shift, and he suddenly threw up all over the control board. Jeff was walking past and saw it happen. He ran in to see what was going on, and Pete was on the ground. He wasn't breathing. Jeff called 9-1-1."

The paramedics rushed by my window just then.

I cleared my throat again. "What do you think is wrong?"

Harry ran his hand through his hair. "I don't know. He was eating lunch, even though Marcus has threatened to kill him for eating in the studio. Oh, damn. I'm sorry, Amanda."

"That's okay. I guess. I don't know. I don't know what I feel about this." I took a deep breath. "I mostly feel weird. Kinda glad, but guilty for not feeling bad about someone dying. Are you sure he's dead?"

"No. When Jeff called 9-1-1, I ran in here to let you know. But it sure didn't look good. We'll know by how quickly the paramedics leave with him."

But before the paramedics left, police officers showed up. Harry left to see if he needed to do anything, but Marcus, Pete's program director, and Catherine, the general manager, were in charge.

The paramedics notified the police because it looked like Pete had been poisoned. He was dead, although they wouldn't officially call time of death until he reached the hospital and a doctor made that decision. The uniformed officers were talking to Marcus and Catherine and Jeff when the detectives arrived. All sorts of police.

The police took the leftover spaghetti in the margarine tub, as well as samples of the vomit off the control board.

I looked at the time and was shocked to see that it was about time for Jeff to come into our studio to voice-track his afternoon shift, just after 2 o'clock. I was just going to look for Harry to ask if I should record the first hour when Jeff showed up, followed by a detective.

"Are you okay?" Jeff asked me.

I shrugged. I really didn't know. I didn't have to fake shock and anxiety because I was anxious about being caught. Especially with the police detective in the studio.

"You're Amanda Montana?" she asked me. "You used to be married to Pete Steele?"

"That's my air name. My real name is actually Reed. Pete's is—was?—Smith," I said. "And yes, I used to be married to him."

"I'm Lisa Nesmith," the detective said. "Let's go into the general manager's office. She said I could use it for a while."

Detective Nesmith sat behind Catherine's desk. I sat in the guest chair. She didn't pussyfoot around.

"How did you and your ex-husband get along?" she asked.

I took a deep breath and followed her lead. "Not well. He was verbally abusive when we were married and the same after the divorce. His boss and my boss threatened to suspend him for bothering me at work."

The detective nodded. "That's what everyone said, although they were more circumspect about it."

I shrugged. "I figured as much. It was no secret. Lately he was harassing me for recipes."

"Recipes?"

"I'm a good cook. He wanted some of the recipes I made when we were married. I finally gave him my spaghetti sauce recipe, just to get him to leave me alone."

Detective Nesmith looked at her notes. "That's what he was eating today, spaghetti with meat sauce." She looked back up at me. "You seem more upset than I would have imagined, given your relationship."

I nodded. Scared is more like it, but I didn't say that out loud.

"It's all very unsettling. The way Harry described it, it sounded like a nasty, violent death," I said. "But to be honest, I won't lose much sleep over him. I don't know what to think yet."

"Thank you for being direct. I appreciate that in this business."

Her phone rang.

"Thanks for your time. Please stick around for a while, okay?"

I was talking with Jeff and Harry in the bullpen when the detective came in a few minutes later. Marcus was using our studio to record voice tracks for Pete's afternoon shift, since his studio was not only a godawful mess, but also still a crime scene.

"Pete Smith was poisoned with oleandrin," Nesmith said.

"Oleandrin?" Jeff said. "Is that related to the oleander bush?"

"The very same," Nesmith said.

"Oleander leaves look a lot like bay leaves," I said. "Bay leaves are used in most spaghetti sauce recipes."

Everyone looked at me.

"Pete used to brag about harvesting bay leaves from Yosemite National Park," Jeff said.

Harry nodded.

"Isn't that a violation of federal law?" Nesmith asked.

"Yeah, but Pete didn't care. He was just so proud of himself for recognizing the bush. Arrogant asshole. He was always lecturing everyone on whatever was on his mind. He thought he knew everything."

"Obviously not, if he mistook oleander for bay," Harry said.

"Would he use a random leaf in cooking?" the detective asked.

Jeff barked a laugh. "He would if he thought he was right."

Nesmith looked closely at each of us, but she didn't say anything else. She excused herself and left to talk to other members of her team who were still wandering around the office. Harry and Jeff left, too. I stayed in the bullpen, shuffling through papers. I tried to read through public service announcements, but my mind was too jumpy to concentrate.

Detective Nesmith told Catherine that she would be back after checking Pete's house to see if he made the spaghetti himself. I was ready to leave for the day when she returned a couple hours later.

Everyone gathered in the lobby. Nesmith said there was no evidence, for or against, as to whether he cooked the spaghetti sauce, but she found a pantry full of canned goods and spices, as well as a cupboard with a full set of pots and pans, and there was a skillet soaking in the sink that appeared to have been used for scrambled eggs, so it looked like he actually did cook, as unusual as that was for a divorced man.

She was going to recommend the coroner list the official cause of death as accidental poisoning due to misadventure. Nesmith left, and I figured I was home free, until Jeff motioned for me to come into the studio with him.

"I noticed some things today," Jeff said. "Pete was eating spaghetti with what looked like homemade meat sauce. If it hadn't been in a margarine container, I might have thought he'd stolen your leftovers."

He gave me a look I couldn't decipher. I didn't know what to say, so I didn't say anything.

Jeff continued. "But I know you don't ever use margarine, only real butter, so you wouldn't even have a margarine tub."

I cleared my throat. "What's your point?" I tried to sound calm.

"No point, I guess. Although I'll bet that we can bring our lunches again and know they'll still be there at lunchtime."

Jeff gave me a hug. "Cookies tomorrow? I'll bet baking would be relaxing."

My heart skipped a beat. I smiled. "Butter cookies made with real butter for sure."

I thought I heard a whisper from Nancy Sinatra. Maybe Jeff would like almond-flavored cookies, just for him. I'm sure I could scrape up some almond flavoring somewhere.

Wooden Ships
by Jeanne DuBois

(based on "Wooden Ships," Crosby, Stills & Nash, 1969)

Clare Cecarelli didn't know what her son Anthony or his wife Jennifer were thinking. The beach in August? No tent or sunblock known to man was going to keep six-month-old Liam from looking like a seventeen-pound cooked lobster after about five minutes under Florida's UV rays. And Emmy, Jennifer's ten-year-old from a previous marriage, with skin so white it was almost blue? She was going to fry like an egg. Or drown. Rip currents pulled unsuspecting swimmers to their deaths all the time along Florida's First Coast. As it turned out, it wasn't the sun or surf that got her.

Of course, Clare was thrilled when Anthony said they were spending five days in St. Augustine Beach before heading to Magic Kingdom. At the time, she thought they meant to stay at her place. She floated on cloud nine for a week. Her only child lived in New York so she rarely saw him or her grandbaby. Silly Clare. Her house couldn't compete with the new Embassy Suites by Hilton and its beachfront views, outdoor pool, signature restaurant and twenty-four-hour gym. Not that Anthony was all nose-in-the-air now that his IT career shoveled hundred-dollar bills at him. No, his hard-headed wife was the one plucking those strings. Well, Clare would paste on a happy face and dance to Jennifer's tune.

The morning after their arrival, Clare was awakened by her neighbor Jim, a retired postal worker and divorcee who sometimes slept over. Since well before the big five-oh Woodstock anniversary, he'd been reliving a youth cut short by the Royal Oak draft board in 1968. Which explained the motorcycle, the ponytail and the tie-dye shirts, though not what he was talking about now.

He stood at the door of her bedroom, hugely resplendent in green and red spirals, going on about something. "...and I've looked everywhere."

Clare sat up, yawned, and glanced at the clock. "What?"

Jim raised shaggy gray brows. "My CD player?"

"Isn't it on the table by your sliding glass door?"

"Nope."

"Then I don't know."

Jim walked away. "Those little rascals..."

Clare was heading out the front door when she heard the opening chords of "Wooden Ships"—Jim's favorite track on his gold "Crosby, Stills & Nash" CD—from somewhere in the distance. And then, silence. She laughed to herself. The snippet of music was a tantalizing bit aimed at getting Jim to run around the neighborhood trying to locate his missing player. No telling where he'd find it. Two of his grandchildren lived in the neighborhood and loved to mess with him. They'd been teasing their grandfather about his music CDs for weeks.

*

Clare caught up with Anthony and his family in the dining room of the hotel, then followed them to a shade tent on the beach, hungering for a chance to hold the baby. But, same as when Clare visited their home in April, Jennifer guarded Liam like a miser protects his gold. Clare finally managed to steal a peek at the baby's sleeping face, felt a rush of adoration, and fell into a happy memory of her own mothering days. Grown-up Anthony broke into her reverie with an absent-minded hug and sent her chasing after Emmy with a container of spray sunscreen. Clare remembered Jennifer's daughter from the wedding, but that was about it. Emmy moved full-time into Anthony's house during Clare's spring visit, but headaches kept the girl in bed for most of Clare's time there. Jennifer blamed them on allergies.

Emmy wanted to swim. Anthony was on his phone. Jennifer was busy hoarding the baby. The child couldn't go in the water by herself. Clare threw off her dress, shoes, sunglasses and hat, and trailed the girl into a not-so-calm ocean. After a long time spent diving under breaking waves or riding them to shore, Emmy tired of the water. Weak-kneed, Clare followed her out, handed her a towel for drying off, and sprayed her all over again with sunscreen. Clare then accompanied the ten-year-old on an erratic walk along the beach, filling the pockets of her beach-dress with the pound of shells Emmy collected, for who-knows-what-reason. Emmy didn't chase or tease the resting terns or skittering plovers, didn't squash the lavender jellyfish, or kick aside the shy little ghost crabs. Clare made sure to praise her every time. Emmy finally stopped to look at Clare, who felt like an Earthling being examined by an emissary from beyond the Milky Way. Emmy's eyes were a penetrating wash of bluish gray, her lashes bright fringes of corn silk.

Clare must have passed the test-from-outer-space because when they returned to the shade tent and Jennifer informed them of the next items on the day's agenda, lunch followed by a nap, Emmy asked if she could go to Clare's house instead. Clare had hoped they would eat lunch as a family, but Anthony was still prowling the beach on the phone with work, so she accepted her fate and went with Jennifer to exchange Emmy's swimsuit for a t-shirt and shorts.

The suite was spacious and cool. Jennifer dropped into a chair beside the telephone and perused the room service menu. Liam slumped in his carry-seat at her feet, asleep. Clare longed to stroke his dark wavy hair. She contented herself with a loving smile.

Jennifer smiled back.

Was it Jim who explained to Clare recently how a smile meant the same thing all over the world? Behind Jennifer's, lurked a smug little, that's *my* baby. Peace and love, not.

"No screens," were Jennifer's parting words.

"I know," Emmy said. "I left my phone in my backpack."

They were halfway across the parking lot when Clare recognized the rattle coming from Emmy's pockets. "You brought shells?"

Emmy skipped beside her. "We can make art, can't we? Tony says you're an artist."

Was it the casual way she tossed off a nickname Clare's engineer son would never use? Or the fact he'd called his mother an artist?

Either way, Clare's heart warmed to the child. "I wouldn't go that far, but I did teach Art in elementary school while Anthony was growing up."

"That's what Mom said. She's always telling me how Tony grew up without a dad. He died of cancer, right? When Tony was eight?"

Clare hesitated. "Yes."

Emmy turned to look at her. "Bet you didn't go out and marry somebody else right away."

Or ever, Clare reflected.

*

Jim's motorcycle was in his driveway. Clare wondered where he'd gotten to in his search. She didn't hear any music, but the cul-de-sac where Jim's grandsons lived was several houses away.

Emmy and Clare went inside and washed their hands at the kitchen sink. Emmy admired Clare's windowsill garden—fat little succulents, all shapes and colors—then wandered around the combination living/dining room checking things out. Clare lined up whole-wheat wraps and mayonnaise, opened a can of tuna, and retrieved a yellow bowl from the cabinet.

"What's this?"

Clare turned to look. Those little buggers. She was going to have to put a broom handle across the bottom of her sliding glass door. Perched on one of the two chairs at her tiny kitchen table, revealed now that Emmy had pulled the chair out, was Jim's portable CD player. When Clare explained, Emmy acted like Clare was speaking another language. "What does it do?"

Clare dried her hands, placed the player on the counter, popped the lid, saw gold, closed it again, and pressed play. "Suite: Judy Blue Eyes," a song with nary a mention of either Judy or blue eyes, filled her kitchen. Clare turned down the sound.

Emmy furrowed her brow. "Where's this music from?"

"The Sixties." Clare placed a green and a blue plate on the counter, handed Emmy the pickle jar, a fork and a bag of chips. "Want to help?"

The first two tracks earned three stars each from Emmy, "Guinnevere" earned four, the next songs two each.

The sixth track, "Wooden Ships," began with breaking waves and chatty seagulls, then incorporated a series of chords. The first line of the lyrics said something about a smile meaning the same thing all over the world. Ah hah. Clare cut a lemon into wedges and squeezed one into the tuna salad. When the song ended, Emmy asked to hear it again. Jim, Clare reflected, would love, love, love this little girl.

Clare set the player to repeat the sixth track. Either Jim wasn't home, or the music was too low for him to hear. Clare turned up the sound, set the plates on the table, and added two glasses of iced water flavored with lemon.

After the third time, Clare said, "Again? Or the next ones."

"The next ones, please."

Clare switched off auto-repeat, grabbed napkins, and sat at the table. They listened as they ate. The CD ended. The light on the silent player beckoned, so Clare turned it off.

"What kind of game were they playing?" Emmy said.

It took Clare a minute. "In 'Wooden Ships'?"

Emmy nodded.

"No game. There was a nuclear war." Clare put their dishes in the sink and turned on the hot water.

Emmy leaned on the counter. "They didn't know who won?"

"Nobody won, that's the point."

"Oh."

"They dropped bombs on each other until they all died." Clare squirted dish soap on a sponge.

Emmy made a face. "I don't understand how a song can sound so beautiful and be about a war."

Clare gave her Jim's take on the lyrics. "It's about the power of peace and love. The survivors from both sides sail away in wooden ships to start a new world together, leaving the fighting behind, all happy and free."

Emmy mulled this over as she pulled shells from her pockets, placing them in groups on the kitchen table. Clare gathered arts-and-crafts supplies from various closets. And then things got weird.

The front door slammed open. A young man in jeans and a black t-shirt rushed into the kitchen and lifted Emmy off her chair. Clare grabbed at him, but he knocked the wind out of her sails with a swift backhand. Emmy's body was slack, her mouth open in surprise. Clare leaped onto the man's back. He threw her off, elbowed her hard in the stomach, and whipped Emmy into the air like a bag of laundry. Clare struggled to breathe. With Emmy over his shoulder, firefighter style, he ran outside and shoved her into the back seat of a black sedan.

Clare was right behind him. She dove in the car, slid across the tan leather seat, and pushed Emmy out the other side. "Run! Keep going, no matter what!"

The driver, a skinny guy in a Yankees cap, caught Emmy and flung her back into the car. Both back doors slammed. Clare tried to open hers. No go. Stupid childproof locks.

Clare banged on the window. "Help!"

Black-shirt waved a small pistol where she could see it. "Sit back and shut up or the kid gets it in the face."

Clare dropped her hands into her lap and shut up. The car squealed around in the cul-de-sac and raced back toward Beach A1A. Clare patted her pockets. Several tubes of paint, a palette knife, two paint brushes, some hot glue sticks. No cellphone. That was still on the counter in the kitchen. Of course it was.

*

Jim stood spread-eagled, holding the wooden playset's crossbeam steady while his son-in-law's next-door neighbor tightened the bolts. Jim's daughter Mary crossed the yard with bottles of cold water—Tervis, not disposable plastic ones—and one grievance to share. "Clare just drove by in the back seat of her son's car and didn't even wave."

"Maybe she didn't see you," Jim said, taking a water bottle with a grateful nod.

"She saw me. Is she mad at you about something?"

Jim gave Mary an exaggerated look of surprise. "How could anyone ever be mad at me?"

She rolled her eyes. "Seriously?"

"Look out," her husband Frank said, wiping sweat from his face, "here comes trouble." He took the proffered water bottle and chugged.

Jim's twin grandsons ran across the grass.

One said, "PopPop, did we make Aunt Clare mad at us? 'Cause we put your CD player in her kitchen?"

"Cuz she just drove by and gave us a real mad look," the other one said.

"So that's where it is," Jim said. "I got sidetracked with this beastly playset. Let's give her a call and if so, you can apologize."

When Jim's calls repeatedly went to voicemail, he walked down the street with his grandsons at his heels, and found Clare's front door hanging open. Two pairs of flip-flops, both blue, different sizes, rested in the entryway under a table holding hats and sunglasses. Clare's phone was on the kitchen counter. A kitchen chair was overturned. Shells were stacked in small piles on the table. He checked the bedrooms and backyard. The twins followed him next door.

Jim shoved his feet into a pair of heavy work boots leaving the laces half-tied. "Tell me about the car."

"Black BMW M5 sedan," one twin said.

The other said, "Tan headrests. Blue license plate."

Jim said, "Remember the number?"

Both boys shook their head.

"Two men in the front," the first one added.

The second one said, "Aunt Clare and a girl with a blonde ponytail in the back."

Jim said, "Anything else?"

"The driver was wearing a black New York Yankees cap."

"They turned left at the stop sign."

Jim donned a hand-painted rainbow helmet, a gift from Clare on his seventieth birthday, and mounted his motorcycle. "You did a good job. Now keep an eye on Aunt Clare's house. Call me when she gets back." Not that he expected that to happen, but hope was a positive feeling and it gave the kids something to do.

He kept as far above the thirty-mile-an-hour speed limit as he dared. Somehow, he managed to hit the crosswalks after everyone had crossed. He rolled through the lot at Embassy Suites and spotted a black sedan with tan headrests driving away from the light at Pope Road.

Jim hit the curve going sixty. He merged right with the traffic going to the Oldest City via the Bridge of Lions and caught up with a black BMW M5 bearing a blue license plate. The driver wore a Yankees cap. A dark-haired woman and a girl with a blonde ponytail were in the back. Clare and her step-granddaughter? The driver could be Clare's son, a New Yorker and possibly a Yankees fan. But then who was the man in the passenger seat? And why was Clare's phone on the kitchen counter, her shoes and hat in the vestibule, her front door wide open?

Jim tailed the BMW over the bridge to Vilano Beach, staying a few vehicles behind. Two sun-hatted women waiting to cross at the intersection forced him to reconsider his plan to run the red light at A1A. After it changed, Jim negotiated the corner in time to spot a black car turning away from the ocean about a mile ahead. Jim followed. At the end of the street, brake lights flashed. Three rolling stops later, Jim made the same turn. No sign of the black car. The only vehicle in sight was a white truck making a right at the other end of the street.

*

The men ushered Clare and Emmy into the dark cottage and switched on a ceiling fan to circulate the musty air. Clare's stomach tightened.

Black-shirt said, "You got stuff in your pockets. Put it on the table."

Clare piled tubes of paint, paint brushes and hot glue sticks, then sat next to Emmy on a lumpy loveseat covered by a beach-themed throw. The cottage was fairly neat and clean. There was an appropriate number of chairs, tables, shelves and ocean pictures plus three shaded windows, one in each of three outside walls. A doorway and an empty rack for storing surfboards shared the fourth wall, separating the main living space from the rest of the cottage.

Black-shirt ambled around the room, fiddling with things on the tables and shelves. Yankee-cap paced in and out of the doorway. They were both young, not much older than twenty, and except for a small amount of facial hair, fairly clean-cut. Still, appearances can be deceiving.

Clare cleared her throat. "So, what happens now?"

Both young men looked at her, surprised. Yankee-cap opened his mouth to speak. Black-shirt silenced him with a cutting-of-the-throat gesture.

The two men sat finally, ignoring their captives, fixated on their phones. The ceiling fan wobbled on every third turn. The not-so-distant ocean sounded like a fleet of trucks barreling down A1A.

"Are we waiting for someone?" Clare said.

Black-shirt said, "Lady, you're a real pain, you know?" He pulled the pistol from his pocket and laid it on the table beside him. "Don't push your luck. You're not even supposed to be here."

Faint music sounded from Yankee-cap's phone. Clare cocked an ear, but it wasn't a ring tone. Meanwhile, scenarios were playing themselves out in her mind, way worse than reality, or so she hoped. She tried to block most of them as soon as they appeared.

The one she kept, despite its obvious flaw, had Anthony paying a huge ransom to a third party who then telephoned for their release. She and Emmy would make their way back to St. Augustine Beach, barefoot and thirsty, but none the worse for it. The problem with that scenario, and it was a biggie, was neither of the men were wearing masks and the license plate of the white truck was etched in Clare's mind.

She glanced again at the pistol. Kidnapping was a major felony in Florida, with or without a deadly weapon. Convictions resulted in lengthy prison sentences, as much as thirty years, as well as hefty fines. No doubt witnesses with good memories weren't welcome survivors.

*

Jim cruised the two blocks, checking the mostly undeveloped wetlands to his right, then the other side of the street where three- and four-story houses claimed riverfront views. At the last one, he spied a patch of black through the bushes. He left his motorcycle around the corner, walked back, and found the BMW in a covered driveway. It sat empty, an eighties model in excellent condition, except for a ruined steering column. A white cockle shell rested on the back seat.

Jim walked around the house, peeked in windows, saw no one, and worried about the car with its missing occupants. A long pier over the wetlands led to an empty dock. A white-haired man around Jim's age, but not nearly as big or robust but still intimidating because of the wooden baseball bat he carried, met Jim in the front yard.

"Hey, now," Jim said, palms out, "whatever happened to peace and love, Brother?"

"Don't come any closer." The man showed Jim a flip phone. He was close enough for Jim to catch the smell of cigarettes. "I already called the police."

"And told them…?"

"I told them how you stole my neighbor's car while he's gone for the weekend. Just brought it back, didn't you?"

Jim chuckled. "That'd be a good trick, driving a car and riding a motorcycle at the same time. Tell me, did you see what happened to the four people who were in the car?"

The man glowered. "Nobody here but you and me."

"You must have been getting the bat." Ignoring the man's advance, Jim squeezed through the hedge to the lot under construction next door and found footprints in the sand. Some had been made by bare feet. Tire tracks obliterated them on a path to the street. He found a black scallop shell in the sand near a roll-off container.

Jim returned to the covered driveway. "You see a white truck parked over there?"

The man stuck out his chin. "Maybe."

Jim strode away, oblivious to the man's angry protests. Why does someone steal a valuable car only to return it? Maybe to commit a different crime. Clare's son was a wealthy man these days. There were things here a kidnapper/car thief might find useful. Vacated home in a secluded area. Upscale car with a pre-nineties ignition. Nearby hiding place for a getaway vehicle. Nosy neighbor, not so much, but everything has its downside.

Jim pulled on his helmet, kick-started the engine and roared around the corner. Clare could be close by. Squeezed between the ocean and the river, the island wasn't that wide. All he had to do was ride the grid of streets until he spotted a white truck. Jim passed the man with the bat and flashed him the peace sign.

*

After what seemed like hours, Emmy touched Clare's arm with a clammy hand. "I don't feel so good."

The girl's ghostly pallor sent Clare to her feet. "Where's the bathroom?"

Without looking up, Black-shirt said, "One at a time."

"I don't think so," Clare said. "She's going to be sick."

As if to emphasize the urgency, Emmy fell onto her side, gagging.

"Kiddie vomit, eww." Yankee-cap shuddered.

Black-shirt sighed and gestured toward the open doorway. "End of the hall."

Yankee-cap's long legs blocked the doorway.

"Excuse us," Clare said.

He bent his knees without taking his eyes off his phone. On the way, Clare gathered a few unused brown napkins from beside an empty pizza box hanging out on the kitchen stove, just in case. She needn't have bothered. There were towels and washcloths on hooks in the tiny bathroom and more rolled into a rack under the sink. The white enamel fixtures were old but clean. The window above the toilet was open a few inches, letting in fresh air through a screen.

Clare left the lid up after her spot-check and squeezed past Emmy to hook the door closed. When Clare turned around, she caught Emmy putting down the lid. The girl flashed a mischievous grin as she climbed onto the toilet. Emmy's hands reached the window, but she couldn't budge the sash.

Clare turned the cold water on in the sink and made splashing sounds. Emmy groaned a few times for effect and exchanged places with Clare who quickly located the screws on both sides of the window that limited the sash's movement. Clare removed the palette knife from her pocket and used it like a screwdriver.

Emmy hissed a warning. Clare looked around. The pointed blade of a pocketknife was between the jamb and the door, moving up to knock the hook out of its eye. There wasn't time to change places. Clare sat on the toilet, grunting. Emmy bent her head over the sink and made genius plopping noises in the water with shells from her pocket. They only could see part of Yankee-cap's head, but the look on his face was priceless. Clare put her face in her hands and tried to sound like she was crying, in order to hide her laughter.

Adrenaline was making her too giddy. She stifled herself. The door closed. Emmy leaped to reset the hook. Clare stood on the toilet.

Once the screws were removed and the sash raised, the window screen remained the only obstacle. Clare couldn't find the tabs that would allow her to pull it out, so she slashed it along its taut edges while Emmy ramped up the being-sick sounds. When she was done, Clare stood on tiptoes and peeked out. The coast was clear.

Clare went out the window feet-first, scratching both legs and forearms in the process. Once safe on the ground, she took hold of Emmy's hands, guided the girl's wiggle through the opening, and caught her when she broke free. It was like helping a big baby be born, without all the fuss and muss.

The fence at the back of the property was galvanized chain link and the path to it, loaded with burrs. They avoided them, as best they could, while hopping clear of fire ant mounds. Clare imagined she heard Jim's motorcycle nearby. Not likely. Shortly afterward, a crash came from the direction of the cottage. Spurred on by the sound, Clare shoved her toes into the chain link and boosted herself to the top rail next to Emmy. Unlike Emmy, whose feet fit perfectly, only two or three of Clare's toes made it into each diamond-shaped space at a time. Some wayward wire twists on top grazed Clare's leg as she swung it over and blood trickled down her leg. Emmy appeared to be unscathed. A car rounded the cottage and came to a screeching halt two yards from their perch.

Emmy cried, "Daddy!" and jumped off the fence.

Clare swiveled her head expecting to see her son, but of course it wasn't Anthony. An unfamiliar man in a Panama hat was sliding out of the driver's seat of a blue sports car.

"Peaches!" the man said in response. "My boys been treating you okay?"

Emmy stopped short. "Wait, you know them?"

"Well, yeah. Why else would you be here?" Her father laughed. "It's not your uzsh hang-out, is it?"

"I don't believe it."

"I know, isn't it great? I told you I'd see you again soon."

"One of them pulled a gun on Tony's mother and threatened to shoot me in the face."

He noticed Clare for the first time. "Tony's mother?"

Emmy said, "Yeah, and guess what? She's not insane."

Her father frowned. "What's she doing here?"

"Your boys kidnapped her, too."

"First off, nobody kidnapped anybody, okay?" His hard tone quickly turned cajoling. "I had to get you away from your mother, didn't I? Figured we'd hang out here for a few days, until the heat's off, you know, then hit the road together. It'll be just like old times."

Emmy crossed her arms. "Like last time when you left me with Grams and she locked me in the cat room and I had to go to the hospital 'cause I couldn't breathe?"

"Aw, Peaches, she forgot you were allergic."

"Or the time before when I dropped my lunch over the fence at the zoo and Grams sent me into the enclosure to get it?"

"Nothing bad happened."

"Only because the gorillas weren't out yet."

"Forget Grams, okay? New day, you know? Just me and you, happy and free."

Emmy stared at her father for what seemed like a long time. When she finally spoke, her voice was almost too quiet. "You don't really want to be with me. Sending your boys to pick me up was just you dropping another bomb on Mom."

He looked baffled. "What?"

"You heard me. Your car's no wooden ship, Daddy. There is no happy and free for you and me without Mom."

He looked accusingly at Clare. "What have you been telling her?"

Clare shrugged. "I didn't say a word."

He gave his daughter a pouty look. “I went to a lot of trouble to set this up, you know. Renting the surf shack for a week wasn’t cheap and neither was hiring the boys.”

“What did you think Mom would do when I went missing?”

“Well, I thought she might carry on a bit, but she has a new kid now, you know, and I figured after a few days, she’d be ready to move on. They got tickets to Disney, don’t they?”

Emmy shook her head. “You’re not telling the truth, Daddy. You hoped she'd worry herself to death.”

At that moment, Jim called from out front, “Clare, are you here?”

Clare’s happiness immediately turned to fear. She shouted back, "The one in the black shirt has a gun!”

Jim’s response was gleeful. “Not anymore, he don’t.”

By the time Emmy caught up with Clare and they rounded the corner of the building, the circus in front of the cottage included three police cars with blinking light bars, an unmarked car in the street, blocking traffic, a white-haired man with a baseball bat, a victorious Jim with a kidnapper’s arm in each hand, four uniformed police officers, two curious passers-by, and a happy black dog who just wanted to play Frisbee on the beach.

Emmy’s father made the mistake of trying to drive through the assemblage. Clare stepped in front of Emmy so the girl wouldn’t see him being forcibly removed from his car. He loudly echoed the others’ claim that since no one had asked anybody for ransom, he couldn’t be accused of kidnapping. The police politely explained, one more time that it didn't work that way in Florida.

*

While Jim and Anthony presided over Clare’s propane grill and Jennifer nursed Liam in the air conditioning, Clare sat beside Emmy at the shady picnic table snacking on grapes and cubes of mozzarella cheese.

Emmy said, "Were the purple berries in 'Wooden Ships' more like grapes or blueberries?"

"That's a good question." According to Jim, the lyrics referred to iodine pills the survivors were taking to ward off radiation sickness, called Purple Berries because of their color, like other pills in the '60s, Black Beauties, Red Devils and Orange Sunshine, to name a few. Clare didn't want to get into that discussion.

"It doesn't matter," Emmy said. "When the people were sharing them, they were sharing peace and love, right? Here, have some of my purple berries, Nonna." Emmy held out a small bunch of red grapes.

So choked with emotion she couldn't speak, Clare reached for the grapes with a smile. Peace and love, Granddaughter.

Emmy went on breezily, "I asked Tony if I could call you that and he said I could. It means grandmother in Italian. It's nice having one who's not insane, you know? Not every one of our visits will include a near-death experience, if you know what I mean. The one yesterday doesn't count against you, by the way. Fear and danger are the 'uzsh' whenever Dad's involved."

Clare pulled the girl into a hug. A clever granddaughter with a sense of humor who liked to make art? What a treasure.

Holding baby Liam? Just a matter of time.

It Ain't Me, Babe

by Terrie Farley Moran

(based on "It Ain't Me, Babe," Bob Dylan, 1964)

Cully, night bartender at the Dive Inn, emptied my ashtray and chased a few stray ashes along the mahogany with a wet bar rag. "Jake, I don't get it. Every other guy in here needs to wave around serious cash or drive a muscle car for the girls to notice he's alive. You, you're a natural Babe Magnet." Then he dropped his elbows on the bar, leaned in, and whispered, "So tell me, what's your secret?"

I shrugged like it was no biggie and said, "It's my personal charm, at least that's what the babes tell me. If I could, I'd trade you a smidge for another long neck." And I pushed my empty Budweiser bottle toward his side of the bar.

I was watching the sports roundup on the ten o'clock news when the front door opened and I felt a blast of cool night air. The guys at the pool table, arguing about who made the best bank shot, went dead quiet, which was enough to make me glance in the mirror on the barback.

Her black miniskirt was dangerously short, and she was wearing those shiny white boots girls had been stomping around in for the past few months. A ton of eye makeup played up her green eyes but her lips were pale. She swiveled to the line of bar stools separating me from two rum-dumbs at the far end. If she wasn't some weirdo interested in old guys, I figured I was a sure thing. She pulled out a seat and perched, her long blonde hair swinging against the torn red plastic edge of the stool.

Cully was practically drooling at her cleavage when she ordered a Bourbon Sour. He looked puzzled but his brain must have recovered what he learned in bartender school because after a few beats, he gave her a smile and said, "Coming right up."

She tossed a pack of Parliaments on the bar, pincered one between long slim fingers tipped with blood red nails and pointed toward my pack of Lucky Strikes.

"Got a light?"

"Sure thing, Babe."

I flicked my gold-plated Ronson and she moved closer to catch the flame.

That's how it started. It didn't take long for us to be making out right there at the bar, and by midnight I was driving her home, got invited in and Bam! we were a couple.

At first it was all laughin' and lovin' and I was convinced that Lola was the ultimate babe. I knew I wasn't a forever kind of guy, but I thought we could have a good run. Sooner or later she was going to find out that new Bob Dylan song, "It Ain't Me, Babe" was written about guys like me.

The first hint I had of the amount of trouble she could cause was the night we stopped at the Dive Inn for a drink on our way to the Lux to see the latest Steve McQueen western. Cully delighted in making a Bourbon Sour for Lola and it annoyed me that I had to remind him to bring my beer. He was too busy ogling her and dreaming of what could never be his.

At a table by the jukebox, five or six soldiers roared when one spilled half a bottle of beer down the front of his fatigues.

Lola said, "Glad they can laugh now. They won't be laughing when they're in the jungle over in Nam. What a waste that war is."

The light went out of Cully's eyes. "My brother, Cal, was killed by sniper fire at Dak Tô early last year. He was supposed to be training the locals how to kill. Instead he took one straight through his brain. You telling me he died for nothing?"

Lola reached to pet his arm but Cully pulled away. She tried again but he walked down to the other end of the bar. Her magic touch couldn't overturn what she'd done.

She looked to me for support. "All I am saying…"

I cut her off. "Let's not be late. I wanna buy some popcorn. Bound to be a long line."

There was no point in talking. She'd insulted my favorite bartender. Tough move for a babe to survive.

She let it go until after the movie. On the drive home, she started telling me about the French government, global colonization, rubber plantations and who knows what all. I got more than a little angry when she said, "And you. How is it you didn't defend me when Cully got nasty?"

"Defend you? Why? You were wrong to bring up that anti-war bull, especially around here. You know how folks feel. And you went mouthing off to a guy who lost his brother fighting for the cause. Not my job to defend you or anyone else."

"I'm your girlfriend. You're supposed to stand up for me, no matter what."

I shook my head. Not the way I saw it.

That was the first time a date between us ended in her giving me a peck on the cheek with no invite to come in. I figured it was a peaceful ending. She could go her way and I could find a new babe. They're easy enough to come by. Before I had the time to look around, Lola called and offered a half-hearted apology along with a little afternoon delight. I figured what the heck. She likely learned her lesson. If not, this would be a sweet goodbye.

As it turned out we did spend more time together. I avoided taking her to the Dive Inn which left a lot of room on our social calendar. When she wanted to go to a dance club just over the county line, I decided to put up with her friends and the raucous music while I focused on planning a really good end to the evening, if you catch my drift.

Lola's girlfriends were nice looking but clearly not in her league. After a while I realized that was the whole point for Lola. She needed to be the star. Out on the dance floor the girls formed a circle to do the Shimmy. Lola jumped in the middle. The other girls were laughing and dancing, but Lola kept an eye on the onlookers.

Anytime she wasn't getting the bulk of attention she would elevate her shimmy until she had every guy in the place wishing she was with him.

I sat at the table listening to the guys talk about which teams were likely for this year's World Series. The Yankees fan was booed loudly while the poor sap who thought the Baltimore Orioles had a solid chance got pity looks. I tossed the St. Louis Cardinals out there and was pleased to get a few nods.

Suddenly Lola was by my side, pulling on my arm, yanking me out of my chair. She pointed to the edge of the dance floor. "You see the creep in the gray sharkskin jacket? He rubbed up against me when I walked past him. You better straighten him out."

I looked at the dance floor filled with twice as many people as it could realistically hold. And the guy Lola pointed to was dancing with a redhead. He seemed really into her.

"Babe, it's crowded. The guy didn't mean it. Probably didn't know what he did." If he did anything, I thought.

Lola specialized in sulking. After a group trip to the ladies' room, her girlfriends took turns whispering among themselves and shooting dirty looks my way.

I stood. "Early morning for me. Time to hit the road." I looked at Lola. "Ready, Babe?" I had enough of being the bad guy for no reason at all.

Everyone at the table looked at me. Then their heads swiveled to Lola. For the first time since I met her, she looked uncertain.

Then she picked up her purse and took my hand. "Sure thing, honey. But I hope you aren't *too* tired."

A couple of guys snickered at her tone, while the girls looked surprised.

We were halfway through the silent car ride to her house, when she started. "How could you humiliate me in front of all my friends? Would it have killed you to take a swing at that…that creep who grabbed me like that?"

"Didn't seem worth a big fuss." I said mildly.

She slouched in her seat. "You mean I'm not worth the fuss. Is that what you are saying? Here I am your steady girlfriend and you're willing to let any guy manhandle me. What's that say about you?"

I pulled over to the side of the road. I knew what I had to do, and I suspected her response was going to be bothersome, but I learned long since that it's the way these things go.

"Listen Babe, you know I like you and we've had some good times together but I kind of think the good times are over. Why don't we just call it a day?"

She sat up straight and leaned toward me, green eyes flashing. "You're dumping me? Like hell. No one dumps me. I am the hottest thing this town has ever seen. You're lucky I gave you the time of day. And don't you forget," she shook her finger in my face, "the rest of what I gave you. Mostly, you didn't even have to ask."

I could see this wasn't the time or the place. "Calm down, Babe. Maybe we ain't done. But for now, I have to get up early tomorrow and I need my sleep."

She crossed her arms and leaned back to her side of the car. "Glad you come to your senses."

After I dropped her off, I drove home slowly. I'd dealt with the breakup problem before. Who hadn't? But this babe was different. Somehow she thought she should be in charge. How the hell did that happen?

My phone rang the next morning while I was still shaking the sleep out of my eyes. All sugar, Lola said she was sorry for carrying on the way she did and she hoped I would come for dinner that night. She was so full of apologies that I thought I may as well get a decent meal and a final roll in the hay. Then I'd make sure this babe was history.

It didn't quite go as planned. On the way, I pulled into the Texaco station and left the gas jockey to check the oil and fill the tank while I slipped inside to pick up some cigs. I grabbed a pack of

Luckies and, on a whim, picked up a pack of Parliaments for Lola. Sort of a parting gift you might say.

She was gorgeous, gotta give her that, and she did her best to strut her stuff. When she opened the door, I got a whiff of some fancy perfume. Her skintight pants and snug sweater showed every curve of her body. I knew for certain she wasn't wearing a bra. She reached in to give me a kiss and the next thing I knew we were in her bedroom. By the time we came up for air, I was exhausted but happy.

Lola rested her head on my shoulder. "You really don't want to give this up, do you?"

And at that moment the only answer I could think of was, "No, Babe, I don't."

I should have known better. I didn't realize that she thought my answer gave her total control.

Then there were the cigarettes. Instead of being happy I bought her the Parliaments, she used them to guilt me into showing up with flowers once in a while. Then she started making random phone calls that always started suggestively. "Why don't we…" but as it turned out we'd end up spending time with those girlfriends I'd come to think of as her clique, all of them constantly watching me to make sure I treated the queen the way she deserved.

The final straw came—loud and clear. I'd made plans to watch the Friday night fights on my brother-in-law's new color TV. Just before I left my apartment the phone rang. I had a bad feeling, but I answered anyway, ready to turn down whatever she had to offer.

Lola was sobbing. "You have to come, right away. I need you."

"Hey, I already told you I'm going to my sister's. What's wrong? What can't wait?"

She snarled like a cornered cat. "There is always something more important than me. What about your baby? Is he more important than me?"

"What baby? Oh God, are you…" I couldn't even say the word.

"Just come now. Please."

I slammed the receiver down so hard I knocked the telephone off the table. How could this have happened? I was always careful when I was with a babe. Was there a time I wasn't careful enough?

I drove slowly to Lola's house. What part of "I'm a good time guy and don't get entangled" did she not understand? As soon as I parked, the front door flew open and Lola was down the steps, throwing herself in my arms.

This wasn't going to end well.

I coaxed her back inside and we sat on the couch. I noticed she'd conveniently left off the heavy eye makeup, which was my first clue that this was a setup. Why spend time putting it on if you were only going to mess it up with tears?

She looked down at the wad of tissues she was shredding in her lap.

I decided I could outwait her. I was totally numb inside, waiting for the worst news of my life. I wasn't going to rush it.

Finally she spoke. "I know that deep down inside you love me…"

Where did that come from?

"And I've been really good to you…"

So have dozens of other babes.

"I thought I was pregnant…scared I was pregnant…"

Thought? Only thought?

"And we both know it could have happened…"

Could have?

"So I think we should get engaged. You know, in case it ever does happen." She turned to me, her eyes welled up with tears that were ready to run down her cheeks.

There it was. She sprung the trap, setting me up so I couldn't dump her without looking like a bum—even to myself. Once we were engaged, there'd be no turning back. I'm sure we'd have peace for a while and then she'd want to seal the deal with the ring that would shackle me for life—a little gold band.

Lola had long ago made it clear that she saw my role as being the one to solve her problems, use my fists to straighten out anyone who bothered her, and blast anyone who disagreed with whatever she said. I was damn sure that wasn't the life I wanted. Not with her, not with any babe.

I pulled away but she just snuggled closer. I petted her head while I considered my options. Finally I heaved a long loud sigh. "Okay sweetheart. Give me a couple of days and I promise you the most romantic engagement this town has ever seen.

I had a plan and I needed to set it in motion.

The following week I invited her to go for an afternoon ride. When I picked her up, she asked, "Today? Is it today?"

I smiled. "Wait and see. Might be a big surprise ahead."

I drove out to the state park, eight hundred acres of cliffs and valleys. The day was overcast, so when I pulled into a nearly empty parking lot, Lola looked around. "What are we doing here?"

I turned off the ignition. "We are going to have a life-changing afternoon."

I popped the trunk and pulled out a picnic basket.

Lola clapped her hands. "A picnic! Even in this drizzle, that's romantic." She opened her umbrella and took my hand. "You know, there's a band shell by the lake. We could sit under there."

"I have a better spot." I took her arm and led her up a trail inclining its way through a stand of Ponderosa Pines.

I was afraid all the walking would bring out her whiney self, but I guess she was too excited, waiting for her big surprise. When we cleared the pines, I was happy to see the rain had stopped.

We came across a small sitting area of log benches surrounded by hawthorn bushes. I knew it well. I'd once made it with a girl named Irene, Eileen, something like that, on one of the benches. Turns out she got a few splinters and then wanted me to pull 'em out for her. No way!

"It's so cute, why don't we have our picnic right here?" Lola gave me her wide-eyed pretty-please look.

"Babe, I've been planning this for days." I tapped the pocket of my biker jacket like it was holding something special, "I know exactly where I am going to spring my surprise on you."

She got giddy, reached up to kiss my cheek. "I am going to take such good care of you. See if I don't."

I led Lola past a dense area where Southern red oaks mixed with white oaks, and kept her busy by asking if she could say which was which.

By the time she was bored with the guessing game, we reached a clearing on the top of a flat granite cliff with a sheer drop on its far side

"Here we are." I was so enthusiastic that Lola let go of my hand and spun in a slow circle eyes darting as she tried to find what made this place so special. Finally she looked at me and before she could ask, I answered.

"Thirty years ago momma and pop came to this very spot for a picnic. While momma was looking over the edge admiring the valley down below, my pop snuck up, took her hand and slipped a ring on her finger. And, well, here we are."

Lola threw her arms around me, gave me a soulful kiss and snuggled close. "That is the most romantic thing I have ever heard. You brought me here and so...what's next?"

I stepped away from her and said, "Well if you do what momma did, maybe I'll do what pop did."

It took her a minute, but she got it. She walked to the edge of the rock, looked down into the valley a hundred feet or so below us. Then in a tiny voice she said, "Honey, come look, the treetops are so pretty from up here."

I moved closer, swung the picnic basket smack into the middle of her back and she flew off the cliff. I watched as she twirled, faster and faster, falling deep into the valley. The sound of the thud when she landed bounced off the rocks of the surrounding cliffs.

By the time the echo reached the top I was hiking back the way we came.

So now I'm speeding along State Road 40 following the signs that point north to Highway 61. Lola, this was all your fault. You just didn't get it. I hummed a few bars of "It Ain't Me, Babe" as I drove.

Aliens in MacArthur Park
by Heidi Hunter

(based on "MacArthur Park," Richard Harris, 1968)

"See? There it is again." Andrea pointed toward MacArthur Park.

I saw a flash out of the corner of my eye, but when I glanced up, it was gone. "What?"

Andrea Emerson slumped in her deck chair and stroked her mastiff, Hairy, on the neck. "That light. In the woods."

I handed my best friend the margarita I'd made. On this sultry July night, we were swarmed by bugs attracted to the porchlight overhead. The crickets nearly drowned out the soft-playing radio tuned to an oldies station.

"Oh, Cassie! Maybe I'm losing my mind." Andrea didn't acknowledge her drink.

"I'm sure it's just kids looking for a place to party." Although they shouldn't, since the park closed after dusk and no one was supposed to be wandering the unmarked woods after midnight. When did that ever stop kids?

Andrea's back patio overlooked MacArthur Park. A small area with open space for picnics, a playground, and a ball diamond, the attraction was the many acres of woods, some with accessible paths, some with trails made by the tread of years of hikers. The woods sprawled gently uphill, then back down toward the river.

"I keep hoping it's Paul," she went on. "Afraid to come home."

I didn't know what I could say to comfort a friend whose husband disappeared several days ago. Who left for work one morning in his grey Toyota and never arrived. Then the story broke of embezzlement at Carson Asset Management, Paul's employer, and his possible guilt.

Andrea hadn't left the house since then, due to the gossip in town. Holdingford was split as to whether Paul was guilty of theft, if he ran off with another woman, or both, using the money to fund his new life. Now, Andrea mostly slept during the day and wandered the house at night. I wished I could do more to console her. An after-midnight visit for drinks on the patio wasn't enough.

"I don't see Paul as the type to camp out in the woods," I admitted, taking a sip of my margarita. Well, maybe, glamping.

I found it hard to believe Paul would abandon Andrea. They seemed like the models for the Barbie and Ken dolls. Both tall, fit and blonde. I was the exact opposite of Andrea in every way, including in the lucky-at-love department, and sometimes it galled me.

The radio began playing "MacArthur Park"—the horrible disco version.

"Ugh." Andrea reached over and switched it off. "Paul hates that song. We almost didn't buy this house because it's across from a MacArthur Park, even though it isn't the park the song was based on. How silly. I found the original Sixties recording on a 45 on eBay and bought it for him as a joke our first Christmas here."

We finished our margaritas without seeing the light again, if it ever existed.

After my late night, keeping Andrea company, I was barely coherent when I arrived to open my coffee shop the next morning. I had purchased Let It Drip with my rat-bastard ex-husband's divorce settlement. I included Cassiopeia Dalton, Proprietor, in large letters below the name on the sign, so whenever my ex walked by, he'd know where his money went.

"Hey, Cassie!" Megan, my morning employee, a college student off for the summer, greeted me. She was far too perky for six o'clock on a Tuesday morning. Once inside, she unboxed pastries dropped off by the local bakery while I took down the chairs from the few tables we had available for slow sippers.

My first customers, as usual, were businessmen and the police. Megan served the businessmen, who took one of the tables in the corner.

"Hi, Rod," I greeted Detective "Rod" Rodnitski of the Holdingford Police Department. He always stopped by, pre-shift, for a black coffee spiked with a shot of espresso, dubbed the "eye-opener." "Anything new with the embezzlement?" I hoped for some positive news to take back to Andrea.

"Not much. Still looking for the money, and Paul, whichever we find first." Rod took a sip and nodded absently in approval. "Dead ends all around. I've been working on that petty theft wave we've had lately. Seems to happen a lot in the summer."

"What's been taken?" I hadn't heard about the crimes. I'd been too busy consoling Andrea. Maybe I needed to keep a closer eye on the shop.

"Oh, nothing valuable. Clothes disappeared off a clothesline. Someone shoplifted items from Axon's Drugs and food from the grocery store. Nothing big. You shouldn't worry."

"It's the aliens, Detective. I told ya." Nadine, Holdingford's own "colorful personality," approached the counter. Dressed in a floral muumuu with a straw hat, at least she hadn't donned the foil hat I'd heard alien conspirators wear. "Espresso, Cass," she ordered, as if she needed more caffeine, and turned back to Rod. "They landed a week ago. I saw their lights in the forest. I called the station right away."

"And we searched the woods," he assured her. "No spaceships to be found. Don't worry." He said to me, "It might be that homeless guy we've had hanging around town. If you see him, let us know. We'll make sure he gets some help. We don't want anyone lighting fires in the park."

With that, he left the shop. I set Nadine's espresso in front of her. "It *is* the aliens," she insisted.

I doubted it. Aliens lurked in cornfields, not trees, right?

"I've been sayin' it for years. Ever since they snatched my poor Jimmy." It was well known Nadine's husband ran off with the jailbait waitress at the Fill and Eat station a decade ago. That's when

Nadine's obsession with aliens began. "I knew they'd be back. And now they've got poor Paul Emerson."

My mouth fell open. "What do you mean?"

"Oh, I didn't believe for one second Paul stole that money from Carson's. And he would never run off with some floozy. No, it was the aliens that got him. I'm going out there tonight. Maybe they brought my Jimmy home." With that, she nodded firmly to me and tottered out of the shop.

"I'm not sure how welcome aliens would be here in Holdingford," Megan said as she finished serving a county road worker his black coffee. "My dad says he'll shoot any on sight because they'll eat our cows."

I shook my head at all the crazy alien talk.

"Aliens didn't get Paul," the county worker said. "Did they? He took the money and run. Hey, Derek!" he shouted to one of the businessmen who was making his way out of the shop. "You work with Paul. What's the word at Carson's?"

Derek was dapper in a tailored grey suit, white shirt, and grey and white striped tie, a look few businessmen seemed to wear these days. He froze, as if sensing everyone in the coffee shop was waiting with bated breath for his reply. "Paul was an exceptional employee for a decade." Derek and his coffee companion shared a look. "We cannot believe he might betray us like this." Derek charged to the door, forestalling additional questions.

As Derek exited, I spotted a man lingering on the sidewalk outside the shop. He turned away as Derek strode by. I didn't recognize him, although I couldn't tell much with the hat pulled low over his face, and the too-baggy clothing, which I suspected were swiped from a clothesline. The homeless man? I decided to leave him some of our unsold pastries on the back stoop in case he got hungry.

That night, I was back at Andrea's. I had been hoping to catch up on my sleep; however, she woke me complaining the light was back, and Hairy was growling at her back door.

We sat in matching Adirondack chairs, silently watching the woods for signs of life—alien or human. Hairy was sound asleep at Andrea's side. I wondered if her imagination was in overdrive. All that time alone with your thoughts can make you a bit crazy.

Then I saw it. A flash of light. Brief, but I was certain I didn't imagine it.

"There it is again. I'm not crazy, am I?"

"No." I had to agree it wasn't Andrea's imagination. "Though it's probably Nadine. She said the aliens have landed, and she was going out there tonight to visit."

Andrea nodded as if that was a logical explanation.

To take her mind off the light, I changed the subject. "A man was in the shop today who works with Paul. Derek?"

"Derek Rasmussen? Hair gelled to within an inch of his life? Probably born wearing a suit?" I nodded at her accurate description. "Yeah, he's Paul's boss, the Chief Financial Officer."

"He was with another guy. Older, puckered face?" I didn't get a real good look at his companion.

"If he looks like he ate a bag of lemons and it disappointed him, then it was Simon Granger. He's the Head of Customer Experience or some such nonsense. A long-time friend of the owner. Not sure he does anything at the company. I had the misfortune to meet him at the last holiday party."

Another flicker of light, so brief it might have been a firefly.

"Carson's has been supportive during this ordeal." Andrea didn't mention the light. "They've called daily to find out how I'm doing and if I've heard from Paul yet." Her shoulders sagged. "They know, even if no one else does, that Paul is a loyal employee. We live comfortably. We don't need the money."

I laid a hand on her arm. "I'm positive Paul didn't do this." Even though a part of me—that suspicious, scorned wife part—wondered if he did. As I learned in my marriage, you never really know someone, no matter how long you've known them. "And I'm sure all his friends realize this too. It'll blow over once the real thief is caught."

*

"Cassie!" As I unlocked the front door to the coffee shop the next morning, I heard Nadine call from behind. She trotted across the street toward me, waving her hand. "I visited the aliens last night. You won't believe…"

Her statement was cut off when she was struck by a vehicle speeding down the road. The thud was sickening, and my hands flew to my mouth to stifle a scream. Nadine flew a few feet before crashing to the pavement, motionless. Her packed tote bag burst open, scattering its contents around her. Her straw hat floated down onto the sidewalk.

The driver of the familiar grey sedan didn't stop. Instead, he gunned his engine, racing down the main road out of town. Megan and I gasped in horror and ran toward Nadine.

"Call 9-1-1!" I ordered Megan. Kneeling next to Nadine, I took her wrist, searching for a pulse. It was no use. Her unseeing eyes stared up at me. She was dead.

"Did either of you get a license plate? Or see the driver?" Rod asked us a short time later. A crowd had formed on the sidewalk, held back from the street by police officers.

We shook our heads. "It happened so fast," I said. Megan nodded, her fist pressed to her mouth, tears running down her cheeks. I hesitated, not sure I wanted to say what bothered me the most—that the car looked a lot like Paul's. I added instead, "Just before she was hit, she was saying she visited the aliens last night and saw something. Are you sure nothing's out there?"

"I'm sure aliens did not run her down," the detective said.

Megan finally spoke. "No, a Toyota did."

*

Although shaken to the core by Nadine's death, I still opened my shop, albeit a bit late, to allow the town a place to commiserate.

The shop was soon abuzz with uneasy mutterings, although not what I was expecting to hear.

"...aliens did it."

"...seen lights too."

"...sent one of their scouts...that homeless guy..."

Was everyone losing their minds?

*

"Something suspicious is going on in the park," Andrea declared later as we again gathered on her patio after dark, the sunset doing nothing to alleviate the persistent humidity. Thunder rumbled in the distance. Maybe relief was on the way. "The lights, and now Nadine is killed after going in there. What did she see?"

I hadn't told her I thought the car that ran Nadine down might have been Paul's. Andrea was ready to fall apart as it was. And why would he kill Nadine anyway? "Rod said they found nothing in the park."

"Where are the police looking?" she asked. "The lights were pretty deep into the woods. I know those woods like the back of my hand. I think they may be near the creek where it runs along the foot of the hill."

If anyone would know where the lights originated, it would be Andrea. She and Paul spent a lot of time roaming the unofficial trails forged by other hikers over the years.

"You know, there's a clearing with a small footbridge that crosses the creek," she continued. "That might be where the lights are. I want to go have a look around."

"It'd be a wasted trip." Even though I had to admit, I was curious to know if anything was going on in the park.

"Paul could be in there, afraid to come home." Andrea set her jaw.

We agreed to search the woods the next day, after my morning rush at the shop. I was sure we wouldn't find anything, especially Paul. If he did steal money, he wouldn't be hanging out in the woods. If he didn't steal the money... Well, at least it would get Andrea out of the house.

*

It rained during the night, taking some of the humidity from the air and leaving behind a cool breeze. I dressed in a bright yellow cotton dress to cheer me up following the devastation of yesterday.

In no time, the coffee shop was humming once again with talk of aliens. Excited rumblings rather than the undercurrents of fear I heard yesterday. At least they weren't talking about Paul anymore.

When Derek and Simon arrived, I spotted the homeless man lurking on the sidewalk, watching the shop. He noticed, pulling his baseball cap lower over his eyes. My heartbeat quickened and my hand shook as I handed a customer her change. Was he watching me? Why?

I maneuvered Megan out of the way so I could serve Derek his latte. He seemed the more approachable of the two, and I had a few questions for him about the embezzlement.

"How's business at Carson's?" I asked, fiddling with the latte machine to stall him. "With the embezzlement and all, it must be tough."

Derek frowned and glanced around for eavesdroppers. "We're fine," was his terse response.

"How do you know Paul did it?" I pulled the latte into a cup.

"When he took off and left us in the lurch, we divvied up his files and discovered the missing client funds."

"It was customer funds, not company funds?" That had never been clear. Carson's managed the money of many of Holdingford's old guard. I handed him his latte. "It's no mistake? It was Paul?"

"No," Derek replied curtly, then moved to the corner table where Simon waited.

I turned to Megan. "Can you hold down the fort for me after the rush?"

"Sure, what's up?"

"Andrea and I are going into the woods at MacArthur Park. We've seen the same lights Nadine saw." If something happened to us, I wanted Megan to be able to tell the police where we were headed.

Megan's eyebrows turned down. "Are you sure that's a good idea? Nadine went, and now she's dead."

"Can I get one of those cookies?" Sour-faced Simon, Derek's co-worker, stood at the counter, pointing at the lemon biscotti. Megan plated one for him.

"It's daylight. We'll be careful."

After the rush, I went home and changed into jeans and an old t-shirt my rat-bastard ex left behind, then went to meet Andrea. I brought a flashlight, just in case. Andrea was dressed in the same jeans and jersey shirt she'd worn the last three days. She had Hairy with her, as her "just in case."

We crossed the street to the park, Hairy sniffing every scent he encountered. A lot of scents, based on his slow pace. On this gorgeous summer morning, the playground was full of mothers trying to keep active toddlers busy. Hairy watched them as if he wanted to join in but didn't pull on his leash. We strolled past picnic tables, where a couple of old men played Chinese Checkers, and onto one of the paved paths. Andrea unerringly knew when to step off the main route onto a barely visible trail into the woods.

As we hiked deeper among the trees, noise from the playground, the street and the town faded away. The only sounds were the wind rustling leaves on the trees, and the occasional cracking branch, which I assumed was a rabbit or deer and not little green men. The woods reeked of decaying vegetation, wet from last night's storm.

My thighs began to burn the more we hiked, and my breath came out in huffs. Andrea, however, seemed fresh as a daisy. I glared at my friend's back, briefly hating her for having so much energy while I felt like a limp dishrag. But she was a woman on a mission. After what seemed an interminable amount of time, we finally heard the soft tinkling of the small creek. The trees thinned. My foot trod on something squishy, and I nearly fell.

"What is this?" I had stepped on a soggy box discarded at the edge of the clearing. Inside was a sodden cake with "We—," the rest of the words melted away by last night's rain. A welcome cake for the aliens? A gift from Nadine?

We stepped into the large, circular clearing spanning both sides of the creek. A small footbridge crossed the water. We stopped, stunned.

Fresh holes had been dug in the clearing all around the bridge.

"Well, this isn't at all suspicious." For the first time, I thought maybe Nadine and Andrea were right about something unusual going on out here.

"Maybe animals did it?" Andrea suggested, her voice expressing doubt. As if to prove his owner right, Hairy sniffed at a few of the holes before doggedly digging one of his own.

"No, someone's looking for something. That must be the lights we've been seeing. Someone holding a light while someone else dug."

"For what? Buried treasure?"

I examined the holes. They were more sizeable than a dog might make if digging for a bone, but not large enough for a grave, which I had feared. Maybe the size of several shoeboxes stacked together.

"We have to tell Rod about this," I said.

However, upon returning to Andrea's house, we discovered her back door had been jimmied open. Andrea ran into the house before I could stop her. What if the thieves were still here?

Fortunately, the place was empty. Still, the intruders had left their mark. Shelves emptied. Contents of drawers flung to the floor. Paul's beloved record collection scattered across the carpet. We had only been gone a couple of hours, and the house had been hastily but thoroughly searched.

"Anything missing?" I asked.

"Paul's computer." Andrea pointed at the empty desk in the spare bedroom/office. "But my jewelry is here, as is the TV and stereo." She gazed around her house, shell-shocked. Hairy snuffled about, occasionally growling as if he didn't like what he was scenting.

"Oh, Cassie. What is going on?" I knew she meant more than just the house break-in.

"Maybe the thieves were here hunting for what they couldn't find out there." An idea was forming in my mind.

"What?"

"Money."

"What money?"

"The money they think Paul took from Carson's."

"Why would they look for money in the woods?" Andrea was confused. "Wouldn't you look in a bank?"

"Not if the thief didn't want it traced back to him. The question is why they're searching by the bridge."

"At least they came in when I wasn't here." Andrea shuddered.

"Yeah." That was a coincidence, and coincidences were suspicious to me. Who knew Andrea wasn't going to be home? I thought back to this morning. Anyone who was in the shop when I told Megan to cover for me was a suspect. However, Megan could have told anyone who came in afterward. In this small town, everyone probably knew.

Rod arrived with a couple of officers. When I let them in, I spied the homeless man standing across the street. Was he the one who broke in? Or did he see who did it? On impulse, I started toward him, and he took off down the street.

"Hey! Wait!" I ran to catch up with him. "I want to talk to you."

But the man was fast. When I reached the end of the block, he was nowhere in sight. Maybe he was an alien to be able to disappear so quickly.

We reported the discovery of the holes in the woods.

"Animals," Rod dismissed with a shrug.

Andrea was sobbing by the time Rod left. "I—I think something bad happened to Paul." She hiccupped.

"No, you can't think that way." I hugged her, inside wondering the same thing. If Paul didn't take the money, and if he didn't run off with another woman, then where was he? Dead? Being held against his will? Did he know something about the embezzlement that required he be silenced?

"I want this to all be over." Andrea sniffled against my shoulder. "I don't have the stolen money. Paul didn't take it, and he didn't run off with another woman. Someone killed Nadine and maybe Paul. And the police aren't doing anything about it."

"Okay, we'll do something," I said, more to comfort her than to make a real plan.

However, Andrea took me at my word. "Tonight. They'll be back in the woods if they didn't find what they were looking for here. We'll go find out who it is and demand to know what's going on."

"No, they're dangerous. We'll see who it is, then call the police."

So that night, I arrived at Andrea's armed once again with a flashlight—and a broom handle. Andrea had her dog, a flashlight and a hammer.

We hurried to the park, deserted at this time of night and a bit spooky. Shadows flitted among the trees, almost making me believe aliens were waiting for us. The woods were not silent. Owls, crickets, snapping twigs, rustling leaves. And something else. Shuffling through the leaves. The hair on my arms stood at attention. Footsteps? I swung around and brandished my flashlight at the trees. I caught what might have been a dark mass shifting behind a tree, but it was hard to tell. Maybe it was just a shadow. Or my imagination. Or aliens.

A murmur of voices and the thunk-thunk of a shovel hitting dry earth warned us we were nearing the clearing. We flipped off our lights and crouched down just inside the tree line. Two people were in front of us, one digging and the other swinging the flashlight along the ground. The trees blocked out most of the moonlight, so I couldn't make out who the people were, though I thought the voices were both male. I touched Andrea on the shoulder, who shook her head. She didn't recognize them either.

Hairy sniffed the air and gave a low growl. I put my hand on his side to comfort him and keep him from revealing our hiding place.

"They have to be here," the guy handling the flashlight said. "Paul said they were in MacArthur Park and led us right to this spot."

"We've dug up the whole area." The digger grunted. "He led us on a wild goose chase."

A snap of a branch across the clearing spooked the men. They stopped digging and extinguished their light, plunging the area into darkness.

"I hope it's not more alien hunters," one of the men snarled. "I thought getting rid of that crazy bitch would scare them off."

Andrea gasped.

"I told you that was a bad idea. Just brought more heat down on us."

"I say, if we don't find those documents tonight, we take the money and leave. By the time Paul makes his way back to wifey, we'll be drinking rum in Fiji."

"Paul's still alive!" Andrea whispered.

A more deliberate rustle of leaves sounded from across the clearing. The men swung in that direction. Hairy took that moment to lurch out of the woods at the men, snarling. Andrea leaped out right behind him, me right behind her.

Hairy and Andrea pounced on digger-man, who lost his grip on the shovel. I whacked flashlight-guy in the back with my broomstick. It startled him but didn't bring him down. He spun around, grabbing my weapon. He yanked me toward him, jerking me off balance. He twisted the broom handle so I was no longer facing him. The broom handle disappeared, replaced by an arm around my throat and something sharp poking it. Jeez, this guy had some moves. I'd be impressed if I wasn't about to pee my pants.

"Where is my husband?" Andrea demanded, leaning down and waving the hammer in the digger's face as Hairy snarled at him, teeth bared. "What did you do to Paul?"

"Get off Simon and call off your dog," my captor said. "Or your nosy friend is dead."

Simon? The sourpuss? So, my captor must be Derek Rasmussen, he of the gel-slathered hair. I broke out in a cold sweat and clawed at his arm, desperate for air as it tightened against my throat. The jab on my neck intensified and I felt something wet trickle down it. Blood? I froze. Having killed once, I knew he meant business.

Andrea grabbed Hairy's collar and stumbled backward, raising one shaky hand in surrender.

I wracked my brain to find a way out of this mess alive when a blinding light lit us up from above.

"What the…?" I heard Derek mutter.

I couldn't look up to check it out, not with the sharp whatever poking me more insistently in the neck. Instead, I watched Andrea, who was staring at the sky, gaping. Glancing back at me, I saw her eyes widen just before I heard a thump. Derek's grip loosened as he fell behind me.

I spun around and saw the homeless man, holding the shovel, which he had used to whack Derek. Seeing Derek unconscious, Simon attempted to run. Andrea let go of Hairy, and he leaped on Simon, and stood over him, showing teeth.

The spotlight, which had assisted in our takedown, darted away and disappeared, leaving us again in near darkness. We all stood in silence, wondering what we just witnessed. What silent aircraft was the source of that light? It couldn't have been a helicopter. A blimp? A spy plane out for a test flight? No way was I going to believe aliens just saved our lives in MacArthur Park.

"I—I don't know how to thank you," I stammered to the homeless man. "Who are you? What are you doing here?"

"Name's Ted. Had myself a nice little setup here in the woods," he jerked a thumb in the general direction of his camp, "until these two yahoos showed up. I could tell they were up to no good, what with dragging that third guy around and threatening to kill him and all, so I've been watching them."

"So, you were at the coffee shop and Andrea's house…"

"Watching them. Yup. And I was right. No good."

"They're looking for documents Paul told them were in MacArthur Park," I said to Andrea. "If the documents aren't here, where are they?"

A big grin broke out on Andrea's face. "I know where they are."

*

The following afternoon, I was back at Andrea's house sitting in the living room with Andrea—and Paul!—feeling like a third wheel. I had to hear Paul's story, though. He had come out of hiding when the news broke that arrests had been made in both Nadine's murder and the embezzlement. Andrea glowed and clutched her husband's arm as if afraid he would disappear again.

"Why did they go after you?" I asked.

"Because I discovered some anomalies on my client accounts. Weird transactions I didn't put in orders for, for shares in a company I didn't recognize. I started downloading the documents to a flash drive, only Derek interrupted me before I got everything I needed. I took home what I had and hid it."

In MacArthur Park, just like he said. When Andrea and I had arrived home the previous morning, she had gone right to Paul's music collection and pulled out the sleeve containing the 45 recording of "MacArthur Park." A small flash drive was taped inside the center hole of the record. We immediately presented the evidence to Detective Rodnitski.

"I had hoped to get the rest of the documents early that morning before Derek got in, but he and Simon anticipated me. Intercepted my car before I even made it to the freeway. Stuffed me in the trunk then took me…somewhere…and left me locked up. In a shed, maybe? Later, they came back and said they "uncovered" the embezzlement and reported to the police that I did it, and now I was missing. If I returned the documents, they wouldn't press charges. Ha! I knew when they got the evidence, I wouldn't be left alive."

Andrea wiped a tear from her eye.

"I told them I buried the evidence in MacArthur Park, and the spot was difficult to find, so I'd have to show them. After dark, I led them up to the bridge. They made me dig. My hands were tied in front of me, but my feet were free, so when I had my chance, I hit Derek with the shovel and ran. I know the woods, they don't. I managed to hide until morning, get my hands free of the rope, and hike out. It was too late. I read in the paper I was the prime suspect in the embezzlement."

"Why didn't you go to the police then?"

"I thought I'd be arrested on sight, and I didn't know if I had enough to prove myself innocent. Some of the victims were my clients. It could easily have been me."

"You should have come home." Andrea stroked her husband's stubbled face. "We would have faced it together."

Paul smiled lovingly at his wife. "I figured Derek and Simon wouldn't rest until they had both me and the documents. I didn't want to come home and put you in danger."

Aww, there were still some good men in the world, unlike my rat-bastard…

"I hitched a few towns over and hid out in a seedy motel," Paul was saying. "Seedy" for Paul was probably a Hilton.

"And now, with the flash drive of evidence and your car, they can prove Derek and Simon did the embezzling and killed Nadine, and you're free." Paul's damaged Toyota was found in long-term parking at the airport, as if meant to show Paul had fled the country. Simon's fingerprints were found inside.

"Yep. I never thought I'd be thankful for 'MacArthur Park.'"

You Better Not Tell
by Merrilee Robson

(based on "Little Children," Billy J. Kramer and the Dakotas, 1964)

It was that song that gave me the idea.

I didn't even like the song. It was all about some guy wanting to kiss his girlfriend and I thought the whole thing was kind of yucky.

But when Billy J. Kramer started singing about giving a quarter and candy to the "Little Children" watching him, to make them go away, I had a super idea.

So it was the song that gave me the idea but, really, it was the record player that started it all.

I don't know why I ever thought Linda would let me use it.

"Don't be ridiculous, Bobby," she said, with the look all big sisters give their younger brothers. I don't know if they have to practice it or if it just comes naturally.

I was used to that look but there was no reason to be so mean about the whole thing.

I loved that record player as soon as she unwrapped it on her sixteenth birthday.

It was in a great big parcel.

I was sure it was going to be some dumb girl thing. She'd been talking about this mohair sweater she wanted, or a new purse in pink patent leather to match her new sling-back shoes. I thought clothes were a pretty stupid present, but Linda talked about them so much I could sure picture that purse she wanted and the exact blue of that sweater she kept on and on about.

The box looked too big for a sweater. Or a pink patent leather purse that would match sling-back shoes.

Linda was unwrapping it so slowly, lifting up the tape so the paper didn't rip and then folding the wrapping back and patting it smooth, so it could be used again.

At first I only got a glimpse of bright orange. Then the white plastic handle and the two small speakers on the front. It seemed to take forever before Linda finally removed all the wrapping paper and flipped open the shiny locks on the front.

"That is the best birthday present ever!" I said.

Linda was a lot more restrained. She gave Mom and Dad a big smile and then got up to kiss them on their cheeks.

"I'm glad you like it, honey," Dad said, kissing her back. "It's portable but I imagine you'll just use it in your room."

I saw him wink at Mom.

And then I realized why. Linda had been playing her records on the big Hi-Fi in the living room. As soon as she got home from school, she'd put on those records, as loud as she could.

I thought it was stupid.

But then there were the Beatles. At first there were just a few kids in my class talking about them and I didn't really know who the Beatles were. After they were on *The Ed Sullivan Show*, that was pretty much it. Everybody knew. The girls would giggle about which Beatle they liked best. One of the guys had a t-shirt with their group picture on it.

I didn't want a shirt, or to grow my hair long like some of the guys.

I just really liked the music.

When Linda brought friends home with her after school, they'd take over the living room, playing the same records over and over again, and dancing with each other.

Linda always told me to get lost. Sometimes I'd go to my room, but I wanted to hear the music.

So I started sitting at the kitchen table, pretending to do my homework while Mom got dinner ready, but I was really listening to the music. I could see Mom roll her eyes when Linda played "She Loves You" for the tenth time, wipe her hand over her forehead as she stood by the stove, and then holler at Linda to turn the volume down.

But then I discovered, if I was careful, I could creep down the hallway, behind the couch, and then under it. The skirt around the bottom hid me pretty well but I could lift it up enough to see, if I wanted to.

It turned out pretty handy when I wanted to sneak down when Mom and Dad were watching *Bonanza* and I was supposed to be in bed.

But when I saw Dad wink at Mom, I knew Mom wouldn't have to complain about how noisy the records were anymore. Linda would be in her room, with the door closed.

And I wouldn't be able to hear the music. At least not very well. It was a pretty solid door.

"There's that cupboard on the landing," I said. "It would fit perfectly in there. And I could get some records. Then we'd have a lot more music to listen to."

Linda gave me That Look. "You're not going to get any records. You spend your allowance as soon as you get it."

Which is true. But the movies on Saturday afternoon cost 35 cents, and extra if I want popcorn. And by the time I've bought some licorice or a chocolate bar on the way home from school, my allowance is always all gone.

"I'll get a paper route," I said. "Please Linda, I'll be really careful. I just...."

"You're not going to touch my record player, Bobby, and you know why."

Okay, I knew why she said that.

There was that time I'd put her Barbie dolls in my cars to roll them down the stair railing and watch them careen off.

The dolls weren't broken exactly, but they got some scratches and some of their clothes got ripped. Accidents happen.

But I was really little then. She should have forgiven me by now.

Okay, I admit there was the time I found her pink lipstick in the medicine cabinet of the bathroom we shared. It was supposed to be peppermint flavored.

I tried it just once to see if it tasted good. And it was pretty cool, so I ate a little bit to see if it really tasted like peppermint candy.

It didn't.

But then it had tooth marks on it, so I tried to smooth them out with toilet paper. And then the toilet paper got stuck on it and I ended up flushing the whole tube down the toilet so she wouldn't find out what I'd done.

And then Dad had to call the plumber to unblock the toilet. And he got mad at Linda 'cause he thought she'd done it.

So, yeah, I knew why she didn't want me to touch her things. But sheesh, that was months ago. I was way more grown-up now.

And I would never do anything to damage that record player. Just thinking about that shiny orange case made me happy.

I was positive if I could buy some new records, ones she didn't have, she'd let me use it.

So when Linda got a new boyfriend, I remembered the words of that Billy J. Kramer song. It talked about the guy giving money to the kids to go away so he could kiss their sister.

How hard could it be?

I really couldn't see why Linda liked the guy.

He had the kind of greasy hair guys used to have before everyone wanted a Beatle haircut.

He did have a motorcycle. That was pretty cool.

But Mom told Linda she couldn't go for a ride on it, so what was the point of him being her boyfriend?

I didn't think even Linda liked him very much.

They had to sit in the living room. Mom wasn't letting him go upstairs to Linda's room, so she was playing the records on the old Hi-Fi again.

But they didn't dance together like she did with her girlfriends.

Sometimes he'd throw his arm around her shoulders. Linda would usually shrug it off.

Then she'd get up to flip the record over.

When she came back, she'd sit a little farther away from him.

In a way, I was kind of glad.

'Cause I thought he looked kind of mean.

And I thought watching them kiss would be really icky.

But it had seemed like such a good idea. And I really needed that money.

So I kept it up, sliding into the living room and under the couch, every time he came home with Linda.

Good thing he never really stayed long.

'Cause it was really boring.

I wasn't getting any quarters, or really any reason to ask for them.

He didn't even kiss her when he left.

I had to swivel around under the couch when they went to the front door to say goodbye.

I hoped they wouldn't hear me moving around, not until I had a good reason to ask for those quarters I needed.

In fact, I was starting to worry that he wouldn't give me any money, even if he did want to kiss Linda.

He looked like he might be more the kind of guy who would rather hit a kid that was bothering him, not give him candy or money.

Anyway, I wriggled around, so I could see the front hall when they said goodbye. I was real careful to just lift the ruffle around the bottom of the couch just a little bit, so I could see out with one eye and not be seen.

I thought he might try to kiss her then. And maybe he would have.

But Linda stepped back from him.

Then she did the strangest thing.

She reached out and handed him something.

And I could have sworn she was giving him money. She dropped something and I thought I might be going to find some money after all. But she bent down and picked up whatever she'd dropped and handed that to him too.

And he passed something to her. It was in a bag so I couldn't tell what it was.

And that drove me crazy.

Maybe it was nothing.

Maybe he'd just picked up something for her, some makeup or hairspray, and she was paying him back.

But then why did they both look around the hallway, like they wanted to make sure Mom and I weren't around.

And why did Linda run up to her room as soon as he'd left and close the door.

I really wanted to know what he gave her.

Maybe it was candy. I used to know where Linda hid candy, but she'd changed hiding places after I ate everything she got for Halloween one year.

When she got that big chocolate Easter egg last year, with her name written on it in pink icing, I just took a few bites.

Apparently, that was even worse. I don't know why.

So now Linda had another different hiding place.

I searched her room. I wanted to find out what was in that bag.

I went through her drawers but it wasn't there.

I did find some things I didn't know she had. A charm bracelet and some big gold hoop earrings.

I didn't know why she had them hidden in the bottom drawer of her dresser, under her winter sweaters, and not in her jewelry box.

I wondered if that was what the boyfriend had given her. But I didn't think so.

I thought I'd found the perfect hiding place when I noticed one of the stuffed toy animals on her bed had a zipper.

But there was nothing in it but her pajamas.

I kind of liked the stacks of magazines with pictures of movie stars and singers. I wasted a bit of time looking through them. They weren't as good as comic books but still they were interesting.

Linda had cut out some of the pictures and taped them on her wall. I wondered if she'd let me have some, but I guessed not.

I tried not to leave any trace. But I wondered if Linda knew.

She kind of smirked at me a few times, as if she thought she was way smarter than me.

Sure, she was older, but that didn't make her smarter.

All she ever seemed to think about was her hair and makeup and clothes, and that was kind of dumb. That's all she seemed to talk about with her friends, anyway.

I knew that 'cause I kept on spying on her when she was with her friends too. Not just when her boyfriend visited.

That was way harder now that she had her own record player.

They'd go up to her room to play records there. She was allowed to have girls in her room, but not boys. Linda always closed the door and I could hear her friends giggling.

I'd go out into the hall between our rooms and try to listen, mostly for the records, but I thought it might be kinda neat to hear what they were saying.

But somehow Linda always knew I was there.

Or maybe she just guessed.

"Go away, Bobby," she'd yell. Sometimes she'd yank open the door and throw one of those stuffed toys at me. I didn't mind too much, but then she started throwing her textbooks at me.

That hurt.

So I stayed in my room, with the door open just a crack. I couldn't hear much talking but at least I still got to hear the records.

And I'd see Linda and her friends if they went to use the bathroom. But I didn't think they noticed me. I was just a gleam of an eye in the small crack of a barely open bedroom door. I wasn't something a teenage girl would notice.

I thought I had found out something useful when I smelled a whiff of cigarettes, and I knew that Linda and her friends were lighting up in her room, blowing the smoke out the window so Mom wouldn't smell it downstairs.

I could have threatened to tell about the cigarettes, but I thought finding out about what she got from her boyfriend would be better.

I saw the same thing a few times, Linda passing him money and him handing her something in a bag.

And sometimes she'd go out with him. Not on the motorcycle; Mom still wouldn't let her do that, but walking off somewhere.

And then Linda would run upstairs as soon as she got home.

I still couldn't find what it was, even though I searched her room whenever she was out.

I did find her package of cigarettes and tried one, hanging out the window of my room until I was coughing so hard I had to stop.

Maybe that's what the boyfriend was giving her, but I doubted it.

And then I finally saw her.

Her friends were leaving, saying goodbye, and one of them was stuffing something in the pocket of her ski jacket.

After they'd gone Linda went back in her room and came out again. She looked around and then cocked her head, listening for any sound of Mom or me.

Then she stuffed the bag into that cupboard on the landing, behind the stack of old photo albums Mom put there after Grandma died.

I had to give Linda credit for thinking of that hiding spot. I'd never have thought of looking there.

But when I finally had a chance to look at it, I was really disappointed.

The bag just had a bunch of dry leaves. Sort of like the houseplant Grandma had given Linda a few years ago that Linda never watered. It smelled kind of like that plant too.

I was pretty sad about that.

I couldn't figure out why Linda would want it. Or why she would hide it.

And most importantly, I couldn't think how I could get her to give me some money for not telling on her.

I think not knowing just bugged me too much.

That's the only reason why I can think of for what I did.

Maybe I was just trying to be helpful. That would be good.

Mom was making spaghetti for dinner.

She was a bit nervous, I think. She had made it before but not when Dad was home. Dad usually only wanted steak or chicken and potatoes.

But Mom thought he should try something different.

I thought it smelled pretty good. It was making my mouth water.

And then she said, "Oh, I don't have enough oregano."

I looked at the remaining leaves in that little jar. It looked like the kind of stuff Linda was hiding.

So I don't know if I was trying to help Mom, or if I wanted to get Linda in trouble.

Or if I just really wanted to find out what she was hiding.

But I said, "Oh, I think Linda has some," and ran upstairs to her hiding place.

And Mom was looking at the stuff, and sniffing it, saying, "I'm not sure this is oregano, Bobby," when Dad came home.

And Dad frowned.

And when Linda got home, he kept asking her where she got it and then she cried and told him about the boyfriend.

And then Dad put on his coat and went down the street to talk to Mr. Simpson, who was a police officer.

And then things got bad.

I mean I had heard about marijuana and how it leads to using heroin.

So I guess they had to stop the boyfriend from selling it to Linda. And then some of the other parents found out that Linda had been selling it to her friends.

So I guess they had to stop them.

Mr. Simpson clapped me on the shoulder and asked if I wanted to be a policeman when I grew up. He said I was smart to keep an eye on what was going on and tell someone about it.

And Dad told me I'd done the right thing.

But he looked sad.

And then Linda had to go away.

Mom told me she was going to boarding school to get away from "bad influences."

But I think maybe she was at some jail for teenagers.

Because I could hear Mom crying at night, and sometimes she'd cry even in the day while she was cooking dinner.

And I started to remember how Linda used to be when I was little. How she'd read stories to me and put on tea parties for me and her dolls and stuffed toys. And how she'd cuddle me when I was hurt. And she'd even carry me when I got tired, even though she wasn't a lot bigger than me.

Dad told me I might as well use the record player while Linda was away.

But I didn't want to.

I don't think it was my fault, though.

It was all because of that stupid song.

Spirit in the Sky
by Claire A. Murray

(based on "Spirit in the Sky," Norman Greenbaum, 1969)

Jerry rushed to the hospital, worry etched into his brow as he sped through a third yellow light, raced up the hill, and found a narrow parking spot on the far end of the lot. Breathless from running when he reached the emergency department, he gasped his father's name at the information desk.

"Oh, Mr. Allen is being seen by the doctors right now. I'll let them know you're here and they'll tell you when you can see him."

Jerry paced in the waiting room until a young doctor called his name. She said everything looked fine, but she wanted to keep his father for several hours of observation. Jerry said, "Pops…my dad, he's really okay?"

"It wasn't a heart attack, if that's what you mean. We think it was anxiety. He won't tell us much. He doesn't seem to like hospitals."

"Last time he was at one was when my mom died. That was thirty years ago. He hasn't been in one since."

"I understand, Mr. Allen. Those memories could add to his stress. Seeing you might help. Please keep him calm. Before you go in, do you know of anything upsetting in his life?"

"No. Nothing. Things are just…normal, far as I know. He's retired. I run his store now and it's doing well, so there aren't any money problems. He's got friends. We have dinner together a few nights a week. Everything has seemed fine for a long time."

"Well, that's a good reason for us to observe him, and in case he has another attack. He was a little dehydrated so we're giving him some fluids. Seniors are vulnerable, especially in the summer. We put in a call to his VA doctor but haven't heard back yet. We won't transfer him to the VA hospital unless he needs to stay overnight. We can talk about that later. It's early in the day."

Jerry put on a calm face and followed the doctor into a long room with curtained cubicles on each side. A few were occupied. Nurses and technicians adjusted equipment and wrote on charts, giving the room an air of busyness. The doctor spoke softly as they approached the far end. "We put him down here where it's quietest. You can stay as long as he remains calm."

Pops looked embarrassed when Jerry stepped behind the curtain and sat beside his bed. "They didn't need to call you. It was nuthin', just nerves, I guess. I must have forgotten to take my cholesterol medicine this morning."

"It's okay, Pops. They said you'll be fine and out of here in a few hours."

"I thought it was the big one, ya know? That I was gonna see the spirit in the sky and meet Jesus…that I'd see Ellie again." Tears formed in the older man's eyes and he wiped them before they could run down his speckled brown face, skin toughened from years of outdoor activity and wrinkled by time.

Jerry was nervous and talked about the weather, the shop, baseball, anything except the reason Pops was here. Still, Pops seemed cranky and secretive, mangling the edge of the sheet, and not meeting Jerry's gaze. No topic got a good response so Jerry finally stopped talking. They just waited. The test results and clean bill of health eventually came. Pops' VA doctor phoned in a mild anxiety medication and made an appointment to see Pops a few weeks later. Jerry took his dad home in time for dinner, then slept on the couch after Pops went to bed, still muttering that he "didn't need no nursemaid."

*

The next day, Pops made an effort to behave as usual. While Jerry cleaned up after breakfast, Pops sat in his easy chair and played a favorite recording. From the opening distorted guitar riff, through the drums and gospel elements, right to the end, Pops sat motionless and listened. "Spirit in the Sky" had lived in his heart through war, his friendship with his Vietnam buddies Tony and

Smitty, love and marriage with Ellie, the birth of Jerry, then Ellie's death. Fifty years after he had first heard it, the song no longer brought him to the sense of all being right with his world. The sudden change was jarring.

He pulled a folded sheet of paper from his pocket to look at the drawing, the layout of an out-of-town mall. He moved to the old rolltop desk, opened the secret drawer, shoved the map inside, and hearing Jerry's footsteps, quickly closed it. He was straightening a pile of bills on top of the desk when Jerry entered the room.

"What're you doing, Pops?"

"Oh, nuthin'." The older man dropped the bills back on the desk and settled into his easy chair.

"How much you need to pay those overdue bills?"

"I don' need no handout or no one hovering over me. They told you at the hospital, it was just anxiety. I got these pills to make sure it don't come back." Pops grabbed a book from his reading pile. "I'll pay those bills come next social security check. Was just checkin' ta make sure I got 'em all in order."

"Okay. I just worry about you. I want you around for a while longer, you know?" Jerry looked over the old man's shoulder and read the title, *Dark Canyon*. "You really like that Louis L'Amour guy. How many times have you read this one?"

"Four. Five if you count this time. Now lemme read."

Jerry returned to the kitchen where Pops heard him set up dinner for that evening. He thought, Jerry will work late. I can call Tony and Smitty, get 'em to come over to talk about that damned map without Jerry overhearing. When the back door closed and he saw Jerry's car back out of the driveway, he set the book down, closed his eyes, and let his mind drift back in time.

*

It was 1969. Pops was home to visit family after one tour in Vietnam. While in town, he rekindled a romance with his high school sweetie, Ellie. He was surprised to see she'd let her hair go natural. "No more straightening for me," she told him. He especially liked how the Afro created a halo around her head.

They went to the drive-in, danced to the latest music, and he tried to forget about the war-torn country, the rice paddies, fish diet and oppressive, damp heat. After all, he had to go back. At the airport, between kisses goodbye, Ellie promised to write often and wait for his return. Then she pressed a package into his hands. "Open it on the plane," she said.

After takeoff, he discovered her gift was a small player/recorder, several cassettes, and a playlist for each. She'd recorded dozens of songs, including his new favorite, "Spirit in the Sky." She'd put it on several of the cassettes. They'd listened to it so many times, feeling the beat, hearing the simple words, and understanding if you live right, you shouldn't be afraid to die.

The song captured his confused feelings about his role in Nam. His faith in his decision to serve had been shaken during his first tour. News articles, protests and demonstrations, violent dreams of war when safe at home, and being told by hometown friends he was a murderer had jolted him during his leave. He didn't want to abandon his commitment or dishonor those he'd fought alongside. "Spirit in the Sky" helped ground him. He was prepared to die, if that was to be. He was not a sinner. His spirit would lift upward.

Back on the battlefield, sleep was difficult those first few weeks. The quiet nights of home were replaced by constant artillery fire, followed by deafening silence. Nature filled the void with chatter from lizards and birds. When they got quiet, he knew to expect more artillery. Whether the sounds were real or dreams, he wasn't always sure. He'd put the cassette player on low and listen to "Spirit" several times before shutting it off and returning to sleep. His tent mates never complained.

War brought Pops together with two unlikely friends, Tony and Smitty. Tony always had his mind set on how to get rich. Smitty was a relentless womanizer. The two were often in trouble. Pops was their grounding wire, keeping their antics at bay, and getting them out of trouble or talking their lieutenant into giving a lesser punishment. It wasn't a surprise Smitty and Tony never rose in rank. Pops made sergeant.

The lieutenant once told Pops, "You'd rise farther and faster if you weren't so close to those buddies of yours."

Pops' response was, "Someone's gotta look out for them."

His song became their song. Once, after a week of particularly heavy fighting, Tony said, "I don't know as I believe Jesus is my friend, but I know I'm going to heaven when I die 'cause I'm living in hell right here." Thus, they hardened themselves to the constant presence of death and fought with valor, earned medals for bravery, and accepted that they would either live or die. War brought them together; the looming specter of death cemented their bond.

The three survived Vietnam and returned home with minimal physical scars, still friends. After attending Pops and Ellie's wedding a year later, Smitty and Tony moved to Pops' town, and he kept an eye on them. Jerry called Tony and Smitty "uncle." Pops opened a secondhand store and made enough of a living over the years to buy a small house and help Jerry pay for his books for business school.

Pops and Smitty often had to bail Tony out after one of his get-rich-quick schemes failed. Sometimes he was just broke and needed money. Other times, he was truly in jail. Smitty, womanizing more as he grew older, fell hard for a woman with few scruples. She took all his money and left him deep in debt. To dig himself out of that hole, he and Tony cooked up a scheme to rob a bank in a nearby town. Unknown to Pops, he was the get-away driver They'd told him Smitty was there to cosign a loan for Tony. Ellie got sick and instead of meeting the guys, Pops took her to the hospital. Tony and Smitty ended up in jail, while Pops worried at his Ellie's bedside, laying her to rest a month later.

Jerry, by now on his own and successful, stayed with Pops for several days after the funeral. A neighbor told Jerry about some of the misadventures Pops and his friends had gotten into—small things mostly—the neighbors wondered and worried about. Grateful that Pops hadn't been in on the botched bank robbery,

Jerry resolved to keep a closer eye on him. He sold his house, left his job, and bought a condo less than a mile from his childhood home. He told Pops he'd take care of the shop, which was now open only three days a week. "I'll get it back open full time, Pops, wait and see."

Jerry opened every day, even on Saturdays, while Pops stayed with the three-day schedule he was used to. They worked well together. The shop was still in Pops' name, but Jerry managed it and handled all the paperwork. His business degree and experience made him a savvy businessman who knew how to assess items, haggle with customers so they both felt they got a good deal, and still turn a profit. Jerry tucked away some of that money for the day when Pops could no longer live on his own.

Years passed and Pops retired, leaving the store fully in Jerry's hands. He modernized and expanded it, adding selected antiques. One corner, though, he kept much as it had been during his father's heyday. Posters from the '60 and '70s were behind the cases. Other sale items included vintage radios, jukeboxes, vinyl records, music cassettes and players, buttons and bumper stickers. In the center display case, not for sale, was Norman Greenbaum's "Spirit in the Sky" single, and photos of Pops with friends, mostly from his service days in Vietnam, including Tony and Smitty.

*

After leaving Pops to his book, Jerry saw Pops' neighbor watering flowers in the front yard, and stopped to update her on his dad's condition.

"Mrs. Peach, got a minute?" As a child, Jerry and her son Peter had played together. She'd called the ambulance yesterday after seeing Pops stagger past her house.

She turned, her brow furrowed, "Jerry, how's your father doing? I've been so worried. Was it a heart attack?"

"No, nothing like that. It was anxiety, they think. Say, does he walk by here every day?"

"Oh, yes. Just about every morning and evening. We wave to each other."

"He never told me. In fact, he doesn't tell me much lately. That's why I stopped. I'm worried about him." Jerry remembered she was the neighborhood busybody and would know if something fishy was going on. "He's getting older. I don't want to hover, but he's my dad..."

She shut off the water and hung the hose on a hook. "Come inside and I'll fix you a cup of coffee. I made brownies. Would you like one?"

"Sure. That would be nice." Jerry followed her to the kitchen in the back. Through the curtains, he could see the blurry outline of Pops' kitchen. Jerry asked about Peter, and that got Mrs. Peach on a long-winded track he wished he hadn't started. He finally steered the conversation back onto his father. She had little to offer, and he didn't want to say anything that would lead to gossip. She agreed to call him if she heard or saw anything suspicious.

Driving to the store, his thoughts centered on Pops' anxiety attack, why he'd become so cranky, and whether his mental faculties were still intact. Jerry knew decline was hard to spot in someone you were close to and saw daily. If Pops needed medical or long-term care, would there be enough money? Pops had some antiques at home and in the store. Internet research, and a talk with Pops' VA doctor, were definitely in order.

At the store, he surfed Internet sites for rolltop desks and learned Pops' desk was hand built, which likely dated it to before the 1860s. That could fetch a good sum, even with the wear and tear of life in the Allen home. There wasn't a time Jerry couldn't recall it being there. He'd sat at it to do his homework, played under it with his trucks. Pops had bought it when he first opened the shop, then kept it for himself. He might not want to part with it, but if the time came, Jerry would sacrifice that desk to make Pops comfortable. He saved his search and closed the browser when a customer came in. He was busy through the rest of the afternoon and into the evening. He called Pops to make sure he'd taken his medication and got a scolding in return, not like Pops at all. He closed up and went home, still worried.

*

That same evening, Pops answered the door to let Smitty and Tony in. They sat in the living room and clinked their beer bottles together before Tony asked, "So, you in or not, Pops? We gotta do this soon."

Pops shook his head and said nothing.

"It's foolproof. We can do this," Smitty said. "We did it all the time in Nam."

"You got caught a bunch o' times in Nam," Pops said,

Tony said, "Only those times you weren't there. You're our Jesus factor."

"You mean you used me—" Pops said. "Got me all figurin' we was never gonna get caught and if we did, well, it was all right anyway. I finally got some sense and stopped. But you two kept right on goin' and I kept rescuin' ya. I was a fool to let you play me, let that song go to my head."

Smitty said, "We're doin' it, with or without you. If just me and Tony do it and get caught, that's on you."

"I don't know. Too risky without Pops. We ain't young like back then," Tony said.

"See, Pops? We need you," Smitty said.

Pops banged his beer bottle down on the coffee table, sending a spray of drops onto the wood. "Go away. I gotta think on this. I been bailin' you two outta trouble for fifty years and you still don't learn." He led them out the door and cleaned up the empties, muttering all the while. "They think Jesus or me is gonna get them outta their scrapes. I swear, I don't know no longer where I'm goin' when I die. I wish Ellie was here. She always set me straight after them two was around."

*

Pops' checkup at the VA was normal for a man of his age. Cholesterol was still a little high, heart normal, blood pressure good, and blood tests from the hospital had come in and were fine. There was nothing physically wrong. "Has anything been worrying you, Mr. Allen? Do you get enough sleep? Have enough money to pay your bills? Is anything unusual going on at home?"

"Nuthin's bothering me or like that. I got enough money and Jerry here runs the store good, made it run better over the years. I don't know why I had that attack, if that's what you're getting at. I just want to go home and go about my business."

The doctor said Pops should stay on the anxiety medication awhile longer, switch to decaf and take his blood pressure daily. On the trip home, Jerry said, "Look, Pops, if something's been bothering you, tell me. I love you. I don't want to lose you. Whatever it is, we'll get through it together."

"There's nuthin' to get through, Jerry. I'm fine. Just take me home and go back to the shop. You don't want that college kid running it too long. He might sell the whole store too cheap."

"He won't. He's a business major and likes working there. We should stop and get dinner. We haven't been out to eat in a while."

"No. I want to go home." Pops stamped his foot on the floorboard. "I got things to do. You go about your business."

Jerry dropped Pops off at the house and returned to the store. During lulls, he pulled up his research on antique desks and learned some of them had hidden cavities or drawers. He'd never explored Pops' desk, just played beneath it. He did more research and made notes on everything he could find about possible locations.

*

The next morning, Pops met Smitty and Tony at a diner on the outskirts of downtown. "Jerry has been dropping in on me without callin' sometimes. I need to talk with you two without him around."

"Sure, Pops," they chorused back. The waitress brought water and offered menus. "Coffee, gentlemen?"

Tony and Smitty said yes; Pops asked for unleaded, his name for decaf. They ordered without looking at the menus. When she was out of earshot, Pops faced his two comrades and kept his voice low. "Look. You knuckleheads have gotta cut this out. I ain't always gonna be around to bail you outta trouble."

"What're you saying, Pops? You sick or somethin'? You was at the hospital." Tony looked closely at Pops, who calmly unrolled flatware from his napkin.

Smitty settled back in the booth and pointed at Pops. "Naw, Tony, look at him. He's the picture of health. He's just being cautious, like always."

"I'm bein' smart. This plan of yours ain't gonna work. Things are different today. Too much technology. Too many cameras. There's no Jesus gonna take you to the Spirit if you keep on actin' like fools and gettin' inta trouble. And I ain't gonna be there to get you out. I'm done." He sipped at his coffee and rummaged in the condiment bin. "All this non-sugar crap's gonna kill me. Where's the damned sugar?"

The waitress returned with their orders and the three dug in. Between bites, Tony and Smitty tried to talk Pops into helping them. As the lunch crowd began to filter in, Smitty threw down his napkin and said, "All right, Pops, we get it. You won't help us. Give us back the map."

Pops looked at his friend. "You're gonna go through with it?"

"Hell, yes. It's my lifeline. I got nothing left to lose."

Pops looked at Tony. "And you're gonna help him?"

"You bet. I'm ashamed you won't. Thought you was our friend."

"I am your friend, both of you. I'm tryin' to save you from yourselves."

Smitty said, "Give us the map, Pops. We'll handle this on our own."

"Didn't bring it. Thought I could talk sense into you two. Thought maybe you'd grow up some day, especially after last time.

Then you come up with this fool plan. Well, whatever happens, I ain't gonna have no part in it and I ain't bailin' you outta jail when you gets caught."

Tony got up and threw some money on the table. "Tonight, Pops. We're coming over and you'll give us what's ours. C'mon Smitty. Mr. Right needs his privacy."

Smitty threw a few more bills on the table and left with Tony. Pops sat for several more minutes, tears streaming down his face. The waitress brought the check and more decaf. Seeing his sadness, she asked, "You all right, honey? Did those two do something to you?"

"Oh, I'm okay. Just sad. Some folks don't never grow up. Always have to be the fool, ya know?"

She put a hand on Pops' shoulder, "Yeah, I know. See it every day. Look, let me take this. You don't pay for your breakfast. Let me do that for you." She picked up the loose bills and let him compose himself.

Pops left the diner and went to the town common where he walked the length of it and back. He couldn't give them the map. It was too risky. They'd get caught, and at their age, the time they'd spend in jail, well, it would kill them. He sat on a bench, head in his hands with his elbows propped on his knees.

A young man came and sat down next to him. Pops looked up into a set of green eyes that almost matched the camouflage uniform he wore. Green Eyes said, "You okay, mister? You look kinda sad."

"Yeah. I am."

"Wanna talk about it?"

"You military?"

Green Eyes pointed to the name stitched on his right pocket flap, "Lieutenant Greenbaum, at your service. Two tours in Afghanistan."

"I was a sergeant…in Nam."

"It's an honor, sir."

"Hmph. That's something I never heard when I came back. You still in?"

"Recruitment center," he pointed across the street, "right over there between the diner and the pizza shop. You look like a man with a problem. Maybe I can help, sir."

Those green eyes said, trust me.

"Call me Pops," he said.

They sat and talked for hours. Pops went home with a light heart and the beginnings of a smile on his face. He had a friend in Jesus after all.

*

When Pops walked in the front door, he was surprised to find Jerry there, rummaging in his rolltop desk. "Pops, did you know these old desks can have hidden drawers and compartments? I'm looking to see if you've got one."

"You leave that alone. That's mine. You can explore it when I'm dead."

"Pops, don't say that. I want you around for a long time. But don't you see? There could be something important, something valuable, in this desk. It could add to your retirement money."

"I said leave that desk alone." Pops shoved Jerry away from the desk.

Jerry stood and stared at his father. "You've never talked to me this way before. What's gotten into you? I only want to help and lately all I get from you is argument and 'leave me alone.' Crap like that. That's not you, Pops. What's wrong?"

Pops shook his head. "I'm sorry, son. I got some things on my mind, that's all. Nuthin' to do with you."

Jerry led Pops over to his easy chair and helped him sit down. "Tell me. Please. Let me help."

"Naw, I got me some help. It's gonna be all right. Now get out of here. Tony and Smitty are comin' over and I don't want you here."

"Those two. I bet this has something to do with them. I'm not leaving until I know what it is."

"I was worried about them, but I tell you, I got this covered. Now let me be. You'll spoil everything if you stay."

"Pops, you got to tell me. I think maybe you aren't yourself. You had that attack a few weeks ago and something is worrying you fierce. I don't want to see you back in the hospital. I'm not leaving until you spill it all."

Pops relented and told Jerry about the hidden drawer. He retrieved the map, showing the location of alarms at a store with a safe that Tony could crack, and revealed Tony and Smitty's plan.

Jerry was shocked. "You mean they've been doing stuff like this for years? Man, can you keep secrets."

"Now you know why I didn't want to tell you. It'll spoil everything. I don't want them to go to jail, but I can't help them do this."

"So what're you gonna do, Pops, give them the map?"

"Yes."

"That's crazy. They're bound to get caught."

"I know. But I can't help them this time. I told them so today."

Pops swore Jerry to secrecy and ushered him out the door. He sat in his easy chair and waited for his two friends.

*

After Smitty and Tony left with the map, Pops sat in his easy chair listening to the one cassette from Ellie he'd managed to keep intact from his days in Nam. The cassette began and ended with "Spirit in the Sky." Pops closed his eyes. It didn't matter any longer if he lived or died, he was once again at peace, feeling that all was right with his world. His heart no longer thumped loudly when he thought about Tony and Smitty and their plan.

He wished he could be a fly on the wall where the robbery was to take place. It would certainly be tonight because once those two had their hands on the map they would spring into action, each never quite trusting the other with sole possession. That's why they'd left it in Pops' hands. They'd done similar things over the years, always pulling Pops into their plans even though he wouldn't go with them on their escapades. He was the one point of total trust between them. It had been that way since they'd met.

His phone rang at midnight. After the call, he sat back and smiled, then sighed. He hoped this would be it: the final crazy, stupid, jackass idea from his two buddies. He picked up his car keys and drove to an old warehouse downtown.

"Pops, glad you could make it." Lieutenant Greenbaum, in dark clothing and no military insignia, stepped out of the darkness and shook Pops' hand. "Want to see the interrogation?" At Pops' nod, he led him to a small room with a one-way mirror and they watched as first Tony and then Smitty were interviewed separately. The two clearly thought they'd spend the rest of their days in jail although they couldn't figure out what police station they were in and kept demanding their right to a phone call.

Pops looked at his new friend. "You didn't rough 'em up none, did you?"

"Nope. My buddies treated them right. You won't find a bruise or mark on them. I've stayed out of sight all along, so they'll never know, even if they see me on the street."

"That's good. Thank you. What happens next?"

"That's up to you. You want to go in there and talk to them? Separately? Together? Spill it that this part was your setup?"

"Won't do no good. They'll take it as me bailin' 'em out. Had an idea, though, while waitin'."

Lieutenant Greenbaum agreed to Pops' plan and after a short while, Jerry met them in the warehouse. "Jeez, Pops. How'd you manage all this?"

"Not me. Him." Pops pointed to his new friend, then looked at his son. "Now, got your story straight?"

"Yup. You told me about their plan. I listened to a police scanner and learned when they'd been picked up. I talked the police into letting two Nam vets go on account they got no brains between them."

"Yeah. That'll work. Just make sure they know the cops are on to them and will be watchin'. If they ever pull anything again, they're toast."

"Got it."

After Jerry met with Smitty and Tony, Lieutenant Greenbaum's buddies blindfolded and led the two out of the warehouse. "For your own protection," they told each man when dropping them off at their homes. "We don't ever want to see your names on any arrest warrants or even see you in our station again."

*

The next day, a subdued Tony and Smitty had lunch with Pops after he called and said to meet at the diner. The same waitress took their order. She looked closely at Pops and he winked.

Smitty handed the map to Pops. "Burn it, eat it. Just destroy it before it destroys our lives. We decided to pass, not just on this one. We're done, for good."

"Sounds like you two growed up sudden-like."

"Yeah. You could say that," said Tony. "I'll find another way to pay off my debts."

Pops said, "You could start by takin' some advice 'steada all them schemes you come up with." He slid a piece of paper, with several resources on it, over to Tony. Pops didn't say where he'd gotten the list, but Lieutenant Greenbaum had come up with it right after Pops had met him.

"Yeah. I shoulda' been listening to you all along, Pops. You've always tried to help us, teach us. Guess we never appreciated how smart you are."

"Not smart. Practical. And I listen to smart people."

Smitty said, "Pops, can you forgive us for what we said yesterday? It was mean. I realize, Tony realizes, you was watchin' out for us like always, like we're still a team."

"Yep," said Pops, "that's what it takes, a team." Pops nodded ever so slightly to Lieutenant Greenbaum, watching from the booth behind Tony and Smitty.

Jimmy's Jukebox
by Michael Bracken

(based on "I'm So Lonesome I Could Cry," B.J. Thomas and the Triumphs, 1966)

"Don't do it!" shouted half a dozen voices as a young man new to the neighborhood shoved a quarter into the jukebox and entered a selection.

Those of us who were regulars knew better then to play the jukebox at Jimmy's. The bar's owner had long ago rigged it to play one song and one song only, despite whatever selection was entered: B. J. Thomas and the Triumphs' 1966 recording of the Hank Williams classic "I'm So Lonesome I Could Cry," which climbed to number eight on the Billboard Pop Singles chart the week of April 9, 1966.

I don't know if it was the most depressing song recorded during the '60s, but playing it always put a pall over the room. New customers frequently asked Jimmy why he chose that song, but he never said. Instead he smiled his sad smile, bought the questioner a round, and moved away to serve someone less inquisitive.

The week Thomas' version of the song peaked, two long-haired young men wearing ski masks walked into a numbers bank in Chicago armed with a cut-down double-barrel shotgun and a snub-nosed .38. Outside, in a red four-door 1961 Chevrolet Impala, sat a young woman—sister of one of the men and wife of the other. She kept the engine idling and the radio tuned to an AM station playing the hits of the day.

The numbers game is an illegal lottery. Back in the day, bets placed at bars, barbershops and beauty parlors were delivered to the bank by runners carrying small slips of papers representing the bets. With the odds of winning 999:1 against the bettors, and the winners only paid 600:1, the bank always won, and profits any given day could be significant.

That day—payday for most of the people in the neighborhoods surrounding the numbers bank—cash on hand was somewhere north of a hundred thousand dollars when the two young men followed one of the runners inside. Their entrance surprised the muscle stationed at the door, a thick-chested crew member who had grown lax believing no one would dare try to knock off one of the Mob's numbers banks. The twin shotgun barrels jammed into his spine taught him different.

The young man sporting the .38 threw a green canvas duffel bag at the unarmed men inside the windowless room, and they stuffed it with all the cash on hand.

When the song ended, a soft-spoken young woman of mixed heritage leaned against the bar next to me and tried to catch the bar owner's attention. "Mr. Jimmy?"

Jimmy poured two beers for an elderly couple at the far end of the bar before he made his way back to where we sat.

"What can I do for you, Darlene?"

She couldn't meet his gaze and instead stared at the water rings marring the worn wood of the bar. "I—I can't make my rent, Mr. Jimmy. It's due tomorrow but I don't get paid until Friday."

"How much do you need?"

"Just ten dollars, Mr. Jimmy," she said. "That's all. Just ten dollars."

Jimmy was a soft touch and everyone knew it. He had helped many people in the neighborhood, and those he hadn't helped were related to or friends with the people he had. "What about that baby of yours?" he asked. "You got food in the pantry?"

Darlene looked up, meeting his gaze for the first time. "I do, Mr. Jimmy," said. "My baby's not going hungry. I just need a little help with the rent, that's all."

Jimmy pulled a crumpled twenty from the pocket of his white apron, pressed it into her hand, and clasped both of his hands around hers.

"Thank you, Mr. Jimmy," she said. "I'll pay you back, soon as I get paid."

Jimmy smiled, gave her hand a pat, and said, "Now stop your worrying and get on home to that baby of yours."

As Darlene walked away, Jimmy glanced at my beer mug. "Top you off, Pete?"

Everyone else called me RePete because I occupied the same stool every night—the one in the back corner under the neon Pabst Blue Ribbon sign—and had for near as long as Jimmy had owned the bar. Though Jimmy ran a tab for me, I had never paid for my drinks and likely never would. "Sure, Jimmy," I said. "I'd like that."

He topped off my beer and returned to the far end of the bar. Just as I had never missed a night holding down my stool, Jimmy had never missed a night behind the stick. He knew all of the regulars by name, knew their favorite drinks, and asked after their families when given the chance. New faces weren't new for long, and Jimmy soon knew the life stories of anyone who visited his bar more than twice. None knew his.

The two young men backed out of the numbers bank, jammed the door closed with a broken broom handle, and dove into the waiting Impala.

"We did it, Sheila!" they shouted as they slammed the doors. "By God, we did it!"

Sheila shoved the transmission into gear, popped the clutch, and sped away from the curb. None of them anticipated the crew member who stepped around the corner just ahead of them and fired his .38 at the windshield. Before either young man could return fire, Sheila upshifted, spun the wheel left, and slid the Impala around the corner, leaving the crew member behind them, the hammer of his .38 snapping down on empty chambers.

They were well east of the city, deep into Indiana, wind whistling through the bullet holes in the windshield, before either of the young men noticed that Sheila had been shot. Her brother, sitting in the rear seat with the money-filled duffel bag, had been more concerned with counting the cash. Her adrenaline-fueled husband, sitting beside her, had been talking a mile a minute, telling Sheila how they could finally settle down, get a place of their own, buy a small business, adopt a dog, have a baby. "We won't ever have to do anything like this again."

A falling star lit up the night sky as the Impala drifted to the side of the road and slowed to a stop. Sheila slumped to the left, her head against the window.

Her husband reached out. "What's wrong, honey?"

He drew back a hand covered with blood.

As soon as they realized Sheila was beyond help, the two young men tumbled out of the Impala. One had lost a wife. The other had lost a sister. They argued. They blamed one another. One threw a punch. The other threw one back. They beat on one another until they were too tired to continue.

Leaning against the Impala, struggling to catch his breath, one said, "We can't leave her here."

The other said, "Well, we can't take her with us."

They left her in the stolen Impala, parked outside a funeral home in Portage, Indiana, with two thousand dollars in singles, a note on the seat beside her, and B. J. Thomas on the radio. Then, tears in their eyes, they stole a Ford Fairlane and continued eastward.

Knocking over the numbers bank had not been the trio's first robbery, but it had been the most financially rewarding. When the two young men parted company just outside of Pittsburgh, they each walked away with more than fifty thousand dollars. Sheila's husband headed north. Her brother continued east.

Jimmy's had been in the same location in Buffalo since it opened in the 1920s, and it survived prohibition by selling bathtub gin and booze smuggled across the Niagara River from Canada, but the current owner wasn't the original Jimmy. When he purchased the place, he changed his name to Jimmy rather than change the name of the bar.

Early one Sunday morning, after the bar had closed and all the Saturday-night customers should have been gone, I stepped out of the men's room and heard unfamiliar voices. One asked, "Davy Thompson?"

Jimmy had not answered to that name in more than fifty years, and he didn't answer to it then.

"Chicago, 1966," said a second voice. "We didn't forget."

I peeked around the corner and saw two men the size of linebackers gone to pot. Neither was as old as Jimmy, but fifty was clearly in their rearview mirrors. One carried an aluminum baseball bat. The other snatched an empty PBR bottle from the bar.

Jimmy reached under the counter for the cut-down shotgun he had never fired, and they didn't give him the opportunity to fire it then.

I slipped out the back, into the alley, and used my cellphone to call 9-1-1. By the time a patrol car arrived, it was too late. Jimmy was dead, the bar was destroyed, and his two assailants were gone.

The police questioned me for several hours, asking again and again what had happened and if I had any idea why it had happened. I stonewalled as best I could, but I knew. I knew those two young men could not hide from the Mob forever, and that the remaining young man would soon experience a repeat of what had happened to Jimmy.

After the police released me, several of the bar's regulars helped me clean up the place before we held Jimmy's closed-casket wake. Everyone from the neighborhood crowded into the bar to pay their respects. We drank and we played B. J. Thomas and the Triumphs on the jukebox until we wore out the grooves in the 45 and everyone ran out of quarters.

After the last mourner left, I found myself alone with my brother-in-law's casket, and for the first time in years, I was so lonesome I could cry.

Little Old Ladies from Pasadena
by Maddi Davidson
(based on "Little Old Lady from Pasadena," Jan and Dean, 1964)

A law-abiding citizen with nary a parking ticket, Rose DiMello's descent into the criminal underworld had been breathtakingly rapid. A mere four months earlier she'd been a common housewife pushing her shopping cart of frozen TV dinners along the road of life with a drab husband of longstanding in tow. Harry had been her rock—some would say anchor—right up to the point when he muttered that Rose had put too many onions in the meat loaf, after which he clutched his chest and keeled over, dead of a heart attack, leaving Rose with his unfinished Schlitz beer, the dirty dishes and a ketchup stain on the rug.

Now knee-deep in a bank heist, Rose's hands shook violently, the deadly end of a Colt .45 oscillating between the tellers and customers huddled in front of the bank counter and a five-foot tall sign offering a "Free Toaster with New Checking Account." Her peripheral vision, somewhat obscured by her wig's red curls, caught the movement of the bespectacled assistant manager as he inched toward the end of the counter. Rose suspected he was attempting to trigger the alarm. Under orders not to speak, she swung the gun around and pointed it in the manager's direction. He made eye contact with her, but continued toward his objective.

Rose aimed the Colt over his head, closed her eyes, and squeezed the trigger. The shock of the recoil and roar of the discharge almost caused her to drop the gun. In the ensuing pandemonium, shrieks of terror cut through the air and—only God knows why—a deluge of water burst from the sprinklers in the ceiling. Rose opened her eyes. Through her water-streaked spectacles she could see several bodies on the now wet floor including that assistant manager, blood oozing from his temple and washing down his face.

A wave of nausea swept over her.

"Move your ass!"

A bag of cash in each hand and dripping wet, the bellowing Dot appeared around the corner advancing at full gallop. Well, maybe not full gallop, but darn fast for a sixty-five-year-old woman whose primary exercise was trying on high-heeled shoes. Quicker than one could say "Wilma Rudolf," Dot was out the door with Rose on her heels, praying for God's forgiveness.

*

After Harry's death, Rose drifted in a long, dark and lonely tunnel whose only light was watching *The Dick Van Dyke Show*. Not only did she ache for her husband, but women she once counted as friends no longer invited her to potlucks, bridge parties, slide shows of summer trips or garden club meetings. Only the other neighborhood widows, Dot and Willa Mae, offered Rose sympathy, understanding and the occasional glass or three of red wine.

"It's not you," Dot said one morning as she, Rose and Willa Mae were having a coffee klatch at Willa Mae's bungalow. "Married women view widows as a threat. Even a wife who despises her husband fears losing him. That's why neither Willa Mae nor I have been invited to neighborhood events since we lost our husbands."

Rose flushed in embarrassment; she'd not asked either woman to her home when Harry was alive.

Willa Mae added two tablespoons of sugar to her cup and rhythmically stirred her coffee. "I know it's been two months since Harry passed, but it ain't doing ya no good to sit around and mourn," she said in her unmistakable Appalachian twang with "it" pronounced "hit" and "ain't" as "hain't." Putting her spoon on the scratched-up, oak table, Willa Mae finally took a sip of her coffee and sighed. "After Earl passed, I learned to just 'do my own thing,' as the young people say."

Willa Mae's thing included jettisoning her nylons and dresses for the comfort of stretch pants and jeans she wore everywhere, even to church where she served as a greeter. "Life is eighteen times better without a girdle," she oft said. She'd become enamored with pop music, particularly the California Sound of Jan and Dean whose records she played almost non-stop.

Following her friends' advice, Rose volunteered at the local library and Red Cross. On weekends the three women explored neighboring Los Angeles—a treat for Rose since Harry had been forever too tired to take her anywhere. Although the evenings were still deathly quiet, for several hours each day Rose forgot she was a widow. Especially those days when she could sit with her friends in the sand on Venice Beach, one of Willa Mae's favorite spots to watch the surfers and hum pop music.

At Willa Mae's home one morning, the women settled at the table with their freshly brewed Maxwell House coffee and the tunes of Jan and Dean when Rose began to cry, tears rolling down her cheeks into her china cup.

"What's the matter?" Dot asked. "Is the coffee too hot? Too bitter? Music too loud?"

Rose responded with loud sobs.

Willa Mae dragged her chair across the linoleum to sit next to Rose and put an arm around her shoulders.

"Go ahead and cry, sweetie. Let it all out."

Amidst the snivels, nose wiping and weeping, Rose haltingly explained that her son, Bill, had called the prior evening. He had reviewed her finances and decided she'd have to move out of the house: she couldn't afford her mortgage. He wanted her to come to San Francisco where he and his wife, Nancy, located a one-bedroom apartment for her less than five miles from their home.

"How could this happen?" she wailed. "Harry was a good earner. He bought a brand-new Cadillac two months before he died. How could there not be enough money?"

Willa Mae rubbed Rose's back. "Don't you want to be closer to kin?"

"No! His wife doesn't like me. She still calls me Mrs. DiMello and sends me dowdy housecoats on my birthday and Christmas. I used to love visiting my grandchildren, but they're teenagers now and they have long, stringy hair, wear strange clothes and have crazy ideas. They think I'm a fossil."

"How 'bout staying with your other son, John?" Willa Mae said.

"I don't want to move to Massachusetts. I can't survive those cold winters. That's why Harry and I left Ohio."

"You could rent an apartment in Pasadena."

Rose dropped her voice to a whisper. "I love my home. It still smells like Harry is there."

Dot cleared her throat. "Just how much do you want to stay?"

"I'd do anything. Anything." Rose surprised herself with the vehemence of this declaration.

"Would you lie to your son about your finances?" Dot asked.

"He won't believe me. He's reviewed Harry's records. Besides, what good would it do if I can't afford the house?"

"There might be, no, there is a way around that," Dot replied. She leaned forward, peering intently at Rose. "Willa Mae and I can help, but you must do your bit."

Dot instructed Rose to inform her son that she'd discovered Harry had another savings account and it might contain sufficient funds to keep the house. She should tell Bill she appreciated his help, but henceforth she would consult an accountant about her finances.

"Bill will want to know how much is in the savings account."

"Make up a number or tell him you only have an old statement. The point is you have to remove him from managing your life or we can't do anything for you."

A few days later during morning coffee while Jan and Dean confessed "I Get Around," Rose reported that she'd talked to Bill. "He didn't sound convinced, but I told him I already had an accountant and he seemed relieved. He still wants to know how much I have in savings, though."

"That can wait," Dot said, "until after the bank heist."

Stunned into immobility, Rose said not a word as Dot explained that she and Willa Mae had been planning for some time to knock over a bank in Burbank. They had all the details worked out, but success required a third member of the gang. "Two of us are needed in the building. The other will remain outside with the getaway car."

"Rob a bank?" Rose said in a strangled voice. "I can't do that!"

"Of course you can," Dot said. "Everybody's doing it. The Los Angeles area has one or two every day. No reason we can't join in. Besides, it's a victimless crime. No one loses anything."

"What do you mean?"

"The bank's losses are covered by the insurance they've paid for. The insurance companies have priced their coverage to handle losses and still make big profits. Everyone wins!"

Rose brightened. "Maybe I can be the driver. I wouldn't actually be robbing anyone that way."

Willa Mae shook her head. "I've been evadin' the police from back in the day when I ran moonshine for Daddy. I'll hot-wire a car for the job be'ens my ol' Studebaker cain't go so fast."

As if on cue, strains of "The Little Old Lady from Pasadena" filled the kitchen with its homage to the Super Stock Dodge. "Wish I had one of them," Willa Mae said. "It's gotta 425 horsepower V-8 that would leave the cops so far behind it'd be like they was goin' backwards."

Willa Mae still had a far-off look in her eyes, dreaming of the Dodge when Rose abruptly stood up, announced she had to "use the ladies' room," and scurried down the hall.

"You're sure she can handle it?" Willa Mae whispered to Dot. "I've seen eyes like hers in rabbits the 'xact moment a hawk grabbed 'em."

"Give her a chance; she's lived a sheltered life. Her desperation will carry her through."

"Fine, then. Just don't tell her everything."

"No chance of that," Dot replied as Rose returned.

"No chance of what?" Rose asked.

"No chance we'll be recognized," Dot said.

Rose took a sip of her now tepid coffee. "Are we wearing masks?" she asked. "Scarves pulled up over our noses?"

"Enter the bank that way and someone is sure to trip the alarm. No, you and I will be disguised as women." Dot replied.

"But we are women."

"We'll wear preposterous wigs, baggy dresses, poorly applied makeup and no perfume—although if you have any of Harry's aftershave left, use some of that. I'll call you George. People will assume we're men badly disguised as women. I'll do all the talking, of course. They won't have any trouble believing I'm male."

Dot had always possessed a gravelly voice—deeper now that she was in her late fifties—and was unusually tall with large hands. She typically wore big hair, frilly dresses and the highest heels she could find in size eleven, creating the impression that she stood well over six feet.

"Of course we'll have to pad your shoulders and waist," Dot said to Rose. "Don't want any of your curves to show."

Rose appreciated Dot's kind words. Her once hourglass shape had begun the slide south years ago, so she now resembled a large beaker.

Rose continued to pepper the other two with questions. "What bank would we rob? Where is it? Have you been inside? How this? When that? What if? Have you done this before?"

"This ain't my first rodeo," Dot said.

Willa Mae nodded. "It's easier than runnin' moonshine. Pays better, too."

Out of questions and overwhelmed, Rose told her friends she needed some time to think about it.

"Of course, dear," Willa Mae said. "Dot and I are jest tryin' to help. It's okay if you cain't do it. I'm sure living near family in San

Francisco won't be all bad. Maybe you and Nancy will become bosom friends."

The next day, bleary-eyed from lack of sleep, Rose committed to the venture.

As the women prepared for the heist, Rose vacillated between optimism for her future and a sense of doom that the plan would fall apart or, even worse, that she'd be responsible for them all being caught. She almost backed out of the venture when Dot announced one morning that Rose would carry a gun.

"But I don't want to hurt anybody," Rose protested.

"Of course not. That's why I'll teach you how to use one. We need the guns to frighten people so they'll do as we say. You'll pull the trigger only if someone starts to get out of line. Now, the first thing is for you to become comfortable handling a weapon."

Rose recoiled at the black handgun in Dot's outstretched hand. Gingerly she touched it, then carefully picked it up and put it in her lap. "It's heavy."

"Over two pounds, unloaded. Pick it up and aim it at the lamp."

Rose did as she was told, her hand shaking like an aspen leaf in a strong wind.

"Hmm. Maybe you should just hold it while I give you instructions."

Rose put the gun back in her lap, her hand resting atop the cold metal.

Dot's technical monologue about the virtues of this particular weapon left Rose confused. Did it hold seven bullets, or forty-five, and why did Dot keep talking about a magazine? When Dot instructed Rose to again aim at the lamp and pretend to shoot, she held up the gun, pointed it in the direction of the lamp and pulled the trigger. Nothing happened.

"Remember, you need to release the safety, cock the gun, and squeeze the trigger," Dot said.

Rose's face was a blank.

"Here, I'll show you."

Dot performed the maneuver and handed the weapon back to Rose, who still appeared clueless.

"I think you're spittin' upwind there," Willa Mae said.

"Right," Dot replied. "Tell you what Rose, I'll cock the gun, you just aim and pull the trigger."

After a few dry runs with Rose, Dot was not impressed.

"Before we go into the bank, I'll set up your weapon. This is important: keep your finger off the trigger unless you intend to pull it. There's almost no chance you'll hit anyone, but just in case aim high and hope for the best."

For their disguises, Dot donated a long, black wig from a witch's costume and a curly, red 'do. "From when I was a very tall elf for Christmas," she explained.

Willa Mae offered to pick up the dresses. "I'll find something at Goodwill on Figueroa on Friday. They don't know me there. I'll get myself a big floppy hat too, so as no one can see my face."

"Have you found a car, yet?" Dot asked.

"Yup, a nice Buick Riviera that sits in a lot near Paradise Way during the day. If it's not there, I know of a good Caddy that parks a block away."

"I thought you were getting a fast car," Rose said. "Like a Corvette."

"All cars are fast when I drive 'em. 'Sides, three old ladies in a Buick is a darn sight less suspicious than in a Vette. That's if we could even fit in a Vette."

"Oh, I see," Rose said. And she did. Her friends had thought of everything it seemed. They really didn't even need her, except to keep an eye on the tellers while Dot went into the vault with the bank manager. Maybe, just maybe, this whole thing would work.

Dot declared they'd hit the bank on the following Wednesday.

That night, Rose's son Bill called. He was taking off work on Friday to fly down and, with the new account she'd uncovered, review her finances with her. "You shouldn't have to rely on an accountant," he said. "It's a son's duty to look out for his mother."

"Nothing I said made any difference," Rose told her friends the next day. "I'm sorry."

"No matter," Dot said. "Willa Mae can pick up the disguises this afternoon. We'll do the job tomorrow."

Willa Mae, her lips tightly pressed together, said nothing.

"What can I do?" Rose asked.

"It's your volunteer day at the library, so go. If anyone asks what's new, tell them you are excited your son is visiting," Dot said. "And really, really try to sound happy."

"You okay?" Dot asked Willa Mae after Rose left.

"We picked a Wednesday morning cuz there are fewer customers in the bank then. Now it'll be Thursday when there are more witnesses."

"We don't have a choice."

"How 'bout Rose callin' her son to tell him she has the flu."

"I trust Rose's acting ability as much as I trust her aim," Dot said. "It has to be tomorrow or not at all."

*

Rose pounded out of the bank and slid into the back seat beside Dot. Willa Mae took off, the car's momentum slamming the door closed.

"Down!" Willa Mae yelled as the car squealed around the corner and roared off. After a few minutes of high-speed driving and screeching turns, Willa Mae slowed to a sedate twenty-five miles per hour.

"Have we lost them?" Dot inquired as she and Rose raised their heads.

"Nope. Weren't nobody behind us. I just wanted to drive fast," Willa Mae said. "It felt real good, too."

Ninety minutes later, the women were back in Willa Mae's kitchen. The Buick had been returned and the disguises dumped in various trash containers along the route home. Two bags of money sat in the cupboard under Dot's sink. The women were again huddled around the kitchen table and Willa Mae had poured each a tot of gin.

"You'll need to deposit your portion of the money this afternoon," Dot said to Rose. "So you can show your son a bank balance."

Rose, who hadn't said a word since the heist, didn't respond.

"Did you hear me? Rose? What's the matter, honey? Are you feeling okay?"

"Is she in shock?" Willa Mae said. "Did she get hurt when I was rippin' 'round corners?"

"Thank you for your efforts," Rose said, her voice barely a whisper. "I promise not to reveal your names. I'll make up some story. Or maybe just not talk, but I have to give myself up."

Dot jumped to her feet. "What are you talking about?"

"I killed a man. The least I can do is surrender. Do you think I can donate my portion of money to his family?"

"You couldn't have."

"I shot him when he went for the alarm. I tried to miss, but I didn't. Got him in the head. He must have died instantly."

"He ain't dead," Willa Mae said.

"Certainly not," Dot said. "Listen Rose, there were blanks in your gun. I couldn't trust you with a loaded weapon. I'm sorry."

"But his head?"

"Hit it against something, I expect," Dot said.

"Oh."

A pregnant pause ensued. Finally, Rose spoke. "Did we get enough that I don't have to move?"

Willa Mae smiled. "Enough to cover your mortgage and a new car for me."

"What about you, Dot? What will you buy?" Rose asked.

"Nothing. I don't want the money."

"Dot did it for me," Willa Mae said. "Earl promised me a hot car one day, even makin' a down payment on a '59 Ford Thunderbird. When he died, the last thing he done said was, 'Willa, promise me you gonna get a good car for yo'self.' I tol' him I would. Couldn't 'ford to 'til now."

"Ever since Jan and Dean came out with the song about the lady from Pasadena driving a Super Stock Dodge," Dot said, "Willa Mae's been mooning about that car. I told her I'd help her get the money for it. Robbing a bank seemed the easiest way."

Dot raised her glass. "A toast, ladies. To our successful first and last bank heist."

In the process of reaching for her glass, Rose froze. "But, but, but…you said this wasn't your first time."

"I lied. Didn't want to make you any more nervous than you already were," Dot replied.

"Oh," Rose said.

The three women clinked their glasses together and drank.

Rose drained her glass and set it carefully on the table. "More."

"Do you think that's wise?" Dot said. "You still have to drive to a bank this afternoon."

"No, I don't," Rose replied. "I'll take care of the money some other day. And when my son shows up tomorrow, I'll be very nice, but firm. He needs to know that my life is my business and I can get by just fine"

Willa Mae got up from the table and disappeared into the living room. A moment later, the kitchen was filled with the sweet harmony of Jan and Dean singing, "The Little Old Lady from Pasadena." "To us," Willa Mae said, "three little old ladies from Pasadena." They raised their glasses and their voices, "Go, Granny, Go, Granny, Go, Granny, Go!"

Mercy

by Joseph S. Walker

(based on "Oh, Pretty Woman," Roy Orbison, 1964)

Before our father set it on fire, my big brother Stevie amassed what was possibly the largest collection of 45 singles in our town. He started buying them when he was 7. By the time he was 12 he was nearly obsessive, funneling the money from a paper route and his grudgingly tendered allowance directly to the local record shop. When he was 15, he scrounged scrap wood from around the neighborhood and built shelves of his own design to hold the hundreds he'd collected and lovingly maintained, allowing me, his worshipful little sister, to touch or play them only in his presence. At 16, he brought home "Penny Lane" and "Strawberry Fields Forever" on the flip side and spent one blissful Saturday listening to the two songs over and over again.

At 18, his number came up in the draft lottery.

I sat on his bed and watched him pack. By then we'd started to hear about boys who ran off to Canada rather than risk Vietnam. I knew Stevie wouldn't, but, watching his slender fingers folding shirts, I was heartsick at the thought of him in uniform. To distract me, I think, he made me promise I would take care of the records while he was gone. He said I could choose one of them to have as my own as payment for being their guardian. He probably expected me to pick one of the new songs, a mind trip from the Beatles or a grinder from the Stones.

I ran my fingers along the alphabetized rows, letting the corners of the paper sleeves rustle under my nails. When I chose, it was a record he'd had for more than five years, one of the first ones I remembered loving, I handed it to him shyly.

"Monument 851," he read. "'Oh, Pretty Woman,' by Roy Orbison and the Candy Men. B-side 'Yo te Amo Maria.'" He looked at me. "How come?"

"I like the way he says 'mercy' at the end of the first verse." As I said the word I tried, without much success, to imitate Orbison's teasing delivery, the playful lasciviousness layered over something that wasn't play, something I didn't yet understand. "And then the growl after the second verse." I didn't even try to replicate that.

Stevie laughed. He picked up a pen and turned the record over.

He had written his name on the back of the sleeve of every single in his collection. In later years, when I worked in a record store myself, I learned this reduces their value. I don't think Stevie would have cared about that, if he'd known. He didn't want the records for money. He wanted the records for the records.

On the back side of "Oh, Pretty Woman," he wrote, under his name, "Traded to Lila Benson for services rendered." He signed and dated it and handed it to me, grinning.

Five months later I came home from school and saw the telegram from the Army on the kitchen table. Dazed, I walked to the window and saw our father in the backyard. He had stacked Stevie's records in a pile and poured the gasoline from the shed over them and now he stood there while they burned, not even seeming to watch as the sleeves darkened, came apart and drifted away, black scraps edged with fading red embers.

*

For years, I tried to feel some sympathy for my father. He was widowed when I was born, left alone with an infant daughter and a two-year-old son. It must have been hard in ways beyond my comprehension. I couldn't use it to explain or justify, though, the ease and speed with which he reached for his belt, or the feeling of the back of his hand across my face. It couldn't undo the jolts of pain or erase the ugly purple welts everyone at school looked away from.

Stevie intervened when he could, often accepting bruises meant for me. After Stevie was killed, my father's cold rage filled the house, seeking a target, finding one as often as not in his strange, quiet daughter. It grew all the stronger as he started to suspect what

I'd discovered for myself years earlier. My complete disinterest in the boys on the football team. My not-quite-casual-enough ogling of Mary Ann on *Gilligan's Island* and Goldie Hawn on *Laugh-In*. There would be no strapping, beer-guzzling son-in-law to take me off his hands.

I hid the Orbison single, the last remnant of Stevie's collection, under a floorboard in my closet, alongside the lurid paperbacks about fallen women, shoplifted from The Book Emporium. I started spending as much time as I could manage anyplace else but the house where I'd grown up. On a good day I didn't have to see my father at all.

*

A couple of years after Stevie died, I was out of high school and working on being out of the house for good. I clerked part-time behind the counter at Music's Last Stand, the record store where they remembered me as the little sister of their all-time best customer. I crashed on friends' couches when I could, slept at home when I had to, took a couple of classes at the community college, and spent a lot of time in the town square, hanging around in what was half a homeless camp and half a permanent protest against the war. There was a lot of pot, a little bit of LSD, and always music, but we didn't think of ourselves as hippies. Altamont had happened by then. Manson had happened. We had lurched into the '70s. It felt like the hippie thing was over, but we still had Nixon, and we still had the war, and we sensed it was still our duty to hold up the signs and chant once in a while. A lot of towns would have run us out, but the police chief had lost his youngest son during Tet. As long as we didn't panhandle or hassle people going about their business, he let us be.

One May morning I was perched on the low wall circling the square. I hadn't been home in a couple of weeks. I'd saved a little bit of money and I was wondering if I could manage the rent on my own apartment and who to ask to be my roommate. I stopped thinking about all of that when a woman I'd never seen before walked around the corner.

I forgot to breathe. The world reoriented itself around her, like loose playing cards returning to order as you tap them against the table, edges all lined up. In that instant I understood everything about Roy Orbison's growl.

Her short jet-black hair swept up into an Elvis pompadour. She wore a leather jacket over a white t-shirt and tight jeans, her eyes hidden behind sunglasses blacker than Spiro Agnew's soul. She carried no purse, wore no jewelry, but her mouth was outlined with neon red lipstick, one corner turned up in the barest hint of a smile. Her clothes clung to her in a way that made Goldie Hawn drop clean out of my mind, but it was her walk that slayed me, smooth and confident, moving fast while barely seeming to move at all. A guy would have said she walked like she owned the place, and he would have said it with a bit of a sneer, but that wasn't it. She didn't walk like she had a claim on the world.

She walked like it had no claim on her.

I had ten seconds to look at her after she rounded the corner and before she was past me. I didn't turn my head, because I didn't want to watch her disappear around another corner. I wanted to save her, whole in my mind, always coming toward me. I closed my eyes and a voice spoke, right at my elbow. "Hey, pretty girl," it said.

It was her. The corner of her lip had lifted a little more and her head was tilted. I had the feeling she knew everything I'd just been thinking, and I felt my face flush.

"You look like you know what's what," she said. "Where can I get a good breakfast around here?"

I had to swallow a couple of times before I could answer. "McCoy's Diner," I said. "A couple of blocks."

"Cool," she said. "You want to come have breakfast with me?"

"Yes," I managed. I had just enough dignity not to add please. I stood up and nodded in the direction she'd been going. "It's this way."

"Lead on," she said. We started down the sidewalk together, my heart hammering. I felt like an oaf next to her. I had on a Monkees t-shirt I pretended to wear ironically and a flowered skirt that already seemed like some kind of costume, a pretentious bit of Woodstock playacting. I tried desperately to think of something to say that wouldn't make me seem like the clueless dolt I was. I couldn't come up with anything. We covered a block in silence, my humiliation growing with every step.

Halfway to the diner we were passing the mouth of an alley when she put her hand on my elbow and pulled me into the opening. She spun me up against the brick wall and put her forearm against the wall next to my head and leaned toward me. Her right hand slipped casually under the hem of my t-shirt and there was the electric touch of her warm fingertips against the bare skin of my side.

"What's your name?" she asked.

"Lila," I got out.

"Lila," she said. "I don't want coffee on my breath the first time I kiss you."

It was slow and sweet and warm and when it was over, she pulled back, tipping the dark glasses down, and for the first time I saw her blue eyes.

"My name's Mercy," she said.

*

Mercy had a green VW Bug she'd been driving around the country for two years, working odd jobs and waitressing, moving on whenever she wanted. She had a set of tools to keep the Bug running and a switchblade knife to keep overly helpful men at bay. She had a rock she'd picked up on the beach at Key West that she worried with her thumb when she was thinking. She had a dream of settling down and running a little bookstore, somewhere in Arizona. She had an atlas she hardly ever looked at, a box full of Green Lantern comic books she reread constantly, and parents in New York City who had made it clear they never wanted to see her again.

I didn't learn all this at that first breakfast. I learned it, and much more, over the course of the week we spent together, starting right then. I had to work a shift at Music's Last Stand, so she sat on a stool next to mine behind the counter, swinging her legs and teasing the customers, one hand resting on my thigh. When the shift was over, I took her to the back room of the house where I was crashing. I won't talk about that. There are moments that are only for the people who are in them.

Mercy took her time revealing herself to me, sharing her stories. I took my time too. It was five days before I told her about Stevie. I thought I had cried all the tears I had for him, but telling Mercy made it new and raw again and she held me as I found there were a lot more.

When I was all cried out, we held hands, lying on our backs and looking up into the sky. It was the wee hours of the morning and we were on the roof of Music's Last Stand in a big sleeping bag she kept in the Bug. She liked being under the stars, even though we couldn't see very many of them with the town's lights in the way. It's why she wanted to end up in Arizona. Out there, she said, there were hardly any lights at all, and you could see the whole Milky Way, spread out just for you.

"So the record's still there," she said, after a time. "Hidden in your old closet."

"Yes," I said. "When I have my own place, where it can be safe, I'll go get it. I don't want to carry it around. It's all I have of him."

"Well," she said. "We'd better go get it soon."

I took a moment to savor the "we," and then looked at her silhouette in the darkness. "Why?"

"I'm about ready to move on," she said. "And you can't leave it behind."

"You want me to come with you?" I didn't know how to think a thought that good.

Mercy laughed.

"Oh," she said, "pretty woman." And she rolled and reached for me.

*

We went to the house two days later, at a time I was pretty sure my father would be at work. He was a warehouse foreman and his shifts sometimes got moved around, but early afternoons had generally been a safe time to be there, even back before Stevie left. I thought the house looked smaller than I remembered, shabbier. As far as I was concerned, the place was already receding into my past.

The inside was a mess. I'd given up cleaning for him months ago, and there was a smell I didn't remember, a combination of dirty laundry, empty beer cans and full trash cans. I opened a window to get some air circulating and led Mercy to the back of the house, resisting the urge to hurry. I wasn't trespassing. This was my home too, and if this was going to be my last time in it, I wasn't going to sneak.

My room felt hollow, staged, and I realized it had been a long time since anyone had really lived there. It was like a museum exhibit of what a girl's room might have looked like in an unimaginable past. Mercy drifted along looking at old school portraits and sketches from my high school art class. I could tell she sensed it too.

I remembered a cheap suitcase I'd had for sleepovers in grade school, still under the bed. "I'll get the record," I told Mercy. "Will you pack some clothes?" I showed her the drawers where she would find things that still fit. In the closet, I knelt and did the tricky push and slide, the only way to move the loose floorboard.

The record was still there. I realized I'd been afraid he would have found it and started another fire. I set it by the door and looked at the other treasures-in-hiding. A glass piggy bank full of pennies. A doll my father had called ugly and threatened to throw away. A journal I'd written two entries in and then stopped, lacking the language to express the things I was feeling. And then three paperbacks that had expressed them too well, paperbacks I had slipped into the waistband of my skirt and smuggled past the bookstore register, heart pounding. I picked up the top one. The title was *Private Rooms*, and the blurb on the cover asked, "What turn in the road sends normal women down the twisted paths of lesbian lust?"

I turned to show the book to Mercy and saw my father standing in the doorway.

*

Mercy was folding my underwear, her back to the door. I dropped the book, and at the sound she looked up at my face and then spun to see him.

He was still a big man, but the hard muscle that had defined him was beginning to soften, and his stomach bulged a little against his shirt. The tight buzzcut was iron grey now. I'd known these things, known he was getting old, but seeing him now, with Mercy there, was like seeing him for the first time.

He didn't look at me or Mercy. He looked at the record.

"Guess I missed one," he said. Somebody who didn't know him might think he sounded mild, thoughtful.

"It's mine," I said. I picked up the record and stood, my back to the wall. "Stevie gave it to me."

"It wasn't his to give," my father said. "Everything he had became mine when he died. If I want that record, you'll damn well give it to me."

"I won't. It's mine." I was breathing hard but I made myself think of Mercy and of Stevie. "I'm leaving. For good."

He shook his head, and for the first time looked at Mercy. "Who the hell are you?"

"My name's Mercy," she said. She sounded calm. Resolved. "I'm in love with your daughter."

For a second, I forgot to breathe again.

My father's face twisted. "Don't be disgusting. You're not going to bring your sickness into my family."

"We're just here for a few of Lila's things. Then we'll be leaving."

"You will be. Not her." He looked back at me. "Give me that record."

I put it behind my back. "No."

"You think I can't take it? I'm not that old yet." He took a step forward. Immediately Mercy glided between us. She held up her left hand in a stop gesture and with the right hand pulled her switchblade from her jacket pocket and flicked it open.

He stopped, staring at the knife and then her.

"I don't want to hurt you," Mercy said. "But we are leaving, and we are taking the record."

I find myself back in that moment, all the time, in my dreams. The three of us, frozen in place, all of us waiting to see what would happen.

After a second, I stepped away from the wall and stood right behind Mercy, putting my hand on her hip to let her know I was there. My father watched me do that, looked at my hand, then turned his back and walked out of the room.

Beneath my hand I felt the tension in Mercy marginally ease. "Hurry," she said. "Before he comes back." I went to the bed and put the record in the suitcase and closed it. She hadn't gotten to all the clothes but I didn't care. I wanted out of this room, out of this house.

I took her hand. "Let's go," I said.

We walked down the hall. Maybe everything would have been all right if we'd gone into the garage and left by the back way. But we went the way we'd come, into the living room, and my father was sitting in the chair he always sat in, and in his hand was a gun.

He lifted it and pointed it at us. "Sit on the couch," he said. "Right now."

Mercy hesitated, just a beat, and he pulled the trigger. There was the loudest bang I'd ever heard, and I swear I heard the bullet pass through the space between our heads. We both jumped.

"Couch," he said again.

We moved to the couch and sat. I put the suitcase between my feet.

"Don't do this," I said. "Where did you even get a gun?"

"I'll let you know when you can talk," he said. "Toss the knife on the table here in front of me."

Mercy tossed the knife gently. It came to rest on the coffee table a foot and a half in front of my father. I saw he was sweating.

"Did you know that they're less likely to take only children?" he said.

Mercy and I looked at each other, confused.

"The draft," he said. "They'll try not to take an only child." He looked at me. "First you took my wife," he said. "She died trying to bring you into the world. Then you took my son. If he'd stayed an only child, I'd still have him."

I could hear Mercy's breathing. I wanted to take her hand but I was afraid. I would die before I let him hurt her. What terrified me was, I was sure, entirely sure, she was thinking the same thing.

"You took everything," he said. "And now you're going to, what, shame me? Take my good name too? Make sure everyone knows I raised a pervert?"

"Dad," I said.

"Don't call me that."

"Just let us go," Mercy said. "We'll never come back. Nobody will know."

"I'll know," he said.

"We love each other," I said.

"Oh, I can see that," he said, his lips twisting. "If you call that love."

"Yes," Mercy said. "We do."

He shook his head. "You took everything from me," he said again. "So now I'm going to take everything from you."

I pulled my feet back and leaned forward, preparing to jump at him, to put my body between the gun and Mercy, but instead of lifting the gun, he picked up the phone on the little side table by his chair. Working left-handed, he dialed 0.

"Operator," he said. "Give me the police. This is an emergency."

Now he did lift the gun, pointing it at us.

"Police," he said, his voice rushed, panicky. "My name is Tony Benson. I live at 435 Sycamore. I just came home and found a woman here with my daughter. Her name is Mercy and she's robbing the place. She has a knife. A switchblade—yes, she is threatening me. Listen, I think she's brainwashed my daughter. She's some kind of sick pervert and my daughter says they're in love, but I think this Mercy woman has her all turned around. She's a good girl, she's not like that. Please come. I think this Mercy wants to hurt me. I've got a gun and I fired a shot to scare her, but I only had the one bullet. Please come fast. I think she's going to—"

He broke off and dropped the phone to the floor. For the first time I saw he had a handkerchief. He leaned forward with it and grabbed Mercy's knife. She understood a second before I did and jumped for him, too late. Looking at me, smiling for the first time I could remember, he brought the knife up and cut his own throat.

*

I told my story, again and again, to everyone, even when I knew they weren't listening. I told them Mercy had tried to save him, that she was covered in his blood because she'd tried to hold it in him with her bare hands. I told them he had been lying, we weren't robbing the place, we didn't threaten him. None of it mattered. His call to the police had been recorded and as soon as the jury heard "brainwashed," it was all over. The prosecutor was happy to remind them of the women who'd sat outside the courthouse during Charlie Manson's trial proclaiming their love, making up alibis, still willing to kill for him. Now our little town had its very own lesbian Manson, and a martyred father who had tried to save his little girl. Every cop and reporter in town preferred that story.

So did the jury.

*

The one saving grace turned out to be the gun. Because my father had it, the lawyer appointed to Mercy's case argued there was an element of self-defense and got murder reduced to manslaughter. With good behavior, Mercy will be out in June of 1983.

Five years down. Six more years to wait.

I visit every week. The guards have gotten used to me. They let us hold hands across the table. At first, Mercy told me not to wait for her, that I was throwing my life away. Now she holds my hand and we count the remaining days together.

I sold the house and everything in it. I still have Stevie's record. I live in a tiny apartment, work at the record store and save every penny, except for what it takes to keep Mercy's Bug running. In my spare time I go to the library and read up on possible places to live in Arizona and the economics of running an independent bookstore.

One of the things everyone loves about "Oh, Pretty Woman" is the irresistible opening guitar riff, a stuttering, immediately repeated rendition of the opening notes of the progression that drives the rest of the record. Legend, as told in record stores, says it sounds like a mistake because it was, the guitarist not quite getting the full riff right the first time through. Orbison decided to keep it, and that gleeful little false start became the key to the record, That's how I think of the week Mercy and I had together. A little false start before the real music begins.

I'll be there in 1983, with the Bug fully gassed and ready for the road, a route to Arizona marked out in that same old atlas. The door will open and there she'll be, a few lines at the corners of her eyes, a touch of grey in the pompadour, but that same gliding step that every guard will turn to look at. I'll hold out my arms, and my Mercy will come walking.

Back to me.

Under the Boardwalk

by Dawn Dixon

(based on "Under the Boardwalk," The Drifters, 1964)

A steamy breeze ruffled Spanish moss in the giant oak tree as Mary Lizzie squinted through the screen door. On the front porch stood her last stepmother, Ruby, the one who'd murdered Mary Lizzie's daddy a few years back.

"Long time no see," chirped red-haired, red-faced Ruby as if they were best friends. A sheen of sweat covered her freckled skin as she stood there, a stick figure in her denim cutoffs, halter top and red flip-flops. Two beers dangled in a plastic handle that usually held six.

"Have you fallen off the wagon again?" Mary Lizzie glanced at the Jeep in the driveway and wondered how Ruby avoided getting stopped on the interstate. That rehab in Charlotte must not have done its job well enough.

"Is this how you say hey to someone you haven't seen in years?"

"Sorry, it just popped out."

"I'm used to it. Besides, I only had a couple beers on the way. See?" She waggled the cans in the air. "I got all that under control now. Beer don't count anyway."

"Uh huh."

Ruby had been thirty years younger than Mary Lizzie's father, Pete, when they'd wed. This infuriating turn of events "made her six years younger than me," Mary Lizzie had complained to her friends at the time. "I could read and write by the time Ruby screeched her way into the world."

Unbeknownst to Ruby, that's how Mary Lizzie still described her former stepmother whenever she became a topic of conversation. Ruby the Screecher.

When Pete brought his child bride to the family home in North Carolina, Mary Lizzie raised all kinds of Cain.

"For the love of God, Daddy, where is your mind?" Mary Lizzie hissed. "You only clapped eyes on her seventeen days ago. You know nothing about her. No one gets married after seventeen days, except maybe movie stars or rock and roll singers and you're not either one of those. People live in sin these days."

But Pete was old school; they'd slept together, therefore they'd married. End of story. He saw no reason to wait. Mary Lizzie knew he believed in marriage. Ruby was wife number four.

He'd grabbed his daughter's elbow and hustled her outside to the patio after her outburst.

"Keep your voice down, Sugar," he said. "Ruby is very sensitive. You'll hurt her feelings."

Mary Lizzie rolled her eyes, doubting the existence of Ruby's feelings. She'd seen the gleam in her eye when the woman sashayed up the sidewalk scanning the house and surrounding prosperous neighborhood with a chin-raising I've-come-up in-the-world expression.

From the patio, Mary Lizzie and Pete peered through the picture window in time to see Ruby make a beeline for the bar in the den. Her pile of russet hair, teased to within an inch of its life and rounded, resembled a fallen sweet potato soufflé. Ruby stared at the colorful lineup of alcohol and liqueurs like a kid in a candy store before selecting the Beefeater London Dry Gin and heading toward the kitchen.

"That's odd," Pete remarked. "She hasn't touched a drop of alcohol in all the time I've known her."

Mary Lizzie just looked at him. All the time you've known her?

"Y'all got limes, Pete?" Ruby screeched from the kitchen. "I'd kill for a gin and tonic."

Mary Lizzie checked her watch. It was 9:30 a.m.

During the Pete-and-Ruby semi-sober marriage years, Mary Lizzie had either witnessed or heard tell of many loud, drunken Ruby sprees and vowed not to interfere, although this had sometimes proved impossible.

She now shook her head to banish the hurtful scene with her father. This was a new day and a new life, she reminded herself. She'd always thought of herself as somewhat of an opportunist. So, when he died, she took flight from the situation and moved to Reprisal, South Carolina, because it was a historic sleepy town—and far away from Ruby.

"You was hard to track down," said Ruby. "Gone Girl was what I was callin' you to your friends. You know, like that movie? Why'd you move to this godforsaken place? Long drive from Charlotte for one thing and no decent mall far as I can tell."

"I wanted to live near water. It's fascinating, really. The moon, the sun, the earth's rotation and everything in flux. I swim at the beach or take the boat out at high tide. I love walking on the boardwalk every night," Mary Lizzie said, deep-sixing the knot in her throat, something she hadn't had to do in a long time. She mentally patted herself on the back for not screeching back at the Screecher and her whining about Reprisal's lack of retail amenities.

Ruby followed Mary Lizzie into the kitchen.

"I read up on Reprisal the other day when I knew I was comin'. For sure, a whole heap of water lives round here. Gives me the creeps because I cain't swim and you got ocean, three rivers and a bay at your doorstep. Makes it like a sauna, don't it, with mosquitoes and all?"

Ruby picked up Mary Lizzie's latest *Garden & Gun* magazine and fanned herself with it. "Lots a slimy snakes and gators out there, too. And sharks? I ain't put a toe in the water since *Jaws* came out in the '70s."

Speaking of jaws, Mary Lizzie prayed for Ruby's mandibles to stop clacking.

"Lookie here," Ruby said, patting the stainless-steel countertops and throwing open my prized reclaimed wooden cabinet doors with a flourish. "Is this what all them high-falutin' decorators call the rustic look? 'Minds me of Granny's cabin down near Gumdrop,

Georgia. Got lots of splinters whenever we visited her. But to each her own, I always say."

"To each her own," I repeated.

"I noticed in your den you've got your daddy's old stereo equipment and what looks like a typewriter that came over on the Mayflower."

"Um, yeah. I like vintage."

She wrinkled her nose.

"Like a drink, Ruby?" Mary Lizzie tried to swallow but her throat was dry. "I sure could use something."

"Always told Pete you were sharp as a tack. I'm parched. Gin and tonic would go down real fine about now. I drove straight here over all them potholes on 521. Didn't even stop at a 7-11. How about you fix us a drink whilst I visit the little girl's room?"

Mary Lizzie gathered tall glasses and bottles and assembled their drinks. Ice water for herself and the ubiquitous gin and tonic for Ruby. She dropped a lime slice in each glass. The silence was a relief, but Ruby wasn't gone near long enough.

"How long you here for, Ruby? Not to be nosy or anything."

"Hopin' to stay for a couple days if that's OK with you and that handsome hubby of yours. He at work right now? Anyway, just sold the house, and I've gotta see my sister down in Folkston. That's where me and your daddy got married, you know."

"You sold my house? I mean…the house in Charlotte?"

"Yeah. They say it's a tear-down. Good riddance to the fifties. That house was butt ugly no matter how I tried to fix it up. They'll probably build one of those big old stucco jobs with arched windows that are so popular right now."

Mary Lizzie's breath caught. Her mother had loved that "butt ugly tear-down." The mellow old brick ranch house, broad and sturdy under the oaks. Azaleas in the spring, gardenias in summer, chrysanthemums in fall and camellias in winter, just for starters.

Mary Lizzie coughed past her anguished nostalgia, knowing that Ruby always spoke her mind even if there wasn't much in it.

"Let's go sit on the front porch," Mary Lizzie said.

"I thought I heard a rocker callin' my name out there," Ruby said. She grabbed her drink and headed outside.

They settled in the white rocking chairs. A young couple pushing a double baby carriage past the house waved to them. Across the street, a little old lady holding a plastic bag urged her dog to take care of business. The air sweltered, but the breeze Mary Lizzie noticed earlier was still stirring.

She sipped her ice water. "Did you get a good price for it?"

"For what?" Ruby slurped a mouthful of gin and tonic. "Ah, real nice. I like 'em strong."

"For the house. Did you get a good price for it?"

"Not your business, is it, Sweetie? But never mind. Oh, I did find a couple boxes of old junk in the attic. Thought you might want 'em. Anyway, that's one reason I came. And I kinda wanted a chat about, well, you know the accident."

The accident Ruby survived in an inebriated crash through a damaged guardrail and into a murky lake, thought Mary Lizzie, the one that killed Daddy. Again, she marveled at someone who couldn't swim getting herself out of that sinking car and up to the surface.

"Fine." Mary Lizzie bit her tongue to keep it polite. A "chat" about Daddy's unnecessary death would tickle me pink, she thought.

They rocked silently for what seemed an eternity to Mary Lizzie. Ruby finished her drink and hopped up asking if she could make herself another.

"Knock yourself out," Mary Lizzie said. She held her sweating glass against her cheek and wondered if it was only the extreme heat making her uncomfortable. She had long ago decided to put tragedy behind her, to face the world with a smooth face even if a volcano seethed just below the skin.

Ruby plowed through the screen door with two G and Ts and reclaimed the rocking chair.

"It was an accident, Mary Lizzie. I swear to God."

"You were blind-ass drunk."

No answer.

"You said you were arguing and slapping each other but you claimed you couldn't remember what it was about."

Ruby took a long gulp of her drink. Mary Lizzie wondered how much tonic was in it.

"God dammit, Ruby, you were driving. Daddy told me how many times you'd scared him to death driving like a homicidal maniac." She muttered "Screecher" under her breath.

Ruby's rocking chair sped up; her feet banged on the wooden porch on the downswing.

If only that rocker was an ejector seat, mused Mary Lizzie; I could launch her into outer space. Or at least back onto the highway.

Ruby said, "You always did hate me."

Nothing could be accomplished by agreeing with her, so Mary Lizzie ignored the remark.

"I didn't believe you when you said he had a heart attack right before the crash and that's why you swerved all over the road," she said to her former stepmother. "You only said that after you learned he'd had a heart attack. But you know good and well, he had that heart attack after you hit the guardrail. You were playing the sympathy card, going for a shorter sentence and rehab." Mary Lizzie felt her heart ease a tiny fraction after that rant.

"So what?" Ruby said. "It worked. You'd have done the same, am I right? He was dead. At that point, what did it matter exactly how, when or where?"

Mary Lizzie felt ice snaking its way through her veins. "So, now we know you lied."

"Shit happens."

Mary Lizzie gnashed her teeth, but Ruby didn't notice, what with a couple of gray-haired, bandana wearing, senior citizens on Harleys roaring down the street.

"Didn't aim to come here to get you all riled up." Ruby shook her head. "Maybe I should find a no-tell motel after all." She stopped rocking. "Let me get those boxes out of the car."

"Look, we're both adults here," said Mary Lizzie raising her voice a notch as Ruby wobbled to the Jeep, now slurping the third drink. "Nothing will bring my father back, so this whole chat, as you call it, is pointless."

"He wasn't perfect, you know," Ruby hollered from inside the vehicle. "Far from it. You still keepin' him on a pedestal, seems to me."

The woman just couldn't let it go.

Mary Lizzie remembered standing on his big feet as a little girl. They both wore socks and shagged to beach music in the living room of the Charlotte house, as if there was sand on the wooden floor. Was he on a pedestal? she wondered. Maybe it was just that she craved those snug, golden times.

"If you marry someone thirty years older," Mary Lizzie pontificated to Ruby as she trundled back up the porch steps, "you've got to expect some friction in the relationship. Of course, no one is perfect. Not even my father."

"He pissed me off that day."

"Did he find out about a boyfriend? Surely you had one."

Ruby's eyebrows shot up as she slammed the car door shut with her hip, but she dodged the question. "Whoa. Again, not your business."

"Whatever," said Mary Lizzie. She stayed put in the rocker. Etiquette told her it was rude not to help, but she was tired of the whole hot mess that was Ruby. She swallowed, pushing another rising knot back down her throat.

"Put them in the foyer and I'll go through them later," said Mary Lizzie. Just in case the boxes contained nostalgia, she didn't want to get emotional in front of the Screecher.

Ruby and Mary Lizzie decided to stroll down Main Street, which was only a hop, skip and jump from the house, and access the boardwalk to get a bite of supper. Beau's fried shrimp with black beans and rice sounded good to her. Early in the evening, the sidewalks were crowded with tourists and local folks peeping in shop windows, but this being a weekday, the area would be deserted by ten o'clock.

"What about Hank?" said Ruby. "You not waitin' for him to get home?"

Mary Lizzie pointed to the paper mill in the far distance. She never got over the irony that it looked like a castle in a medieval forest at night, when the steam wreathed it in white and the lights twinkled in the sunset. "Hank used to work there. But he's gone now."

"What do you mean, gone? Are y'all divorced?"

"The dearly beloved has definitely departed. No one knows where. Water under the bridge, really," said Mary Lizzie. As her bright smile looked like it was about to crack, Ruby changed the subject back to herself.

"I am looking forward to the shrimp basket here," she said as the two women walked into the crowded restaurant.

An hour or so later Ruby stumbled out with Mary Lizzie holding her up. Darkness engulfed Reprisal except for the boardwalk lights and the streetlamps on Main Street.

"Feel like walking to the end and seeing my boat?" Mary Lizzie asked. "Or have you had too much to drink?"

"I told you, I'm doin' fine in that department. Just on vacation, you know. I can jump on the wagon later. Doesn't hurt to tipple on special occasions is my motto."

The wind working through the halyards of a sailboat sounded like bamboo chimes as Mary Lizzie and Ruby made their way down the dock. It was darker on that end, but the Aurora was clearly visible, bobbing in the gentle swell.

Just before reaching the Aurora, Ruby stopped to read the alligator warning sign nailed onto the wooden railings. A plump alligator was pictured at the top.

Alligators May Live Here
Be Gator Safe:
Warning: It Is Unlawful to Feed Alligators
Feeding, Harassing or the Unlawful Killing or
Taking of Alligators May Result in Substantial Fines
And/Or Jail Time.

Ruby thought the sign was "cute" and took a picture while Mary Lizzie watched.

"There used to be the sweetest baby alligator under the boardwalk when we first got here," Mary Lizzie explained to Ruby. "Everybody fed it because it almost looked like a toy."

Ruby shuddered.

"Is it still down there?" She peered over the railing at the murky water.

"I think the police finally enforced the feeding thing before the alligator got too big. It would have been destroyed eventually for safety reasons, so I'm hoping it swam off and is living like an alligator should," I replied.

Mary Lizzie climbed aboard the 18-foot Pioneer and helped Ruby jump across from the dock.

"I think I have something we can drink here," said Mary Lizzie, opening a cupboard in the center console. Behind the life jackets, a big bottle of blueberry vodka and plastic cups were stored in a box along with paper towels and cleaning products.

"Not supposed to have alcohol on the boat or at least when you're using it. But..." Mary Lizzie poured two small cups full to the brim and handed one to Ruby.

"So, what do you think of her?" Mary Lizzie said with a sweeping motion of her hand. "Ship shape and ready to go. Except for life jackets. They're old and torn up. I've got some on order."

Ruby ran a finger along the console. "Not a speck of dirt. You always were a neat freak," she said before downing her vodka in one shot. Mary Lizzie poured her another.

"I do like to tidy up. Don't like to leave a mess," she replied. "So, yeah, I'm still curious. What were you and Daddy arguing about the day of the…the day he died?"

"It's complicated, you know?"

"Seems to be a good time to simplify it."

Mary Lizzie raised the vodka bottle, and Ruby held the plastic cup up for a refill.

"Maybe I should stop drinking now." She took a sip. "Nah, maybe not. Like I said, it's all under control."

Mary Lizzie stowed the vodka back in the console anyway. They both gazed over at the paper plant, a bright, steamy vision in the dark sky.

"That plant ever smell?" asked Ruby. "There was one in Georgia used to stink like rotten eggs sometimes. Then there was that god-awful waste treatment plant in Charlotte."

Mary Lizzie said, "It doesn't smell that often. Depends on the wind. Doesn't bother me. Though it feels like you're changing the subject. About your argument with Daddy?" said Mary Lizzie.

"Lord help us, girl, OK OK. I been thinkin' that since you and Hank aren't together anymore…"

"Yes?"

"It's a good thing. Y'all bein' apart now. He was a cheater, Mary Lizzie." She stood and looked down the boardwalk toward the restaurant and lights. She shivered. "It's dark as hell this end."

"What has that got to do with Daddy's death?"

"He accused me of doing the dirty deed with Hank. Said he was going to tell you. Said he was gonna kick me out."

Mary Lizzie stayed remarkably calm except she felt a blood vessel jumping wildly in her right temple.

"So, you decided to kill my daddy?" Mary Lizzie said not moving a muscle. "You drove for the guardrail full speed ahead?"

"Christ, I was hammered, and Pete's remark went all over me. I wanted to kill him. He shoulda been fighting with Hank the Scumbag, not me. I grabbed the wheel and all."

"You and Hank then? Only once, right?"

Ruby cackled, so drunk she started to choke. "Ain't you just a innocent lamb? That man...well, let's just say he was horny as hell most of the time. Didn't y'all ever do it?"

Mary Lizzie crushed her cup of vodka in her hand and vaulted onto the dock in two big leaps.

"Wait up!" shouted Ruby as she staggered in the boat and started to climb over the side.

Mary Lizzie turned in time to see Ruby frantically grabbing at air as she stood in the stern and tried to leap on the dock from there. But as inebriated as she was, she fell sideways and cracked her head on the sailboat beside the Aurora and then fell in between them. There was no sound except the water sloshing faintly and the boats bobbing and sliding into each other.

Frozen in shock for several seconds, Mary Lizzie finally ran back to the slip and peered down at the water. Nothing.

"Ruby? Ruby, where are you?" She re-boarded her boat and walked all around it to see if she could spot Ruby. She listened for a long time for any burbling screech from the water. Then she cleaned up the boat and wiped the surfaces down with damp paper towels and glass cleaner. After a while, she eased her cell phone from her pocket and called 9-1-1.

*

A week later, Mary Lizzie was rocking on her front porch sipping lemonade. One of her neighbors walked her Yorkshire terrier down the sidewalk in front of the house. She paused to let the dog tinkle on a corner of the lawn. When she saw Mary Lizzie on the porch, she waved enthusiastically.

Mary Lizzie was now something of a celebrity in the quiet neighborhood. After all, who else had relatives come to visit who then up and drowned in the river? It had been in all the papers, and everyone had been around to sympathize and drop off casseroles, even though Mary Lizzie had protested it wasn't necessary.

They shook their heads about the girl's bad luck. Back when her husband took off, they were surprised, because the two of them had seemed so cozy, going out on the boat a lot. Hank had been an avid fisherman. When he left town without a word to anyone, they scratched their heads for a while and then got on with it. His truck finally turned up in a field near the Charlotte airport some weeks later. So, it looked like he'd taken off for parts unknown and it seemed right in character. No one knew anything about his family. From out West, was it? He'd often yarned about prospecting in old silver mines in Colorado and making a fortune. "That was Hank," they said. A nice boy, full of piss and vinegar, but a bit of a ne'er do well just the same. Mary Lizzie had overcome it, though; rose above, they opined. She was a go-ahead type of girl. And didn't she keep her garden and home as neat and tidy as a doll's house?

Mary Lizzie's second piece of bad luck seemed a downright shame to them. But still, the night of the accident had been an exciting town event. The fire truck, police cars and ambulances all came screaming into the area after they'd been alerted by Mary Lizzie. People deserted their beds to see what all the hullabaloo was about. Police had a time keeping them behind the crime scene tape, even if it didn't appear to be a crime, not in the usual sense.

Divers didn't find Ruby that night, though, just her red flip-flops. Folks speculated that eventually she would wash up somewhere with the tide unless she was tangled underwater in the marsh grass or had been carried out to sea. Behind their hands, they whispered about alligators, but no one wanted to go there. Besides, they said, wasn't it a good sign that the flip-flops weren't chewed up?

Mary Lizzie explained what had happened to her former stepmother, that she'd been very drunk and she'd had a time walking along the boardwalk with her. When they'd gotten to the boat, Ruby had insisted on trying to board, against Mary Lizzie's pleas to just go home. With the result of the fatal accident. The authorities had been sympathetic.

But tonight was a lovely night, no night to dwell on such terrible events. Mary Lizzie rocked on the porch for a bit longer to watch the sunset in horizontal shades of pink, yellow and orange against a purple sky. When she got up, she decided it was finally time to examine the boxes that Ruby had brought all the way from Charlotte.

One box contained memorabilia from her high school and college years that she'd forgotten were in the attic. Before she lifted the flaps of the second box, though, she felt a rush of adrenaline because she knew what was in it. Daddy's albums.

She gently lifted "Under the Boardwalk" out of the box. The candy colors of the cover were faded and the cardboard tatty. She drifted like a sleepwalker over to the stereo and put the album carefully on the turntable, turning up the volume and waiting for the scratchiness from being played so many times.

She removed her tennis shoes and slid around on the wooden floor in her socks as the music began. She put one arm where her daddy's shoulder would be and one around his waist, careful not to mash his feet too much. With closed eyes, she flitted about the room in a trance.

Oh, when the sun beats down and burns the tar up on the roof
And your shoes get so hot, you wish your tired feet were fireproof
Under the boardwalk, down by the sea, yeah
On a blanket with my baby is where I'll be....

Lovely, Just Bloody Lovely
by Karen Keeley
(based on "Fool on the Hill," The Beatles, 1967)

So we gets this phone call at the precinct telling us they got a dead body at Wreck Beach, that spit of land out near the university. The beach has always been a popular place for the kids to party on the weekends. Sometimes those lookin' to groove to the music brought a transistor radio, the dial tuned to one of two radio stations what played '60s music. My oldest, she's a fan of Red Robinson, a popular DJ with CFUN, her always listening to the Beatles or the Stones or the Dave Clark Five. This week, her new favourite was the Fab Four's "Fool on the Hill," the damn fool song played on the radio all hours of the day and the night, even the one what we got at the precinct.

Me and my partner, Hank Williams, and yes, that's his name, we made the drive to Wreck Beach. Hank did the driving. The beach was accessible if you knew where to look, an overgrown path of weeds and long grasses what goes from the road along the top of the cliff down to the water. If you didn't watch your step you were likely to go ass over tea kettle, take a hard tumble all the way to the bottom only to land face first in the sand.

Hank pulled in behind a couple of squad cars parked at the top of the cliff, them vehicles having arrived first, strobe lights winking in the black night. It looked like a scene out of *Dragnet,* half a dozen boys in blue standing around with flashlights in hand. Two more beat cops leaned against a tree. Tailor-made filters hung from their lips.

The medical examiner's van was parked beyond the squad cars, what meant Doc Peterson was there and probably making nice with the dead guy. Hank tossed me a flashlight from the trunk of our four-door sedan. We nodded at the boys in blue and then walked the steep path down to the beach, slipping and sliding most of the way on the wet grass.

It was a cold night, a wicked north wind cutting to the bone. I found myself wondering if my fake Alligator shoes were gonna hold up, nothing but drizzle the past couple of weeks. My trench coat too, offered little warmth on such a harsh night.

When we arrived at the bottom of the path, it was all wet sand and driftwood, rocks and pebbles, broken seashells and barnacles. We also saw a ton of garbage. I gets to wondering where it comes from—the garbage. People must use the beach to dump their garbage or maybe it was washed ashore by the incoming tide. I then gets to thinking it was probably a bit of both.

Down here, standing on the wet sand at the base of the cliff, we were out of the wind, what made it almost pleasant despite it being the month of October. My partner Hank headed over to Doc Peterson, the medical examiner. Peterson was bent down taking a good look at the dead guy, no more 'n eighteen, maybe nineteen if you were lookin' to be generous. The kid was dressed in ratty old bell-bottom jeans, the jeans spattered with mud. His wrinkled long-sleeved knitted shirt was shoved halfway up his belly, no coat or jacket. His mangled dark hair was coated with wet sand, blood matted at the side of his skull.

"Could be he tumbled down the path," I said. "We chalk it up to a terrible accident."

Doc Peterson poo-pooed that idea. "It's more likely someone hit him with a chunk of driftwood. I got wood splinters in the head wound. I'll know more when I get him on the table and do a proper postmortem."

A big burly fellow, one of the boys in blue what arrived before us must've slid down the cliff to the beach 'cause he approached me, holding out a chunk of driftwood, his timing impeccable. "Found this over there," he said, pointing. "Near the waterline."

I shone my flashlight and we could see what looked like bone matter, skin, blood and hair. Lots of sand too, matted in with bits of seaweed and kelp.

"Bag it for evidence," I said, knowing the copper already knew the drill but I liked to be thorough and state the obvious. Another copper having made the descent stood near the remains of a campfire, maybe fifty, sixty feet away. A girl with long brown hair was vomiting. A second girl held her around the middle, offering support. Two skanky lookin' dudes sat near them, possibly their boyfriends, squatted down on the sand, them too, with a dazed look in their eyes.

Hank asked the doc, "How long dead?"

"An hour, maybe a bit more," said Peterson. "No rigor as of yet." Peterson wore his signature charcoal gabardine suit, shiny at the knees, and wire-framed granny glasses what made his eyes look bigger. It was like conversing with a wise old owl.

I followed the copper what found the driftwood to the water's edge. No footprints but his. If the driftwood was the murder weapon, it had likely been tossed toward the water, the would-be assailant thinking the outgoing tide would carry it off.

I hollered back at the doc, "Who found him?"

The doc pointed to the group squatted by the campfire. "That tall one on the end, the guy with the love beads. When I got here, he told me he'd climbed the cliff and called it in. There's a pay-phone just up the street where the road curves, leading toward the university dorms."

Nice to know the doc had a lay of the land clearly mapped out in his head.

I asked Hank, "So—whaddya think? One of them four?"

Hank nodded. "It's the dead of the night when most God-fearing Christians are home asleep in their beds. Yeah—I figure it's one of them."

"Me, too," I said, and with that, the night's inquiries began.

Doc Peterson and two of his men loaded the dead guy on a gurney. I didn't envy them that job, trying to maneuver the gurney weighted down with a dead body over rough terrain in the dark, shoving the gurney up the steep incline toward the top of the cliff.

Eventually they made it without any mishap, job accomplished.

I told the two beat cops to stick around, their job would be to see that the kids were taken home after me and Hank spoke with them. They both nodded, lit up cigarettes of their own. I picked up a piece of driftwood and stirred the embers in the campfire, flung the wood on top and flames licked around the wood, giving us additional light to see by. A transistor radio was propped on a blanket, the radio playing that Beatles tune—"Fool on the Hill." For some reason, the song bothered me, the lyrics referencing some dumb fuck living alone and without friends.

I requested the radio be silenced. The girl what hadn't upchucked her cookies did me the favour. She had the look of Lady Godiva about her, long flowing tresses the colour of melted butter. Like her friend, she too, wore a peasant blouse and an ankle-length tie-dyed wraparound skirt.

"Who's the dead guy?" asked Hank, his question about as subtle as a gorilla at an Irish wake.

"Leo Gordon," said the long-legged dude with the beads. He was wearing blue jeans, a wrinkled crew-neck t-shirt and Jesus sandals. He looked older than the others. I was thinking he was maybe a university student. He held a stick and was poking it in the sand.

"And you are?" asked Hank.

"Bobby O'Brien. I'm a student at UBC, health sciences. I live on campus."

Hank and me, we both nodded. Neither him nor me had any idea what health sciences meant but I logged that detail in my notebook anyway.

"The five of you, you partied here this evening," said Hank. He was obviously including the dead guy Leo in the numbers count.

All four nodded again. The long-legged dude continued to poke the sand with his stick. He then stood up, tossed the stick into the fire. He had to be six two, maybe six three, taller than Hank and me by a good three inches. He looked me square in the eye. I figured he was taking me for a fool, couldn't see the forest for the trees while the other three started to tell us they were all together when Leo went missing. They had no idea what had happened. It had to have been a terrible accident.

Bobby then interrupted, taking the lead on the narrative. "We were sitting around the campfire listening to Becky's transistor radio, groovin' to the music," he said. "Leo wandered off. He said he was gonna go look for more driftwood for the fire. It was me what heard the holler, a kind of muffled shout. I went to look for him, thinking he'd fallen. That's when I found him."

"You didn't hear or see anyone else on the beach?" I asked.

All four shook their heads. "It was just us," said Bobby, keeping control of the narrative. "We should'a stayed in my dorm but Leo wanted to come to the beach. He said he liked to watch the waves when the wind was up, especially when smoking a doobie. He said the weed made it all the better. Got him into a psychedelic mood, the waves crashing against the boulders."

"And what kind of a mood would that be?" asked Hank.

"Weird shit—colours and motion," said Bobby. "Like watching a lava lamp only it's the waves and the stars and the moon. Leo said it would give him ideas for his artwork—he's a visual artist, a painter."

"So you say," said Hank. "And what's a lava lamp?"

"I'll tell you later," I said, privy to the workings of a lava lamp because my oldest had one in her psychedelic bedroom.

"You others," said Hank. "You were all gettin' high. I see a couple of empty bottles. You been drinking on top of the weed?"

No one spoke. The two girls had huddled together, hands clasped, united in grief. The other guy sitting across from them appeared to be having trouble pulling his eyes from the flames of the fire. "We can get blood samples," said Hank. "THC will show up, what's called tetrahydrocannabinol by its chemical name."

Hank was good with stuff like that. He always remembered what Doc Peterson shared with us when discussing a case. Hank was no fool even if he didn't know what a lava lamp was. I also knew we couldn't really take blood samples. We didn't have the equipment or proper authorization. "We're not gonna bust you for smokin' pot," I said. "Or for the underage drinking. We got a murder to solve."

The dark-haired girl, the one what up-chucked her cookies started to cry. "Murder? You sayin' someone deliberately killed Leo? It wasn't an accident?"

"I doubt he clobbered his own head," said Hank. "He had help."

"Oh God," she wailed. "It's all my fault! I never should've come. Leo only wandered away because of me!"

"And you are?" asked Hank.

"Christine Evans," said Bobby. "She's with me."

Christine nodded. "Me and Leo, we were an item," she said. "I broke it off to take up with Bobby."

Bobby put his arm around the girl, a protective gesture, held her close. "It was no biggie," he said. "Leo supported Christine's decision. He said he just wanted her to be happy. Besides—he was the one lookin' to get high. He told us he'd scored the other day when he was downtown. Bought a nickel bag off of some guy outside the Greyhound bus station."

"Any name?" asked Hank.

All four shook their heads.

"We shared a couple of doobies," said Bobby. "We had Becky's transistor," he was looking at the other girl, the one with the blond tresses who'd managed to keep her cookies down. "We were groovin' to the music, playing it cool, letting it all hang loose."

My notebook was filling up. So far we had Leo Gordon, deceased. Bobby O'Brien, the tall lanky dude with the love beads, current boyfriend to Christine Evans. "You other two, what's your full names?" I asked.

Bobby stuck with the script, the self-appointed spokesperson. "That's Becky Hawthorn, she owns the transistor radio, the one we were listening to."

"Any relation to Andy Hawthorn?" I had a sick sour feeling in the pit of my stomach.

The girl nodded. "He's my father." She was staring at the dying flames, at the driftwood I'd added as kindling. Lovely, just bloody lovely! Andy Hawthorn was the city's Chief of Police. "And you are?" I asked the second dude.

He'd finally managed to pull his eyes from the fire. He stood up, pushed a straggly strand of hair back behind an ear. I figured the last time he'd had a decent haircut was when John Diefenbaker was still Prime Minister. "Becky's brother, Robert—Robert Hawthorn," he said.

"You ever go by Bobby?" I asked.

Robert shook his head. "That's Bobby." He pointed to the tall lanky dude. "We only got one Bobby. I've always been a Robert."

Of course you have, related to the top cop in the city. Like I said, lovely, just bloody lovely!

After getting addresses and phone numbers to go with the names, we told the four of them to accompany the two beat cops—they'd take them back up the path and ensure they were returned home to their families, or in Bobby's case, to his dorm. Me and Hank, we'd be contacting them in a few hours, to not leave town, to not discuss the case in detail with anyone outside the scope of the investigation. Hank and me, we then returned to the precinct to write up our preliminary report. When that was done, we called it quits and left the report on the boss' desk.

The next day, midmorning, after me and Hank got a few hours of shut-eye, we were back at the precinct and we gets hauled into the boss' office, him yelling at the two of us, he'd just gotten off the phone with the Chief of Police. Orders were, we were not to follow up with the Chief's two kids—they were not to be part of any murder investigation. In addition, any reference to smoking pot or underage drinking was to be expunged from the record. Like I said, lovely, just bloody lovely!

Me and Hank, we stood there, our sweat-stained fedoras in our hands feeling like a couple of delinquent punks raked over the coals by the school principal. Our boss then hollered for us to follow up with any and all other leads, what left us with that tall lanky dude, that Bobby fellow and Christine whatchamacallit, in addition to trying to track down the guy at the Greyhound bus station what sold the bag of weed to Leo Gordon.

The boss figured it was possible the seller had been on the beach making an additional sale what led to the altercation ending Leo's life. Hank and me, we knew the boss was well-known for his theories, often tempted to jerry-rig the facts to fit the case, not the way me and Hank played it but we kept quiet, allowed the boss to blow off steam.

When we left the boss' office, we gets the notion to drive out to Kerrisdale and see Leo Gordon's parents. We needed a picture of Leo to use with our inquiries. The coppers what broke the news to the parents in the wee hours had neglected that duty. Both the mister and the missus were still pretty cut up when we arrived, understandable, losing their only son. We introduced ourselves, explained our involvement. A radio was playing somewhere in the kitchen, and again, that Beatle's tune—"Fool on the Hill." Why was it every time I heard a goddamn radio playing it was that song!

My nose caught a whiff of fried bacon strips and greasy eggs along with burnt toast, plates sitting on the kitchen table, the food untouched. Ellie Gordon, Leo's mother, took us into the living room and rifled through a photo album after we made our request. She found Leo's high school grad picture and pulled it from the album, gave it to Hank. It was a good likeness. Leo's hair was shorter and he wore a white shirt, a sweater vest and a skinny tie making him look a lot more preppie than what we'd seen when he'd been lying face down in the wet sand at Wreck Beach. We thanked the missus for the photo, again conveyed our condolences, telling her the city police were doing all they could to find the culprit what ended her son's life.

Al Gordon, Leo's father, walked us to the front door. Ellie, the wife, stayed seated on the living room couch. She was wiping more tears from her red swollen eyes while clutching that old photo album tight to her chest. I figured she'd be doing a lot more of that over the next few days. Me and Hank, we knew Leo was their oldest, three others still at home, all girls, squirreled away somewhere in the house, probably hiding out in their upstairs bedrooms, them too, showing little interest in food.

"Leo got mixed up with some kind of a cult," said Al Gordon as he pulled open the front door. "Somewhere out near Cultus Lake. Me and Ellie, the wife—the girls too, none of us have had any contact with Leo these past months, not since he graduated. I wanted him to come into the business with me. I run a hardware store downtown, but he'd have no part of it. He said he had to find himself, whatever that meant. It near broke his mother's heart. And no…we didn't know any of the people he knew. We did hear it was some kind of a hippie commune. One of those places young folks hang out doing nothing more than smoking that wacki tobacci or dropping acid or groovin' on magic mushrooms."

Coming from Al Gordon, the lingo sounded like a foreign language.

"I got the lingo from my girls," he said, with a forced smile. The smile then cracked—his grief apparent. "Jesus—what's this world coming to?"

Me and Hank, we had no answer.

We each gave Al Gordon a firm handshake and Gordon calmly closed the door.

Me and Hank then gets to standing on the front porch for a moment, each of us breathing in the October air, colourful autumn leaves starting to litter the lawns and the sidewalks. I was thinking it was a nice change to all the rain we'd had. We glanced up and down the street, a street like any other in our fair city.

"You think it's the music?" Hank asked. "That's what's messing with kids' minds, along with the drugs and the booze. It's all some existential search for something meaningful in their lives?"

"I don't know about existential," I said. "But you—I know you. Don't go getting all sentimental on me." Hank shrugged. I followed suit. What the hell did we know?

Every generation had their own thing. When me and Hank were teenagers, we hung out at our favourite malt shop with our best girl, sipping an ice-cream soda or a chocolate milkshake while listening to the jukebox what played rhythm and blues, swing and jazz, tunes by Nat King Cole, Ella Fitzgerald and Louis Armstrong. Now we had the British Invasion happening in the States—the Fab Four the next best thing to Jesus Christ, to hear them tell it, although I was pretty sure the media got that one wrong, some comment taken out of context.

My oldest was a big fan. She had most of the Beatles 45s and vinyl LPs, purchased with her babysitting money. She also bought the latest teen magazines, emulating somebody called Twiggy, black eyeliner, white lipstick and fishnet stockings. Lovely, just bloody lovely! She was my child and I no longer knew who she was. Sometimes she hiked up her skirt, made it shorter, said all the girls were doing it, called it a miniskirt. She too, wore her hair long and straight, hiding her pretty face. Nancy, my wife, she said our oldest wanted to look like Paul McCartney's girlfriend Jane Asher—me wondering, who in the name of Christ was Jane Asher when she was at home? And then I understood. I knew nothing about kids these days. I hardly ever saw my three, the job always came first. Nancy, my wife of sixteen years knew that—knew it when we married, knew it when the kids came along, knew it as the kids grew older. She had the job of raising them. We'd made that deal, sealed it with a kiss and a wedding ring. I would earn the weekly pay-cheque and keep the city safe. Things like raising kids were best left to the women. Even Hank agreed with that despite his never having married.

I plunked my well-worn fedora on my head, turned up the collar on my trench coat, and sallied forth. Hank followed, his heavy tread on the wooden steps bringing up the rear.

Back at the precinct, we gets the sketch artist to play with Leo's high school grad picture, make his hair longer and give him the makings of a mustache and a Jesus beard, what the kid looked like when we found him dead at Wreck Beach. The sketch artist did a bang-up job and we gets copies made and handed them over to the beat cops with our request they take a run out to the Greyhound bus station and ask around, had anyone seen Leo, seen whoever he'd been talking to?

That taken care of, me and Hank then decided to make a run out to Cultus Lake. It would take us a good hour to make the drive, out toward Chilliwack in the valley, lots of farm country and dairy cattle. Me and Hank, we hadn't been on the highway in donkey's years and we knew it would feel great to get out of the city.

The drive did just that, lifted our spirits, and we finally found the commune after a couple of wrong turns, a group of twenty or so living in army surplus canvas tents and A-frame shelters. They'd set up on Crown land at the back end of Cultus Lake, away from the country cottages and dwellings owned by city folk. A cooking fire was set up near one of the tents. A big cast iron pot hung over the flames, the pot filled with something bubbling inside. A woman with long hair plaited into two thick braids leaned over to stir the pot's contents. She stirred the pot's contents with a wooden ladle. She had a baby strapped to her side, the kid swaddled papoose style in some kind of soft mesh fabric, what made the kid look like a grub in a cocoon. We asked after who was in charge. The woman pointed toward a wooden dock fifty, sixty feet away. She told us to ask after Jake.

We found Jake sitting cross-legged at the end of the dock, a tall lanky fellow who reminded me of Bobby O'Brien, except Jake was older, pushing thirty, blond, with a mustache and a beard. He had a fishing line in the water. The way his red bobber was floating, I figured he'd have little to no luck catching a decent sized fish. He must've seen the skepticism on my ugly mug. "They hide under the dock," he said, unwinding his long legs while offering a sincere smile. "Gives them protection from the sunlight."

"You've done this before," said Hank, showing him his credentials, telling him who we were.

"I'm a fisher of men and of fish," said Jake, now standing, him too, looming over Hank and me by a couple of inches. "We're on public land. We abide by the rules of nature. We live in harmony. We don't destroy."

"You think the fish see it that way?" asked Hank.

"Nature provides. We are but the vessels," said Jake.

"One of your vessels has gone and got himself killed," said Hank.

Jake pulled the fishing line from the water, wrapped it around his wrist and set the tangled mess on the dock. There was a hook on the end of the line along with a sad looking worm attached to the hook. I wondered what the worm thought about nature providing.

"Killed," said Jake. "Who was killed? When, how?"

Hank gave Jake the details. I stood back and watched. Again, somewhere far in the distance a transistor radio was playing that damn fool song "Fool on the Hill." I gritted my teeth. The fillings in my back molars vibrated. Why did that song throw me for a loop?

"Leo Gordon—how terrible," exclaimed Jake. The idea of communing with nature and being a fisher of men and of fish seemed to have withered from Jake's vocabulary. He was now speaking plain English.

"How did you come to know Leo?" asked Hank.

"One day, he simply arrived out of the blue," Jake told us. "He was walking down that laneway there, carting a duffle bag and a sleeping bag. He stayed throughout the summer months. When he arrived, he said he was looking for a friend, a guy named Bobby. We told him Bobby had been with us for a time but unfortunately, we'd had to ask him to leave. Bobby's negative karma upset the flow of the commune. But Leo stayed. His karma meshed with ours, make love, not war. I thought he'd stay longer but come September when the weather changed, he too, took off. He said communing with nature was lovely as long as the weather cooperated. I took him for the real deal, but in the end, he was what we called a fair-weather friend."

Hank nodded. I followed suit. The twenty or so who belonged to this Cultus Lake commune didn't seem to be doing anything worthwhile except figuring out how to befriend the weather. They were sitting on their backsides, cross-legged, all of them staring at the clouds, humming a kind of mantra to themselves, rocking back 'n forth—all except the lady with the baby, her stirring whatever was bubbling in that cast iron pot hanging over the fire. If this was the way of the future, I figured the future was fucked.

"When did you last see Leo?" asked Hank.

"Like I said, September," said Jake. "One day, he just upped and left. He took his duffle bag and his sleeping bag and high-tailed it out of here, helped himself to my stash."

"And what stash would that be?" asked Hank.

"As if I have to spell it out, detective." Jake's grin resembled the cat what ate the canary, his blue eyes twinkling. For a guy living in the rough he had beautiful straight teeth. "We all have a stash. If you want to bust us for possession, fill your boots. But we're not hurting anyone. We keep to ourselves, finding bliss with each other, with nature, the wind and the rain, the heavens and the stars."

"You get angry about Leo stealing your stash?" asked Hank.

Jake shook his head. "Anger solves nothing. Peace and harmony, that's our mantra—all of God's creatures are linked to peace and harmony. It's just a matter of dialing into the right frequency."

So we were back to that again, the language of the cult. Talk about a fool on a hill. This guy took the life of the commune to a whole new level. Or maybe it was the brownies talking. Hank and me knew all about brownies, a dash of weed added as the secret ingredient. We'd made a few busts on brownieville over the years, mostly in Stanley Park or down at the docks, them what come in off the ocean-going vessels.

We thanked Jake for his time and departed. I wondered if government officials were gonna make a bust on this commune in the near future. As a group, they were squatting on Crown land, what meant they were living at Cultus Lake rent-free while legitimate land owners paid their property taxes, all of them not wanting property values to plummet after winning their hard-fought battle for democracy, thanks to WWII, where capitalism was the name of the game.

When Hank and me gets back to the precinct, we find that our brethren in arms had located a fellow by the name of Miles Henderson who'd seen Leo Gordon at the Greyhound bus station. They'd delivered Henderson for questioning, had him holed up in an interview room. Hank and me, we tossed our coats and our hats on our desks. I hollered at whoever was listening to turn off the damn radio!

"I'm listening to the news," a voice hollered in return. "I'm waiting for the cash call. We might get lucky, them calling us. It's up to eighty bucks!"

Hank grabbed my arm. "What's eating you?" he asked.

I shook off his arm. "Nothing," I said. "It's just a song I keep hearing. The lyrics keep rattling around in my head."

"You certain you didn't inhale a whiff of that Kickapoo Joy Juice?" said Hank. "What that lady was cooking up in the pot?"

"I didn't get a whiff of anything," I told him.

The whiff we did get was Miles Henderson giving us Bobby O'Brien. Miles said he'd seen Leo talking with a tall dude at the Greyhound bus station, the two of them arguing outside under the awning. The tall guy was wearing love beads and Jesus sandals. Hank and me figured we'd make a personal call on good old Bobby O'Brien, him a university student in health sciences. If we got lucky, we'd find out what health sciences entailed and get a confession. But first, the answer to the question, why was Bobby arguing with Leo a few days before Leo's untimely death?

Tracking down Bobby O'Brien took some doing considering the university covered a ton of acreage home to more buildings than Carter had pills, all geared toward giving those who could afford it, an education. We finally got lucky, ran into Christine Evans—she was headed to Bobby's dorm, telling us his classes had ended at four o'clock and she was on her way to hang out with him. So far, so good—we'd managed to keep the Hawthorn kids out of the equation, meaning our boss wouldn't be yelling at us anytime soon, and the Chief of Police wouldn't be asking for the return of our detective shields.

Bobby must've taken us for a couple of fools because he started to run when he saw us. Anyone with half a brain knew that action usually meant guilt. Hank always could run faster than me. He took off like a whippet at a Colorado dog race, grabbed Bobby by the back of his denim jacket and threw him to the ground.

"Why the footrace?" I asked, fighting for oxygen once I caught up to the fracas. Christine Evans was right on my heels, yelling at Bobby, what had he done?

"Yeah—Bobby. What did you do?" asked Hank, sucking in air, making a sound like a beached whale trying to breathe out of its blowhole. I handed Hank his fedora. He'd lost it during the footrace.

"He brought it on himself," said Bobby, him too, out of breath and struggling to breathe. "Wouldn't leave it alone. Kept telling me he was gonna make a play for Christine, get her to see reason and go back to him."

So that's what it boiled down to—a fool and his love interest. And guilt—gotta love it when guilt comes into the equation. Bobby then spilled the beans, him and Leo getting into an argument after smoking one doobie too many; Christine, Becky and Robert all passed out, too much weed and too much booze; Leo laughing at Bobby, telling him he was a dork. When Christine finally came to her senses, she'd see Bobby for what he really was, a health sciences nerd selling out to the establishment.

We escorted Bobby O'Brien to our four-door sedan, him in handcuffs while Christine Evans pranced along behind, her sobbing and wringing her hands. She was gonna go and find her best friend Becky—tell her what had taken place. She kept screaming it was police harassment, police brutality! I knew what our boss and the Chief of Police would think of that, but right now, they weren't our concern.

Christine's wailing got me thinking of the night Ed Sullivan introduced the Beatles for the first time to a TV audience of more than 70 million and my girls lost it, sitting cross-legged on the living room carpet, squirreled in front of our black 'n white, them screaming and shaking their hands like they were possessed by demons and only a Catholic priest performing an exorcism could've helped. At the time, I'd lifted the newspaper, hiding behind the newsprint not knowing whether to laugh or to cry.

Maybe today's youth knew something I didn't know—the reason for the wild hysteria, the illicit drugs, the idea of free love and freedom songs, them wanting to make a stand against what they saw as social and civil injustice. Maybe the conflict in Vietnam wasn't designed to stop the threat of communism expanding throughout southeast Asia; maybe it was unscrupulous politicians thumbing their noses at democracy, their goal to line their pockets with cold hard cash, a by-product of a Yankee war machine, what meant, if it were true, Christ help those in need, we really were fucked. All I knew, I had a family at home, my oldest wanting to look like Jane Asher, and yes, I'd finally seen a picture of my daughter's idol, not bad lookin', and my wife doing her best to raise the girls while Hank and me, we did our best to keep our city safe.

Hank turned on the car radio during the drive back to the precinct. This time we listened to a Hank Williams tune, "I saw the Light." That got us both laughing. Bobby O'Brien moaned from the back seat, his head hung low. Whether it was Hank's nasally twang or our laughter, who knew? I was thinking about that tune "Fool on the Hill," secretly glad I didn't have to identify with those lyrics anymore, some dumb fuck living alone and without friends. Jake, the guy what led that commune called it dialing into the right frequency. You gotta love it when you see the light and call on Jesus for help. Hank and me, we do a lot of that, a prerequisite what comes with the job.

Can't Find My Way Home
by Paul D. Marks
(based on "Can't Find My Way Home," Blind Faith, 1969)

> *Author's note:* Some of the language and attitudes in the story may be offensive. But please consider them in the context of the time, place and characters.

I Shall Be Released—2000

They say "you can't go home again." They were right, but sometimes you have to find out for yourself. Proust had his madeleines to conjure up memories of a life. For me it was a song, "Can't Find My Way Home," by Blind Faith. I couldn't find my way home, but hearing that song started me on the journey that brought me here today.

I had contacted a young woman through a dating site. I learned everything I could about her and made sure I became her sounding board and confidant. And then we decided to meet.

I stood in shadow next to a booth in the Rex Café, one of those trendy places on Melrose, hoping the sun wouldn't move too fast and shower me in a blaze of bright light. I prefer the shadows. I am an interesting-looking man. Not quite handsome, but striking in my own way. I had dressed for the occasion. I don't go out much so I don't have a lot of good clothes. What I do have is of particular quality and fashionable. I was wearing my gray Armani suit with a vintage hand-painted Art Deco tie. It couldn't hide everything, but it hid enough.

I looked around the Rex. It was both familiar and not, at the same time. One of those places that had been here for years, an L.A. landmark that had changed little over time. I'd changed, but the Rex hadn't. The rooms and smells remained familiar.

The young woman entered. I knew it was her, not just because I'd seen her pictures on the World Wide Web, but because of the way she held herself. The way she dressed. The way her face reminded me of someone else. She stood in a wedge of light the same way Jane Greer had in the film noir *Out of the Past,* wearing all white like Greer. I watch a lot of old movies—like I said, I don't get out much.

She had agreed to meet in a public place. She knew I was older. She knew I walked with a limp and a cane. She knew about the facial scars. But something had clicked between us in our online chats. In her early twenties, she wasn't a minor, though I knew her mother would disapprove of a man in his fifties, someone she'd met online, someone broken. She'd met me under my handle, Sinbad. I'd told her my name was Edward Farina, though my real name is Edward Durand. Her name was Valentina.

"Edward," she said with a warm smile, offering her hand. I let her come to me. Even though she knew about the cane and the limp, I didn't want her to see them. I didn't want her pity. I gave her my hand.

"Please, have a seat."

She slid into one side of the booth. I worked my way into the other side. The conversation flowed as easily as the wine. We got along well. I knew we would. I made sure we would. I knew everything about her, thanks to the web.

"I'm older than you thought?"

"You're fine." The smile in her eyes told me she was infatuated. Some women like older men, she might be one. I felt a certain power over her, but it wasn't a particularly good feeling.

I couldn't help thinking I could take her back to my hotel room—I had one, even though I had a very nice house in the Hollywood Hills. I could take compromising pictures of her and put them out on the Internet or send them to her mother. I could get her stupid-drunk and take advantage of her. Or I could put a knife through her chest…if I wanted to.

Somebody Got Murdered—2000

"Pretty clean," the older detective said, looking up and down the alley.

"This?" The second detective waved her hand at the litter-strewn back street.

"Well, the alley isn't, but the deceased is. Single gunshot to the head. Clean."

The body was found in a Skid Row alley, not far from the tall and gleaming power centers of downtown L.A. Rats eagerly waited for their chance from the sidelines. Unfortunately for them, someone found the body, called it in before they could feast on it. The Three Cs: cops, criminalists and coroners, were all over the scene.

"Nothing," she said, leaning over the body, poking through pockets with gloved hands.

"No ID?" He shielded his eyes from the sun.

"Why should it be easy?"

"This sure as hell ain't Joe Friday's L.A." He slipped his gloves off, wadded them into a ball.

Things We Said Today—1968

"I'm going to miss you," Adrienne said, her eyes wet with tears.

"I'll be home before you know it."

"Hope so." She squeezed my hand, didn't let go. "I'll be waiting."

Adrienne Cooper and I pledged to get married, all the way back in third grade. We'd dated other people, but we knew. We both knew.

I looked from Adrienne to Joe and his girlfriend Debbie, standing nearby. We were behind the garage, near the ancient incinerator that had been dormant for years, like a silent volcano just waiting to erupt.

Joe Carr and I had been best friends since kindergarten, playing with army men on the floor. Playing in a rock band when we got a little older. We had seen the Beatles on *Ed Sullivan*. We knew we had to be in a band. He played lead guitar like George Harrison. I played bass like Paul McCartney. Two other friends filled out the band. We all sang, though maybe we shouldn't have. The first song we learned was "She Loves You." We even played a few backyard gigs—not that we were any good. We knew we'd need something else to do with our lives. What Adrienne, Joe, Debbie and I didn't know as we rode the jungle boats at Disneyland, was that there was another jungle in our future.

"Save Your Heart for Me," by Gary Lewis and the Playboys, blared from the speakers inside the house. That's where the party was. We had our own party-within-a-party out back. We each had a Coors in hand, even though none of us was old enough to be drinking.

"Well, if you're old enough to go to war," Joe said, "you're old enough to have a beer."

The four of us clinked bottles. Swigged. The buzz felt good. A mini escape. I wished Adrienne and I could have been alone. But we were buddies, the Four Musketeers. I'd have some alone time with her soon.

"Good luck," Joe said, glancing from me to Adrienne.

"I'm gonna need it."

"Don't say it like that," Adrienne said. "You're like Superman, bullets bounce off you."

Joe leaned into me, sour beer breath reminding me of all the times we'd snuck beers behind the garage. "Y'know, I talked to my dad. He did what he could."

"I know, Joe. No sweat."

"Well, I feel guilty, man. I mean, I got my deferment, but he couldn't get one for you." On the Selective Service board, Joe's dad got Joe a medical deferment and had tried to get one for me. Joe looked over at Adrienne. Back to me. "Kill some gooks for me."

"Gooks?"

"That's what the soldiers call the Vietnamese."

I would come to know that term all too well.

"Hey," Joe said, grinning. "They say Saigon is the Paris of the Orient."

"How do you know so much about it? You don't even have to go." I gave Joe the look. His eyes wandered from Adrienne back to me. He and Debbie went into the house.

Adrienne and I sat on the low stucco wall behind the garage, holding each other close. Making out. I was set to leave L.A. in the morning.

"You be careful."

"Yeah, sure." I looked up at the black sky. "Vietnam. I don't even know where it is."

We Gotta Get Outta This Place—1968

Tracers and Willie Petes, AKs and M-16s, Agent Orange and punji stakes. The fog of war.

I was the FNG—the Fucking New Guy. I didn't know my ass from my elbow, and hardly knew which end of the gun to point at the enemy. Okay, I exaggerate, but not by much. I tried to get out of going, but I didn't try very hard. I wasn't a hippie or a peace freak, I was just a kid trying to get by and not land in jail for draft dodging. I also didn't want to "ki-il," like the character in "Alice's Restaurant" says. But when somebody's shooting at you, well, you shoot back.

We'd landed at Da Nang. There's three things about being in-country I remember more than anything else: the heavy, wet, oppressive air; the red clay mud that caked onto our boots ground into our uniforms, stained our hands; and the camaraderie of my buddies. Oh, I have other memories, but those are the first things that come to mind. And if Saigon was the Paris of the Orient, I didn't want to see Paris, France. Maybe Saigon was nice at some point, now it was jammed with pushcart vendors hawking strange foods, motorbikes, a blue haze over the city and that fetid, oppressive air. And a reminder of home, Coca-Cola.

I was in the thick of it before I could blink. Three firefights and barely a scratch. I acquitted myself well. At first, I couldn't do anything right, but you learn fast or else. And soon I wasn't the FNG anymore.

I Feel Like I'm Fixin' To Die—1968

We were diddy boppin' down a trail. Lazy. Careless. Anxious to get back to base.

Crack! The sound of an AK-47. Distinctive. Several of them, all firing at once. We hit the deck.

Thwack! I took a bullet in the leg. Busted, I knew it. I went down—I guess I wasn't bulletproof like Superman after all. The RTO called it in.

I saw the grenade flying towards me. Tried crawling away. Not fast enough. Frags lacerated my face. I cried out.

Waiting for dust-off, holding Charlie at bay as long as we could. Until finally, they overran us.

Play dead. Breathe, shallow breaths. Don't let your stomach rise and fall. Don't let them see you breathing. The pain from the bullet seared. Even with all the hell around me, all I could think of was Adrienne. If I died now, I'd never see her again. Would she miss me? What would happen to her?

"Ahhhhhhh!" The sting of a bayonet in my wounded leg. Charlie shouted something in Vietnamese, prodded me to my feet. I was a prisoner of war. I could barely walk, but the jab of the bayonet in my back was motivation and I managed to drag my broken leg behind me. Stumbling. Limping. Falling. Two E-3s from my squad grabbed me on either side, helped me along. Sometimes I wish they hadn't. Sometimes I wish I died in the bush.

The camp they took us to was an old French plantation mansion in the middle of the jungle. From the outside it didn't look so bad; on the inside it was hell. Just for fun we took to calling it the Chateau. They gave me the least amount of medical care possible, then tossed me in a small room by myself. Might have been a maid's room back when the French were sipping champagne on an evening's sunset here. My first meal, I picked insects out of the watery rice. By the second day I had given up on that and ate them.

And let me tell you, one night in this Paris of the Orient—okay it wasn't Saigon, but you know what I mean—was like a year in any other place. The only thing worse than the physical torture was the isolation. I've never felt so alone, so scared, not before or since. Hell couldn't have been any worse.

As the last orange rays of the sun snuck in through the crevices in the boarded-up windows, I could close my eyes and picture Adrienne. The perfect oval face. The peaches and cream skin. The deep blue eyes. I held it as long as I could. Eventually, it dissolved on me. The guards had taken all my personal belongings, including my photos of Adrienne. The only one left was the one burned into my brain. I wouldn't let it go.

Bitterness invaded my body and soul like the damp had invaded my skin, rotting me from the inside out. It doesn't happen all at once; it creeps up on you, so that you hardly notice. The only thing that kept me going was Adrienne.

I was alone, as so many of us were. I broke. We all broke, almost all. I had no intel for them. Torture was just an enjoyable way for them to pass the time.

After three days in my cell—or maybe three weeks or three months, who could tell?—I heard tapping on the wall. At first, I didn't know what it was, but then I recognized it as Morse code. It was the prisoner in the next room, the next cell. I knew a little code and we began talking to each other when we thought the guards couldn't hear. His name was Abner Farina, Abby for short, from Venice Beach, on the edge of L.A. A couple of L.A. boys in the middle of nowhere. He dropped out of Stanford, lost his deferment. A girl he called Susan-on-the-West-Coast-waiting was waiting for him. I told him I had a girl named Adrienne—she was the only thing that kept me going. We talked about everything. That's how I kept any shred of sanity. And then one night he tapped:

"You seen *The Graduate*?"

"Dash dot dash dot." I tapped the letter C, the shortcut for yes or affirmative.

"Scene where guy says the future is plastics?"

"Yeah," I tapped back.

"Wrong—computers. I'm gonna do computers. You too. You smart, get rich. Think about it."

That was the last I ever heard from him.

Sky Pilot—1973

The war was over...sort of. At least our part. We were headed home.

I looked for Farina on the plane. Didn't see him. Maybe he made it out on another Freedom Bird? A C-141 isn't the most luxurious plane in the world, but to me, and all the other POWs on board, it was a swooping angel from heaven. The sky pilots, medics and stews did what they could for us, but all we wanted was to get home. First stop: Clark AFB, in the P.I.

I limped to the open airplane door on crutches the medics gave me, stood at the top of the ramp, scanning the crowd for Adrienne. I didn't see her, but maybe it was too far to see? Maybe she hadn't gotten my letters? Maybe it was too hard for her to get a flight to the Philippines? Or maybe civilians were off-limits here? I didn't really know. They might have told us, but my head wasn't right and everything was spinning.

I was helped down the stairs, still scanning the crowd. No sign of her. I knew my parents couldn't make it—dad was sick, mom taking care of him. But I was hoping to see Adrienne.

I wanted to call home. I wanted to have an ice cream sundae and a cheeseburger, in that order. I wanted to get married. What I got was an officer who debriefed me and was my liaison back to the world. He had a file of letters from home. Pictures of my parents. I tore through the letters—nothing from Adrienne. I hadn't gotten any letters from her in some time. That was to be expected in prison, but I hadn't heard from her for several months before I'd been captured. We all looked forward to mail call. Sometimes mail had a hard time catching up to you. Mine should have found me by now.

I recuperated in the base hospital. It wasn't heaven, but compared to the camp, it was. I tried calling Adrienne at her parents' house, but the number had been disconnected. My parents said they hadn't heard from her.

"Father," I said to the chaplain.

"Yes, son. Yes, Edward," he said, reading from his clipboard.

"I want to pray for a friend of mine. I think he died in the prison."

We walked to the chapel, the chaplain holding my elbow to steady me. I was already walking with a cane instead of crutches—progress. The Vietnamese hadn't done much to fix my busted leg. It had to be rebroken in surgery and properly set. Even with that I'd never walk normally again.

We knelt—or I did the best I could with my wrecked leg. I said a silent prayer for Abner Farina. I knew he was dead. And I knew without him I would have been, too.

*

I lay in bed reading a Superman comic after my most recent surgery, a minor thing on my left knee. The prettiest nurse came in. She was nice, attractive in that wholesome all-American toothpaste ad way. But mostly she was a reminder of home.

"Maybe you'd like to read something a little more challenging?" she said.

"I can give it a try."

She looked through the books on her rolling cart. "Here, try this one."

She pulled a thick, old-looking, musty-smelling book from the cart. Set it on the bed. After she left, I thumbed through it. Something about a count in olden times.

Can't Find My Way Home—1973

I finally made it home. Home to what? My parents were frail, had aged beyond their years. I hadn't heard from Adrienne. My insecurities started to make me doubt myself. Maybe I'd fantasized my whole relationship with her while I lay hopeless and delusional in my prison cell. My face was disfigured and I had a hard time walking. Why would Adrienne want to be with someone like me? I was repellent, ugly. Damaged.

I didn't know for sure that Farina had died that night we tapped about *The Graduate* until after I got home. I wanted to do something for him. Talk to Susan-on-the-West-Coast-waiting, but I had no idea what her last name was or how to find her, and the military wouldn't share any of his personal information. They say war is hell. My war was as much hell as any other, but a lot less popular.

*

I didn't want to, but I moved in with my parents. They loved me and wanted to help me, but I wasn't feeling love and I didn't want help.

"Where're you going?" my mother said, the evening of the day I came home.

I stood there. I didn't want to respond.

"You're going to Adrienne's."

Nodding, I reached for the door.

"Are you sure that's such a good idea?" she said.

"Why? Because I look like this?"

"Because you haven't heard from her." Mom just looked sad.

"Let him go," my dad said.

I walked out the door, the cane steadying my gait. I knew my face was a mess. I still had several surgeries ahead of me. But I had to find her. I had to know. I put the keys in the ignition of my dad's Cutlass. I could have walked. In the olden days—BW: Before the War—I would have walked. And maybe I would again. But right now my leg was aching.

I drove the three blocks, parked in front of Adrienne's house, just sitting there for several minutes. We were going to be married; we'd known it all our lives. I also had a gut feeling something wasn't right. I limped up the sidewalk, knocked on the door. Mrs.

Cooper answered. She stared at me for several seconds, then finally spoke.

"Eddie, is that you?"

Did I look that bad?

Her husband came to the door. They tried not to stare, to sort of look beyond me. Invited me in. We chatted, just small talk for several excruciating minutes.

I finally said, "I've tried calling Adrienne, but her number's changed. Your number's changed."

"We had some issues with a prank caller," Mrs. Cooper said.

"Adrienne's not here, Eddie," her husband said.

"She got her own place? I haven't heard from her in some time. I think my mail's gotten lost."

"She sent you a letter."

It was the way she said it.

"You better tell him," Mr. Cooper said.

Mrs. Cooper hesitated, then, "Eddie, Adrienne's married. She sent you a letter. Didn't you get it?"

I didn't understand at first. "A Dear John letter?"

When they couldn't look at me, I knew.

I'd lost Adrienne. I'd lost everything.

*

It took months, years, and several operations to be able to not look so repellent that people turned away. I took to wearing hats and scarves to hide the scar tissue that remained. Still walked with a limp and used a cane. My parents said it made me look distinguished. I wasn't sure if they meant the limp or the cane.

I moved out and was living on my own in a crummy apartment in West L.A. to be near the VA Hospital in Westwood. I still needed a tune-up every now and then. I put on the radio while I was moving my stuff into the place—KMET, the Mighty Met.

Underground. FM. The first song I heard that day was "Can't Find My Way Home." And it struck a chord.

In talking with some high school buddies, who I no longer had anything in common with, I found out who Adrienne had married: Joe, my best friend. My "I'm sorry my dad couldn't get a deferment for you, too," buddy. My good friend, who was looking out for me and taking care of my girl while I was getting my ass shot off.

I thought about ending it all. Instead, I wandered through life like I was underwater, and in some ways I was. At the very least, I was just going through the motions.

I drove by Adrienne's and Joe's apartment in Palms several times a week. I wanted to stop in. To congratulate them, I told myself. But who was I kidding? I was afraid of what I might do, afraid of what her reaction to my face would be. I'd seen the look on her mother's face, in her father's eyes. They were relieved I wasn't the one she married. I never saw Adrienne or Joe coming or going. Who was I to think that Adrienne would wait for me? And how long had she been seeing Joe? Maybe since before I left? I remembered the looks he gave her on our last night together.

I didn't know what to do with myself. I sat in my stuffy apartment reading Hemingway's *Soldier's Home* over and over, until the pages of the cheap paperback separated from the spine. I had the GI Bill, and even though college seemed kind of pointless, I finally enrolled in some courses at Santa Monica Junior College, just for something to do. After Nam everything seemed so tame, so meaningless. I let my hair grow so I'd fit in better, and to avoid the pity, the hate, and the "baby killer" taunts.

I didn't know what to major in, but Farina's words came back to me: "the future is computers."

*

"You've made the right decision," the instructor said the first day of class. "Computers are the wave of the future. Soon you'll have TVs as big as your wall and computers the size of your hand."

"No way," one of the students countered.

I kept my mouth shut. Sat in the back with my head down and did whatever was asked of me.

The girls ignored me; I wasn't pretty anymore. My face was a little lopsided. I walked with a limp. At night I went home to an empty apartment.

I thought about calling Adrienne every day. Every day I started to dial. And every day my rage and my pride crippled me.

You've Got to Hide Your Love Away—1978

Nothing to do and nowhere to go. Didn't know what to do with myself so I studied computers and programming language. I tinkered with them in my apartment. I bought parts at Radio Shack and through mail order. When I wasn't in school, when I wasn't studying, I tinkered.

I avoided people. I saw the looks, some filled with pity, others with disgust and revulsion. I heard the muffled comments, "freak, monster." I retreated to my crummy apartment. I covered the windows with contact paper. I listened to music, watched old movies on TV. *Double Indemnity. Tension. Phantom of the Opera. The Invisible Man.*

I yanked the mirrors off the wall, smashed them into pieces. Could my luck get any worse?

I drove to the ocean, thought about walking in. Walking in and swimming out—so far out I'd never be able to make it back—like Fredric March in *A Star is Born*. I thought about revenge. I thought about taking out Joe.

I didn't do any of that. I just worked harder at my little inventions, my programs. And I seethed. I watched revenge movies. I watched every version of *The Count of Monte Cristo* I could.

Then IBM came calling. They bought six of my patents and I was rich beyond my wildest dreams. Rich. But invisible. Lonely. Angry. Seething. And plotting.

Your Time Is Gonna Come—1999

They say, "revenge is a dish best served cold." It was twenty-six years after I'd come home. Time for Y2K—I was planning my own Y2K.

I was sure Adrienne and Joe hadn't thought about me for years. Or if they had I was just a blip on their radar. A high school fling for Adrienne. That's what I thought. What I hoped was that she did think about me once in a while, maybe wistfully. Maybe wondering what I was up to or what life with me would have been like instead of Joe. But that was fantasy.

Reality was that Joseph H. Carr Securities and Investments took up the twenty-first and twenty-second floors of the Menjou Bank Building in downtown Los Angeles. His clientele was a Who's Who of Hollywood, Beverly Hills, Bel Air, Malibu, Pasadena. On paper, the company had a net worth of three-hundred million. I was only worth a fraction of that, but I was only one person. No payroll. No overhead.

No wife.

No family.

No Adrienne.

Joseph H. Carr had a wife and two daughters. A house in Beverly Hills. He and his wife both drove Mercedes, and they had a Rolls in the garage for those special outings. They flew private. They partied with David and Victoria Beckham. They partied in New York, Biarritz, the French Riviera. At the Playboy Mansion. They'd known Princess Grace. They were a long way from drinking cheap beer behind the incinerator.

I learned all of this and more from the World Wide Web. I knew the web inside and out. Some of my programs and inventions helped run it.

I drove by their house, hoping for a glimpse of Joe or Adrienne, but I couldn't see behind the hedge that shielded their circular driveway.

I had business cards printed up in the name of Edward Farina. I joined the Jonathan Club, and all the other chichi clubs where the cream of L.A. business hung out. I got friendly with Joe and Adrienne's friends, but I made excuses and departed if I saw Joe or Adrienne coming. But I got to know all about them.

"I don't think everything's on the up and up at that firm," one of their friends told me over brandies at the club.

"Really?"

And he poured an earful on. That's what a little brandy will do for you and I'd made sure the waiter kept the brandy flowing.

Paint It Black—2000

They also say, "Before you embark on a journey of revenge, dig two graves." They can go to hell.

I no longer lived in the crummy apartment, but I continued to pay rent on it for sentimental reasons. It had been my refuge when I first got back from Nam. I had a beautiful house in the Hollywood Hills. I could see the lights of the city below. A whole wing of the house—yes it had wings—was devoted to my research. I had the most powerful computers money could buy.

I hacked into Joseph H. Carr Securities and found he'd been borrowing from Peter to pay Paul. His whole business looked like a giant Ponzi scheme to me.

I created a special worm just for him, sent it in to his system, and the house of cards came tumbling down. A few days later the *Wall Street Journal* headline read "Financier Joseph H. Carr Indicted for Fraud." Sweet. The fact that I'd waited and not tried to get revenge years earlier added to the sweetness. Joe and Adrienne had more to lose now, more money and more status. They were higher on the social ladder with a much longer and harder fall before hitting bottom.

Two days later, Joseph H. Carr's body was found in that alley near Skid Row.

*

I stood in the shadows at the Rex again. I watched Valentina from a distance. I'd seen her several times. Chaste, mind you, though I think she was interested.

She was already seated. I walked to the table. Stood at its side. I'd had a custom suit made for this occasion. I had my fancy ebony cane with the sterling silver handle. I looked as good as I ever could.

They looked up at me, Valentina and her mother. Valentina had wanted me to meet her, especially after her father died. And I wanted to meet her.

"Mother, this is Edward."

Adrienne wore black, still in mourning. She put out her hand. I took it, gently. She stared. "I'm sorry for staring."

"Don't be, everyone stares."

"It's not your...your—" She looked away.

"—scars. It's okay to say it."

She turned to Valentina, asked her to run to the car to get her sweater. Nobody needed a sweater in the Rex that day. But Valentina went.

"You—you look familiar. Edward Farina...Eddie." The smallest tear formed at her eye. "I never stopped loving you."

"You just stopped waiting for me."

"I..." Her voice stumbled.

"Did you ever try to find me?" I couldn't take my eyes off her. I'd seen her photos on the net a thousand times. Even in her mourning black, they didn't do her justice. The restaurant went silent. There was no one else there, only Adrienne and me. And for a moment, but only a moment, it was as if the decades had never slipped by. "I tried finding you—until I found out you were married. To Joe."

"It just happened, Eddie."

"You were going to wait."

"I thought you were dead. MIA."

It was a lie. I knew it. She knew I knew it, but I let it stand.

"You did all this." She pointed to her black mourning clothes. "Destroyed Joe's business. Our lives. What happened to you, Eddie? Where did you go—you're not the same person."

I said nothing.

"You don't have to tell me, I know you did, and I know why. I know he was a cheat and a thief."

She was right. Joe might have killed himself. I might not have pulled the trigger on the suicide gun, but I murdered him. I pulled the trigger that set everything in motion. "But you lived well."

"I was never comfortable with it."

"Comfortable enough."

"Yes, Eddie. We were comfortable enough. I have two daughters, Valentina and Ashley. I did what I had to for them. I don't want to see them hurt."

I looked at her—two daughters who could have been mine.

Adrienne stared at me, or more accurately through me.

"Are you happy now?" she said without affect. Flat. Emotionless. "You got back at us, at Joe and me. You almost stole Valentina. You could have ruined her, too."

"But I didn't. And I wouldn't have."

Valentina returned with Adrienne's sweater. Her eyes flitted from her mother to me. "What's going on?"

"We'll talk about it later," Adrienne said, an edge in her voice.

"Edward?" Valentina looked into my eyes.

I felt something cold in my chest. My face tightened into a mask. "Your mother will explain." I turned on my heel, headed for the door.

I'm So Lonesome I Could Cry—Today

And they say, "Be careful what you wish for."

I never saw Valentina again. I never saw Adrienne again. And it's true what they say—"you can't go home again." I finally learned that.

Three weeks after that day in the Rex, a lawyer representing a mysterious benefactor who claimed to feel bad for Joe Carr's kids donated a million dollars each to Valentina and Ashley Carr.

The same lawyer contacted Susan-on-the-West-Coast-waiting. Her real name was Susan Gladden. She had never married. He told her that one Abner Farina had inherited money from a long lost relative and that they'd discovered he'd named her as his beneficiary. A million dollars was deposited into her account.

I wasn't happy. I wasn't fulfilled, but I did have a good life in some ways. I owed that to Farina.

I played that Blind Faith song one more time and vowed never to play it again.

I am still lonely and alone. But comfortable. More than comfortable. I still can't really find my way home. I don't know if I ever will. But I can still wait. And I can still hope.

Nights in White Satin
by Wendy Harrison
(based on "Nights in White Satin," Moody Blues, 1967)

In spite of the perfect weather for an April wedding in Southwest Florida, the marriage was doomed. I had photographed and reported on the war in Afghanistan, and I knew disaster when I saw it. Jazmine Kennedy had hired me to create a record of the way she had found to humiliate her disapproving parents. What could possibly go wrong?

I climbed the steps to the expansive covered front porch of the Beverly House. The old mansion sat on a grassy plot surrounded by native palms and splashes of color from bromeliads and hibiscus. A broad expanse of lawn behind the house led down to the seawall and the long white pier that stretched out into the Caloosahatchee River. It was a long way from the wars I had covered, but not far enough from the flashbacks that still haunted me.

As I bumped my rolling camera case over the doorstep and into the lobby, I patted the pockets in my black cargo pants to make sure I had extra batteries, even though I knew they were there. It was a habit formed when I'd been in the field.

Passing two women arranging large displays of rare orchids around the entry, I spotted Sarah Summers, wedding planner and harried best friend of the bride. "Where's Jazmine?" I called out.

"Upstairs." She sighed and pushed her hair off her face with both hands. Her forehead was a mass of wrinkles, an unfamiliar sight. She always seemed cool and in charge in the other weddings I'd photographed for her. Dark shadows under her eyes were a new addition.

"What's up?"

She sighed again. "Lots of drama. Fair warning."

I wasn't afraid of wedding drama. I knew what real drama was. Sarah gestured to the white curving staircase on the left. I hauled my case up the steps, grabbing the ebony bannister for balance. It wasn't hard to find Jazmine. I could hear her screams through the closed door to the right. Muted by a heavy oak door, I still recognized her angry voice. I had heard it often enough during the wedding planning. She could easily have played a Bridezilla on TV, although she was a little old for the typical stressed-out control freak whose entire life hung in the balance by the color of her flowers. Monster bride wasn't a good look for someone in her mid-thirties.

I hesitated, not really wanting to find myself in the middle of the crazy. I was saved when the door was thrown open hard enough to crash against the wall. The father of the bride, Maximillian, Max to his friends and Mr. Kennedy to me, wore a pinstriped suit that cost as much as my very best camera. Hell, his haircut cost more than my little digital. He rushed past, not really seeing me, and almost knocked me back down the stairs. That caught his attention. He stopped, regarded me with surprise spiced with a dash of disgust, and went on, the mother of the bride in his wake. Struggling to regain her composure, she attempted a smile. With all the work she'd had done, it probably wasn't unusual for her face not to move. "Oh, hello dear," she said and then followed her husband down the stairs, her right hand trailing lightly along the bannister, head held aging debutante high. The hedge fund manager and the socialite, not thrilled with their 35-year-old daughter marrying a 23-year-old Irish cop. Not surprising.

I walked into the spacious dressing room, designed for a bride and her attendants to prepare for a wedding, but this was a party of one. Jazmine, swathed in white satin, stood in the middle of a spray of broken glass surrounding an intact heavy crystal vase on the floor. Her reflection was an interrupted jagged picture in the mirror she had attacked with the vase during the fight with her parents. She looked exhausted and older than her years.

A voice came from behind me. "What now, honey pie?" I turned to see Jazmine's sister Lily, the young pretty one who relied on a Southern drawl to get her through. "Not done drivin' pater crazy? You made your point. Time to call it off."

Jazmine shook her head. "Not until the pictures make the social section. Our dear momma is going to love hearing 'Oh Clarissa, dear,'" she cooed. "'How old is that young man? And a policeman? How...different,' from all her society friends."

Lily sighed and fluffed her golden hair. "Who're you really punishing?"

When her sister didn't answer, I told them to fix Jazmine's makeup and I'd take some photos. We were interrupted again, this time by Sarah. She stopped in the doorway, her face tightening as she saw the broken glass and the strangely intact vase. Jazmine glared at her, daring her to say something, but she turned away. "I'll get someone to clean this up," she said as she walked out of the room. "It's time for you all to come downstairs."

Even the small wedding chapel on the first floor was too big for the tiny wedding party. Jazmine had vetoed an outdoor ceremony. I never asked why, but I could guess the sparse number of guests wouldn't be a good look. I took pictures of each of the people distributed in the pews as we waited for Jazmine to make her entrance. First, the bride's parents, sitting in the back row. Max, his arms folded, looked like a candidate for a heart attack. Clarissa fussed with the lapels of her blue silk suit, making it obvious she'd rather be somewhere, anywhere else. Poor Peter O'Brien, the groom, uncomfortable in his rented tux, was having difficulty remaining upright, clearly feeling the effects of partying the night before. His close-cropped red hair set off a pale, choirboy face. Peter's friend, Bruno Cavallo, did double duty as the best man and minister. A fellow cop, his primary job appeared to be keeping Peter from falling into a floral arrangement. Lily made an effort to help but seemed more interested in having Peter's arm draped over her shoulders. Sarah stood off to the side, looking as if her dog had just died.

I did my best, trying to capture moments that were less funereal, more wedding-like. Finally, Jazmine entered and walked down the narrow aisle alone. Bruno fumbled through the ceremony. With a perfunctory kiss from the groom, the marriage was sealed. I was relieved that the groom had managed to stay on his feet. Sarah announced luncheon would be served in the dining room in half an hour. Jazmine headed up to the dressing room. I went into the dining room alone to take pictures of the food and beautifully arranged table. I didn't see where the others had gone. I wouldn't be surprised if they had all quietly escaped out the back door, unwilling to stick around for the artificial celebration ahead.

Half an hour later, the others straggled in. Recorded music floated in from the adjoining room where the cake waited. The small dance floor would no doubt go unused. I recognized the song. "Nights in White Satin" seemed an odd choice. I turned to Sarah. "Who picked the music?"

"Jazmine just couldn't make up her mind. Finally, we ran out of time so I chose. When I was a child, it always seemed to be playing when I visited my grandmother. I loved the lyrics. They seemed so romantic. Especially the white satin." She turned away to adjust the place cards around the table, but not quickly enough for me to miss her tears. I was guessing she was in the Max and Clarissa camp of opposition to this unlikely marriage.

When everyone else was seated, it became obvious one place was vacant. The one for the bride. When no one commented on the empty chair, I asked, "Has anyone seen Jazmine?" There was a collective shaking of heads and an apparent lack of concern as the conversation continued. "I'll go find her," I told them and turned away, starting to look first in the room where the music was playing, to be sure she wasn't there.

An over-frosted cake, decorated with sugar orchids like those Jazmine had in her bouquet, sat on a cart draped in white. For a moment, I couldn't absorb what I saw. What I first thought was a drapery covering the cart was a white satin gown, still worn by Jazmine. She was face down and lifeless across the top of the cake.

Rushing to her, I felt for a pulse. The damage to the back of her head made it clear it was a futile gesture. Without thinking, I lifted my camera and photographed the scene. Nothing nearby looked like a weapon, but on the floor, under her dress, were several handwritten envelopes addressed in purple ink. I was careful not to touch anything. I felt a little guilty about my instinctive reaction to take pictures. I wasn't on a breaking story or a battlefield anymore, although the sight of the body left my heart pounding and my hands trembling.

I called 9-1-1. "I want to report a murder." I closed the door behind me as I left the room and decided not to alert the others before the police arrived. It would be chaos, and evidence should be left untouched. I wondered if any of them would mourn Jazmine.

In the dining room, I leaned against the wall next to the door. I watched Lily, sitting a hair's width from Peter, her blond hair brushing the shoulder of his tux. He was drinking champagne, spilling some as her arm nudged his, and they both laughed. Max and Clarissa were across from them at the round table. Max's face was red, and he looked as if he were about to leap across the table at Peter. Clarissa tried to calm him but wasn't having much effect. Finally, Max burst out. "You." He pointed at Peter. "Don't forget you have a prenup. Not a penny if Jaz has regained her senses and left without you."

Peter shrugged. "She tore it up."

Lily laughed and fiddled with his hair. "That's right, daddy dearest. I saw her do it."

Fortunately, the police picked that moment to arrive in noisy force. Four uniformed officers entered the lobby outside the dining room, followed by a tall athletic man with close-cropped dark hair in a white short-sleeved shirt and a badge pinned to his belt. He looked like a recruiting poster for the police department. When he came into the room, the table grew silent. Then Max stood. "What do you think you're doing? This is a private party."

The plainclothesman looked around the table. "Miranda Evers?"

"That's me." I nodded to him. "In the next room." I turned and the police brigade followed me through the doorway. I heard Max demanding, "Do you know who I am?" No one cared.

I pointed as we walked into the room, although it wasn't necessary. It was hard to miss the crime scene. The uniforms neared the body and stopped, waiting for orders. The detective told them to seal the room and not let anyone leave the building. He checked Jazmine, being careful where he stepped. That's when I realized the letters that had been on the floor were gone.

When he came back to me, he said, "I'm Detective Jason Jackson, Fort Myers Police."

I introduced myself and explained I was the wedding photographer. I described the events after the wedding ceremony and what I had seen and heard of the wedding party. "No one seemed worried that Jazmine hadn't come to the dining room so I went looking for her." I hesitated. Admitting I had taken pictures now seemed creepy, even to me. "I took some pictures before I called 9-1-1." He looked down at me. I was tall for a woman, but he was tall for a guy. It gave him the advantage, which I didn't like. "I'm a photojournalist. I take pictures. Of everything." He kept looking, and I kept talking. "I have the pictures in my camera." I lifted it to show him. "There's something you'll want to see. The letters on the floor? They're gone."

He studied the pictures, which I enlarged for him. The three envelopes had no return address and were to "Jazmine Kennedy" at her condo address. They were printed in block letters with purple ink and no sign of a postage stamp on any of them.

After questioning me closely about the timing of the events I had already described, he had me repeat the exchange about the prenup. "Okay," he said, "don't leave until I talk to you again. And I'm going to need a room to talk to the witnesses." I told him the room where Jazmine had dressed might work for him, and I warned him to watch out for broken glass. "Any pictures of that?" he asked.

Okay. Cheap shot but not surprising. I had to admit I had taken shots of the mirror and the crystal vase on the floor.

I was sure I could see a suggestion of a smile, but it never expanded from the corner of his mouth. "I'll need copies of everything." He gave me his card with his email address and cell phone number. Detective Jason J. Jackson. What had his parents been thinking? I promised to send them right away, afraid he might confiscate my camera if I didn't. As I turned to leave the room, the medical examiner arrived. The crime scene crew arrived right behind her, and I was happy to leave the growing crowd.

The dining room occupants were noisy with outrage at being held prisoner, as Max put it, but then the detective followed me in. He stood there until they became quiet. "I'm sorry to tell you that Jazmine is dead."

I watched for the reactions. Clarissa gasped and turned to Max, whose anger melted from his face and left it frozen, as if it would crack if he showed any emotion. Lily cried out, in a wordless protest. Peter looked stunned, but I saw him exchange a look with Bruno as if he had a question he didn't dare ask. Detective Jackson told them they were not to talk to one another. Each would be questioned upstairs, one at a time. He nodded to a beefy uniformed cop who moved closer to the table, glaring at the guests, who, at last, sat in silence.

I turned to Sarah who had come into the room when the police arrived. "Do you think you could shut the sound system off?" I asked her. The music was on a one-song loop that was wearing on my nerves. She nodded and slipped away. A few moments later, there was abrupt quiet.

I sat off to the side and organized the pictures in my camera to send to the detective, who had gone upstairs. I decided to send all of them. Let him sort out which ones might be useful. Shortly after I sent them, I heard the ping of a response. "Thanks." A man of few words.

I asked our guard if I could go outside and get some air. I was starting to feel trapped, and that wouldn't end well. He mumbled into the radio clipped to his shoulder and then nodded. The air was a relief, and being alone was an even bigger one. It seemed likely one of the people around the table had killed Jazmine. For the first time, I felt sympathy for her, unable to walk away from whatever bitter family history had driven her to marry for spite.

I walked around to the back of the house. There were half a dozen police there, doing a methodical search of the area, walking a grid that went from the seawall along the river and slowly along the lawn and gardens. I paused as I heard the battery in my camera start to chirp. After replacing it with a spare from my pocket, I flipped open the lid of the nearest of the trash cans that sat in a line against the house. As I went to drop in the wrapper from the new battery, the flash of a prism reflecting the light caught my eye. I looked down and saw the vase that had been on the floor of the dressing room. Either that or its identical twin. And there was a smear of red along the opening on the top. For the first time, I saw the words etched along the rim. Hand in Hand.

I called over to the nearest cop and beckoned her to join me. Clearly, the police department didn't have a minimum height requirement. She was small but solid and looked strong enough to handle anyone who challenged her. I introduced myself and told her what I had found. She used her collar radio to report to the detective. "He said to wait here," she told me. And so we did. In silence. Maybe she thought I was a suspect, and she didn't want to endanger any confession I might be moved to make. Maybe she just didn't have anything to say.

When Detective Jackson arrived, I explained what I had found. "I was going to throw this away." I showed him the packaging I still had in my hand. He nodded and looked in the can. He hesitated. "I really need pictures of it before I remove it." I waited. "Would you mind?" he finally asked.

"Not at all." I turned my back on him so he wouldn't see me smiling. After shooting several photos, most in close-up mode, I stepped away.

"You should go back to the house," he said. Not what I wanted to hear, but he didn't look as if he was interested in an argument.

When I returned to the front of the house, I sat on the porch. There had been blood on the vase. You didn't have to be Sherlock Holmes to figure out it was probably the murder weapon. It seemed to make it likely the murder was a spontaneous act. It wasn't the sort of thing you'd carry around on your way to kill someone. But how did it get from the dressing room downstairs to where Jazmine was killed?

My crime-solving attempt was interrupted when Peter appeared. He looked like an awful combination of hung over and newly drunk. As he lurched toward the stairs, I jumped up to steady him as he missed the top step off the porch. Pulling him back to the wicker couch, I told him, "Sit for a minute. Did they say you were okay to leave?"

He nodded and allowed his knees to buckle until he landed on the cushion. "It's starting to sink in, dude," he said and dropped his face to his hands.

"How did you and Jazmine meet?" They seemed such an unlikely couple, I had trouble imagining how their paths had crossed.

He answered slowly at first, but then sat up and told me the story. They met at a fundraiser for a police-sponsored youth organization. She was a generous donor, and they had worked on a project for an after-school program for at-risk kids. Jazmine had told him she had been a wild child and had a juvenile record followed by stints in rehab as an adult that her parents never let her forget.

"Nothing she did could ever make it up to those people," he said. "They couldn't let it go. Her getting arrested had made the papers and that's all that mattered to them. She wanted to punish them. All she could think of was to make the papers again and embarrass them with their country club friends." He paused. "It sounds stupid now."

I wasn't sure. What better way than a wildly inappropriate marriage splashed on the society pages to get back at her parents. "I did think it was nuts even then," he said, but he agreed to help in return for a financial settlement when either of them chose to end the marriage. "I figured it would be a hoot, and besides, I could use the money."

"What happened with the prenup?"

"I couldn't believe it. She was going on and on about her parents and then grabbed it and ripped it up." He stared at me through bloodshot eyes. "Man, that was crazy. I was happy with what she was already going to give me." He added, "I liked Jaz. She had a raw deal from her family. It seemed like a good joke on them, and it worked. Her parents were furious."

"And Lily?"

He looked down. "It looks pretty bad, doesn't it? But we just hit it off, you know? Jaz didn't care as long as no one found out. But the way Lily was acting today, Jaz was really angry."

Before I could ask what happened between the sisters, there were footsteps behind us and Bruno joined us. "I told the detective I was sneaking a cigarette and saw you and Lily together outside when I headed out," he told Peter who nodded. Three alibis for the price of one. Interesting.

Lily came out next. She spoke softly, and her eyes filled as she talked about Jazmine. "I can't understand how anyone would want to hurt her." I didn't point out that having a sister carrying on publicly with her new husband would've been painful to any bride, even if not fatal.

The last to leave were Max and Clarissa who glanced at the four of us and sped down the stairs without a word. I had no doubt that in their interviews, they pointed the finger at Peter. If he was the one who had killed Jaz, he wouldn't be able to inherit from her.

The others left, Peter and Lily holding hands. Not a good look under the circumstances. I was the only one left on the porch when Sarah appeared in the doorway. She looked exhausted. "They said you can go," she told me. "Something about a time stamp on the pictures of the table."

I had inadvertently created an alibi for myself. I started to smile but when I took a closer look at her I said, "I think we're both ready to leave." We started down the steps and turned toward the parking area behind the house.

As we walked, Sarah told me that she and Jazmine had been friends since childhood. She seemed genuinely distraught over her death, unlike any of the others.

We walked past the parking area as we talked and veered down toward the river. The police appeared to have finished searching the area, and we were alone. We stayed for a few minutes, soothed by the water lapping against the seawall, and the seabirds calling overhead. It was usually one of my favorite spots, but I couldn't shake the memory of the bloodied head in the white icing of the cake.

She sighed, and as we turned to leave, I reached out to shake her hand as we said goodbye. Her fingers were marked with traces of purple ink. She saw me staring and her eyes widened as I asked, "Sarah? The letters?"

Her shoulders sagged and she nodded. She wept as the story burst from her. "I was so angry when I saw she had thrown the vase at the mirror. I gave it to her on a trip we took to Paris. When I saw she had come downstairs to check on the cake, I went up to get the vase. I wanted to bring it down to show her, to remind her how happy we were. I guess I needed to finally tell her how I felt about her." She began to shake.

"And the letters?" I asked gently.

"I had written letters to her for months but never had the nerve to send them. I had them in my purse. But when I took them out and told her what they were, she was horrified. She said I was like a sister to her. She turned her back on me." She was trembling so hard I was afraid she'd fall over. "I don't know what got into me. I never understood how people could see red. But I did. A red cloud. I was so angry. I raised the vase, and I hit her as hard as I could. I couldn't believe the noise it made. It was awful." I knew what it was like to live in a world of remembered sounds of horror. She'd never be able to forget it. She shuddered. "All the blood. I couldn't believe what I had done. I ran behind the house and threw the vase in the trash. When I went inside, I remembered the letters and got them when you went back into the dining room." She looked at her hands. "I didn't realize the ink had run."

When she looked up at me, her face was twisted into a portrait of desperation. Suddenly, she pushed me hard with both hands, and I fell back over the seawall, grabbing her as I tumbled into the river. We struggled in the water. With the advantage of surprise, she was able to push me under her. She held me below the water with her hands around my neck. There was a moment when I thought it might not be so bad to let go and leave the memories of war and loss behind. Like going to sleep and not waking up. But my instinct for survival wasn't having it. I could see her face, distorted by the water above me, and I was sure she didn't have an end game, other than to stop me from talking to the police. We thrashed around until I felt us collide with the seawall. I was out of air when suddenly, she flew up out of the water. I had a momentary flash of anger that she was going to heaven after what she had done. Then I felt hands grab me and everything went black. When I came to, I was on my side on the grass, spewing river water on the detective's shoes.

"She killed Jazmine," I gasped, and allowed the darkness to return.

*

It was another sunny day, two weeks later, when I returned to Beverly House. I had hesitated when Peter and Lily asked me to come to the funeral for Jazmine. There already were enough flashback triggers in my life. I didn't need to risk this beautiful house becoming another one. I finally gave in, hoping that facing it would help me find a path through the landmines of memory.

Peter greeted me at the door to the chapel. "I think she would like this," he said, and gestured to the crowded displays of the same kind of orchids she had carried in her bouquet.

"I'm sure she would," I said. As I entered the chapel, I saw the glossy white coffin in the front of the room. I walked down the aisle to the casket and looked down at Jazmine's peaceful face, her red lipstick shining brightly in contrast to the white satin lining surrounding her. It was the first time I saw her face free of the anger and anxiety that had driven her during the wedding planning. But seeing her once again in her wedding gown brought back the image of her ruined head buried in the icing of the cake.

I shuddered and turned to see the same cast of characters that had been at the wedding. Peter and Lily, seated closely together in the front. Max and Clarissa, sitting a foot apart on the back pew. Their body language suggested their marriage might not survive the death of their daughter. Bruno was there too, looking uncomfortable but sober. Even the detective had made an appearance. The only one missing was Sarah, and I knew the only event she'd be attending in the near future would be her trial.

When I was seated, Peter stood and walked to the coffin. He turned and faced us, looking down at the notes he had written. "Jazmine was a special person. We're all going to miss her." He looked up, relieved that he had made it through without stumbling. "Thank you for coming. Now please don't get up until we play her favorite song."

I braced myself. No one had told Peter that it wasn't Jazmine who picked the song that played at the wedding. The sound of "Nights in White Satin" came in from the hallway, and as my hands began to shake, I knew that The Moody Blues were permanently off my lifetime playlist.

Breaking Up Is Hard to Do
by Mary Keliikoa

(based on "Breaking Up Is Hard to Do," Neil Sedaka, 1960)

When I arrive at my second-story office, a man stands in the hall, hands in his suitcoat pockets, examining the embossed letters on the glass door: Kevin Simon, Private Investigator. There's a red envelope taped below the word Kevin.

"Can I help you?" I ask. The wind has been fierce this morning. I swat a stray hair that floats across my face. He gives me the once over. Yeah, yeah, I look like hell. Too much whiskey. Not enough coffee. Whatever.

"Looking for your boss," the man says.

I glance over my shoulder, then back at him. "You found her." This guy did what most have done over the years. Thought I was a man. Kevin isn't a woman's name. I relish his surprise.

His dark, piercing eyes widen.

"What can I say? Dad had a sense of humor." He'd also been a demanding taskmaster. Held the bar so high, my fingertips never touched. S.O.B. died last year robbing me of my last chance to make it right.

He smiles. "That'll work."

His woodsy aftershave is strong enough I can almost taste the bark. My father wore cologne like that. Entering a room before he was seen; leaving a reminder he'd been there long after. My stomach twists.

I yank the red eviction notice and shove it in my pocket before opening the door to my one-room office and flick on the fluorescents overhead. The room buzzes as the lights grow brighter. A card table acts as my desk. The floor is covered in bankers boxes of old cases and research. Not fancy, but it suffices. I lean against the shelf with my sleeve and lift a layer of year-old dust. George, the building cat, used to climb up there to sleep. He disappeared about the same time as Dad died. Haven't cleaned since.

"Don't let the mess scare you away."

"As long as finding someone is in your wheelhouse, I couldn't care less. Name's Jacob Riley."

He doesn't pull punches. That works for me. I settle into my chair and motion Mr. Riley to take a seat, noting his chiseled features and expensive haircut. I wrestle a legal pad out from under a pile of papers in a nearby floor stack brushing up against a flask. A swig would take the edge off my gnawing headache. I turn my attention to my potential client. "What brings you here, Mr. Riley?"

His scooch of the folding chair across the Formica floor echoes as he comes in closer. "My wife, Meghan, left me last week. I want you to find her."

I was hoping for something special. Finding people who've skipped is routine. Years as an insurance investigator honed those skills. Not that my boss appreciated it. Or maybe it was the payoff I'd taken to turn the other way on an arson case. What was the big deal? The building was slated for demolition anyway. Dad didn't think much of that either. Told me I only chased a buck. I'd never be as good as him. No moral compass. The whiskey helped ease that slap. Until it didn't. Still, I could find someone curled under a rock and dressed in gray, even in a drunken blur. "Why'd she leave?"

"She's a tramp, a whore. Who knows why? I want a divorce, and to get papers served on her as soon as she's found."

Breaking up is hard to do when the other person is on the run. The old Sedaka song plays in my head. "No clue?" There's always a clue. Signs. Arguments. Small annoyances that grate on your nerves until they're full-blown explosions. I wince at the echo of disappointment in my dad's voice playing like a record in my head.

"We've had our problems for sure. One thing I am certain of. My family hates Meghan. She left me. Might as well make it official."

"You always do what your family wants?" I never did. Or I'd be a bank clerk, smiling through gritted teeth saying, *Would you like to make a deposit?* Punching a clock nine to five. Fighting off nausea for having to be so respectable. Instead, I'm living the dream. It's an adventure. How do we keep the lights on today?

"No. But if she wants out bad enough to run away, then so be it."

The hair on the nape of my neck prickles. Dad wanted to be far away from me. I'd like to oblige instead of wearing this millstone of guilt around my neck. But hey, he wasn't perfect either. He drank too much. Womanized. Mom had plenty of complaints. Who was he to judge me?

Good thing he'd never know it's been two months since my last job. Or that the second notice for electric arrived yesterday. My credit was rescinded during the last employment drought. Rent is due on the tenth. It's the fifteenth. The landlord can be such an ass. His red letter proves it. Yeah, breaking up is a real bitch sometimes.

"Fee is a thousand up front," I say.

Mr. Riley reaches into his wallet. I note a bum hand, wrapped in gauze. He counts out ten one-hundred-dollar bills, placing them on the table as if it's nothing. I should have asked for more. "Start immediately."

When I opened this business, it was a given I wouldn't like every client that came through the door. This guy is one of them and he leaves a sour taste in the back of my throat. "Does she have any credit cards?" I scoop up the cash.

"All cancelled. She might have one, but not likely. She sucked me like a leech. Doesn't work. Never has. Lived off my trust for the last fifteen years. Unless she's got a stash somewhere, she couldn't have gotten far."

"I'll need her full name, social and anything else you have." I hold out a pen and push the notepad in his direction.

He lifts his bandaged hand. "Do you mind?" his eyebrows raise. "Tripped on a stair and broke my hand."

Counting money must be easier than writing. Won't complain about that. I'd almost taken myself out a time or two on a damn step. "No problem." I jot down the information he gives me.

With his good hand, he tosses his wife's picture onto my desk. "You find her, and there'll be another grand in it for you." He says he'll call in a day or two.

Given his charm, no wonder his wife split. Standing, I smooth my hand where the creases used to be in my slacks and lead Mr. Riley to the hall. He takes the backstairs. Maybe he wants to be discreet, but something doesn't feel right about him. Like having a popcorn shuck stuck in my teeth, I can't quite get at what. I stroll back into my office and find that whiskey-filled flask and take a drink. Hair of the dog. Works every time. My headache eases but the question doesn't. Wealthy man who can hire anybody, hires me, to find a wife so he can serve divorce papers. Why not give me the papers to serve the moment I find her? By the time I relay her location, she could be gone. Or does it matter? Dad always said I'd do anything for money.

I tape the cash to the bottom of the table. Maybe he's right. The money is green, and it'll take care of the rent for a month with the bonus of keeping me warm.

This is a job like any other. Only better paying than the last few. I gaze down at the photograph of a thirty-three year old Meghan Riley. A woman a couple of decades younger than I am and in a different league. A sun-tanned blonde standing at the wheel of a yacht, the mister's arm draped across her shoulder. She's about five-two. Beautiful. I didn't question Mr. Riley's desire for a divorce. I'd seen it many times. Still, there's no harm in finding out more about my client before I go further. A call to my cousin Cecily at Castle Rock Police gives me some answers.

"You mean you've never heard of the guy?" Cecily says.

"No."

"His family is only one of the wealthiest in the state."

"Doing what?"

"The first generation made their money in real estate. They practically own half of the Pacific Northwest. Now they run cattle and wheat in eastern Washington. Basically, they're loaded."

No wonder his family's money is important. "You know this because?"

"I read *Forbes*."

"You're kidding."

"Castle Rock isn't a crime mecca, you know. I have time on my hands. There's also this new thing on the Internet called Google. You should try it."

"Yeah. Yeah. You won't catch me typing in questions and trusting a machine to get the answers." Having feelers out, that's what finds people. "But glad you're on top of these things. Thanks for the info." I rub my forehead. Nothing out of the ordinary about Mr. Riley. My misgivings about him are unfounded. I bring my focus back to the matter at hand. "Cecily, I need another favor."

Within minutes of giving Meghan Riley's name and social, Cecily tells me she has a list of charge cards crawling up her computer screen in Meghan's name. I'll be buying Cecily coffee for a month for her breaking protocol. Having been more like sisters than cousins since we were 10 has its advantages.

And given the information Cecily is sharing, Meghan's husband doesn't know his wife well. A few charges have been made in the last week. One at the ritzy but out of the way Hamilton Hotel several miles north.

After a bite to eat, I make the drive. The Hamilton Hotel is old-style glam. I slip a twenty to a bellhop and flash a picture of Meghan. It garners me a maybe I've seen her. "It's only a missing person case," I assure him. His palm out flat, I slap another twenty in it.

"Suite 821."

Meghan Riley is holed up in large corner suite. Having learned early not to entirely trust an investigative lead, even those paid for, I want to confirm it is her room.

Down the hall, a maid's cart is pointed in my direction. The maid must be working her way towards 821. I knock on the door. "Maid service."

A faint voice answers, "Please come back later."

"Could I at least offer you clean towels, Mrs. Riley?" I wait for the woman to confirm her identity. Nothing. Then the door creaks open a crack. The same blonde woman from the picture is dressed in a terry robe. Dark circles shadow her eyes. A bruise taints her cheek.

Her eyes narrow and she jerks away from the door. "Who are you?"

My heart wrenches at her appearance. If that bruise on her cheek is due to Mr. Riley, Meghan has a very good reason to leave him. Which means I can't lie. "I'm a P.I. Your husband hired me to find you. Are you okay?"

Wide-eyed, Meghan scans the hall behind me before opening the door and yanking me in by the sleeve. "My husband sent you?"

"Well, yes," I stammer.

"Please, don't tell him I'm here." Her eyes and the tone of her voice beg for my silence. "I'll pay you twice what he's offering to forget you found me."

My Dad would listen to her. He was good at that. I need to know what I am dealing with before making a judgment.

She leads me to the sunken living room and a leather couch where she sits next to me and sobs.

I offer her a tissue.

She whispers her story. The purchase of a Gucci luggage set Mr. Riley flipped about. Fists. Bruises. A gun in a drawer that frightened her. Her flight to safety. She sobs into her hands.

I'm not a hugger, but this woman could do with a hug. The minute I put my hand around her shoulder, more comes pouring out, the words only just comprehensible between the sobs. They finally subside.

"He says he wants a divorce," I say. "I assume you do as well."

She sniffs. "Is that what he told you? Divorce?"

I nod.

"That's not what he has in mind. He's back in his family's good graces, I bet." She leans in close. "They'll only release his trust funds to him if I'm dead. The family won't risk my getting a cent. Divorcing me means I get half his trust, and that will never work for him. Or them. They hate me." More sobbing. More tissues. "My death is the only way to ensure he receives all the money. They cut him off, see? That's what pushed him over the edge. He blames me. I'm terrified…" Her face crumples, and she dabs her hand on her bruised cheek. "Completely and utterly terrified of him…"

Nausea rolls through me. That explains Mr. Riley's aloofness. Why he paid cash. Was the injury to his hand even real? He might have hurt it from beating his wife. Or did he not want any proof of his coming to see me? Clever. No fingerprints. No handwriting. That's why he'd used the backstairs. To think my own greed almost causes me to lead Mr. Riley to Meghan.

A knock sounds on the door causing us both to jump.

"There was a cart out front," I say to comfort the poor woman. "It's probably the maid." I rest my hand on the gun that I keep holstered inside my coat. Habit.

She nods. "I really would like some clean towels, but..."

I wave my hand. "Sure." I walk to the door. "Who is it?"

"Housekeeping," a husky-voiced woman responds. I turn the doorknob. A body from the other side crashes in. The door smacks my forehead and drops me hard to the floor. Dazed, I have the presence of mind to yell, "Meghan, run!"

I scramble onto all fours. There's a man in a ski mask, holding a gun in his right hand. He hurtles towards Mrs. Riley who is braced. Her feet apart. Her gun raised. Her aim sure. A crack echoes across the room. My eardrums shatter.

The man's body comes to a jolting stop in midair and crashes with a thud, his gun skittering away from him. The kick from the .44 Magnum has sent Mrs. Riley's gun flying. It lands in front of me. Mrs. Riley bends over the intruder and yanks the mask off. Jacob Riley. A wry smile crosses Meghan's face as she leans in. "Breaking up is hard to do," she whispers into his ear. She gazes down at me. "Self-defense. You saw it. He wanted me dead."

"How did you know he'd follow?"

"He's predictable. I was just smart enough to protect myself."

My jaw tightens as I stand and square my shoulders. "You mean you wanted him to find you. Otherwise you would have registered under a different name." Desperate to keep the lights on, I let the obvious slip by. The whiskey hadn't helped.

Meghan shrugs. She wipes the perspiration and crocodile tears from her cheek with the sleeve of her terry robe. She drops her hand to her side. It's covered in reds and blues. Her face is streaked with the blend of purple makeup.

Bile claws its way up my throat. "It was a trap."

Her eyes flash for a second. She realizes what she's done but doesn't miss a beat. "So what if the bastard didn't beat me?" She wipes the rest of the makeup off her face. "He still tried to kill me."

"You could have gone to the police for protection."

"You're so naïve. This way I don't have to hide. Besides, his entire trust fund is better than half. And you should be thankful. He could have waited until you left. He didn't intend to leave you alive either."

My eyes narrow and my lip curls. I'm sneering at her but can't stop myself.

"By the way, my offer to double his still goes. You're the perfect witness. In fact, make it triple." She kicks the rug over her dead husband to cover his face.

Would greed make me an accessory to murder? Words stick like a bone in my throat. "The money's that important to you?"

"You don't love money?

"Not today." I answer both our questions. And my father's.

I kick her gun away from me and turn to leave. I'm almost to the door when another ear rattling crack sends me diving to the floor. I lift my head. Mr. Riley has her gun. He's finished the job he came to do. His body goes limp.

After a quick inventory to make sure I haven't been hit, I get to my feet and walk out of the room. I punch the elevator for the lobby. The shrill of sirens approaches from the distance. I wait for them downstairs.

Two hours later, testimony given, statement signed, I return to my office. Key in the door, I push it open when I feel a brush against my shins. A ball of gray and white fur circles my legs. I'll be damned. George is back. "Where you been, Mister?"

He walks into my office like I should know. And I do.

All the Lonely People
by Maxim Jakubowski
(based on "Eleanor Rigby," The Beatles, 1966)

He actually once saw the Beatles, live and in person.

He was living in Paris at the time, following at a distance, the emergence and triumphs of the Fab Four. When they embarked on their first European tour, he had managed without too much difficulty, to obtain tickets for their show at the Olympia on the Boulevard des Capucines. It was the Paris venue where all major international acts performed, long before stadiums came into play. The concert turned out to be a disappointment—he was seated towards the back of the ground floor auditorium and the musicians were just a blur in the distance. In addition, he could barely hear them at all over the endless screaming of the predominantly female audience. He did buy himself a Beatles wig at the merchandising stand, which he thought he might wear as a joke for parties, but never had the courage to do so. Not that he received many party invitations.

In the years that followed, he would always acquire each new Beatles album as soon as it was released, although sharing his musical loyalty between them and the Rolling Stones, as well as early Bob Dylan.

He had first heard "Eleanor Rigby" on the radio and found it truly haunting and beautiful, and ached to listen to it again and again, but the *Revolver* album wasn't being released for another fortnight in France. That conflicted with a vacation he had arranged to Spain with his best friend, the illustrator Michel, whose younger sister he had once briefly dated. Throughout the drive south the tune and the words of the song haunted his waking dreams. It didn't even sound like the Beatles! It was a thing of beauty, and he knew he was dangerously attracted to beauty. Maybe he saw it as redemption because at heart he knew he was a bad person or, at any rate, had the potential to become one.

In real life, he had not yet killed anyone, but in his dreams he had, all too often. Many times, he would wake in the dead of night from circular nightmares of deepest anxiety, panting, sweating with fear that the hypothetical bodies he had buried were being discovered and now he must race in overdrive to cover his tracks. The dreams were particularly vivid, although they were all about the aftermath of crime, never the act itself. In his mind, he was all too aware of his guilt.

As a child, he had once killed a cat.

He was staying with his aunt in East London for the summer. She had no children, but she did have a cat, whose name he had long forgotten by now. He harboured a deep resentment against it, not so much for the fact his elderly aunt lavished so much love and affection on it, but because he found the overweight creature sly and evasive, always seeming to give him the evil eye. One of his favourite hobbies at the time was painting by numbers, from sets he had been allowed to buy during regular pilgrimages to Hamley's on Oxford Street. That week he was meticulously filling out the hundreds of areas on the canvas that traced "The Laughing Cavalier." On completion of his day's efforts, he would soak his brushes overnight in turpentine. His aunt always left a saucer full of milk on the stone patio outside the kitchen for the damned cat to drink from, and this is where he dripped a few spoonfuls of turpentine one evening, and then vigorously stirred the revolting cocktail so that it still looked like just milk to the eye.

The following morning, the beloved cat was lying tummy up on the grass, to his aunt's sobbing dismay. He feigned concern, but not too much, so as not to draw attention to himself. He was never suspected. He had always concealed his hatred for the pet, just seething inside but outwardly affecting indifference.

His first kill.

Fortunately, the apartment they were borrowing on the Galicia coast had a radio, and whenever he and Michel were not at the beach by day or roving from bar to bar in the main street at night, he kept it switched on in hopes a track from the *Revolver* album might be previewed. Over the fortnight they stayed in Spain, "Eleanor Rigby" was only played twice, alongside other tracks from the album, mostly "Yellow Submarine" which he took an instant dislike to.

He had published his first handful of short stories in diverse science fiction magazines during the course of the previous three years, and the song played on his imagination, although he couldn't quite yet see how to conjure up a story of the fantastic involving Father McKenzie, churches, weddings or the sad death of Eleanor Rigby herself. It might have worked in a crime story, but it would be several decades before he switched genres.

They met two young German women on the beach. Christel and Claudia. One was from Hamburg and the other from Hannover, but they knew each other from university, which they had both attended in Frankfurt. One now worked as an administrator for a heavy machinery manufacturer, while the other was a teaching assistant.

Both Michel and he had come to Spain not just for a break from their respective Parisian jobs but also with a view to hopefully enjoying a sexual fling or two. Michel worked in the record library of the French radio and television headquarters, churning out paintings and surrealist illustrations on the side, while he himself toiled in a foreign bank, as his earnings from writing were still minute and not in a position to even pay half his monthly rent, let alone feed him. It was the end of the summer season and the skies veered between blue and grey, the heat still lingering in the air, the waves rushing towards the beach with rough elegance until they broke against the sandy shore. Tourists were few and far between, so both couples were fated to meet, having travelled here for similar reasons.

They clicked. Turning the charm on in their case; smiling broadly and sometimes giggling when it came to the young German women. Neither he nor Michel spoke German and the girls didn't understand French, so it fell to him to carry most of the dialogue in English, which Michel had never studied but both young women spoke semi-fluently. He had to translate most of Michel's words, often making him feel as if he was engineering a double seduction. But there was little seduction to be done. They all understood the language of lust and quickly established the primary reason for their sojourn in the Spanish resort.

Soon after introducing themselves, both he and Michel had agreed which of Christel and Claudia they preferred. His friend was into blondes, while he had more of an attraction to dark-haired women (it was only, later in life, that his predilections would change and he would become a hopeless sucker for lanky blondes…) so he concentrated his attention on Christel while Michel actively pursued Claudia. Fortunately, the young women had apparently shared a similar conversation and seemed to be happy with the way they would pair out.

Christel wore her hair short, almost page-boy style and her features were delicate—pert nose, delicately outlined cupid bow pink lips, and striking green eyes amongst her pleasing assets. Her one-piece azure swimming costume adhered to her pale body like a second skin, emphasising her waspish waist, the hillocks of her breasts and strong swimmer's shoulders. Strong-thighed, freckled, there was something about her that made him think of an archetypal Mittel-Europa peasant girl, but she had a disarming smile. Her friend Claudia, on the other hand, was by general parameters of beauty prettier, but carried a blandness he knew he would soon find annoying had they come together.

They had arranged to meet for drinks in the central plaza following their initial encounter on the beach. The women were staying in an all-inclusive resort so had declined their obligatory dinner invitation. This didn't displease them, seeing they were both holidaying on a limited budget. Fortunately, the bar prices in town were cheap in comparison to Paris.

Michel, Christel and Claudia drank beer, while he stuck to his Coca-Cola. He'd stopped drinking booze a year before, having ruled he neither enjoyed alcohol nor needed it. Beer, wine, spirits, they all tasted awful to him, and why should he persist in drinking them on a purely social basis?

"Ach, you just want to get us drunk, no?" Claudia joked.

"Why else would we have invited you out?"

Both the women laughed. They were halfway inebriated already, as the quartet had sampled the first three bars scattered along the steep, noisy road that led down from the plaza towards the seafront promenade; a road that featured seventeen bars or cafés, as they had counted them on their first night in town, and agreed they would visit every single one before they returned to Paris. The girls had been most amused by their ambition, and swore they would do the same.

By the fourth bar, the Estrella de Gijòn, Claudia was whispering sweet nothings in Michel's ears and Christel was winking suggestively at him in complicity, in approval of her companion's attempts to communicate, remindful of the fact she was aware that Michel understood neither German nor English.

They staggered back to the apartment block overlooking the beach where he and Michel were staying. The place was owned by an uncle of his and hadn't cost them anything. It only had one bedroom though. Following much fumbling in the living room, the girls agreed to follow them into the bedroom, where they had arranged two beds at either end of the room. They switched off the lights, each couple tiptoeing to their respective bed, undressing, and jumping between the thin covers.

They fucked.

It was not an ideal situation; listening to the noises from the other bed just a few feet away was distracting, and although it was nice to be making love to willing women again, there was also an odd element of discomfort for all involved. And comparing impressions in the morning after the German girls had departed back to their hotel to shower and change before meeting them on the beach in the afternoon, he and Michel weren't sure whether to laugh or be ashamed at the promiscuity they had indulged in. But if the women didn't mind same-room sex, why should they? Although it did feel as if it was a step in intimacy too far.

In the morning post-coital light, he felt there was something harsh about Christel's features, and when "Eleanor Rigby" came on the radio as they were all having breakfast together, she talked her way through it, and distinctly spoiled his pleasure.

But as they discovered, they all still had a whole week left staying at the resort, and the free availability of sex on a regular basis was a luxury they were reluctant to jettison, even as both Michel and he already knew they would not retain any contact with the two German women after this holiday fling. They were enthusiastic lovers but, deep down, they had little in common. The two men were of one mind and agreed they would not provide Christel and Claudia with their Paris addresses. What happened in Galicia would stay in Galicia.

On their third night together, it was agreed that all having sex in the same room was too distracting and uncomfortable and it was agreed that, at night, one couple would use the apartment and the other would move to the women's hotel room. It might have been the swinging '60s, but both Michel and he were still a touch conventional in their attitudes. Later, they would mourn the '60s, but by then they had loved, fucked and learned.

It was the final day of the vacation. By now, they had all tired of each other to some extent. Michel had a bad cold and stayed back in the apartment, while Claudia had a stomach upset and remained at the hotel, so that he and Christel found themselves at the beach alone. It was a grey, windswept day and there was no one else on the sands in close proximity. They sat on the large beach towel, lost for words, with little to say to each other. Today, she was wearing a white bikini.

"Pity it's not too warm today…"

"We'll remember the other days when it wasn't too windy…"

"Yeah…"

"And the nights."

"Of course."

"Did you enjoy it?"

"I did. A lot. You. The sex. Good fun."

"Would you rather have slept with Claudia, no?"

"What a strange question."

"She told me the other morning that she would actually have preferred to go with you, you know…"

"Really?"

"But you have no regrets?"

"None at all."

"I'm sorry I talked all over that song on the radio on that first morning. I realised only later, when you mentioned how much you liked it, that you felt it very deep."

"Very deep?"

"In your soul, you know…"

"That's true."

"My father is a choirmaster back home. In my family, we've always been more into choral and classical music."

"The motive played on the violins in the song sounds almost classical, no?"

"Maybe."

"When I get back to Paris, the first thing I plan to do is visit Gibert Joseph on the Place Saint Michel and buy the *Revolver* album. They will have it in stock by then; it was released just four days ago everywhere in the world. I'll listen to that song for hours on end, memorise its lyrics, understand its story, the characters. It feels like more than a song. It has a story, like a whole novel, you see. I can picture that church, the priest, forlorn Eleanor… What's the first thing you plan to do back home?"

"Go see my fiancé. His name is Thomas. We plan to marry next year."

"Oh…"

He was taken back by her admission.

By her confession of infidelity.

There was no jealousy involved, but more a sense of resentment that he had been used, had had the table turned on him in some devious manner.

"A last swim?" he suggested.

"It might be a bit cold, but why not?"

They were both strong swimmers and ventured out beyond the line of the gulf where the beach stood.

He could see her head bob up and down in the calm waters beyond the break point of the waves.

They say that hate is the opposite side of love. He certainly didn't love Christel. In fact, she was the first woman he had slept with whom he had not fallen in love with. Not that there had been that many at that stage in his life.

She was now floating on her back, catching her breath, peering at the sky and some dark, approaching low clouds.

He moved towards her, placed his hand flat against her face and pushed her under. At first she barely struggled, maybe thinking it was just a joke, if a silly one. By the time she realised what he was trying to do, it was too late and she couldn't summon the necessary energy to combat the downward pressure as his other hand gripped her waist and kept her underwater.

Bubbles of air began to rise to the surface and her legs danced a deathly maritime tango, faster, faster and then weakening, slower until she was inert, her head still held firmly under water, her eyes wide open with an expression of horrified surprise.

He felt nothing.

He had not taken pleasure in killing her, drowning her, extinguishing her soul. It had just happened. It wasn't sexual, or done in anger.

He let go of her body and swam back to the shore. He sat, watching the sea for a further hour and then picked up his clothes. He walked the short distance to the hotel where the young German women were staying and took the elevator up to the room they shared.

He knocked.

Claudia opened the door. She was wearing a partly transparent nightie and he could see the dark stain of her nipples through it. She made no attempt to cover herself and he remembered how Christel had said that Claudia had fancied him.

"Maxim?"

"Hi Claudia. There's a problem…"

"What?"

"It's Christel. We were on the beach…"

"I know…"

"She wanted to go for a final swim. I was too tired so I stayed back on the beach. Must have dozed off, but she never returned."

"Oh dear…"

The hotel reception called the Guardia Civil, the local police. A boat was sent out but no body was found that day. They all had to delay their departures while he was interviewed and further search parties were sent out. Christel eventually washed to shore a few miles down the coast when the high tide came. The verdict was that she had succumbed to fatigue and drowned. Nothing pointed to anything else.

He tried to appear sad.

His first real kill.

He didn't feel any different. Was the same person he had been before that fatal swim with her. He hadn't changed.

Back in Paris, he duly memorised the lyrics to "Eleanor Rigby." But for him they were now intimately connected to what had happened on that late summer Spanish vacation. And would always be. And the song was still a thing of beauty.

Many years later, he even wrote a story about the song, after he had become a crime writer, of course.

I'll Be Seeing You

by James A. Hearn

(based on "I'll Be Seeing You," Frank Sinatra, 1962)

December 31, 1999. Santino's Café, Golden, Colorado

With all due respect to Don McLean, the day the music died was not February 3, 1959, when the plane carrying Buddy Holly, The Big Bopper and Ritchie Valens crashed soon after takeoff. A musical tragedy, to be sure, and one worthy of singing dirges in the dark and lifting bottles of whiskey and rye.

But, no. For me, the day the music died was—and will always be—May 14, 1998, when the greatest singer of the twentieth century passed away. I'm talking about The Chairman of the Board, Ol' Blue Eyes, The Sultan of Swoon.

Francis Albert Sinatra, God rest his soul.

My name's Jimmy Valentine, otherwise known as Simply Sinatra to the patrons of Santino's Café in Golden, Colorado. By day, I sell real estate to retirees, a cozy business in this sleepy Denver suburb. By night, I don my black tuxedo and entertain the patrons at Santino's on my portable karaoke jukebox.

I am many things—retired U.S. Marine, divorced father of twin daughters, a grandfather (the poor but fun one, my grandkids say), a man who likes a whiskey and a cigar after making love, a sentimental fool—but what I am not is a Frank Sinatra impersonator.

Sure, I wear the tuxedo (or sometimes Frank's midnight-blue suit and hat), and I sing his songs like nobody's business. But I don't prance around like a Las Vegas Elvis, a cheap imitation of an original. When I perform, I do my best to carry myself with the same class that personified Sinatra, that perfect balance between refinement and braggadocio.

My act is a tribute to the man who brought joy to millions, including my mother. Growing up in the '60s in Dallas, Friday nights in the Valentine household were a sacred retreat from the chaos of politics, protests and wars. After a long day waiting tables, Mom would make spaghetti, put one of Frank's albums on the record player (usually "Come Fly with Me"), and the two of us would cook, eat, laugh and dance the night away.

Frank was a surrogate husband to her and a father to me, after my own father was gunned down in the line of duty outside a honky tonk that long since burned down.

When I perform as Simply Sinatra, I see Mom's face and hear her laughter. I remember the taste of a Bolognese sauce I'll never be able to duplicate, no matter how many times I try. I sing, tell a few jokes, drink some Jack Daniel's, and put out a tip jar seeded with my own money. Some people clap politely, some keep talking and eating like I'm part of the decor. Either way, it keeps me in beer money.

Tonight, the crowd at Santino's is sparse for a New Year's Eve. I see some regulars, a few truckers in search of a hot meal, and two out-of-towners in black suits. One is thick and bald, with the scarred knuckles and cauliflower ears of a brawler. The other is shorter but wiry, with close-cropped brown hair and a wispy moustache. Chicago, by their accents.

I imagine most folks are staying home to ring in the new millennium, given the weather reports. A blizzard out of the north, the storm of the century according to our local meteorologist. Outside, snowflakes are starting to fall, swirling in and out of golden shafts of light from the streetlamps—schools of strange fish glimpsed through portholes of an undersea craft in the gloomy depths of a wine-dark sea.

Inside, the fireplace is blazing and spices linger in the air, the sweet dance of garlic and oregano. The tables are set, the maître d' is hustling the specials, and the wait staff is up-selling wine and champagne.

Near the stage, Mrs. Riordan's reserved table is ready, just as it always is on New Year's Eve. Every year, the reclusive widow, in a stunning red dress, ventures forth from her high-security gated community and graces Santino's with her presence. North of fifty, she's still a knockout, blonde hair turning to white, graceful long legs, elegant hands, and one monstrous diamond wedding band. In the ten years I've been performing, I've never broken the ice beyond taking a request for "I'll Be Seeing You."

"I don't want you to sing it like Sinatra," she told me when we first met.

I remember staring into her eyes, dark blue pools, falling into them like some schoolboy.

"Mr. Valentine?"

I stammered in embarrassment, "You, ah, realize this is Simply Sinatra?"

"Of course. That's why I came here tonight." She smiled a little smile, no less dazzling for its sadness. "Steven and I had our first date in Circus Maximus at Caesars Palace. The year was 1969. We flew to Las Vegas, saw Sinatra, and got married that very night."

"What a wonderful story," I said. "Your husband is a lucky man."

She did her best to hide her wince, coughing politely, her eyes averted. I knew I had stepped in it. Recovering, I said, "What's wrong with Sinatra's versions of 'I'll Be Seeing You'?"

"Nothing. They're too…" Her voice trailed off.

"Peppy?" I offered.

She nodded. "They're wonderful, but too fast."

I knew what she meant. Of the many versions of this song, there were really only two ways to sing it: one was jazzy, up-tempo, hopeful. The other was low and slow, ala Billie Holiday or Jo Stafford. One said I'll be seeing you, in memories, though separated by distance. The other did not.

"I'm limited by technology, I'm afraid." I patted the karaoke machine that pumped out the music to my repertoire. "My version is pre-programmed, and it's Frank's way or nothing."

She placed a bill in my tip jar, and I tried not to ogle Benjamin Franklin's face staring back at me. "Will you do it my way, acapella?"

She could've asked for the moon, and I would've said yes. "Certainly," I said.

"Thank you, Mr. Valentine. And start at the beginning of the song, not the refrain. With the cathedral bells tolling."

And so I sang "I'll Be Seeing You," channeling Jo Stafford, and I have done so every New Year's Eve, for ten years.

This evening, Samantha Riordan's table is once again set for two, though her dinner companion is a memory. Whatever became of Steven, no one really knew. The small-town rumor mill occasionally churned out a theory, each more outlandish than the last. One said he was the son of a steel magnate; another, that he was a former mobster turned informant; another said he was, of all people, the long-lost D. B. Copper. In all versions, he was very rich, and very dead.

In preparation for Samantha's arrival, Santino has already lit two beeswax candles and iced a bottle of Monte Cristo Brut 1969 Cuvee. Tonight, one of the original 2,000 bottles of this rare champagne will be opened for $18,000 (procured especially for her, paid in advance). She will order rosemary polenta served in gorgonzola sauce, spaghetti alla carbonara, and tiramisu. Where this feast goes on her slim frame, I have no idea. She will drink her expensive champagne, listen to my songs all the way through "Auld Lang Syne," watch lovers young and old kiss, and leave after the stroke of midnight to disappear for another year.

But not tonight. When the revelers are counting down the end of a millennium, I will approach Samantha's table. She will lift her eyes, curiously at first. I will drink a toast with her and offer to dance the last dance with her. Ten years is long enough to mourn, isn't it?

"Time to get started, Jimmy," says Santino. I have my doubts about his Italian lineage, given his flaming red hair and last name of

O'Malley, and the fact that he used to manage an Olive Garden in Colorado Springs. He refreshes my glass of Jack Daniel's and leaves the bottle.

"You got it, boss."

I grab my microphone, check the sound levels, and survey the room. Still no Samantha Riordan. I glance out the windows, where the snow is falling in earnest now. Anyone arriving late might find the roads impassable.

The two men from out-of-town—in my mind, I have named them Tweedledee and Tweedledum—have ordered wine, salads and double portions of lasagna. They laugh raucously at ribald jokes and stare down anyone who looks their way. Despite their celebratory mood, their eyes are contemptuous, as though everything displeases them.

"Hello everyone, welcome to Santino's. I'm Jimmy Valentine, otherwise known as Simply Sinatra. Let's get swingin' with one of my favorites, 'Fly Me to the Moon.'"

That one always gets the crowd going. The buzz of conversation dies, the clatter of silverware ceases and toes start tapping. Couples reach across tables and hold hands, eyes smiling in a way that says, you are the only person in the world right now. In other words, kiss me.

I follow with "The Best is Yet to Come," then "It's Only a Paper Moon." I tell some jokes, sip my whiskey and recite some Sinatra trivia. ("Did you know that Frank was buried with a bottle of Jack Daniel's? He also took a pack of Camels and a roll of dimes to call his friends. Who knew Heaven had pay phones?")

The night grows old, measured out in some of the greatest songs ever written. One dinner crowd leaves, braving the drifts of snow, and another arrives. All the while, Samantha's table remains empty. I catch myself singing "Empty Tables," though Santino hates that song because it's such a downer and reminds him of leaner years in the restaurant business.

Samantha's candles have burned down to stubs, wax dripping over the edge of the candlesticks like stalactites. The ice chilling her champagne has long since melted to slush. Where is she?

After "Drinking Again," Tweedledee, the out-of-towner with the wispy moustache, staggers tipsily toward my stage. He reaches into a pocket and pulls out a money clip loaded with crisp $100 bills.

"The food's bad, but you're pretty good," he says. The compliment is hedged, as if he's reluctant to admit finding anything in Santino's to praise.

"Thank you," I say coolly. "Do you have a request?"

Dee glances back to his table, where Dum is attacking another plate of lasagna with gusto. "My friend wants to hear 'Chicago.'" Dee places a hundred in the tip jar, with a self-satisfied smile. He's a small man that mistakes generosity with ostentation.

The accent is unmistakable. The men in black suits are from the Windy City.

"My kind of town," I say. "You boys from there?"

"Born and bred," says Dee.

"Thanks for the tip," I say. "There are two songs ahead of you, so you'll have to wait."

Dee scowls, his body stiffening. He stabs a knobby finger into my chest as he says, "My friend don't like to wait. In fact, he wants to hear "Chicago" from now until the time we leave. Understand?"

I glance over at Santino, who is behind the bar and watching us. One hand is hidden from view, no doubt grasping the pump shotgun he keeps for "emergencies." I wonder if he kept one at the Olive Garden. He nods to me.

"I have a song you'll like better than 'Chicago,'" I say to Dee. "One better suited to you and your fat friend. It's called 'Here's to the Losers.'"

Dee splutters in fury, a man unused to anyone challenging him. His finger comes up to poke me once again, but I grab it with my right hand and bend it backward, bringing the little man to his knees.

"Leggo! Leggo of my finger!" Dee reaches with his left hand for something under his left armpit, a gun I'd guess. I grab his other hand at the wrist; it's as thin as a boy's, and my fingers wrap all the way around in an iron grip. I tell him to be still, lest I snap his trigger finger all the way back. Dee's snarl turns into a compliant whimper, and he sags to the floor.

When the room goes silent, Dum looks up from his plate, startled to see his partner on his knees. He stands up and his chair flies back, as if eager to be out from under his ponderous frame. As Dum reaches under his jacket, the unmistakable racking of Santino's pump shotgun cuts through the air.

Chuk-chuk!

Patrons and waiters scramble under tables as trays of food crash to the floor. Instantly, Dum's hands go up in surrender. I have to laugh at how quickly the big man caved. Was this a lesson learned in Criminal Behavior 101, or was it a fixed action pattern coded in their genes? When a shotgun racks, throw up your hands.

"We don't want no trouble," Dum says.

"Is he right?" I ask Dee. "If I let you up, you'll be a good little boy and walk out the door?" For good measure, I bend Dee's finger back a fraction.

Dee swears to God he'll be good, and I believe him. When I let go, he scrambles away, rubbing his injured hand and he heads back toward Dum. Meanwhile, Santino has advanced from behind the bar, shotgun levelled at the men in black suits.

"Get out of my place," says Santino in an Irish brogue. "And don't ever come back."

Dee has regained some measure of composure. He straightens his suit and tie, as though seconds ago he wasn't squealing on the floor. His narrow-set eyes shift between me and Santino, calculating odds. Dum fidgets with his wallet, pulling out a few bills that he places on the table.

"Willy," whispers Dum, "we got what we came for. Let's go before the cops show up."

"Shut up, Peaches," says Willy.

"Listen to your partner," I say, advancing. "Or I'll take your little gun away, the one beneath your jacket, and teach you some manners." Maybe it's the Jack Daniel's talking, or maybe I've watched *The Maltese Falcon* one too many times. Either way, I mean what I say.

Willy looks away from me, cowed. "C'mon, Peaches. We got a long drive in crappy weather, and we ain't stopping until we're on our own turf." He spits on the floor, turns on his heel, and walks out the door. Cold air blasts through Santino's, the snowstorm's rage like an animal's howl. Darkness and swirls of snow swallow Willy less than two feet from the door. Peaches follows, but not before nodding at Santino and me with a modicum of respect.

After they leave, I walk to the door and peer out, catching a glimpse of their black Cadillac Eldorado fishtailing down the street. No snow tires I'll bet, and it's a long drive to Chicago. They'll probably end up in a ditch somewhere. Too bad.

The patrons return to their tables, and Santino has declared that everyone's meals are on the house. Men are calling out for free booze too, and Santino tells them not to push their luck. He appears at my elbow, still holding the shotgun.

"Jimmy, the show must go on." His Irish brogue remains.

"I knew you weren't Italian," I say.

"What was your first clue? Now, get up there and sing "The Last Dance," and settle this crowd." He claps me on the back and heads back to the bar.

I approach the stage, then pause by the one table that's been empty all evening. The two unused place settings look indescribably sad. Where was Samantha Riordan?

Sighing, I take the stage and queue up "The Last Dance." I begin the song, remembering a fantasy I'd had to dance with her tonight, to rescue her from her self-imposed exile from happiness.

As I cradle my microphone, leaning into the song, it all falls into place. Her husband's mysterious and untimely demise, Samantha's unusual absence from dinner, the appearance of the two thugs in the restaurant. They came from Chicago and tracked her down.

But was she alive or dead? Was she bound and gagged, tucked away in the trunk of Willy's Eldorado? Or dead in her home? Peaches' gravelly voice springs to mind: We got what we came for. Not, We *did* what we came for.

She was alive.

I jump from the stage and rush to the bar. "Call the police," I say to Santino as I grabbed my coat. "Have them run a safety check on Samantha Riordan. Say whatever you have to say to get them inside. Then give a description of Willy and Peaches' vehicle: black Cadillac Eldorado, probably this year's model. And I'd like to borrow your scatter gun."

Santino asks no questions as he whips out his cell phone and passes me the shotgun. I take it and head to my Jeep. It's a 4x4 with snow tires and a winch, equipped for the worst winters Colorado can dish out.

Outside Santino's, the blinding wind knifes through my coat. Somewhere in the darkness ahead, I will find the answers.

She's Not There

by C. A. Fehmel

(based on "She's Not There," The Zombies, 1964)

Revenants made of dust from the dirt road writhed in my headlights. I mowed them down with my police cruiser. I was off duty, investigating the coldest of cold cases. After twenty-five years, it was the only case that went unsolved in my jurisdiction.

The cassette of one of the interrogations associated with the murder played in the black and white's tape deck.

Sheriff Terrell: State your name.

Lenny: Lenny Teson.

Sheriff Terrell: You're full name, son.

Lenny: Leonard Prentice Teson. But nobody ever calls me that. It's just Lenny.

I'd memorized the interrogation trying to unearth the clue we must've missed. Any tell or slip in Lenny's answers.

Sherriff Terrell: Where were you on August 15th, 1969?

Lenny: (choked up) I was on my way to Yasgur's Farm, man, going to the music festival.

It always struck me odd Lenny didn't say Woodstock, but Yasgur's Farm just like the lyric Joni Mitchell wrote, made famous by the honeyed voices of Crosby, Stills and Nash.

I was a senior in high school when the killing happened. Lenny was a friend of mine and one of my eight classmates. His father was the victim in a locked-room murder. Lenny took his father's death hard—maybe harder since Lenny was the main suspect.

The murder went unsolved for years, in part because one of the other suspects went unquestioned. When it came time for her moment of truth the law found, like that Zombie's tune, she wasn't there. I remembered Chrissie, the way she looked and the way she acted. Nobody talked about her anymore.

I parked the cruiser along the curb on Maple Street. Walking up to the Teson house, painted yellow with bright white shutters, nothing looked more all-American. Near the door, a cement dog had a welcome sign dangling from its mouth. In the fall of our school days, during football season, Colonel Teson used to plant a sign in the yard that said. "Watch my boy on the gridiron." Lenny wasn't much of a player though, more a lover than a fighter.

I knocked on the door frame. The door itself was open and I could smell a late lunch of au gratin potatoes and some kind of beef through the screen door. My pilgrimage was ritual now. When the classic rock station played Jimi Hendrix, Richie Havens, and The Who to commemorate Woodstock, it was a dark reminder to see if Lenny's mom remembered anything that could help find the killer.

Her nurse came to the door, face pruned up with pursed lips. For the last five years, Mrs. Teson didn't remember much of anything. She and the colonel had Lenny late in life, and their only child was his pride and her joy.

"She's not good today," the nurse said.

I took off my hat. The oscillating fan cooled the sweat along my hairline. "I'll just be a minute."

The nurse scowled and took the TV tray with most of lunch untouched into the kitchen.

"Hi, Mrs. T," I began. "I'm Doug, Lenny's friend. How was lunch today?"

"Fine, fine." She squinted up at me as if trying to remember something.

"It's the anniversary of the colonel's death, ma'am. My condolences. I haven't given up the search for his murderer."

"Doug! Have you seen Lenny? He said he'd be right back."

I sat next to her on the faded couch. It was pointless to remind her Lenny passed away just a few years after his father. In a rotten sort of way, it was better for the murder investigation that she still had long-term memories. I tried to walk her through what she'd told Sheriff Terrell all those years ago. She'd been overcome, sobbing and barely audible.

Sheriff Terrell: I'm sorry, Doris. For the official record, can you tell me what happened?

Mrs. Teson: I went to get jack salmon for his dinner. (sob) That's what he wanted, jack salmon, spaghetti and a wedge salad, like always. I went to the grocers. He was in his study with the door closed. (sob) He was still in his study when I got back and went to the kitchen. When dinner was ready I called him and called him, but he never came. I knocked on the study door, but he didn't answer. That wasn't like him. I knocked and shouted (something inaudible). He always kept that door locked. I couldn't get in. I should've had jack salmon in the freezer. I should've been here."

She'd called Sheriff Terrell in a panic. He'd broken down the office door and found the colonel sitting at his desk, shot twice at close range. A cushion had been used to muffle one of the shots. In the crime scene photos foam was scattered on the floor like a freakish snow. The blackened hole in the cushion contrasted with its floral pattern. Nothing was missing.

"Do you remember if anyone was around that day? Or a few days before? Maybe a panhandler or someone collecting for charity?"

"When is Lenny coming? He said he'd be right back."

"On the day of the colonel's death, the Fosters heard a gunshot. Do you remember a gun going off? Maybe as you were leaving the house to walk to the grocers?"

She smiled and nodded, as if I was telling her how Lenny and I had caught tadpoles in the creek.

"Do you remember the murder?"

She stared, her face blank. Her nurse gave me the stink-eye from the kitchen doorway. She didn't appreciate this ritual. It used to upset Mrs. T, but I guessed these memories faded now too. After a brief squeeze of her hand, I got up from the couch replacing a throw pillow that I'd jostled to the floor.

"It burnt the cushion," Mrs. Teson blurted. "The gunshot." Then she turned to the nurse. "Where's Lenny?"

In my cruiser, the August sun seared the vinyl seats and steering wheel. I thought my fingers might blister. I started the car, the a/c blowing warm, and the interrogation started up again with it.

On the tape, Sheriff Terrell learned details of Lenny's trip from Rothville (aka Ratville by its natives) to New York. Lenny described a gas station and a diner where he stopped en route.

Sheriff Terrell: Do you think anyone could identify you?

Lenny: I didn't make small talk, man. To those folks I'm a freak. A hippie.

I watched the cautionary dirt-specters form and disperse on the road before me, warning me off the investigation. Two decades before, Sheriff Terrell told me to leave the case unsolved.

"Careful, son," the sheriff said. "You go turning over every rock it'll be just like in the forest. You'll find wood lice, slime mold, the big, red centipedes that give me the shivers. Once you see it, you can't unsee it, and you'll wish you could."

Sheriff Terrell: Do you know Ollie and Faye Foster?

Lenny: They're my neighbors. They didn't have anything to do with Dad's death.

Sheriff Terrell: They claim you argued with him, the day before his death.

(The tape had some background shuffling and chair legs scraped on the floor.)

Lenny: That's right.

Sheriff Terrell: What was the argument about?

Lenny: Dad wanted me to enlist in the marines. To be a killer, like him.

Sheriff Terrell: What did you say?

Lenny: I told him if I get drafted, I'll be a medic. I don't want to shoot anybody.

Sheriff Terrell: What did your dad think of that?

Lenny: He was pretty angry. He told me I was worthless, and I'd never amount to anything. A real man would join up and fight for this country.

Sheriff Terrell: That's pretty harsh, son. How did you respond?

(background shuffling)

Lenny: I don't remember. I don't think I said anything. It didn't do to talk back to him.

Ollie and Faye Foster were interrogated separately. They corroborated each other's statements about the argument. The retired colonel had the same thunderous voice that he used when he was in charge of new recruits. He was well-feared for his temper. Both Fosters said they only heard the colonel's voice. Lenny had always been soft-spoken. He was the least-likely murder suspect I could imagine. Their statements jibed with what Lenny said.

The Fosters hadn't wholly escaped Terrell's suspicion either. Ollie complained bitterly about Colonel Teson having borrowed his extension ladder, power drill and a shotgun, never returning them. Terrell told me in the end, he assumed Foster kept bringing it up in hopes his items would be returned. Ollie carried on so much at first, the sheriff thought he might've done the killing just to get his stuff back, or maybe Ollie's constant griping drove Faye to pull the trigger.

Directly after the inquest, the Fosters moved back to their farmhouse several miles outside of Ratville. They'd bought the house in town because Faye wasn't well, and they needed to be near help if Ollie was working the fields. They'd chosen the house next door to the Tesons because Faye and Doris were best friends. Perhaps the borrowing without returning ruined their relationship.

Sheriff Terrell: Mr. Foster said your father borrowed tools he never returned.

Lenny: Yeah, a ladder I think. Maybe a drill too.

Sheriff Terrell: Did Mr. Foster ever threaten your father regarding his items?

Lenny: Ollie? He'd never hurt anybody.

Sheriff Terrell: The murder took place in your father's study, the door was locked, but there's a window that faces the Foster place. Being August, the window was open.

Lenny: Sure, man, but geez. It's too small for anybody to fit through. Even Chrissie couldn't squeeze through there, and she's as skinny as Twiggy.

Chrissie, Lenny's girlfriend, was the very person I was going to see. She was in town to attend her mom's funeral, the first time she'd been back in decades. Chrissie had disappeared following the colonel's murder. At the time, her mother claimed Chrissie headed to Mount Holyoke on scholarship in August, so she could settle in before the new school year. When Sheriff Terrell made inquiries, he found Chrissie wasn't at Holyoke on August 15th or ever. Eventually, the sheriff tracked her to a college in upstate New York. Chrissie had written to her mother and told her about the change in plans. Don't bother trying to find her, Terrell had told me.

He never called Chrissie in for questioning, but after Lenny, she was the obvious suspect. She'd dated Lenny for years. When I asked why him and not me, Chrissie said he and I were opposites. I was angry all the time: at my situation, at this dead-end town, at life itself. Lenny didn't mind Ratville. He never wanted to leave; he'd just sit on the front porch and strum ditties on his guitar.

Chrissie could've gotten into the house easy enough. She was at the Tesons' almost every day. No one locks their doors in Ratville. But that study was always locked. It was one of the few coherent things from Doris' affidavit. The colonel had memorabilia from the Asian theater of WWII in his study. A Japanese flag, bayonets, and an enemy soldier's I.D. tags Teson said he'd ripped off the corpse. He worried someone might steal and hock them, though I didn't think they'd be worth all that much.

Sherriff Terrell: Your mother said only your father had a key to the study.

Lenny: That's right. He could lock it from the inside, then shut the door. So even he needed the key to get back inside.

Sheriff Terrell: Was that where the argument the Fosters overheard took place?

Lenny: Uh-huh.

Sheriff Terrell: Did you have reason to enter the study on August 15th?

Lenny: I never went in there on my own. Only when he ordered me to. I hated that room, man, with its paraphernalia of death.

Dusk darkened the sky like soot from a coal fire, as the metallic clap of my lighter chirped along with the crickets. The foxtails lining the parking lot of Red & Stells seemed to wave me off questioning Chrissie, just like Sheriff Terrell. Don't bother trying to find her. Neon lights flashed red and blue off dust-covered pickups tarted up with mud flaps and Confederate flags.

The day's baggage already weighed more than the corpse of the elephant in the room. Janis Joplin's "Piece of My Heart" played to the empty patio. The '80s had been carpet bombed by hairbands in spandex, but at least they had passion. The '90s were wall-to-wall soulless electronic pop confections that stuck with you like cotton candy, and were as about as weighty.

I crunched across the gravel into Red & Stells. Cigarette smoke hovered in a fog, adding to my jaded view of life. I took in what looked to be four drunks hanging on each other next to the jukebox, two guys playing craps at a table in the far corner, and one anorexic hooker I didn't recognize at the bar.

Once my eyes adjusted to the dim light, I realized I had it wrong. The dancers weren't drunk, just two teen couples hanging on each other and maybe copping a feel. The only place to take a date in Ratville, Red & Stells served burgers, but not minors, the only reason I left them alone. The two geezers were rolling the dice, but it was backgammon, not craps. I swung my head left and turned toward the bar. The slim woman with the skin-tight dress wasn't a hooker after all, but who I came to see. I took the seat next to her.

"Chrissie, it's been a long time. Sorry to hear about your mom passing." I nodded to Red behind the bar. He took the cap off a bottled beer and set it in front of me.

Her head turned toward me at vodka velocity. She might have been drunk. She definitely had a buzz. More likely to spill. I thought about the Zombies' song again and the lyric "the way she lied."

"No one's called me Chrissie in a long time."

"What do they call you now?"

"Just Chris. So how are you, Superfuzz Doug?" She looked me in the eye via the mirror behind the bar.

I swallowed the beer while it still had a chill on. "No one calls me that anymore. It's just Doug. Though I always preferred 'pig' or 'copper' to 'fuzz.'"

Chrissie put her elbow on the bar and leaned her face on her hand. "Lacks the internal rhyme of Superfuzz Doug."

"I'm sure that's it."

While she studied her drink, I studied her. She was unnaturally thin. The tight dress showed what crevices and curves there were. She still acted the same, with a nonchalance that once made her seem older, sophisticated even. That had probably helped her get the scholarship for Mount Holyoke.

I guess Chrissie had grown into her attitude. She wasn't one to overreact though. If she shot the colonel, my guess was it would have been premeditated. Chrissie had her alibi of being at a school out of state. When the body was discovered and they started asking questions, they'd find she wasn't there.

Through the decades I tried to figure her motive. Maybe the colonel forbade her to marry Lenny. Maybe he'd made a pass at her. Hell, Chrissie was the prettiest woman that ever came out of Ratville. She was going places. In 1969 she had long hair all the way down her back, yellow and shiny as corn silk. Now it was cut close to her head, spiky like Annie Lennox's or that Swedish singer's from Roxette.

Her next question came out like a proposition. Her tone was like the cigarette smoke. It shifted and twisted and curled into a come-hither gesture. "What's on your mind, Superfuzz Doug?"

My father said if you were pitched a ball with spin, the only way to get purchase was to hit it dead on. So I did. "The murder of Prentice Teson."

An expression of startled surprise hung on her face like a leaf caught in a crosswind, and hung there until...she laughed.

"You think murder is funny?" I asked. "He was going to be your father-in-law."

She took a drink and the truth sputtered out of her. "I was never going to marry Lenny."

"Why not? Did the colonel have a problem with you marrying his boy?" I asked, trying out my first idea for her motive.

"No. If he paid any attention at all, he was probably glad Lenny wasn't gay. But we were never going to get married. Lenny knew I wanted out of this town."

"But you wore an engagement ring he gave you."

She eyed me over her drink. "It was his grandma's engagement ring, yes, but he gave it to me because we didn't have class rings. I wore it because we were going steady. In case you forgot."

I took another swig of beer. It always tasted bitter and antiseptic to me, but it was what cops were supposed to drink. Her last statement was ambiguous. Did she mean in case I forgot in high school they were a couple? Or did she mean in case I forgot after two decades? She was a fool to worry on either count. I still thought about her a lot, her relationship with Lenny, the way she reacted to his father's murder. But grasping her meaning was as elusive as the dust devils on the road.

"So why didn't you ever come back after the murder? Why wait until now?"

Chrissie grimaced. "Why should I? I hated this town as much as you did."

"Your mom was here."

"She came to see me in New York. There was nothing for us here in Ratville." She tilted her head back, "Except to come here."

"You didn't come back for the colonel's funeral. Lenny could've used some support. You did love him, didn't you?"

She nodded in a slow, drunken sort of way. "I did. But when I headed to college, I wanted to make a clean break. No point in tempting both of us when there was no future."

"You didn't go to Mount Holyoke though. Your mom said you were going to settle in before the fall semester."

"Yeah, that's what I told her."

The lyric about lying hit me again. "So where were you on August 15, 1969?"

Red got her another drink. "At Woodstock with Lenny."

"No," I said. "We questioned Lenny. We found witnesses that saw him en route. There was no skinny blonde with him."

"I didn't pump our gas. He didn't either. They had attendants in those days. And at the sandwich shop I waited in the car."

"You were at Woodstock?"

"Yeah. There was no way I was going to miss seeing Santana live. And Janis. And Jimi, though I hardly knew who he was at the time."

I took another swig of beer. "And you didn't tell this to your mom because?"

Chrissie laughed. "It was the Sixties. Mom thought I was a virgin. I doubt she or the Tesons would've approved us going to New York together and getting naked with all those freaks."

None of the witnesses who alibied Lenny mentioned Chrissie. No one told Terrell about her, and she was the kind of girl you'd remember—the way she looked, the color of her hair.

"That's how I ended up in a school in New York as opposed to that prissy all-women's college, Mount Holyoke."

"Can you think of anyone who would be willing to verify you were at Woodstock on the fifteenth?" I asked.

For a moment, Chrissie looked like she was going to be sick. She put her face in her hands. "Dead. All dead and gone."

Lenny had been cleared of suspicion when Terrell found a couple of people who identified Lenny by his t-shirt, the one sporting the Grateful Dead's logo of a skull crowned with roses. Lenny returned to Ratville for his father's funeral, but eventually went to New York to make it big in a rock 'n' roll band. He died two years later.

"I know Lenny passed, but what about somebody else? What about whoever hooked you up at that New York college?"

Chrissie rubbed at her face and then downed her drink in one gulp. "Martha Simington. She was my roommate my first year."

I took out a pad of paper. "Do you keep in touch? If you haven't, I can track her down. See if she can corroborate your statement."

"Elmhearst Cemetery. She went on a trip to India in 1971, drowned in a freak accident."

"You sure have a lot of dead people in your past," I said.

Chrissie swirled her finger in the empty glass. The neon beer signs made her tear-filled eyes bright, though the liquor kept them from being clear.

"Did you see Lenny when he went up to New York? Are you the reason he went?"

"No. I didn't even know he was there. He was in the City. I was north, Watertown near the Adirondacks. It wasn't until he was…lost…his band members tracked me down. Said Lenny was asking for me."

"You didn't go?"

"I went, but he was too far gone. So unfair…he could've made it. He was a great songwriter, he had these lyrics, 'Those with money and not a care/Are only a small percentage/They don't add up to much/Except in collateral damage.'"

I'd never found out how Lenny died. "Was he sick?"

"No. The devil had Lenny by the shorthairs."

"Down at the crossroads like bluesman Robert Johnson?"

She shook her head. "It's the devil you know. Heroin. It takes all the best people. Jimi and Janis…and Lenny."

"Drugs? Really. Kind of cliché. He didn't even recognize you?"

"He was like…catatonic. Never regained any kind of recognition. It was awful."

"So you didn't talk to him?'

She shrugged. "I talked. He couldn't."

From my jaded perspective, this seemed convenient for a murder suspect. "Tell me about Woodstock, something specific." I hoped for something out of the documentary, an incident I could prove wasn't personal.

"Well," she thought for a bit, then laughed. "Somebody peed in Lenny's ear while we were there. Is that specific enough?"

Terrell told me he was trying to find witnesses and stalled for time during Lenny's interrogation so he didn't have to put Lenny in a cell. I remembered that section of the cassette tape.

Sherriff Terrell: Did you enjoy the concert, Lenny?

Lenny: Yes, sir. I missed most of the first day stuck in traffic. But the music was cool, man. They played even when it was raining. That rain, what a mess. I fell asleep and some guy peed on me. He apologized and I didn't make a big deal, but like there was no water, man, just rain. I smelled like piss. At least when he peed on me, I woke up and caught the last songs from Sly and the Family Stone.

If she hadn't spoken to Lenny, there was no way she could've known. Lenny wouldn't have told his mother, a prude when it came to bodily fluids. We both got the willow switch as kids when she caught us peeing against a tree instead of coming inside to use the bathroom.

"There was no water. And Lenny stank," Chrissie continued. "He had pee in his hair and on his clothes. He was trying to dance with me to Sly and the Family Stone, but I didn't want him to touch me. Then some guy came out of nowhere and he had this muscatel. It was a big bottle, and he just let Lenny have it to wash with. I still wasn't sleeping with Lenny after that, but at least he didn't smell so bad. More like grape juice than pee."

Lenny hadn't said anything about the wine, but he had mentioned the incident and that Sly and the Family Stone were on stage at the time.

"Wait," I said. "How do you know Lenny's song lyrics if you didn't speak to him when he came to New York?"

Tears streamed down Chrissie's face like rhinestone earrings. "His bandmates gave me their demo tapes. They couldn't shop his songs since he was gone."

I tossed my beer bottle into the recycle bin behind the bar and waved to Red for another. "So you had nothing to do with the murder?"

"No, but I wanted that man dead. I really did."

Considering she cleared herself based on the shaky evidence of knowing someone had peed on Lenny during Woodstock, this was a bold statement.

"Why? Did he make a pass at you?" This was the only explanation I could think of.

"He was an asshole. He was always bullying Lenny, who was so kind and generous. Yet the colonel was always trying to run his life. Lenny wouldn't have made it in Vietnam. He wasn't like you, a fighter. He wouldn't have survived. It would've driven him mad."

It went with the memories I had in high school. Lenny forced onto the football team but not wanting to tackle his opponents, and the colonel putting pressure on the coach to use him as more than just the kicker.

I sifted through the crime scene photos in my head—the blood-soaked paperwork on the desk. Enlistment papers for the Marines in Lenny's name, but in the colonel's handwriting, probably not even legal. It was moot once the colonel was murdered. Lenny stayed to take care of his mom, so fragile and shaken.

Her account was jumbled after the murder. Two shots were fired, though the Fosters only heard one. Mrs. T claimed to not have heard either. We assumed it happened while she was out of the house. The pillow and its foam on the floor. The burn marks through the pillow like it had been used as a silencer to quiet the first shot, or was it the second? Maybe one shot wasn't enough. Or maybe she was working on an alibi.

The enlistment papers were the clue we'd been missing. Doris would do anything for Lenny. A husband would certainly let his wife into the study. She could've shot him, left the door open, and put the second shot through the pillow to mess with the Fosters' account, and gone into town to establish her alibi. She'd have to be calm, so no one would remark on her behavior. During questioning, she could break down and let the tears flow.

No wonder Faye and Ollie Foster moved back to their farm. Not because a murder took place next door, but because the murderer still lived next door. All this time, I assumed Chrissie left because she was the killer. But she understood Mrs. T's motive, because she had the same one.

The pieces all fit, even the mention of the burned cushion this morning. Chrissie leaned her face on her hand again, hunched over the bar. I stood up to leave. I'd finally cracked the cold case, but the truth left me chilled. No wonder Terrell told me to leave it alone. There would be no arrest. I finally found the killer, but she's not there.

Standing in the Shadow
by Catina Williams

(based on "Have You Seen Your Mother, Baby, Standing in the Shadow?" Rolling Stones, 1966)

You hear things through the years: whispers and strange phrases only half understood. "Don't know why she gave the boy that name... As a girl, she was so full of zest... She was the most beautiful woman, white or colored, to walk the streets of town before...."

Before was the one truth about my mother. She'd been someone before and someone different after. I never knew what splintered Mom into her disparate selves. As a boy, I'd inch closer to those conversations, which ended as soon as anyone spotted my head of tight curls. I wanted to understand why my mother stayed in bed for weeks and why she got that blank, doll-like look in her eyes, no life shining through. More than anything, I wanted to know why I'd catch her staring at me with such hatred. I didn't imagine it. Father saw it too. He'd rush to me, grab my shoulders, and take me for an ice cream. I came to hate the taste, and even the smell, of vanilla.

These were the thoughts in my mind as I sat on the front pew of the First Baptist church of New Eden, staring at the casket that held the woman who birthed me.

My wife, April, and our children sat on the pew beside me and offered comfort on this overcast autumn day. I should have tried to spend more time with Mom after my father's death, but without Dad as a buffer, the distance became unbearable for both of us.

April held my hand.

Deborah Marie Brown was born January 2, 1944, the only child of Lincoln and Frieda Johnson, wife of Daniel who predeceased her. She departed this life to be with her heavenly Father on April 12, 2019 at her home.

The minister read the monotony of her life. Perfecting a recipe for sugarplum pudding was the most noteworthy thing Deborah Marie Brown had ever done, so I included it.

April squeezed my hand. She'd understand how ambivalent I felt. I was supposed to be sad and wanted to be sad, but what I felt was relief. Finally, finally, my mother's reign over my life was over.

Or maybe my wife didn't understand. Maybe she was just following a funeral script for a supportive spouse. A pretender like my mother. Mom pretended to love me because I was her son. The charade scorched more than the neglect.

No, April and Mom were not the same. I never felt any semblance of love from my mother; whereas, my wife was my rock. I married April right out of high school, and we started having babies. She pushed us both through college while taking care of the children. Yes, April was the center of everything that held me together.

The minister was finishing the eulogy.

Left to cherish her memories her devoted son, Leslie Owen Brown (wife, April); three grandchildren, Leslie Jr. (wife, Susan), Antonia and Jordan; and one great grandchild, Piper.

My throat constricted as I heard my name. I tried to swallow to keep it from closing completely and felt April's grip tighten. I hated my name. Friends and neighbors found it the most appalling thing about our family. If I had a quarter for every time I heard, "Why did Deborah give the boy that name?" I'd have enough to buy a Ferrari. My friends started calling me Lob (pronounced liked the Biblical Job). I grasped the nickname like a life vest. To this day, it's how I introduce myself. My wife named our firstborn Leslie Junior She thought giving the name to someone I loved would erase my negative association. It worked, most of the time.

The singular truth of my life was that my mother never loved me. As far as I could tell, she only cared about her rose bushes. Those, she cherished. Year after year, Mom toiled away—rain or shine, blistering heat or chilly air—pruning the crimson-flowered bushes until dirt and scratches covered her hands. The roses were the only thing that brought her out of her depressive funk. Nothing I did or said, nothing Dad did or said, pleased her as much as those roses.

She sang to them—some slow gospel melody. As I sat on the hard pew, I tried to recall the lyrics.

Something, something, passing time.

Tears sprang to my eyes. It pleased me to discover they were not self-pitying tears, but pain at her loss. I wanted a better relationship with Mom, but she constructed the brick wall surrounded by pristine, but thorny rose bushes, like something out of a fairy tale. After a while, I gave up trying to scale it. I loved her because she was my mother, and because something had dimmed her once bright light. Sun glowed through the stained-glass window and reflected off the arrangement of flowers covering the bottom half of the casket, a lush spray of roses and calla lilies. Not as lovely as Mom's roses, but nice.

A Church Mother suggested using Mom's roses for the arrangement. I answered with a harsh no. I remembered all too well what happened when I dared touch her precious flowers.

Maybe it was malicious, or a way to get Mom's attention. It could have been merely my attempt to impress a pretty girl. All I know for certain is I wanted Jennifer Sanders to like me. The date would begin with dinner at Craig's, the only restaurant in town, then we'd go to a movie. At the end of the night, I'd walk Jennifer to her door for The Kiss. For a perfect start, I needed to arrive at Jennifer's house with flowers. Without considering what it might mean to Mom, I cut a half dozen roses. Everything went as planned. The kiss even included a little under-the-shirt action. I floated home on the memory of Jennifer's soft lips, warm breath and small breasts covered by smooth cotton. I wasn't even across the threshold when the blows started. The belt whipped through the air, with a snap. The first lash left welts on my arms. I protected my face, but my back, stomach and legs received so many blows that red, bleeding stripes crisscrossed my body. For the first time, Dad failed to rescue me. I ran away. Going to a friend's house wasn't an option. I was too ashamed to tell anyone what happened. I spent the night under the school's football bleachers. The next morning, I went home. Mom didn't look at me. Dad handed me rubbing alcohol and ointment, then told me to clean myself up. I understood. Dad liked me more than Mom did, but he'd always take her side.

The minister invited everyone to say their final goodbyes. Already slender, Mom weighed 82 pounds at her death. The funeral director had done his best to make her look pretty, but nothing remained of her fabled beauty.

It didn't take long. My mother wasn't the type to make friends. I guess most people came out of curiosity or because they knew me. Aside from family, there were a few members of the church she'd joined in 1960, although her attendance had been sporadic. She must have been 16 when she got saved. Saved? Joining the family of Christ may have saved her soul, but not her mind or spirit. I added Jesus to my list of people who owed me answers.

Sixteen. At that age, I thought I understood my mother's pain. She had been married and widowed before she met Dad. Maybe her first husband beat her. I worked up my courage and asked Dad. He said it was none of my business. I replied, as part of the family, it was my right. A deep pain spread across Dad's face, and I felt ashamed to have caused it. Yet, I didn't back down. Dad looked me in the eyes and said, "You have no rights in this house except those we give you. If you don't like it, you don't have to live here." Then he cupped my neck and jerked me closer. "You're my son. I've kept you from harm. Stay out of grown folks' business."

I didn't ask a second time.

The choir sang "Amazing Grace." My family followed the coffin. I kept my face in a respectfully solemn expression as they loaded the casket holding the remains of Deborah Marie Brown, my mother, my stranger, into the hearse. The song she used to sing tried to surface again:

Something, something, passing time;

Something, all your sympathy.

"Come on.," April tugged my arm.

We slid across cool leather seats into the limousine. The ride to the cemetery would take ten minutes. New Eden was a tiny town without a bank, but with two cemeteries. White folks were buried in Fair Creek, black folks at Coleman. The whole thing reminded me how the people never altered from their ingrained prejudices. The earth didn't care about keeping the dead segregated, but the people of New Eden sure did.

"At least she's not suffering anymore," said Jordan, my youngest.

I nodded.

"You picked a really nice dress for her," Antonia added.

Junior, not to be outdone by his sisters, offered his contribution. "Grandma's hair looked nice."

Everyone stared at Junior with horror. Mom's health had steadily declined over the last year as did her appearance: eyes sunk, cheeks hollowed, and lips thinned. Her hair, which the funeral director had opted to dye jet black, made her look even less like herself.

Jordan dropped her head into her hands and made a choking noise. April was too far away, so it was my job to offer sympathy.

I patted Jordan's knee. "It's okay."

"Her hair," she squeaked.

Jordan wasn't crying. She was laughing. My face cracked. The first joy I'd felt in days. I pressed my lips together and stared out the window. I tried not to picture my mother's hair that looked like the funeral director used black shoe polish.

"What?" Junior said. "Her hair did look nice."

I snorted. The sound was a release valve for all of us and soon guffaws flooded the limo. Not even Junior could maintain his indignation. I wondered what the driver thought of our behavior and that made me laugh harder still.

When the car arrived at the cemetery, we had to regain control of ourselves. It took several minutes. We emerged with tear-streaked faces, appropriate for the occasion.

At the grave, I strained for a pleasant memory of Mom: my fourth-grade American history play. I'd won the role of Thomas Jefferson. Parents were responsible for costumes, including pointy boots, jackets and wigs. Mom threw herself into the project. By the time she was done, I was the best-looking Thomas Jefferson New Eden elementary had ever seen. She even came to school to help me dress and watched the entire production. One uncomplicated memory. I stepped forward and placed a hand on the casket with a silent thank-you.

The minister prayed a prayer and read a Bible verse. I laid a red rose on the casket. My family followed suit.

The minister's wife stepped forward. "Our beloved sister asked me to sing her favorite song. Now, I didn't think it was appropriate to sing in church, but this is a nice time to honor her wish."

My stomach twisted as the minister's wife lifted her voice in song. The melody was slow and soulful.

Have you seen your mother, baby, standing in the shadow?

That was it, the song I'd been trying to remember. No wonder I couldn't recall it. My mother sang to her roses in this half-gospel, half-bluesy rendition of the Rolling Stones classic. The woman's voice lilted and swayed.

Well I was just passing the time

I'm all alone, won't you give all your sympathy to mine?

My fists balled. I pushed aside my resentment at the roses. At least they brought comfort to Mom for the pain of her past, whatever pain that was. Anyone who could have given me answers had died before my mother. Now, she had joined them in death.

It began to mist. People retreated to their cars until just my family and the minister remained. The minister was in his fifties, closer to my age than Mom's. If he knew her secret, maybe he'd disclose the information now that she was gone, when it could no longer cause pain, only solace. I asked.

"I've heard rumors," the minister said. "The Civil Rights movement happened but didn't make it to New Eden. Your momma was a little touched, but life made her that way. My grandmother used to say she wouldn't wish Deborah's luck on the devil."

Was that the answer? I never considered my mother as a hate-crime victim. This should have been enough to ease my mind, but after a lifetime, a possible answer was wholly insufficient.

The house might hold a clue. I'd start in my parents' bedroom. The room remained off-limits—even after Dad died, even after Mom became ill. I could have overruled her, but respect for rules had been drilled into me at an early age.

My parents were dead. The restriction, by necessity, was lifted.

My family and I returned to the limousine, and it dropped us at the house, Mom's home, not so much mine. I reminded myself that not everything was bad. There was always enough to eat, I had new clothes every schoolyear, and Dad took interest. We tossed a football in the front yard, put up the fence, painted it together every other year until he became too old to help. After that, he watched and pointed it out when I missed a spot. I missed a few on purpose, just to make him feel included. Some evenings, the whole family just sat on the porch, listening to the chirping of grasshoppers and smelling the summer scents: pine, honeysuckle, and roses.

The repast would begin soon. People were arriving with platters of food.

I retreated to my childhood room. It was just big enough for a queen-sized bed, a desk, a dresser, and nothing more. April and I squeezed into this room on our yearly visits, while the children piled blankets and pillows wherever they found room. I changed into jeans and a golf shirt, then went to my parents' room before my courage ebbed. Their room wasn't much larger than mine, but they had a king-sized set, which included a rolltop desk. I pulled each drawer from its slot and dumped the contents on the bed.

My gaze landed on my father's old Masonic ring, several rolls of cash secured with rubber bands, and a faded photo of a pretty woman in lingerie. It took a long second to register my mother's face, something I didn't need to see. I flipped the photo over. I picked up the wads of cash and thumbed the rolls. The was at least twenty large. Mom's ratty robe hung off the side of her walker. What had they saved the money for?

I tossed the cash on the bed and sifted through folders, loose photos and worn-out wallets. I found titles to every car my dad ever owned, tax bills stamped paid in large letters and insurance papers. There was my ninth-grade poetry notebook filled with rhymes about love and loneliness. Dad must have saved it. Occasionally, I discovered letters from friends to one of them, mostly dad, mostly from many years ago. I read each with growing desperation. Nothing clued me into what made Mother sick.

"What are you doing?" April asked as she stepped into the room.

I picked up the rolls of cash and held them out in answer.

"Whoa." She weighed one of the rolls in her palm. "You know, I've been really wanting to upgrade our kitchen."

"Take it."

"I'm kidding. Put it away. The house is full of people asking for you."

"I need a minute."

April stepped away. "I understand."

I caught her hand and pulled her into a tight embrace. "I don't need a break from the best part of me, just those people out there."

April returned my hug. "Oh, Love, you only get sappy when drunk or hurting. Take your time. I'll cover for you."

She hugged my waist, kissed my chin and left. I had chosen my life partner well. The simple gesture from April healed all wounds. The lingering press of her lips faded leaving only her words—drunk or hurting. I'd been coping with the hurt for days now; I might as well give the other thing a try.

I hid the cash and went to greet family, friends and the curious residents of New Eden.

Wessemer was a dry county, which meant no alcohol could be sold legally. It mattered not at all. The residents drove one county over and bought anything they wanted. If they didn't want to make the trip, they procured the best moonshine and homemade muscadine wine from Bobbie Richmond. Plenty of liquor, of the store-bought and homemade variety, flowed throughout the repast. I went straight for the muscadine wine.

Mother's church friends gathered around me in clumps of three and four. The kind, gentle, and supportive woman they talked about wasn't anyone I recognized. I nodded and smiled as they told me how she spent her last years directing the children's choir. The kids loved her. I wanted to return to the cemetery and tell the gravedigger to dig up the casket because he'd buried the wrong woman. Except every one of these people mentioned Mother's devotion to her damn roses.

A group of my high school buddies stopped by—big time jocks who would have made it to the majors if the right scouts had seen them. They were a good-natured group who never outgrew chasing pretty girls, which accounted for nine divorces between the four of them. They brought more muscadine wine, and we indulged for old times' sake. In my years away from New Eden, I'd forgotten its sweetness and the kick sixty-proof liquor could pack. As we talked of old girlfriends, mean teachers and silly pranks, my resentment grew. The rose bushes, just visible through the front window, taunted me.

"Are you okay?" April asked, resting a hand on my arm.

"Fine," I slurred.

"I'm getting you some water," she said.

"Water." I nodded. "Mother watered those brushes...er, bushes every Saturday. Never forgot. She couldn't remember to get dressed some mornings, but she remembered to take care of those damn roses."

The anger, hurt and neglect flared to punch me in the gut. I knew what I had to do. I marched, as steadily as my alcohol-soaked brain allowed, to the shed in the backyard and retrieved the ax. I stomped through the house with the ax over my shoulder. A few people scurried away, but most followed, ready for whatever show I was about to put on.

Amid a chorus of objections from Mom's friends and chants of "Lob, Lob, Lob" from mine, I swung. The first whack into the stalks felt better than my first time with April. The second swing felt even better. I chopped until the bushes, all five, lay in scattered debris around my feet.

Mom made the choice to give her love and attention to them. Even in remnants, they refused to grant me peace.

I yelled that I needed a shovel. One of my old friends staggered to the shed and brought it to me. I dug until the roots were exposed and loose, twisted and pulled the roots from the earth. Triumphant, I lifted them into the air, like an athlete hoisting a championship trophy. I let out a roar of victory and smiled at my wife and children. They didn't smile back. April wasn't even looking at me, but at the ground. Surely, she knew why I'd done it. Surely, she wouldn't condemn me.

I followed her gaze and saw it: a tiny skull. Instant sobriety. I dropped to my knees and swept away the too rich, too dark soil. It was an infant, wearing a once-white dress. Tiny roses were stitched around the hem. Above the row of roses, words were stitched in pink thread: Leslie-stillborn, 4/11/68. Good Lord. A grave. The burial place of...my sibling?

Have you seen your mother baby, standing in the shadow?

New Eden—the place where prejudices, grudges and affairs were on parade—would surely crumble under the weight of this knowledge. I lifted the skeleton and placed it gently on the lawn beside me.

Four decimated bushes waited in a line. Blood pounded in my head. Thud, thud, thud.

I turned to the second bush and pushed the shovel into the ground. A solemn quiet had descended over the guests, weightier and thicker than at the funeral. No one moved. No one coughed or shuffled as I uncovered a second skeleton, slightly larger and dressed in the same style gown. The stitching read: Leslie 7/1/69 – 11/17/69. A tiny crack ran along the front of her skull, like something had bashed her head. I fingered the jagged fissure. Maybe I'd nicked the soft bone with my shovel. I deposited the second Leslie by the first.

Have you seen your mother baby…?

I dug around the roots of the third rose bush with more care. A strangled sob tore from my throat when I uncovered the skeleton. Third Leslie's neck had been snapped. Broken. Not snapped. A horrible accident. She wore the same dress. The stitching read: Leslie 2/28/71- 11/8/71. I did not remove her from her grave before going to the next.

Leslie Four's dress only had one date stitched: 12/19/72. No stillborn written beside it. This one had been a live birth, and she'd been murdered on her birthday. Murdered? No. Tragic accidents, they must be.

I barely breathed as I approached the fifth bush. My heart stopped thudding and began to clang. And yet, I dug. No body. Just a dress with a name and date: Leslie-boy 6/16/74.

I knew. I had known since I unearthed the second baby. These were not accidents. Two things were certain: she killed, murdered the babies, my sisters, and she cherished them. Her reasoning could never be understood. Dad had been complicit in keeping her secrets, hiding her crimes. I wept and pressed my face into the filthy fabric of the gown with my birthdate. That's what he meant when he said he kept me from harm. My maleness had saved my life. Arms encircled me. My April. For once, my pain was greater than her comfort could heal.

I'm all alone, won't you give all your sympathy to mine?

Won't You Come Out Tonight?

by Josh Pachter

(based on "Sherry Baby," Frankie Valli and the Four Seasons, 1962)

The envelope was precisely centered on her desk when she returned from lunch at the McDonald's across the street. No address, no return address, no stamp or cancellation. Just her first name, misspelled "Sherry," neatly hand printed in the exact center of the white oblong.

Sheri Lane set down her steaming cup, shrugged out of her parka, and sat. She pulled the lid from the cup, stirred two and a half packets of Equal into her coffee, took a cautious sip. Hot! She parked the coffee, picked up the envelope, and turned it over. The other side was blank, except for the letters "SWAK" printed in miniature on the flap. The acronym took her back twenty years, almost half her life, back to junior-high romances she thought she'd long forgotten.

Sealed With A Kiss.

She picked up the jeweled souvenir dagger she used as a letter opener, slit the envelope open carefully, slid out a folded sheet of cream-colored notepaper. She unfolded it and read the two lines of printing just above and below the fold: "Sherry, baby! Won't you come out tonight?"

Although the office was at least forty degrees warmer than the bitter December day outside, she shivered.

"Well?"

She looked up from a sheaf of projections for next-quarter sales.

The man standing beside her desk, half a step too close for comfort, was vaguely familiar. He was new, she thought. She had the impression she'd noticed him in the elevator once or twice, but she wasn't sure. He was thin, not quite gawky but not far from it, in a suit that had been in style once upon a time and would undoubtedly someday be back in style again. A sprinkling of old acne scars marred an otherwise not unpleasant face. His intense brown eyes were his best feature, but they were almost hidden behind thick lenses in an old-fashioned John Lennon frame.

"Well?" she echoed, pushing her chair back a foot to reestablish proper social distance between them.

"My note," he said, smiling, perching easily on the edge of her desk. "Won't you come out tonight?"

Her face cleared. "That was you," she said. "How did you know?"

Now it was his turn to look confused. "Know?"

"The song. It was number one the week I was born, and my mother had a crush on Frankie Valli, so she wanted to name me Sherry. My father made her change the spelling, though, so it wouldn't be too obvious. One *r* and an *i*."

"Oh, God, I had no idea. I pointed you out to John Testa in Marketing yesterday, and he told me your name. It reminded me of the song, so I wrote the note."

"And the SWAK?"

He grimaced. "Just being goofy, I guess. I hope you don't mind."

She turned away, put out a hand to her McDonald's cup. It was empty, but she knew that. She picked it up and faked a swallow, buying time.

"It doesn't matter," she said at last, dismissing not only the childish kiss but the note itself, and him.

Then, realizing she'd been ruder than the situation called for, she tacked on a questioning, "And you are—?"

He washed a sheepish hand across his chin. "Darrin," he said. "Darrin Stephens."

She blinked.

"No, really," he said.

"You mean—?"

She twitched her nose.

He nodded. "Same spelling, too. Nothing to do with *Bewitched.* My parents swear they never even heard of the show."

"Poor you. You must have taken a lot of kidding, growing up."

He was still nodding. "Yup. So, what do you say?"

"Say?"

"About my note. Won't you come out tonight? For dinner, maybe?"

"Oh." She shook her head. "I appreciate your asking. I've got plans, though. Sorry."

He hitched himself an inch closer. "Tomorrow, then? We could have lunch, maybe, or just a drink after work, if you'd prefer."

She took a deep breath, sighed it out. "Thanks, Darrin, but no, I don't think so."

His broad smile finally began to fade. "Boyfriend?" he asked.

She refused to be drawn into revelations about her personal life. "I don't date men from the office, Darrin. I just don't. But thanks for asking."

He eyed her closely for a long moment, then lifted his hands in an "oh, well" gesture and stood up. "I guess I'll see you around," he said, and walked off before she could say goodbye.

Lynn Kasza squeezed into the chair across the white linoleum table from her, unwrapped her Filet-O-Fish, smothered her fries in ketchup, stripped the paper from a straw and squeaked it through the plastic lid atop her cup. "So?" she demanded. "Is he as geeky as he looks, or what?"

Sheri glanced up from her salad. "I beg your pardon?"

"Don't be coy, girlfriend—enquiring minds want to know." She took a dainty bite of her sandwich, chewed and swallowed, washed the fish down with chocolate milkshake.

Sheri looked at her blankly.

"Mrs. Stephens' little boy," Lynn prodded. "What's he really like?"

"What are you talking about?"

"Duh!" Lynn waved an admonishing french fry. "Your date? With Darrin Stephens? How'd it go?"

"I didn't go out with Darrin Stephens." She frowned. "You know I don't date guys from work."

"Well, that's what I thought," Lynn said. "But Carrie said Lisa said he said you went out."

"Carrie said—? He said we went out? When? Where?"

"To dinner at Angelo's. Tres chic, non? And then you went up to his place and"—she made quotation marks on either side of her face with her fingers—"hung out for a couple of hours."

Sheri tossed down her plastic fork. "That bastard. I did not go out with him, Lynn. I wouldn't—"

"—go out with you even if I liked you, which, believe me, I most certainly do not!"

She stormed out of his office and slammed the door behind her, then turned around and marched back in, leaving the door open. She leaned over his desk, her weight resting on clenched fists. "I'm going to pretend this didn't happen, Darrin. But I swear to God, if you so much as mention my name to anyone here again, I am going straight to Mr. Brownlee, and you will be out on the street so fast your head won't stop spinning for a week."

Darrin smiled, a crooked smile that made him almost attractive. "I don't think so," he said.

Sheri stared at him. "You don't think I'll go to Mr. Brownlee? You just try me, buster, and—"

"I don't think he'll can me." He was wearing the same suit he'd had on the other day, this time with a flamboyant Jerry Garcia tie. The jacket was buttoned, but beneath it Sheri swore there was a plastic holder full of pens in his shirt pocket. "He's my uncle, Sheri. Uncle Bobby, my mother's baby brother. He got me this job in the first place. So who do you think he'll believe, you or me?"

He looked so smug, Sheri wanted to punch him right in the face. "You son of a bitch," she said instead, and went away from there.

The phone was ringing when she got home that evening. There was no one she felt like talking to, so she let the machine pick it up. "I'm sorry," her voice said, "but I can't come to the phone right now. Leave a message at the tone, and I'll get back to you as soon as I can."

There was a long beep, and then she heard him singing: "Sheh-heh-heh-eh-eh-eh- ree-ee, bay-ay-bee, Sheri, baby, Sheh-heh-ree, won't you come out tonight?"

She snatched up the receiver. "I don't care if he is your uncle," she said tightly. "I don't want you calling me, I don't want you talking to my friends, I don't want you following me around. I told you, Darrin, I don't date where I work, and I damn well don't date creeps like you. Just leave me alone, okay? Leave—me—alone."

She paused, breathing deeply, enraged. At the other end of the line, she heard a kissing sound, and then a faint click, and then the dial tone.

"How 'bout that booth over there by the window?" He touched her elbow and tried to turn her, but she jerked her arm free and strode ahead of him to the bar. There were four vacant stools in a row at the far end, but she chose a single between a truck driver drinking Bud from a longneck and two secretaries gossiping over strawberry daiquiris.

Darrin stood too close behind her, unbuttoning his London Fog and loosening his tie. When the bartender came over, he ordered a Manhattan. She had never heard anyone order a Manhattan before. She wasn't sure she knew what it was.

"Scotch," she said. "Single malt. In a glass."

The barman raised an eyebrow. "That was good," he said. "Can you do the thing with your upper lip?"

The truck driver banged down his empty bottle, stifled a belch, and headed for the door, and Darrin settled onto his stool. "What thing is that?" he asked.

She exchanged eye contact with the bartender. "Nobody watches the black-and-white ones anymore," he mourned, and set glasses in front of them.

"Black-and-white?" Darrin said. "What's that all—?"

"Never mind," she snapped. "Just drink your drink." She looked at her watch impatiently. She had to be crazy, coming out with him like this. "One drink, right? And then you'll leave me alone?"

His chocolate-brown eyes glittered. "Promise," he said, his hand on his heart. "I mean, if you have a good time, if you decide you want to go out with me again, well, great—but all I wanted from the beginning was one shot."

"One shot," she said, raising her glass and draining it. The smooth burn almost melted the knot in her stomach. Almost, but not quite.

"Thank you for the drink, Darrin," she said. "It's been real. Good night."

There were a dozen roses in a cut-glass vase on her desk when she got to work in the morning, nicely arranged with ferns and a spray of baby's breath. Her name was spelled correctly on the small envelope tucked in among the flowers.

They don't have to be from him, she told herself. But when she saw the SWAK printed on the back of the envelope, she pitched the whole shebang into the trash—roses, vase, unopened envelope and all. She knew what it would say on the card.

At lunch on Tuesday, Lynn told her it was all over the building she'd slept with him. She debated confronting him again, but what was the use? The man was out of his mind. Not only couldn't he take a hint, he couldn't read a freaking billboard. Lynn suggested the police, but Sheri'd read that the state's new stalker law was a joke.

When she got home that evening, there were twelve white envelopes taped to her front door, all of them sealed with kisses. She was so outraged she opened them. Every single one of them held a cream notecard, and each notecard read "Won't you come out tonight?" in a different color ink.

Something woke her after midnight. She sat up in bed, her head throbbing. She'd finished off almost half a bottle of vodka that evening, watching Darrin's notecards burn in her fireplace.

There it was again.

There was someone at her door.

She grabbed a thick terrycloth robe and shrugged it on, stole down the hall to the foyer, put an eye to the peephole.

Nothing.

She left the chain in place and opened the door a crack. On the porch stood a cut-glass vase holding a dozen red roses. She couldn't see a card. She released the chain and swung the door wide.

There were twelve white envelopes taped to the outside of the door.

She bought the pistol the next day at lunch.

There was nothing in the Yellow Pages under "Firearms," but under "Guns & Gunsmiths" she found three columns of listings and a half-dozen display ads. Metropolitan Arms and Armor was only four blocks from the office. She left her car in the lot and walked.

The salesman, a squat homunculus with a salt-and-pepper spade beard and the unidentifiable edge of an old tattoo peeking out from beneath the rolled-up sleeve of his red flannel shirt, recommended the Beretta .380 ACP, a 9mm short with a magazine holding thirteen cartridges, and offered to throw in a box of twenty Federal Hydra-Shok hollow points to sweeten the deal, but $350 was way more than she wanted to spend, so she settled on a Taurus Model 65 six-shot revolver, a .38 Special. All the caliber numbers and model numbers and firepower statistics were meaningless to her—the salesman assured her the Taurus was easy to use and well suited for self-defense; the price was only $180, and her birthday was at the end of April, so Taurus was her sign.

"Can I—I don't know how to say it—try it out first?" she asked.

He looked at her as if she was insane. "Lady, I don't have a range in here," he said, excessively patient, "and, even if I did, I let you fire it and you decide not to buy it, it's all of a sudden a used gun and I have to knock fifty bucks off the price."

She nodded, understanding, and he showed her at least how to load it and shoot it. When she asked him where the safety was, he sighed and explained that a revolver doesn't have a safety but would in fact be safer for her to carry and use than the Beretta, as long as she made sure to leave it uncocked.

The five-day waiting period law wasn't due to take effect for another four months, so all she had to do was show her driver's license and fill out Federal Firearms Transaction Form 4473. No, she was not a convicted felon, was not currently under indictment, was not addicted to drugs or alcohol, had not been judged mentally incompetent, was not an alien residing illegally in the United States.

She marveled at the inanity of the form, wondering if an illegal alien who had been judged mentally incompetent would be foolish enough to check "yes" in response to any of these questions.

Including $12.95 for a box of Winchester Silvertips—their aluminum-jacketed soft-lead bodies unexpectedly heavy yet comforting in her palm—and state sales tax, the total came to a little over two hundred dollars. She didn't have that much cash on her, so she put the purchase on her Visa card.

She named the gun Bull, after Taurus, and then thought of the tall bald bailiff on Night Court and smiled.

She decided not to carry Bull around with her: at the office; in town, she was perfectly safe. It was only at home that she felt vulnerable, so she kept Bull on an end table beside the sofa during the evenings as she watched television or read, moved him to the nightstand beside her bed when she went to sleep. From time to time, she reached out a hand and touched him, and the cool solidity of him reassured her.

For the next two days, Darrin left her alone, almost as if he knew she had brought Bull into her home.

Did he know? Could he have followed her to the gun shop and watched her make the purchase? It was just as well if he had, if that's what was keeping him away.

Then, Friday at lunch, Lynn said, "I see your boyfriend's back. I bet you're thrilled and delighted."

Sheri stared at her.

"Darrin," Lynn explained. "They sent him to Chicago for the RFC, didn't you know? And I was kidding about the 'boyfriend,' girlfriend. Don't look so stricken."

"When—?" Her throat was constricted, and she began again: "When did he leave?"

Lynn dipped a McNugget thoughtfully into her little cup of sweet-and-sour sauce. "Day before yesterday, I think. Why?"

Sheri stood up and put on her parka and scarf and gloves and left the Mickey D's, her food scarcely touched.

He called her four times that evening, and there were more roses on the porch when she went out to get the paper Saturday morning. She dialed the operator and asked to have her number changed and unlisted, but there was nothing anyone could do about it until Monday morning. She switched off the ringer and turned the speaker volume on the answering machine down to zero.

By 11 P.M., eight messages had accumulated. One was a hang-up, and the other seven were all him, all singing that damn song.

She turned the machine off altogether when she went to bed and kept Bull beneath her pillow, and still she slept badly. When she did sleep, she dreamed of a beautiful witch with a twitching nose, imprisoned in a dark dungeon.

Well, duh, she thought when she awoke, sweating, her blankets hopelessly twisted.

He was listed in the phone book. She waited until eight Sunday morning, and then she called him.

"Sheri?" he said blearily.

"No," she spat, "it's Laura Bush. Now listen to me, you bastard. I don't want you calling me. I don't want your stupid flowers. I don't want your notes."

"Why don't you just go out with me?" he said, awake now. "If you got to know me, I bet you'd really like me."

"I went out with you, Darrin. I got to know you. I really don't like you."

"But I—"

"Shut up!" Her voice was tighter than she could ever remember it. "I don't know what your problem is, pal, and I don't care. But it's your problem, not mine. I have been very patient with you, but my patience is gone. It's time for you to leave me alone."

She slammed down the phone.

Ten seconds later, it rang. She gripped the receiver but stopped herself from lifting it. Instead, she pushed the button to reactivate her machine. It picked up on the third ring.

"Sheri?" Darrin said after the beep. "I know you're there, Sheri."

There was a pause, and then he began to sing.

"Has the caller made physical threats against your person, ma'am?"

"No, he—"

"Has the caller used obscene or abusive language?"

"No, Sergeant, he just keeps asking me out."

"Well, I'm afraid there's nothing we can do, unless he's threatened you or been obscene or abusive, ma'am. Your best bet is to call the phone company's business office and report the—"

"There's nobody there until tomorrow morning, Sergeant, that's why I'm—"

"I'm sorry, ma'am. I'm afraid there's nothing we can—"

*

"—do," she said. "Can you believe it? This jagoff can do whatever he wants, and the police can't do a thing to stop him!"

"Did you try talking to Uncle Bob?" Lynn said. "Maybe he can—"

"Uncle Bobby," Sheri corrected her. "Can you just see the Honorable Robert Brownlee, Esquire, answering to 'Uncle Bobby'? I tried to get in to see him the other day, but Doris just gave me that I-pity-you look of hers and wouldn't even let me make an appointment."

"What about writing him an email?"

"And say what? 'I'm sorry to bother you, Mr. Brownlee, but your sister's little Darrin has been sending me flowers and I want you to make him stop'?"

"Well, you'll have to—oh, gosh, Sheri, there's Donald, I gotta go. You hang in there, girlfriend. See you tomorrow morning."

Sheri set down the receiver, and the phone rang immediately, burning her fingers.

Finally, a few minutes before midnight, she unplugged it and crawled into bed, pulled the covers over her head, and tried to sleep.

The doorbell rang at 1:22 AM, and she plugged in the phone and called the police and reported a prowler. By the time the black-and-white pulled up before her bungalow, though, Darrin was long gone. The officers looked suspiciously at her wild hair and red eyes, made only the sketchiest of notes, and drove off with vague promises.

At 3:41, the doorbell rang again. This time, it took forty-five minutes for the patrol car to arrive, and the same two bored officers stayed less than a quarter of an hour and didn't even bother to take out their notebooks.

At 4:45, only moments after the police had gone and Sheri had returned to her bedroom, the doorbell rang again. She didn't bother dialing 9-1-1, just crushed her pillow tightly against her ears and hummed into her percale top sheet in a hollow attempt to drown out the chime.

When she noticed what song she was humming, she bit her lower lip hard enough to draw blood.

At 7:00, she was sitting on the edge of the living-room couch, waiting for him. When the doorbell rang at 7:16, she jumped up, grabbed Bull from the end table, and strode to the front door. "Leave me the hell alone!" she screamed.

The recoil when she pulled the trigger was enormous, vastly more powerful than she would have believed possible. The revolver bucked in her hand as she fired again and again and again through the panels of the closed door.

At last the six chambers were empty. She stood there in the foyer, shaking with rage, with hatred, with fear.

The telephone rang.

She turned to stare across the room at it, then swiveled slowly back to the door, released the chain, touched the cool brass knob, swung the door wide.

Crumpled on her porch lay the body of a man.

Behind her, her own voice said, "I'm sorry, but I can't come to the phone right now. Please leave a message at the tone, and I'll get back to you as soon as I can."

The man held a plain white envelope in his hand. The letters S-W-A were visible between his splayed fingers. His overcoat was tattered and patched and drenched in blood. He had thinning gray hair and a rough beard.

She had no idea who he was.

"Sheh-heh-heh-eh-eh-eh-ree-ee, bay-ay-bee," Darrin Stephens sang from her answering machine's speaker. "Sheh-heh-ree, won't you come out tonight?"

Suspicious Minds
by John M. Floyd
(based on "Suspicious Minds," Elvis Presley, 1969)

My name's Eddie Warrington, and September 20th is my birthday. This year it was an occasion celebrated by nobody and remembered by nobody (except me), and at the stroke of midnight I observed the end of my special day by sitting behind a bush on the edge of the woods near Rosalie, Mississippi, and peeking out at a rundown shopping center fifty yards away. Beside me, hidden behind a similar bush, was my friend Dexter Holtzhagen. And yes, that's his real name.

"Why, again," Dexter whispered, "are we doing this?"

"We're being cautious. You know what the early bird gets."

"Sleep deprived?"

"Just keep watching," I said.

We could see, from our vantage point near the end of the long building, both the front and back parking lots. They were dark and empty, like the three shops that made up the building. Not a creature was stirring.

"Seriously," Dex said. "She told us to come at exactly 2 A.M. I'm wondering if midnight isn't taking 'early' a little too far."

"Yeah, well, I'm wondering why she gave us a specific time. Why should she care when we do it?"

Dex fell silent then, and I knew he was thinking that over.

"Maybe she knows more than she's telling us?" he said.

"Maybe she does. I don't trust her, that's for sure."

"I thought you dated her."

"Long ago. I never said I trusted her."

"Then why'd we let her talk us into this?"

I didn't bother to reply, and he didn't bother asking again. Both of us knew the answer.

We were doing it because we needed the money. I'd lost my job on the Rosalie police force a year ago and got laid off at the canning plant a week ago, and since I'd been a failure at just about every legitimate endeavor I'd ever tried, well, my chances of immediate future employment were limited. Dexter wasn't much better off. He was a part-time security guard at the Pine Ridge shopping mall in Tupelo, sixty miles away, and barely earned enough to pay for the gas it took to drive there and back. The apartment we shared out near the lumberyard was drafty in the winter and hot as a two-dollar pistol in the summer, both our cars needed new brakes and new transmissions, and we were overdue on most of our bills. Upstanding citizens, Dex and me.

But at least we hadn't resorted to crime. Until now.

Our current adventure had started two nights ago, as we sat in our living room humming along with Elvis on an ancient CD player and eating the remains of a three-day-old pizza I'd found in the fridge. Dex had a beer in his hand and I was slurping a Sprite. I love Sprite. The phone rang—that bill was another one we hadn't paid in a while, but thankfully they hadn't yet cut us off—and when I picked it up and heard the voice on the other end of the line I almost choked on my pizza.

"Eddie?" it said.

Natalie Landers. The voice alone—low, smoky, sexy—was enough to spike my blood pressure. Natalie was an old flame, one that should've winked out long ago but still flickered in the back of my mind. I'd heard she left town and had recently moved back, but we hadn't spoken in years. I motioned to Dex to turn the music down.

"Yeah," I said. Then I listened awhile, staying quiet, staring at the wall. Finally I nodded and replied, "I'll be there," and heard her disconnect. Still holding the phone to my ear, I turned to look at my roommate, who was studying me with narrowed eyes.

"Tell me we won the lottery," he said.

"We won the lottery."

"Now tell me the truth."

I hung up and said, "I've been offered a job."

*

Actually, I'd been offered an interview. According to Natalie, I was to meet her at a city park near our apartment in half an hour, to discuss the specifics. I of course smelled a rodent. A voice from the past? A rendezvous in a park at 10:30 on a Wednesday night? To discuss employment opportunities? Even so, considering the current state of our finances, I jumped at the chance. Also—I admit it—I wanted to see her again.

When Dexter and I arrived, Natalie was already there and waiting, at a picnic table in the streetlight-shadow of an oak tree near a parked gray SUV that I figured belonged to her. She was the only person in sight. We sat down across from her. There were no hugs, no smiles, no How ya doins or Long time no sees. Just solemn faces all around. Solemn or not, Natalie Landers still looked good, even in the dim light.

"Why do I get the feeling," I said, "that this isn't a regular job you're talking about?"

"Because you have a suspicious mind," Natalie replied. Which jarred me a little, for reasons I'll explain in a minute.

"And," she added, "because you're smarter than you look." She turned and fixed her expressionless gaze on Dex. "I don't think we've met."

Dex introduced himself, said he'd grown up here but had gone to a different school, said he and I were roommates now, explained that we'd met in the army a few years back. He didn't explain why we were still running around together, which was just as well, because neither one of us knew. Maybe misery loved company.

"No offense," she said to him, "but I just need one man, for this operation. Not two."

I shook my head. "You hire me, you hire Dexter. Matched set."

Natalie paused a moment, considering, then nodded. "Good enough. But you split your share."

"Agreed."

She sat back and folded her hands on the wooden table. "Here's the deal."

As it turned out, the rat I thought I'd smelled earlier was alive and stinking to high Heaven. What Natalie wanted, she said, was for us to rob the RealQuik Cash office where she worked. I didn't ask how or why she'd thought of me for this task, and she didn't say.

She did assure us it wasn't as risky as it sounded. The safe in the back of the shop, which always contained more than ten thousand in cash, had only two keys, and one of them had gotten lost several weeks ago. The "lost" key was at this moment in Natalie's purse, but nobody else knew that, and the owner was too cheap to change the lock and too dumb to be worried about it. He was also dumb enough to leave early every Friday night, around 6 o'clock, and let Natalie close the place up at 8.

According to her, the plan was foolproof. Two nights from now—Friday, September 20th—Dex and I could come in through the back entrance at exactly 2 o'clock, use her key to unlock the safe, load the money into one of the canvas sacks they kept there for transporting cash, and exit through the same door we'd entered. She would leave that back door unlocked for us, and since the only camera was fixed and aimed at the rear parking lot, she would turn the camera off when she closed the office at 8. It was old and unreliable anyway, and she could later say it malfunctioned. When I asked why we couldn't just come in and leave through the front door, she said there was too much traffic along the highway out front, even late at night, and we might be seen. The back lot bordered the seldom-used Hillman Street, and was otherwise hidden from view.

"Will you be there with us, when all this happens?" I asked her.

"Not a chance. You'll be well paid for your time and effort. I'll be at home, asleep."

I thought for a moment, then said, "Why do you need us at all? If you're there alone for two hours before you close up, why don't you just bag up the money and take off?"

"Because I'd be the prime suspect," she said.

"You'll be the prime suspect anyway."

"No I won't. I always go straight home, and we have security cameras at my house too. If anyone looks, the cameras'll show me walking in from my driveway empty-handed that night at eight-fifteen and then they'll show my husband ten hours later loading his Saturday-morning golf bag into the trunk of the same car and leaving. I'll be in the clear and can say truthfully that someone else committed the burglary, long after I left the office."

We all thought that over for a minute. I wasn't sure that made sense, but she sounded convinced enough to convince me.

"Hillman Street," Dex said. "Where is that exactly?"

She pointed to a ballpoint pen clipped to Dex's shirt pocket, and he handed it to her. On a notepad that she placed in a bright island of light from the streetlamp, she used his pen to sketch the location, including the building, the shops, both parking lots, and surrounding streets. We stayed another 20 minutes, asking questions and looking at the layout and making sure we understood it all, and when we were done Natalie gave us the key to the safe and a hard look and said, "Remember, two o'clock exactly. No earlier, no later. I'll contact you afterward and we can settle up."

Settling up meant giving her the cash and keeping out two grand for ourselves. For ten minutes' work.

What could go wrong?

*

Lots of things, I told myself, squatting there in the bushes a few minutes past 12 o'clock two nights later and watching both parking lots. I remembered those old *Mission: Impossible* reruns on TV. Every week the plan was perfectly laid out, and every week the plan went off the rails. I also remembered, for the second time, what Elvis had been singing the other night on our CD player when Natalie phoned our apartment. His version of a Mark James song called "Suspicious Minds." Coincidence? I wasn't sure.

But if Dex wanted to do this, I didn't want to be the one to back out. After all, I was not only the main reason we were here right now, I was also the main reason we were short on money. Ten days ago, as I was getting ready to take an envelope containing our rent payment down to our landlord—he liked it in cash, for reasons that were probably not entirely legal—a young pregnant woman had banged on our door, and when I opened it she informed me, frantic and sobbing, that she lived downstairs and her husband had just passed out and hit his head and they had no insurance and the ambulance driver was demanding a thousand dollars to take him to the ER. Our rent payment was twelve hundred, and I was standing there holding it in my hand. Long story short, I gave her the money.

I later discovered, after realizing that medical transport didn't cost a thousand bucks and that no emergency team would've asked her for money at that point anyway, that the woman didn't live here at all, and that in fact no ambulance had come to our apartment building in the past six months. I was told this the next day by the landlord, who was unimpressed by my excuses and gastrically upset over my failure to deliver our monthly payment. Also not pleased was Dexter Holtzhagen, who wound up paying our rent when it wasn't his turn to pay it and, as a result, didn't have enough left over to pay our light bill (which it was his turn to pay). So for several days now we'd been expecting to be playing checkers by candlelight one night soon, instead of watching TV or listening to '60s music—and Dex was grumbling once again that I was too soft-hearted. In his view, no good deed went unpunished.

He probably had a point. This wasn't the first time something like this had happened: I'd always been overly generous when it came to helping those in dire need. Not that it had ever gained me anything. I wasn't even a Democrat.

I was deep into this line of thought, and in fact I was thinking that Dex and I were often in dire need ourselves, when I heard the sound of a car motor, and my fellow conspirator hissing at me to pay attention, someone was coming.

A dark SUV approached the building, eased around to our side, avoiding both parking lots, and stopped just off the pavement. The driver stepped out onto the grass. Even in the anemic glow of the strip-mall streetlights I recognized Natalie. She was dressed all in black, like a ninja—or maybe Catwoman. She didn't bother to look around; no one else was supposed to be here yet. She hurried around to the back door of RealQuik Cash, stooped to unlock it, and went inside.

I turned and looked in Dex's direction, though it was too dark to see his face. I think I saw him shrug. I faced front again and continued watching.

After maybe five minutes Natalie came out again, this time from the front door. She had what looked like a heavy bag slung over one shoulder like Santa Claus. Head down, she scurried across the front of the building and around to the SUV, heaved the bag inside, climbed in, started the engine, and gunned it out of there.

When all was quiet again Dexter said, "What was that? Were you expecting that?"

I didn't answer right away. I was thinking.

"You figure she was unlocking the back door for us, like she planned?"

"No," I said. "I figure she was unlocking it for herself." I drew a long breath and let it out. "I think she just stole the money she told us to steal."

"But—why?"

The more I thought about it the more certain I was. "She didn't park in the back lot. Notice that?"

"Yeah," he said. "Think it was because the camera was on?"

"No. I think she went inside to turn it on."

"Not off?"

"I think she turned it on."

"And then left through the front door—"

"So the now-active camera in the back wouldn't see her leave."

I could almost hear the wheels turning, in his head.

"But if it's on now," he said, "it would see us, when we come at two o'clock."

I nodded. "If we were still gonna come at two o'clock." The deal, obviously, was off.

A long silence passed.

"What exactly's going on here, Eddie?"

I stood up in the dark, rubbed my eyes, and looked at the luminous hands of my watch. Twelve-fifteen. My legs were stiff, and I felt old. I was once again reminded that I'd had a birthday yesterday.

"What's going on is a double-cross," I said. "A setup." I paused a moment, putting words to my thoughts. "I figure Natalie just stole most of what was in the safe but left some in there for us to take as well. That way, if things had gone as planned, we'd go in there, we'd see it for ourselves—not knowing she'd already been there—and we'd figure she'd overestimated when she told us how much was in the safe. I think she wanted us to take the rest so we'd be holding stolen cash in our apartment when the police come for us."

"What?!"

"My guess is, she'll wait until early morning, after we supposedly do our deed, and then she'll sic the cops onto us. Not only would we be on video, she'll probably also say she spotted us lurking around outside at two o'clock as she drove past the building on some late-night errand or other. As for the money, she'll already have what she planned to take—the lion's share—safe and hidden away. The cops would find the part that we took when they search our place, and they'd figure that was the whole stash. Remember, we'd have been on camera entering and leaving through the back and carrying a sack of money out. And if we told the cops she set us up to take the fall, she'd just deny it."

"So it'd be her word against ours?" Dex had risen also and was looking at me.

"Yep. And in case you're wondering, you and I aren't exactly believable."

"Speak for yourself," he said, stretching his back muscles.

"Come on—nobody trusts someone with both an *x* and a *z* in his name."

He snorted. "You are such a doofus. At least I'm good-looking."

"Keep telling yourself that," I said.

"Think about it—there has to be something that would connect her to this," he said. "A witness, maybe, to our meeting in the park."

"Forget it, Dex. Nobody saw us meet her."

He fell silent again. The wind had picked up a bit and rustled the fallen leaves around us. It was a chilly night.

"So what do we do?" he asked. "Go to the cops ourselves?"

"The cops around here don't like me much. I used to be one of 'em, if you recall." What I recalled most was that fights with the chief were frowned on, especially fistfights in the squad room, and that's what got me canned. There was a new chief now, but everybody remembered what I'd done. I'd been even more stupid then than I was now. "And you're not exactly their favorite either, since we're together so much. Besides, if we tell 'em to go pick Natalie up, she'll have already hidden the money, and she'll point the finger right back at us."

"What if we just wait till morning, and if she reports a two o'clock theft and says the camera will show who took it, the camera'll be our alibi. We won't be on video because we weren't there."

I shook my head. "Won't work. She'd just tell them we probably came in through the front instead of the back. Like you said, her word against ours."

"So—again—what do we do?"

I thought for a long moment before the answer occurred to me. The perfect answer. I looked at him and smiled.

"We go to the movies."

*

Dexter didn't remember Grover Hammond, but I did. He owned a movie theater here in town when I was a kid. Later, when I was in high school, Grover sold out and moved to Tupelo, about an hour north, and opened a bigger theater, one that offered an unusual but (for some) appealing quirk: it showed all-night movies, ran them straight through from early evening till early morning. The two- or three-o'clock showings were almost empty sometimes, but that didn't bother Grover. He was a night owl anyway, and folks said he often manned the projection room himself, dozing and snacking and reading novels by the flickering lights of the equipment. When he wasn't there, he hired high-school students to run the movies and earn a little extra cash.

The best thing about Grover's red-eye theater, though—at least for our purposes—was that he was security-conscious to the extreme, and had half a dozen cameras overseeing his operation, from the front sidewalk to the ticket booth to the concession stand to the theater itself. He always knew what was going on inside his little realm. And I knew he knew, because I'd done some part-time work, back before my soldier-boy and city-cop days, for a video supply store up in Lee County. As luck would have it, I was the one who had installed Grover Hammond's cameras.

So that's where Dex and I were, between 1:45 and 2:15 on the morning of September 21st. We strolled in, smiled for the cameras that were mounted right where they used to be, and we did the same on the way out. The movie was okay—one of the *Rocky* sequels—but nothing special. We only stayed for half an hour. But security tapes are time-stamped, and our presence had now been established at a location at least an hour from the scene of the crime. We had our alibi.

The only other memorable thing about our trip to Tupelo that night was yet another encounter with a damsel in distress. A young woman in a nurse's uniform was standing beside a car with a flat tire on a dark, empty stretch of road a few miles from the movie theater, alone and in tears and trying to use an apparently dead cell phone. Dex of course didn't want to stop—he was quick to remind me of the other weeping "victim" I'd helped recently, and the way that had turned out—but I was the one who was driving, and I ignored him. We pulled over, changed her tire for her, accepted a bear-hug and her sincere thanks and watched her drive away before resuming our trip. We got back home a little before 3:30 and went straight to bed.

*

At ten minutes past six, I woke up to an urgent pounding on the door to our apartment. I hauled myself out of bed, pulled my shirt and pants on, and got to the front door at the same time Dex did. He opened the door, and we stood there staring at two uniformed cops. Mutt and Jeff—one was tall, one was short. I knew the short one: Lenny Hicks. We tried to look surprised.

"Get your shoes on, boys," Hicks said. "You're coming with us."

Half an hour later we were sitting handcuffed in an interrogation room with sickly green walls and four chairs and a bare wooden table. In the center of the table was an old-fashioned tape recorder, and on the other side were our two arresting officers. We'd already been informed of our rights and grilled about our role in last night's burglary of the local RealQuik Cash office, and our two cops, neither of whom seemed pleased to be here, were also not pleased with our answers. No lawyers were present, and none had been requested.

"Search our apartment, if you don't believe us," I said, for at least the third time. "Search our cars. We don't have any of this stolen money you're talking about."

"We plan to," Tall Cop replied. The name on his badge said FENLAND, like the country spelled wrong.

"And I bet that office you say was robbed has closed-circuit cameras," I said. "If it does, the real burglars ought to be on video. Right?"

"We'll check that too. Meanwhile, I told you, we got an eyewitness says she saw you both as she drove past in the street, saw you sneaking around outside the building. Said she recognized you, from long ago. Gave us your names."

Good old Natalie. Sometimes I hate being right. "You said she claimed she saw us there at 2 A.M.," I said. "If that's true, why'd you wait till daylight to come arrest us?"

"She didn't report it right away. Said she couldn't sleep for hours, for thinking about it, and finally decided to call it in."

"Don't you think that sounds a little suspicious?"

"I think it sounds perfectly reasonable," Hicks said.

"Of course you do. Where's your chief, by the way?

"He drove back from Jackson during the night. He'll be in soon."

"All I can say is, check the cameras," I said again. "My friend and I weren't there."

"Then where were you, at two o'clock? Home in bed?"

"We probably should've been."

"You're admitting you weren't home?"

"We were an hour north of here," Dex said. "Watching a Rocky Balboa movie."

"What? A movie?"

I looked at Hicks. "You remember Grover Hammond, used to live here? Dex and I went to his all-night theater, in Tupelo. If you want to look at cameras, look at Grover's. They'll prove we were there."

The cops exchanged a glance. "Grover Hammond?"

"That's him."

Hicks gave me a strange look. "You didn't see him there, did you?"

"See him? No. What does that matter?"

His face turned smug. "Grover Hammond's dead, Warrington," Hicks said. "Died three years ago."

I felt a cold shiver work its way down my spine. "Well, somebody runs the place. We were there, at exactly two o'clock."

"Somebody runs it, all right. His son, Anthony. I went to school with him."

"So check with Anthony."

"We will—but it won't help. He don't use cameras."

"Sure he does," I said. "We saw them ourselves."

"If you'd been there, I don't doubt you'da seen them. Anthony's probably too lazy to take 'em down. But he don't use 'em. He's too cheap to even pay his people a fair wage."

I felt my shoulders slump. If that was right, our only alibi—our proof—was worthless. I now wished I hadn't depended so heavily on the theater cameras. We hadn't seen or spoken to anyone we knew on our trip that night and hadn't even gotten the name of the nurse with the flat tire. We were back to our word against Natalie's.

"Let's say you're right," I said. "Let's say we can't prove we weren't at the crime scene. You also can't prove we were."

This time both of them smiled. "Actually," Hicks said, "we can."

He placed a clear plastic bag on the table. Sealed inside was a ballpoint pen, and on the pen were the words PINE RIDGE MALL.

"We found this on the floor of the cash office," Fenland said. "Beside the empty safe."

As my heart sank, I remembered Natalie asking Dex for his pen, in the park. She'd been smarter than I'd realized.

"I believe you said you work at this mall, Mr. Holtzhagen. That right?"

Dex's tanned face was pale as a bedsheet. He didn't answer. There was no need to. They had us.

The lyrics to that old Elvis song popped into my head, as clear as crystal. We were indeed caught in a trap. And couldn't walk out.

But, at that moment, someone else walked in.

Chief Joe Sanchez pushed through the door, frowned at us, and then frowned at his two officers. "What did I miss?" he said.

Fenland and Hicks filled him in, beginning with Natalie's call to the police and ending up with the evidence—Dex's pen—that had been "left at the scene." Throughout their pitch, Sanchez leaned against the greenish wall and listened with his eyebrows knitted and his arms folded across his chest. When the officers were done, Sanchez turned to Dex and me. "Anything you boys want to say?"

I gave him a much more positive summary, from our 120-mile round trip to the theater in Tupelo at the time of the reported burglary to the knocking on our door at shortly after 6 this morning. I even told him about our stop to help a young nurse on our way back from the movie. But even I realized how lame it all sounded.

Afterward Sanchez stared at Dex and me for what seemed a very long time. Then he said, "'Scuse me a minute," took out his cell phone, and stepped out of the room.

Officer Fenland, a man I didn't know and didn't like, and Officer Hicks, a man I remembered well and also didn't like, sat there giving us a dark, triumphant look, one that said Your goose is cooked and you know it. And we did know it. I wished I'd strangled Natalie Landers on sight the other night, instead of listening to her.

When Chief Sanchez came back into the room, pocketing his phone, he looked at Hicks and said, "Take their cuffs off."

"What?"

"You heard me. Take 'em off and wait for me outside."

Scowling, Hicks unlocked our handcuffs and left. Fenland followed him.

When the door closed behind them, Sanchez took one of the chairs and leaned back in it, watching the two of us. We probably looked shellshocked.

"My daughter Katie," he said, "lives in Tupelo. She works nights. I just called her, and as it turns out, she saw the two of you, at exactly the time you said you were there. Described you to a T. There'll be no charges."

It took a second for me to process that. "You mean—she saw us at the theater?"

Sanchez broke out a slow smile. "She saw you when you stopped to rescue her, by the side of the road. Katie's an RN. She was on her way to her three-to-eleven shift at the hospital." He took off his hat, ran a hand through his dark hair, and studied us a moment more. "You fellas helped my daughter, my only child, when she really needed help. Maybe saved her, considering where she was stranded."

I didn't know what to say. I looked at Dex. His mouth was hanging open.

"I didn't know you, Eddie Warrington, when you worked here. I came after you left. But I knew the chief you had a tussle with."

A silence passed. Finally I said, in a small voice. "What does that mean?"

"It means I'd like you to think about coming back. Entry-level, but still." He looked at Dex. "We could use both of you."

I blinked. I opened my mouth and then closed it again.

"Consider it, okay? You saw what I have to put up with, in Fenland and Hicks. I need guys like you two."

Both of us were gaping at him like idiots. When I found my voice, I said, "What about the robbery?"

"Well, now that we know for sure you were sixty miles away when the only eyewitness to the crime says you were here...I think we need to talk again to the eyewitness. Maybe ask her why she just happened to be driving past her place of business in the middle of the night."

I silently wished I could be there when they had that conversation. But I didn't say that. What I said was, "Thanks, Chief."

He smiled again. "My pleasure. Let me know about the job, okay?"

Ten minutes later, after Sanchez had taken us back home, we stood together on the sidewalk outside our apartment building and watched him drive away. We were still a little stunned.

"So, what do you think of your birthday, so far?" Dex said.

I turned to face him. "You remembered?"

"Unlike you, I really am smarter than I look."

"Actually, it was yesterday."

He shrugged. "I was close."

*

We sacked out and slept till well past noon. Afterward, Dexter read a paperback Western in his recliner while I sprawled on the couch and sipped from a Sprite can and watched a Saturday football game on TV. Alabama was beating up on somebody, 42-7.

"What do you think," I said, "about this deal? About being a cop?"

From the corner of my eye, I saw Dex look up from his book. "I'm not one, yet. Sanchez said I'll have to take some courses first."

"You'll be fine."

"What do you think about it?"

"I think I'd like to pound on Fenland's door one morning, early. Handcuff him, maybe. See how he likes it."

Dex grinned. "If we're on the force, we'll at least be able to pay our bills again, right?"

"Yep. Maybe even get a decent CD player." I couldn't help thinking of Elvis and his suspicious mind. Maybe it hadn't been a coincidence.

"Or afford a date, now and then," I added.

"A date? What's that?"

Both of us were grinning now. After a pause he said, "If it comes to that, do me a favor. Get an honest girlfriend."

"Good idea."

Neither of us said anything for a while. But he must've noticed the look on my face.

"What?" he asked.

"I was thinking maybe a nurse."

His laugh was drowned out by a burst of cheering from the TV. Alabama had scored again and kicked the extra point—49-7.

I popped open another Sprite.

Our Cool DJs

EARL STAGGS In his lifetime, Earl wrote about serial killers, goats vs. roses, Elvis, Sheriff Molly, and the Black Dahlia, all without offensive language or explicit sex. He said, "If my characters want to talk dirty or have sex, explicit or otherwise, they'll have to go home and do it on their own time."

Earl passed away on January 3, 2020. Author of *Memory of a Murder* and *Justified Action,* two-time Derringer Award winner, he served as Managing Editor of *Futures Mystery Magazine,* as President of the Short Mystery Fiction Society, and was a frequent speaker at conferences and seminars.

JACK BATES knew as soon as he saw the name of the song, he had his story. Mix in a childhood memory of a family reunion, smack in the middle of an unexpected "turn on, tune in" gathering at a local park, and the tale just kind of wrote itself.

He's become somewhat proficient at self-publishing, blending several collections of earlier work with new tales. His alter ego, J. P. Beast, writes romance.

LINDA KAY HARDIE A former oldies station disk jockey, Linda Kay Hardie is an avid reader, writer, freelance editor and speaker. She's old enough to have been an original Nancy Sinatra fan and loves the irony that such a feminist song as "These Boots Are Made for Walkin'" was written by a man.

She teaches English composition and core humanities, both required classes, to unwilling students at the University of Nevada, Reno.

JEANNE DuBOIS A resident of Florida for over forty years, Jeanne rediscovered her song, and some good old friends, at a Woodstock 50th Anniversary party in Haddon Heights, NJ. The host's hippie tie-dyed t-shirt was the inspiration for Jim's, but she's the one with CS&N in her CD player. Peace.

Her first story, "A Troubling of Goldfish," appeared in the *A Murder of Crows* anthology.

TERRIE FARLEY MORAN A relic of the Flower Power generation, Terrie admires the music of Bob Dylan. Her independent streak made "It Ain't Me, Babe" the perfect choice. Moran still dances to the music of the '60s. Peace out!

Recipient of Agatha and Derringer awards, author of the Read 'Em and Eat mystery series, she co-authors Laura Childs' New Orleans scrapbooking books. Her latest novel, *Murder She Wrote: Killing in a Koi Pond,* #53 in the long running Jessica Fletcher series, is available for preorder. (May 2021).

HEIDI HUNTER When Heidi first learned of this '60s rock 'n' roll anthology, she immediately thought of aliens, because who doesn't? She was delighted to discover the popular song, "MacArthur Park," was first released in the 1960s, a perfect setting for her tale of murder, mayhem, and yes, aliens.

After a decade investigating financial crimes, Heidi pursues her love of writing mysteries. Her short stories have appeared in *Mysterical-E, Flash Bang Mysteries* and an anthology, *Crime Travel.*

MERRILEE ROBSON always liked "Little Children" and other Merseybeat music, but had never thought of the song from the point of view of the children. And then Bobby turned up, with that orange record player. It wasn't his fault.

Find her short stories in *Ellery Queen Mystery Magazine, Mystery Weekly, The People's Friend, Over My Dead Body, Mysteryrat's Maze* podcast, and various anthologies. Her novel is titled *Murder Is Uncooperative*. She lives in Vancouver with her husband and two spoiled cats.

CLAIRE A. MURRAY crammed her life into a storage pod and car, left New England in her exhaust, and settled in Phoenix to write. Her story's inspiration was the mural dedicated to composer Norman Greenbaum in his hometown where she'd worked for 25 years.

This is her eighth published short story. Her current project is a fantasy trilogy set on an earthlike planet with a medieval setting.

She's a long-time teacher, manager, disability advocate, animal lover and dog enthusiast.

MICHAEL BRACKEN is a wanna-be musician who has no sense of rhythm and can't read music. Instead, he writes stories. Lots of them. He lives, writes and listens to sad, sad songs in Texas.

Michael is the editor of the Anthony Award–nominated anthology *The Eyes of Texas: Private Eyes from the Panhandle to the Piney Woods,* the *Fedora* series, *Jukes & Tonks* with Gary Phillips, *Guns and Tacos* with Trey R. Barker, editor of *Black Cat Mystery Magazine,* author of 11 books and over 1,300 short stories, plus 2 anthologies for 2022.

MADDI DAVIDSON "Sixties music" brings to mind Motown and the Surf Sound. Since the authors, sisters Mary Ann Davidson and Diane Davidson, enjoy surfing, they based their story around the latter. The need to empty a bank account, anyone's bank account, to purchase a new car inspired "Little Old Ladies from Pasadena."

Their short story, "An Extinction of Dodos," appears in the anthology *A Murder of Crows.*

JOSEPH S. WALKER was raised a Catholic and became an academic, but shows promising signs of recovering from both conditions. He chose "Oh, Pretty Woman" because Roy Orbison's growl is as iconic as anything that came from Liverpool, and his shades are cooler than Mick and Keith combined.

His stories have appeared in *Alfred Hitchcock* and *Ellery Queen Mystery Magazines,* the anthology *Mickey Finn: 21st Century Noir, Cozy Villages of Death* and *After The East Wind Blows: World War I and Roaring Twenties Adventures of Sherlock Holmes,* and *The Killer Wore Cranberry, A Sixth Scandalous Serving.*

DAWN DIXON Amid the marsh grass and humidity of the South Carolina Low Country, Dawn lives cheek by jowl with boardwalks, alligators and ancient grudges. She swears all her stepmothers are either still breathing or they died from natural causes. Sure they did. (Y'all hear "Under the Boardwalk" playing softly?)

Dawn has written for local, regional and national publications. Besides dodging reptiles and downing cocktails on her front porch, she's writing the sequel to her first humorous mystery, *Faux Finish.*

KAREN KEELEY identified with her song throughout high school, groovin' to the music, believing the Fab Four ruled the world. At a 50th high school reunion it became clear most of her fellow grads stayed true to the cause, never suffering fools gladly. Today, they rock on with their grandkids.

Karen's stories can also be seen in *Trench Coat Chronicles* and *Fiction Junkie Vol. 1.* Born and raised in Vancouver, BC, Karen now lives in Calgary, AB.

PAUL D. MARKS Paul is a huge Beatles fan, but just to prove he has other interests, he decided to choose Blind Faith's "Can't Find My Way Home." It just seemed like the perfect song for his updating of a classic story to Vietnam.

Paul's novels include the latest, *The Blues Don't Care* and *White Heat.* He's also co-editor and a contributor to the anthology, *Coast to Coast: Noir from Sea to Shining Sea.*

WENDY HARRISON The longing and mystery in "Nights in White Satin" have haunted Wendy since her wild ride through the 1960s.

Currently living in Fort Meyers, Florida, she's a retired prosecutor. She continues to write short stories and is intent on reviving a promising manuscript found in a drawer. She's pretty sure she wrote it. She has finished 11 half-marathons and a sprint triathlon since turning 60. She is unsure who is chasing her.

MARY KELIIKOA After years hanging with lawyer-types, Mary Keliikoa has seen enough rocky relationships to make her groovy song selection fab. The Pacific NW is her main pad. But when she's not hitting the links, you can find her catching some rays on a Hawaiian beach plotting her next murder…novel that is.

Mary is the author of the PI Kelly Pruett Mystery Series. *Derailed* is available now, and *Denied,* in May 2021.

MAXIM JAKUBOWSKI did see the Beatles perform at the Olympia. He lived in Paris. He traveled to Spain at the time of the release of the *Revolver* album. But not all elements of the story are autobiographical. He says, "Come, sit. You can trust me. I'm quite harmless, really."

He was an editor and owned/operated the Murder One Bookshop for over 20 years. He now writes, edits and translates full-time in London. In 2019, he received the Crime Writers' Association Red Herring Award for lifetime achievement.

JAMES A. HEARN discovered an appreciation for Frank Sinatra through his wife's album collection. It's in his will that "I'll Be Seeing You" will be played at his funeral. He hopes to earn enough through writing to pay for said funeral, assuming he's cremated and no dinner is served afterward.

His fiction has appeared in *Alfred Hitchcock's Mystery Magazine, Mickey Finn: 21st Century Noir, The Eyes of Texas, Guns + Tacos,* and *Monsters, Movies & Mayhem.*

C. A. FEHMEL wanted to be a musician, but her brother got the talent while she got the ambition. She ran a blues show in college; however, in the real world she landed with a thud at an all-news station. Now she writes with her music turned up to eleven.

A prolific writer, Cindy is now immersed in the world of '40s B movies, gangsters and dames, as she pens what's sure to be a blockbuster novel.

CATINA WILLIAMS lives for happily-ever-afters, though her characters rarely experience them. Her obsessions include monsters, fairies, witches, Mr. Darcys and aliens. Suspicions abound that husband Troy and dog Katie are extraterrestrials, or megadroids. Her story highlights a lesser known song from the greatest rock band ever, The Rolling Stones.

Look for her short story, "A Ghost, Turkeys, and a Pretty Holiday Sweater" in *The Killer Wore Cranberry: A Sixth Scandalous Serving.*

JOSH PACHTER The Police's "Every Breath You Take" is a pervy song, but the Four Seasons staked out similar territory twenty years earlier.

Josh sometimes writes pervy stories, and "Sherry" inspired this one. Josh's fiction, pervy or not, has appeared in *EQMM* and many other places for more than half a century. This year, the Short Mystery Fiction Society awarded him its Golden Derringer Award for Lifetime Achievement. He edited, and Untreed Reads published, *The Beat of Black Wings: Crime Fiction Inspired by the Songs of Joni Mitchell.* Watch for more anthologies to follow its success.

JOHN M. FLOYD is a lifelong resident of Elvis's home state and grew up humming The King's songs from the '50s and '60s. One of his favorites was "Suspicious Minds"—and since every mystery character has one of those, it seemed a good choice for a story theme.

By October 2020, John had twenty short stories and one book published, and won a fourth Derringer Award. He has 32 more stories upcoming in magazines and anthologies, including a third appearance in *The Best American Mystery Stories.* He is a superstar contributor for mini-mysteries for *Woman's World* magazine.

SANDRA MURPHY is an experienced editor, finding her way through the patchouli haze, to keep writers from wandering off-topic or getting lost in research, as writers are wont to do. She lives in St. Louis, downwind of Anheuser-Busch Brewing Company. On a hot summer day, the smell of hops encourages her imaginary friends to spin tall tales. The line from a Pink Floyd song, "there's someone in my head but it's not me" is a fact of life for a writer.

She pens those tall tales for anthologies such as *The Killer Wore Cranberry: A Fourth Meal of Mayhem*. Her collection of stories, *From Hay to Eternity: Ten Devilish Tales of Crime and Deception,* is available at Untreed Reads and the usual outlets. "Lucy's Tree" in *The Eyes of Texas: Private Eyes from the Panhandle to the Piney Woods* won the Short Mystery Fiction Society's 2020 Derringer Award. She also edited the anthology, *A Murder of Crows*.

Printed in the USA
CPSIA information can be obtained
at www.ICGtesting.com
LVHW051629200823
755763LV00006B/110